About this Book

"In a perfect world, the federal government would establish a Ministry of Humour and put Terry Fallis in charge of that department. *The High Road* is brilliantly written and hysterically funny. . . . Terry Fallis manages to top his first novel *The Best Laid Plans* with this relentlessly enjoyable follow-up. No small feat, since the original won the Stephen Leacock Medal. Do yourself a favour and pick up this book, find a quiet place to read it, and enjoy . . . you will laugh out loud on almost every single page."

— IAN FERGUSON,
author of *Village of the Small Houses*

"It is a giant talent that can elicit so much fun from the dour world of back room Canadian politics. Battling egos, smear campaigns, vigilante seniors and a dipsomaniac First Lady make for quite a romp up and down the Hill. MP Professor Angus McLintock, the never bending free-thinking Scot, is the perfect foil for all that is inflated in the world of policy and polling. Doing battle with the prigs and prats that rule the halls of power has never been more enjoyable since . . . well, since *The Best Laid Plans*. Thought provoking and funny, here's hoping there are more installments to come."

— JIM CUDDY,
singer/songwriter, Blue Rodeo

Praise for *The Best Laid Plans*

"This is a funny book that could only have been written
by someone with firsthand knowledge of politics in Canada,
including its occasionally absurd side. This is a great read for
anyone thinking of running for office, and especially reassuring
for those who have decided not to."

— THE HON. ALLAN ROCK,
former Justice Minister and Canadian Ambassador to the United Nations

"*The Best Laid Plans* is . . . amusing, enlightening – and Canadian,
and it deftly explores the Machiavellian machinations of Ottawa's
political culture." – GLOBE AND MAIL

"Terry Fallis has found the cure for Canada's political malaise: a
stubborn, old, irreverent Scotsman with nothing to lose. Until
Angus McLintock walks out of fiction and into public office,
where he would surely save the nation, the only
place to find him is right here among *The Best Laid Plans*."

— TOM ALLEN,
CBC Radio host and author of *The Gift of the Game*

"Terry Fallis weaves a funny yet tender tale that gives us all hope
for the future of democracy. Hilarious and thought-provoking,
I literally could not put this book down. I finished it in one sitting,
with a full heart and sore sides. With an insider's knowledge of
politics, beautifully developed characters, and a page-turning plot,
Terry Fallis has written a winner. Get it, read it, now!"

— THE HON. ELINOR CAPLAN,
former Minister of Citizenship and Immigration

THE HIGH ROAD

Also by Terry Fallis

The Best Laid Plans

THE HIGH ROAD

A Novel

TERRY FALLIS

EMBLEM
McClelland & Stewart

Emblem is an imprint of McClelland & Stewart Ltd.
Emblem and colophon are registered trademarks of McClelland & Stewart Ltd.

Library and Archives Canada Cataloguing in Publication

Fallis, Terry
The high road / Terry Fallis.

ISBN 978-0-7710-4787-9

I. Title.

PS8611.A515H54 2010   C813'.6   C2010-901492-8

We acknowledge the financial support of the Government of Canada through the
Book Publishing Industry Development Program and that of the Government of
Ontario through the Ontario Media Development Corporation's Ontario Book
Initiative. We further acknowledge the support of the Canada Council for the
Arts and the Ontario Arts Council for our publishing program.

Published simultaneously in the United States by
McClelland & Stewart Ltd., P.O. Box 1030, Plattsburgh, New York 12901

Library of Congress Control Number: 2010926643

This is a work of fiction. Names, characters, and incidents are the products of the
author's imagination. Any resemblance to actual events, or persons, living or
dead, is entirely coincidental.

A Douglas Gibson Book

ANCIENT FOREST
FRIENDLY

Typeset in Dante by M&S, Toronto
Printed and bound in Canada

McClelland & Stewart Ltd.
75 Sherbourne Street
Toronto, Ontario
M5A 2P9
www.mcclelland.com

6 7   14   13   12   11

For my mother and father

Oh! ye'll take the high road and
I'll take the low road,
And I'll be in Scotland afore ye;
But me and my true love
Will never meet again
On the bonnie, bonnie banks of Loch Lomond.

— "Loch Lomond," an old Scots song

Part One

CHAPTER ONE

Politics is often a millstone around democracy's neck, and it had become a noose around mine. But I had an escape plan. I was nearly free. Granted, I'd botched my first attempt. Or rather, I'd been undone by an eleventh-hour shocker completely beyond my control. But that was then. In a day or two, I'd be in the clear. Really.

I was seriously asleep when my BlackBerry chirped. When my eyes could finally recognize our alphabet, I read "B. Stanton" on the screen. Excellent. I'd hoped never to see that name on my BB ever again. Yet here it was. A call from the Liberal leader's slippery Chief of Staff seldom sent me to my happy place. Just a day or two more.

I spoke quietly, trying not to waken Lindsay beside me. I need not have worried. When she slept, she went straight to the bottom.

"Daniel Addison," I sighed.

"Is that you, Addison?"

"Uh, no Bradley, I just open with that name to confuse callers. I'm actually Tiger Woods," I replied, no longer caring about pissing him off on my way out.

"Up yours!" he roared. "You've got call display. Why can't you just pick up and say 'Hi Bradley'? You knew it was me calling."

"You mean 'You knew it was I calling,'" I lectured. Too often, I corrected grammar on instinct, without thinking. "And 'up yours' is just so . . . last century."

I

"Fuckin' pedant. I'll be gla–"

"And yes, I do have call display," I interrupted. "But I was praying it might be a wrong number from, say, a Bratislav Stanton, or perhaps his brother Benito. But no such luck."

I waited for him to speak but he didn't. So I just kept going. This was kind of fun.

"So what's up?" I continued. "Wait, don't tell me, you're recruiting for *Machiavelli: The Musical* and I made the shortlist. I'm touched, really I am."

"Yeah, that's just hilarious, ass-wipe."

Where was he getting these archaic boys' camp epithets?

"Listen," he went on. "Have you seen the *Globe* this morning?"

"Bradley, it's 6:45. I barely have vital signs at this hour. Why?"

"There's another fuckin' story about you and your crazy mountain man. Are you still working the gallery for these puff pieces? 'Cause if you are, I'll have your nuts," he threatened.

"Um, yours seem to be quite large enough already, Bradley. But before you have an aneurysm, I had nothing to do with the story, whatever it is. And I've not pitched a single journo since the government fell," I said, and meant it.

"Yeah, well, the piece says your hairy friend might run again. I'm waiting for you to tell me that's not true. I'm waiting for you to tell me you're both heading back to your academic sandbox. I don't want to see either of you on the Hill again. I'm just so tired of that 'holier than thou' shit you and McLintock were peddling," Stanton barked.

"Of course you're right, Bradley. Putting politics together with honesty, transparency, and the national interest, it's an outrage bordering on treason," I sneered. "Now you listen. Don't get your boxers bunched up. I can tell you that neither Angus nor I has any plans to make any plans to return to politics. We didn't expect to be there in the first place, and I certainly have no desire to go back. I was trying to get out when all this started, remember? So I'm done, and hearing your warm and caring voice again clinches the deal."

I heard the click as he closed his cell. What a jerk.

Noose or not, the political junkie in me still needed my morning fix. So in a semi-comatose stupor, I tipped myself out of bed and padded to the front door, my fingers twitching for the newspapers. The first faint traces of morning light angled into the second-storey boathouse apartment and pooled on the hardwood floor.

Outside on the porch the papers lay rolled and waiting, just out of reach from the warmth, and shall we say traction, of the front hall. You've heard of black ice – that treacherous and nearly invisible glassy layer that forms on roads when certain meteorological conditions are met. Well, the McLintock boathouse has a similar phenomenon known locally as "porch ice." With no eavestrough, the melting snow on the roof drips onto the porch, only to freeze when the sun drops. Angus had mentioned this danger to me in his typical engineer's dialect, noting something about the floorboards' coefficient of friction dropping asymptotically to nearly zero. Right, asymptotically. So when I slipped out the front door to fetch the paper, I literally "slipped" out the front door.

In life-threatening situations, the "fight or flight" instinct kicks in. Without consulting me, my body chose "flight," in the truest sense of the word, so I was compelled to go along for the ride. I managed to sustain a life-saving hold on the doorknob, my only tether to earth, as my foot left the icy porch floor in a hurry. Now I'm not what you would call coordinated . . . at all. Yet I somehow landed back on the porch without serious injury, my shimmying feet eventually coming to rest more or less under me. But naturally, my momentum slammed the door shut. Scratch that. Locked the door. Think bank vault, or Fort Knox. So there I was, marooned on my own front porch at 6:45 in the morning, the frigid day after Christmas. Did I mention that I was naked? No pants, so no pockets, so no keys.

Bare hands and faces are quite accustomed to braving the harsh temperatures of winter. Other parts of the male anatomy, not so much. I felt December's arctic grip clamp down on my . . .

3

situation. Like pushing an elevator button that's already lit, I tried the doorknob, oh, fourteen or fifteen times just to confirm with each attempt that the door was indeed still locked. It was. I then decided I had two choices. I could simply bang on the door and face the unbridled humiliation of wakening Lindsay to rescue me, or I could pry open, and crawl through, the narrow side window next to the porch. Easy call.

I slid open the window without incident, even on my frictionless bare feet. I'd not thought it possible to be any colder than I already was, until my bare chest touched the window sill. It was aluminum. When I had shoehorned myself halfway through the deceptively small opening, the "humiliation in front of Lindsay" scenario was looking pretty good. But things were going so well with her, with us, I decided that breaking into my own apartment, naked, was worth it.

I kicked my legs gracefully, almost balletically, scraped through, and landed on the hallway floor, my forehead coming to rest on, er . . . Lindsay's bare feet. As I looked up, I saw that "bare" applied not just to her feet. She was holding her stomach and quivering. She was making a Herculean effort to keep her sides from splitting wide open. I was not blind to the humour in all of this, but I did think her hysterics took it a tad too far. In time, she gathered herself.

"I often find the door works quite well also," she deadpanned.

"Yes, well, I was a C-section baby so I'm drawn to windows," I quipped without missing a beat. I jumped to my feet to stand next to her, affecting casual indifference, as if nothing had happened. Tough to sell, with hypothermic convulsions, full-body abrasions, and a shrunken . . . ego. She shivered once, standing so close to my icy body, then headed back to bed. To complete my tribute to the Keystone Kops, the rolled-up newspapers still lay on the porch, mocking me through the window.

After a scalding twenty-minute shower, I returned to bed with the newspapers and all the nonchalance I could muster. Lindsay lay beside me, apparently back in the trough of deep sleep.

4

Boxing Day is one of my favourite days of the year. The chaos of Christmas is over, and the real relaxing begins. Because of the holiday, the papers were thinner than usual, but the story Bradley had called about actually appeared in both the *Cumberland Crier* and the *Globe and Mail*. I hadn't been completely honest with *Darth* Bradley. I knew that André Fontaine, staff writer for our local paper, the *Crier*, was working on a feature and had hoped to get broader placement of it. He couldn't have done much better than our national newspaper.

I propped myself up on my pillows, taking care not to shake the bed unduly, and opened the *Globe*. Four photos accompanied the story. There was a shot of Professor Angus McLintock receiving a teaching award from the U of O Engineering Society. Another showed him sitting in *Baddeck 1*, the hovercraft he'd designed and built in the boathouse workshop below me. Yet another photo, taken just outside the House of Commons, featured Angus flanked by yours truly and Muriel Parkinson, whose smile actually made her look younger than her eighty-one years. Finally, there was a stock photo of disgraced former Finance Minister and Cumberland-Prescott MP, the Honourable Eric Cameron, likely taken after presenting his last federal budget and well before the cataclysm of a couple of months ago.

Lindsay stirred beside me, then was still again.

It was surreal to see my own name in a *Globe and Mail* headline.

McLintock and Addison – Cutting a new path in politics

It was a bit over the top in my view. Then there was the subhead to fill in the holes in the headline.

Behind the partnership that brought down a government

Please. It made us sound so much more purposeful and calculating than we had actually been. Really, I'd had very little to do with it all. The Tories had gambled that the snowstorm of the decade would maroon most MPs in their ridings. It was Angus who had rocketed up the frozen Ottawa River in *Baddeck 1* all the way to Parliament Hill. I was just a spectator in the gallery when he burst onto the floor of the House, his wild grey hair and swirling beard in full fright, just in time to cast the deciding vote. But like the intoxicating aroma that often leads me three blocks out of my way to the nearest Cinnabon outlet, the headline and subhead are intended to seize your attention.

I settled in to read the piece. Lindsay still looked as if she were asleep beside me but her roving hands beneath the comforter told a different story. Focus, Daniel, focus. André's story covered the whirlwind of the last two and a half months, including my abrupt resignation from my speech-writing gig in the Liberal Leader's office and my guilt-driven promise on my way out to find a Liberal candidate to run in my new home riding of Cumberland-Prescott. Never mind that it was the safest Conservative seat in the land.

As I feared, André revealed the bargain I had struck with my new landlord, Angus McLintock. I'd admitted nothing in my interview, but honest Angus had freely confessed he agreed to let his name stand as the no-hope Liberal sacrificial lamb only after I promised to teach his English for Engineers class, a quadrennial duty he absolutely loathed. I was surprised to see that André had included a nice quotation from my PhD thesis supervisor noting how pleased he was that I'd agreed to join the English faculty at Ottawa U.

Lindsay's sub-sheet ministrations moved quickly from distracting to arousing, but I had almost finished the story. The hint of a smile on her tranquil face confirmed that she was not in the throes of some strange, yet wholly satisfying, sleep disorder.

"Just a couple more paragraphs, Linds, and I'm all yours. I'm just getting to the good part."

"Me too," she whispered, still smiling.

She redoubled her efforts as if I'd said nothing at all, which,

6

frankly, worked out pretty well for me.

André had some fun with the leather-studded late-campaign stunner, describing how the wildly popular incumbent MP and Finance Minister Eric Cameron inadvertently went public with his S&M secret. You don't often see words like "alligator clip" and "crotchless rubber suit" living in the same sentence alongside "Finance Minister." So I savoured the moment. Even Muriel made it into the article. André described her as the spirited eighty-something Liberal warhorse who had stood for the Liberals against the Tory tide in C-P for five elections in a row. Nicely put. I wondered how Lindsay's grandmother would take the "warhorse" reference, before deciding she'd probably wear it with pride.

By this time, Lindsay had shed any pretence of sleep and thrown herself into her work. She was quite good at it, too. My concentration flagged as I tried to make it to the end of the article while also thinking hard about baseball. And hockey, and football. Did I mention baseball? Almost there. Just a few more paragraphs. Bear down, Daniel. Down.

The article couldn't quite capture the full impact of Angus McLintock's stunning upset and his honest, forthright, and refreshing approach to public service. Yet it was all true. Against all odds, against more than a century of local political tradition, and definitely against the wishes of Angus McLintock, it was all true. Despite outward appearances of a carefully orchestrated grand plan, we'd simply been lurching from one issue to the next, trying to do the right thing. Who could have foreseen Angus McLintock's Midas touch? I certainly hadn't.

The last line of the feature really said it all.

> *"With the government defeated and another election looming, the burning questions are: Will Angus McLintock seek re-election for a job he never wanted in the first place? And will Daniel Addison still be at his side?"*

"No and no," I intoned out of nowhere, in a louder voice than I'd intended.

Lindsay clearly wasn't taking no for an answer, and launched into new techniques well beyond my thin playbook. I do have my limits. I jettisoned the paper as if it were on fire.

An hour later, when we'd both finished, the *Globe* story I mean, Lindsay set down the paper.

"Well? Did André nail it?" she asked.

"He got the history right, but he's got the future all wrong," I replied. "As far as I'm concerned, Angus and I are heading back to the peace and quiet of the university. He didn't want to win. I didn't want him to win. The collapse of the government just means we can now go back to our regularly scheduled lives."

Lindsay smiled and looked down. I thought I might even have detected a faint shake of her head.

"I'm with Grandma. I think Angus was surprised to discover that he actually liked being an MP. And I think you actually quite liked being his EA."

"Despite what Muriel and you believe, I think I know Angus pretty well. He will not run again," I concluded. "You can flip us both over and grab the barbecue sauce, we're done."

We lay in peace for a time.

"What a wonderful few weeks it's been," Lindsay sighed and rested her head on my chest. No one before her had ever rested her head on my chest. I liked it.

December had certainly packed a punch, and I don't just mean weather-wise. When the government collapsed, we found ourselves with some time on our hands as the Governor General tried to figure out what to do. The government fell, but it didn't automatically mean another election would immediately be called. The GG had another option to consider, particularly since Canadians had endured an election just over two months ago. She could ask the Liberals to try to form a government with the support of the New Democratic Party. But that would be like asking the Hatfields and the McCoys to make nice and move in together. Not bloody likely, but worth a try. Neither party had the seats to survive without the support of the other. So our fearless leader sat down with the NDP Leader and for the last two weeks, they'd been trading horses, trading insults, and nearly trading blows.

Twice the discussions broke down. The first time, the NDP Leader stomped away from the table when our guy refused even to consider a thirty-year-old NDP plank, nationalizing the banking system. It was a non-starter. To get him back to the table, we apparently offered a compromise, agreeing that a Liberal government would strengthen the regulatory powers of the long-neutered Foreign Investment Review Agency. Then three days ago, our enraged leader was said to have thrown an eraser at his NDP counterpart. I've seen the Liberal leader in the heat of a temper tantrum. I'm glad only an eraser had been in reach and not a stapler, let alone a fax machine. It all fell apart over the demand that at least a couple of NDP MPs sit in the proposed Liberal Cabinet. I could understand why the NDP would expect a seat or two at the Cabinet table if they were going to prop up a Liberal government. Unfortunately, I was not invited to the negotiations. Bradley Stanton was running the show. Bradley wouldn't recognize a principle if one landed squarely on his crotch. As for the NDP's Cabinet demand, our leader exhausted all the appropriate clichés (*over my dead body, when hell freezes over*, etc., etc.) and reached for the eraser. After bouncing it off the NDP Leader's forehead, he found there really wasn't much left to talk about. The two negotiating teams gathered up their toys and headed home. It was Christmas Eve by then, yet neither leader was in the gift-giving mood. The Governor General was expected to announce her decision on how to proceed on December 27, giving the political parties, and the nation for that matter, a brief Christmas reprieve from the political manoeuvring.

While much of that was playing out, Lindsay and I had escaped to Quebec City for a four-day break. If you're with the right person, at the right moment in a romance, nothing deepens a relationship like four days strolling through the snow-filled streets of old Quebec. I swear I did not think for even one moment of the political maelstrom we had helped to create and that was now presumably raging in the nation's capital. I couldn't. Lindsay and I connected on a whole new level while in that beautiful city. Without romanticizing it too much, it seemed more a meeting of minds and hearts than anything else, although deep and long discussions were punctuated by the breathless meeting of more tangible parts. When we returned to Cumberland, Lindsay promptly moved into the boathouse with me. It was the most wonderful Christmas gift I'd ever received.

Angus had spent his holiday break in the workshop putting the finishing touches on *Baddeck 1*, the now famous homemade hovercraft that had brought down a government. I'd seen very little of him since Lindsay and I had returned, but as I climbed the outside stairs to the apartment above, I spied through the workshop window that the hovercraft was finally varnished so the blue paint gleamed.

Yesterday had been wonderful. Christmas morning always has a special feel to it. The streets had been deserted as Lindsay and I drove to pick up Muriel, before returning to open gifts and wade through the turkey fumes at the McLintock house. Pete1 and Pete2, two pierced and tattooed punk rocker engineering students, and our only campaign volunteers, made a brief appearance, on leave from their own family celebrations in Cumberland. In true Christmas spirit, Pete1 had attached a jingle bell to one of his cheek piercings while Pete2 had reinforced his red and green frosted mohawk with enough mega-hold gel to support a small sprig of mistletoe that hung perfectly above and in front of his forehead. Nice.

Angus did not once raise politics but outdid himself as merry host. Well, as merry as a crusty Scot can be. He fussed over Muriel as never before and made sure she was settled in a comfortable chair before he passed out the gifts arranged under the tree in the window. It helped that he bears a striking resemblance to Santa Claus in street clothes, although I doubt Santa carried sawdust and sandwich crumbs in his beard, let alone spoke through such a thick Scottish accent.

Angus clearly took delight in giving gifts, despite his curmudgeonly demeanour. He'd obviously given heartfelt thought to each of the gifts he presented. To Muriel, he gave the final typewritten manuscript of his late wife's last book. Muriel had been a great admirer of Marin Lee's writing, long before she knew Angus had been her husband. She was moved to glistening eyes by the gesture. On almost every page, there were notes in Marin's own hand in the margins. Angus had built and varnished an ornate maple box, with a lid and latch that housed the manuscript perfectly.

For the two Petes, Angus had somehow secured two official lapel pins of the mace of Canada's Parliament that must be worn by MPs to allow them access to the House of Commons. I have no idea how he'd gotten his hands on two extras. Using his soldering skills, Angus had fashioned each mace pin into what looked like a big safety pin so they could be worn as body piercings for special occasions. Angus warned them not to show up on Parliament Hill wearing them or the Commissionaires might seize their pins and "escort" them off the premises.

When Lindsay opened the very old Walter Duff sketch of the Canadian Senate Angus had found for her, she just shook her head in surprise and locked him in a bear hug. Lindsay was doing her Master's in political science and her thesis was on the future of the Senate. She was bucking the prevailing wisdom and felt strongly that the Senate could actually become the chamber of second sober thought that it was originally envisaged to be. The sketch was a beautiful piece of art in a simple and classy black frame. She was touched.

As for me, I unwrapped a mint-condition, signed first edition of Robertson Davies's novel *Leaven of Malice*, the only one of his great works to have won the Stephen Leacock Medal for Humour. I have no idea how Angus had known, but this was the only Davies novel I didn't own in a first edition.

I don't know who was more pleased, all of us who had just opened absolutely perfectly chosen gifts or Angus himself, as our unalloyed pleasure washed over him.

Having passed all the gifts under the tree to us, Angus eventually got around to opening my gift to him. He looked at it for such a long time I began to worry. Then he raised his eyes to mine and mouthed, "I thank you." No sound came with his words.

It was a framed photograph taken at Baddeck in Cape Breton in 1918. In the foreground, a dock juts into Baddeck Bay. Dominating the right-hand side of the photograph, Alexander Graham Bell stands with his back to the camera. He cuts a fine figure in tweed knickers and a poor-boy cap. He gazes out towards the bay watching as his hydrofoil, the *HD-4*, races above the waves on its ladder blades towards the world water speed record it would own for more than a decade. Later that night as I sat at my – rather our – kitchen table in the dark counting my blessings, I saw Angus trudging through the snow towards the boathouse, the Bell photo under his arm. Fifteen minutes after he'd entered the workshop below, I heard five faint hammer blows as a finishing nail was driven into the wooden wall so Bell could watch not only his beloved *HD-4*, but also stand guard over *Baddeck 1*.

Enough reminiscing. We'd both finished the *Globe* and the *Crier* and really had no excuse left for still being in bed at that hour. Lindsay leapt up first, newspapers flying everywhere, and threw on a T-shirt and sweat pants. A minute later she was standing in the centre of the living room holding her new Duff sketch and eyeing each wall in turn.

"How about over the bookcase?" she proposed, holding it up against the wall.

"Done!" I replied. "Much better than the poker-playing dogs I had in mind."

Long a believer in using the right tool for the job, I jumped up to swing a heavy saucepan to embed the picture hanger in the drywall. It took me nine swings to make contact once with the nail. I had a much higher batting average hitting my thumb. As for location, I'd have let her suspend it from the refrigerator door if she'd wanted to. Hanging her Christmas present from Angus on the wall, on our wall, seemed to codify that we were actually living together. I liked that too . . . a lot.

We spent the rest of the day squished together on the couch reading, except for about forty-five minutes late in the afternoon when we were squished together on the couch not reading. I was immersed in my signed first edition of *Leaven of Malice*, marvelling at how Davies strung together so many luminous sentences. Lindsay was engrossed in Rohinton Mistry's *A Fine Balance*.

At 6:00-ish, I kissed her on the forehead, descended the boathouse stairs, and ambled up the snowy trail to Angus's front door. I figured he'd spent enough time alone over his first Christmas break without Marin. I knocked.

"You ready?" I asked as he opened the door.

"Aye, but are you?" He let me pass and closed the door on the winter wind.

He was wearing denim overalls above a bright orange Buchanan tartan flannel shirt. It took my eyes a moment to adjust. I'm not kidding. In concert with the chaos of his hair and beard, it put him in the running for the eighth wonder of the world. He took his place at the table next to the window with the frozen Ottawa River only just visible in the fading light. I sat opposite and palmed a black pawn in one hand and a white in the other beneath the table. He chose and I handed him back his black pawn. I much prefer playing white anyway.

Angus seemed distracted but was a skilled enough player to brood on some other subject while still dismantling me on the chess board, whereas I needed to devote all my cerebral energy to the game to avoid spectacular blunders that often spelled defeat in fewer than ten moves. We settled into a standard opening and the familiar rhythm of the game. Time to focus.

"I know I warned you about the ice on the porch, laddie, but I may not have mentioned that there is in fact a spare key to the apartment hanging beneath the railing opposite the door," Angus said, his face expressionless, his eyes trained on the board, but with a twinkle germinating.

I sighed.

"Fantastic. That's just great. How much did you see?" I asked, mortified.

"Oh, I didnae come upon the scene until your hindquarters were lodged in the hall window with your legs windmillin' out of control like a . . . well, like a windmill out of control. An uncommon, even startlin' sight at dawn's first light, it was. It fair put me off my oatmeal."

"You might at least have tried to help me. I might have been hurt," I whined.

"Aye. Well, you also might have worn pyjamas. They're all the rage these days. Even I wear them. Och, calm yourself, professor. I was halfway out the door to render assistance when you managed to wriggle through." Angus was smiling now, but still staring at the board. "I might have come to your aid sooner but it took me a moment or two to find my camera. But damned if I could lay my hands on the tripod. I almost had you in the lens when your flappin' feet disappeared through the window and I heard you thump to the floor, even from this distance. So of course I retreated discreetly, as you would have done for me."

He was enjoying this a little too much so I said nothing, not wanting to encourage him.

"Mate in three," Angus announced.

Great. I confirmed his claim in an instant and toppled my king in surrender.

We played four games. Three decisive McLintock victories, but I managed a draw in the fourth game. Angus refilled his single malt and handed me another Coke before draping himself on the chintz couch. I reclined as much as I could in my extraordinarily uncomfortable arrowback chair at the chess board. It's no wonder I lost, the seat was so hard I'd had no feeling in my legs since halfway through our second game.

"So you know what happens tomorrow, I suppose." I inched towards the issue.

"I still read the papers. I see our feckless leader has sent the NDP packin'. I held out little hope for a coalition but it would have been interestin'. I'm just not sure it would have been good for the country."

"Well, I figure it's a moot point now. The GG will probably drop the writ tomorrow and it's back to the polls we go, whether the voters like it or not," I said. "What I still don't know for sure is who will be the Liberal candidate in Cumberland-Prescott." I took in a breath and held it.

"Well, laddie, if you've no big plans tomorrow, let's have Muriel over for lunch and we'll put an end to it all." He swept his hand over the *Globe and Mail* on the floor, opened to André's article. "We can meet with the university later in the week, but I think they'll be fine if we both return. I foresee no problems."

I exhaled, relieved. It seemed I really was slipping out of the noose. His demeanour suggested I should drop the subject. I've learned the hard way to go with his demeanour. My mind flashed to the university life about to welcome us back.

When I returned to the boathouse, Lindsay was already asleep. I find confirmation in my feelings for her when I watch her sleep. It's hard to explain. A face at peace – free of stress, joy, angst, or happiness. A face at rest. Perhaps it's knowing what the face can reveal and convey when awake that holds my eye and my heart. I was still watching her sleep when I heard Angus slip into the workshop below.

DIARY
Thursday, December 26
My Love,
I've made it through by the skin of my teeth. I cursed the

Christmas traditions we created together as they fell silent for the first time without you. I don't mean that how it sounds. But it fair tore me up these last few days. My saving grace, beyond incessant thoughts of you, was having Muriel, Daniel, Lindsay, et al. over for Christmas dinner. I fear I'd still be deep in the abyss were they not there with me.

I also had some time to tidy up *Baddeck 1* after what the damn papers are calling "its historic run up the river" a couple of weeks ago. Pap and hyperbole. The paint is now done and dried and the varnish kicks off a mighty sheen. I'm now only waiting for an electric starter motor to arrive from Cordova, Illinois, so I can start her from the comfort of the cockpit rather than yanking that cursed pull-cord astern. And then she's done.

As to my current dilemma, I've gathered the clan and will tell them tomorrow. But I think you already know . . . AM

CHAPTER TWO

I found Muriel Parkinson sitting with her coat on in the main lounge of the Riverfront Seniors' Residence. That morning, she looked every one of her eighty-one years. Politics takes its toll, and Muriel had given herself completely to the Liberal Party, running in five consecutive elections in a riding that had never, ever gone red. That is until three months ago.

The curved wall of windows overlooked the frozen reaches of the Ottawa River where a windless day lent the scene the stillness of a photograph. Her eyes were glued to the TV in the corner where the top CBC news anchor and the parliamentary bureau chief were killing time before cutting live to the Governor General's residence.

Muriel sensed me behind her and held up a trembling index finger to preempt me, her eyes still fixed on the screen. I reached for her hand, and we both focused on the talking heads.

"Well, Peter, the negotiations went irrevocably south a few days ago. The two leaders emerged awash in a sea of bitterness and recrimination. Our backroom sources quote the Liberal Leader describing the NDP Leader as a 'washed-up Marxist with forty-year-old ideas' before he stomped to his waiting car," the bureau chief commented.

"And what did the NDP Leader have to say for himself?"

"Well, he was much more succinct, Peter, declaring the Liberal Leader to be 'an imbecile.'"

I sighed at the deep and insightful analysis of live, unscripted television. But wait! There was more compelling news to break.

"Peter, while we have a minute or two to fill, there was a related story on the wire this morning. Apparently, the Sado Masochism Association of Canada, known as SMAC, has just issued a news release naming the Honourable Eric Cameron, the disgraced former Finance Minister, as their Naughty Boy of the Year, bestowed annually on a Canadian who brings honour and glory to what they call the 'S&M cause.'"

Muriel just rolled her eyes and shook her head.

Beside her, an old man, wearing a full suit and cravat, in a wheelchair took great delight in the Cameron story.

"And long may he spank!" he cackled, his shoulders pumping up and down like pistons.

I was struck that the Cameron story was still news after so many weeks and so much political drama. But I suppose I shouldn't have been. The volatile combination of extreme sex and high-profile politicians always made for good ink.

There was a brief but awkward silence before the news anchor finally found a way of filling the dead air.

"Well, um, er, our congratulations to Eric Cameron, wherever he may be, on yet another, um, noteworthy distinction." He then furrowed his brow and nodded his head in sage acknowledge-ment. Eventually, he looked down, giving us a good view of his growing bald spot and placed his index finger on his earpiece. A moment passed. Composed again, he lifted his eyes once more to the camera. "Well, let's now go live to Rideau Hall where the Governor General is expected to announce the dissolution of Parliament, sending Canadians back to the polls for the second time in four months."

Muriel squeezed my hand as a sombre GG read a very brief statement, lamenting that the House of Commons could not come together to sustain a government and calling an election for Monday, January 27. I did a quick count in my head, arriving at a thirty-one-day campaign, shorter than the standard affair. The GG had invoked a rarely used provision in the Elections Act that gives her the latitude in extraordinary circumstances to abbreviate the campaign period. Obviously, she considered asking Canadians to endure a second full campaign, so soon after the last one, to be cruel and unusual punishment.

Shortly thereafter, CBC cut back to regularly scheduled programming.

"And so it is done," Muriel intoned as if presiding over a funeral, although a hint of a smile circled, as if seeking clearance to land. "And it certainly adds some drama to our imminent lunch."

She reached for my arm to begin the sometimes difficult ascent from her chair to a position somewhere between stooping and standing. It is a cruel coincidence that Muriel Parkinson lives with a disease whose name she shares. Muriel clutched my arm as she performed what she called the Parkinson's shuffle out to my battered, aging Ford Taurus. The slow but steady progression of her disease meant growing bouts of tremors and shakes, and restricted her to assisted walking only.

"Just what exactly do you mean, that the election call adds drama to our lunch?" I asked as I eased her into the front seat.

"I mean I don't think Angus is inviting us over just to showcase his culinary prowess."

"Muriel, stop. There is no way Angus is going to run again. It's not happening. Being the accidental MP for a few months was a pleasant little distraction but I think his fifteen minutes are up. He as much as told me so last night. And that means I can finally say goodbye to Parliament Hill and good riddance to partisan politics."

Muriel just smiled and watched the river as we drove out of Cumberland to the McClintock house. In her lap, her index finger rubbed back and forth against the pad of her thumb, unbidden.

"Come on, Muriel, you're supposed to say 'Yes, of course you're right, Daniel. Angus has served Cumberland-Prescott well but it's time he headed back to the engineering faculty.'"

"Daniel, if I believed that I'd say it. But I don't, and because I want to arrive safely for lunch, I'm keeping quiet about it." She turned her gaze to the trees lining the road. "I think I just saw a cardinal."

We drove in silence for a time before she piped up again, ever cheerful.

"I understand my granddaughter and you are now living together in sin in the McLintock boathouse." She was still gazing casually out the window.

I still wasn't used to her directness. News travels fast in small towns.

. "I was going to tell you. We were going to tell you," I stammered. "We had such an amazing time in Quebec City. And, well, one thing led to another, which led to her moving her stuff in when we got back. I hope you're okay with that. You are okay with that, aren't you?"

She reached over and patted my arm.

"I couldn't be happier."

I unclenched.

Not another word was exchanged for the rest of the drive, giving me plenty of quiet time to wonder why I thought I might finally be free of politics. I reviewed the evidence again and again, and convinced myself that Angus could not and would not seek re-election and the world would return to equilibrium. I really didn't think I had the stomach to return to politics yet again. And I was eager to resume my delayed re-entry to the academic world. When Angus won the seat, the University of Ottawa had agreed to hold open my teaching position in the English department so I could accompany the new Cumberland-Prescott MP to Parliament Hill. Working with Angus had been fun, fresh, and even exciting. But like skydiving, I wasn't sure I could do it every day for the next four years, even if Angus could somehow win this seat again without the gift of his new Tory opponent self-immolating just before the vote. It felt like I was done.

When we arrived at Chateau McLintock, Angus was waiting to open the car door for Muriel and arm her into the warmth of the living room. My last act before getting out of the car was to set my BlackBerry to *Vibrate* so we wouldn't be disturbed during lunch. Angus seemed happy. His hair, a cross between Albert Einstein and Bob Marley, was in full frazzle. His beard? Well, it looked not unlike Niagara Falls, just not quite as orderly. Safely ensconced on the couch with a glass of Dubonnet, Muriel looked utterly content as Angus bustled about. I flopped down next to her. Out the window, I could see the boathouse through the trees. Lindsay had gone over to her mother's to help her assemble a bird feeder she'd received for Christmas from a distant and sadistic relative. The kit had more parts than a V8 engine and instructions written only in French, Spanish, Italian, and what Lindsay thought might be Japanese. I'd offered to help, but knowing of my stunted mechanical gifts, Lindsay had wisely declined. For me, it's a very short trip from "do it yourself" to "blew it yourself."

"Angus, I had such a wonderful time here on Christmas afternoon," Muriel gushed in a voice designed to reach Angus all the way in the kitchen. "It was a wonderful celebration."

"Aye, that was a splendid time," Angus replied as he returned with a serving tray of Swedish meatballs. There was also some kind of a sauce and a tiny pewter cylinder of toothpicks. Despite her tremor, Muriel was quite adept at stabbing the meatballs, dipping them, and then getting them to her mouth. I was into my fourth or fifth meatball when Angus headed for the door to the deck.

"Okay, I'm runnin'," Angus said over his shoulder, his Scottish lilt draped over every word, but more like a tarpaulin than a shawl.

"What do you mean? We just got here," I said perplexed. Muriel was smiling in mid-meatball.

His hand on the doorknob, Angus turned to me.

"You're not hearin' me. Or perhaps you don't want to. I said, I'm runnin' . . . for re-election." With that, he disappeared out onto the deck where a bottle of white wine chilled in the snow.

I knew from childhood birthday parties that in moments of

shock, or even hilarity, milk can actually pass from one's mouth up through the sinuses and project out the nostrils. I'd seen it myself and even experienced it once or twice. But I confess I had no idea that a chunk of Swedish meatball could make that same perilous journey. By the time my coughing and gagging subsided, Angus had returned from the deck, wine in hand, his face creased with concern. Muriel just patted my back, smiling and nodding her head vigorously in affirmation. There was a very distinct "I told you so" gleam in her eye. By then, Angus was smiling and shaking his head, happy that the Heimlich manoeuvre was not on the menu.

"What was all that talk yesterday about 'putting an end to it all'?" I sputtered, when I'd finally regained the ability to vocalize.

"The *speculation*, man! I meant let's put an end to all the speculation swirling in the damn papers. I thought you knew where I was," Angus replied.

I thought I knew too.

"Yeah, but you said you thought the university would be fine if we were to 'return.'" I used my fingers to mime quotation marks in the air. "It seemed quite clear to me that you meant 'return' to the university."

"You were listenin' for what you wanted to hear, laddie. I'm sorry. I meant 'return' to the House of Commons. Go back to Parliament Hill. Was I not clear?" he asked.

Silence descended and I tried to figure out my next move. But Angus wasn't finished.

"But there's an iron-clad condition to my decision. I cannae do it without you both. I won't do it without you both," Angus prompted. "That's my immutable caveat."

Muriel leapt in first.

"Of course I'm here for you, Angus," she fairly shouted. "I'm tickled you're up for the fight and I'll gladly carry your sword and shield."

"I thank you, Muriel. I knew you'd be there. Well, that's one down. What say you, Professor Addison?"

Shit. Two sets of imploring eyes turned my way as I sank deeper into the couch, rehearsing in my mind the lines that my head had devised when my heart wasn't looking, in case of just such an emergency.

Angus, Angus, Angus. You no longer need me. You've achieved a great deal and really blazed your own trail. I've actually done very little and I have no doubt you'll be re-elected. But I think my time in politics and on Parliament Hill has finally come to end. I'm excited about my new academic career and the future it holds and I want to get started on it. Of course I'll help you find a good campaign manager and executive assistant, and I'll always follow your exploits with pride, but I think I'm going to sit this one out.

Still, imploring eyes. Then, somewhere between my brain and my mouth, my thoughtful and carefully crafted message took a wrong turn or pulled up lame, possibly both. All I could manage was:

"Angus. I just can't do it again. I'm tapped out."

He stood up, his face clouding over. Muriel gaped at me as if I'd just drowned a Labrador puppy, slowly.

"I'm sorry. It's been a ride and a half but it's time for me to move on," I pleaded. "You don't need me any more. There are plenty of EAs out there. Finding one you like and trust will be easy."

"I've no interest in anyone else. I'm a creature of habit and I like the team we've got," Angus replied. "Dinnae give me your answer right now. Think on it. Talk to Lindsay. Sleep on it. I'll not announce my decision until tomorrow morning but I cannae run if you're not there. I'll not."

How do I get myself into these messes? It was an awkward hour thereafter, even after we moved to the table. Very awkward. I felt terrible. I'd let them down as surely as if I'd crossed the floor to join the Tories. But I'd spent five years of my life on the Hill and it had almost done me in. It was time I started a new chapter. I thought I'd earned that right.

I was relieved when Angus insisted on driving Muriel home

after lunch. I'd dreaded the return trip to the Riverfront Seniors' Residence after disappointing Muriel. They left in a melancholy fog and I slunk back to the apartment. I couldn't just walk out on Angus, so I agreed to organize the news conference for the next morning, even though it wasn't yet clear what Angus was announcing. I sat at the kitchen table and emailed a quick media advisory to the regional media and to the Parliamentary Press Gallery inviting them to the Cumberland Motor Inn for 10 a.m. Asking journalists to attend a Saturday morning newser was quite possibly unprecedented, but the election had already been called. If Angus were not the candidate, another Liberal would have to step up, so there was no time to waste. While I worked on the advisory, I heard Lindsay's cellphone ring. She took it out on the porch, making me think it was either Muriel or Angus.

I'd just hung up from my call to the Cumberland Motor Inn to confirm the small function room when Lindsay came back inside, with a face that said pensive.

"You finished?" she asked. "Let's go for a walk up the river."

Even though I figured I was about to be hit with a full-court press, I still liked the idea of walking on the ice in the sunshine with Lindsay next to me. Besides, that evening she was headed off to Montreal with her mother for a long-planned, post-Christmas shopping weekend, so we only had what was left of the afternoon together.

"One more quick call, then we'll go," I promised.

I called Angus and told him about the arrangements for the morning news conference. I also told him I'd give him my final answer in the morning, though I was pretty sure my position would remain the same. Angus reported that he'd be picking Muriel up early and he'd see me in the news conference room well before the ten o'clock start.

"I just need to know which announcement I'm making," Angus said.

The ice was hard but a thin layer of snow near the shore made it like walking on a snow-covered street. Not a cloud in the sky and the wind had fallen as the sun started its descent. We'd walked in silence for ten minutes before she spoke.

"Why did you go to Parliament Hill in the first place?"

No preliminaries. Right into it.

"It sounds so naïve and corny in hindsight, but I truly believed that I had an obligation to serve. That the government should make the right choices, even if they weren't always the popular choices," I replied, not looking at her. "I remember telling my father that I actually thought of public service as a noble calling. Can you believe that?"

"And why did you want to escape to Cumberland last summer?"

"After five years, I felt as if I'd almost crossed completely over to the other side. I'd become one of them. Image became supreme. Sound bites replaced meaningful discourse. Opinion polls no longer informed policy development, they dictated it. Long-term planning, looking into Canada's future, meant four years at the most. Our vision horizon was forty-eight months. If the government were in year three of the mandate, looking ahead meant twelve months. It finally dawned on me one day that I really was thinking like them. It was time to get out."

Lindsay just walked, nodded, and kept up her questions.

"Was it different working with Angus?"

"Completely different. He's unlike any politician I've ever known. He has more common sense than any politician I've ever known. He doesn't care what people think. He seems congenitally programmed to do what's right even if it costs him support. And he's as honest as they come. He refused to play the political game. Instead, he changed the rules. And he made it work. One man against a powerful political system more than a century in the making. There are time-honoured forces at play on the Hill that Angus simply defied. One man."

"Two, actually," countered Lindsay. "And how did it feel when you shut down that environmental travesty of an aggregate mill or when you helped Sanderson Shoes reinvent itself?"

"I'm not sure I've ever thought about it in those terms but

now that you mentioned it, I guess it felt good. It felt like we actually achieved something in the public interest. It felt, for once, like we'd done what we'd been elected to do."

"How often did you feel that rush when you were writing speeches for the Liberal Leader?"

"Not often enough. Okay, never. Wow, you are good."

Lindsay smiled and held my hand.

"So why is it suddenly okay for you and Angus McLintock to leave the game now that you've started to change the rules? Seems to me we'll be back to 'politics as usual' before the ballots are even counted."

We walked and talked like this for as long as we could. I was not conscious of the passage of time. I told her I was tired. I told her I'd done my part. I told her I was ready for a change. Even though it wasn't directly related to my Angus dilemma, I told her I'd never been happier than since I'd met her. I slipped on the ice, landed hard on my back, and told her it didn't hurt and that I'd meant to do that. She held my hand throughout, apart from the fall. She never overtly passed judgment on my decision, yet her questions deftly focused my thinking in a way that undermined my own position. Finally, Lindsay's mother called her cellphone to remind her of the Montreal departure time. She wanted to get at least some of the drive done in daylight. After I'd driven Lindsay to her mother's, her most pointed comment was delivered just before she got out of the car. She faced me in the front seat and took my hands in hers.

"The university will always be there. Politicians like Angus McLintock won't be," she started. "I'll be with you whatever you decide, because we've got something going on here that I'm really enjoying and that I've really needed. But I don't want you, Professor Addison, to wake up beside me in six months, complain about the state of politics in this country, and idly wonder what Angus and you might have accomplished had you both gone back into the game. Don't you dare do that."

She kissed me and got out. I drove away.

Shit. When we'd started the river walk together, I was committed to my escape plan. A few hours later, as I pulled in the driveway alone, I was waffling so much I could almost smell maple syrup. Gripping the railing, I clumped up the outside staircase and into the apartment. A voice mail from U of O's Vice President, Administration, was waiting for me.

"Daniel, it's Brenda LaChance. I heard on the street that you might be returning to the campus fold sooner than many of us were expecting or, more accurately, hoping. Don't get me wrong. We're looking forward to having you back on the team here. But it was sure nice having two of the university's own ensconced on Parliament Hill. We're all hoping Angus runs again. It would be good for the country and good for U of O. You're welcome back here whenever you're ready, but returning in the middle of the year does complicate matters somewhat. We'll make it work, but are you sure you don't want to take another ride on the McLintock roller coaster? Let me know of your plans."

Another country heard from.

I was still awake at 3:30 in the morning weighing the pros and cons, weighing the options, weighing my future. I even weighed myself on the bathroom scale to alleviate the tedium of just lying in bed weighing things in my head. By the time I fell asleep, around 4:30, as near as I can estimate, I was once again committed to my position. It just wasn't the same position I'd arrived at in the afternoon. I considered calling Angus to let him know, but he was a bear when awakened. I hated sleeping without Lindsay beside me, but I was so tired by the time my mind was free enough for sleep that I'm not sure her absence made much difference that night. I just managed to set my alarm before my coma came a-calling.

When I awoke, the sun was streaming into my bedroom. I heard no music from my clock radio, so I had no idea why I was conscious. I turned my head and saw the dreaded flashing 12:00 on my bedside table – a power outage in the night. That's not good,

I thought. I cursed Captain Murphy and his stupid law and grabbed my BlackBerry. My BB told me it was 9:45! That was really not good. Angus was due to face the cameras in fifteen minutes, and I was not going to make it. He'd be freaking out. I also noticed that my BB was still set to *Vibrate* and I'd missed six calls in the last two hours. Three from Muriel, two from Peter, and one from Lindsay. No time to shower, so I threw on khakis, a white shirt, and my academic-issue tweed sports jacket, no leather elbow patches, though. I couldn't find my dressy trench coat so I went without. I burst through the front door onto the landing at warp speed ready to vault down the stairs two, perhaps three, at a time, to my trusty, rusty Ford Taurus waiting below. But this time, I'd already released my grip on the doorknob when the words "porch ice" skidded into my mind.

My tailbone hit the icy deck and I slid on my back towards the railing faster than a bobsledder on the Cresta run. The origin of the term "breakneck speed" dawned on me.

The Building Code was amended in 1985 to require crosspieces in outdoor railing design to prevent the hapless from sliding underneath and injuring themselves. A sensible change, to be sure. But as I hurtled underneath the railing into space, I remembered Angus telling me he'd built the boathouse in 1983. On instinct, my final act before leaving the landing altogether was to snag the rolled-up *Cumberland Crier* on my way past in case I had time for in-flight reading. I noticed the spare key for the boathouse apartment hanging from a small brass hook on the underside of the railing as I slid by. Good to know.

Mercifully, the relentless and heavy snowfall of the past two weeks meant a feet-first, featherbed fall into a massive drift of wet packing snow some ten feet below. A perfect dismount – and I really stuck the landing. And I do mean stuck. When the dust . . . er, snow, settled, only my neck and head protruded above the surface of the snowbank. It held me tight. I could feel the pressure from the snow on my chest as my breathing approached hyperventilation. My right arm was free, still holding the newspaper high and clear of the snow. Always protect the newspaper.

Had I not been so unaccountably late for Angus's newser, my little mishap would probably have been exciting, even fun. I might well have repeated the stunt recreationally. But entombed neck-deep in snow, with only a copy of the *Cumberland Crier* to save me, I was a little miffed, completely unable to move, wet, and heading fast from chilled to frozen. Boots, mitts, a hat, and a proper winter coat might have been a good idea given the weather, but I hadn't planned on impromptu arctic survival training. On the bright side, I was very much awake. Full immersion in packing snow had elevated me to a higher plane of consciousness than even the Hare Krishnas promised. At one point early in my incarceration, I felt my BlackBerry vibrating in my pocket but I was powerless to reach it.

I'd never felt claustrophobic in small elevators or even when I managed to lock myself in the trunk of the family car when I was just a child. Okay, I was sixteen at the time, researching a project on Houdini; I really thought I'd be able to escape. Even when I'd gone spelunking with a friend at university, I'd been quite comfortable in that dark, dank, and cramped subterranean world. But being held fast and frozen up to my neck in the snowbank's viselike grip, with only my head and arms in daylight, really seemed to push my panic button. The novelty of my predicament wore off quickly. I not only needed to get out fast, I desperately wanted to.

"Stay calm," I said aloud to myself. Actually, it may have been more like "STAY CALM!" as every bird singing in every tree within a hundred-metre radius burst into flight in unison. It was quite a striking sight.

DIARY
Friday, December 27
My Love,
You must find it amusing to see me scuttling about the

galley wearing your apron. I've not yet washed it and may never. You see, there is still your faint scent upon it. It somehow finds its way to me now and then, buffeted by the other aromas of the kitchen. It is a comfort still.

Poor Daniel. All this time I thought we were seated together. But I discovered today we're on different buses going in different directions. Muriel says he'll come around, but time is short and I'll not go without him. Damnation. Just when I'd finally decided to seek that which I already had, but never wanted, Daniel throws in a spanner. I need him. And I need you. What a strange journey it is.

AM

CHAPTER THREE

The appendages that weren't buried and already numb seemed
to be working properly. Barely controlling my anxiety, and using
the folded sports section of the *Crier* as a scoop of sorts, I was
eventually able to claw and crawl my way out of the snowbank
and race for the car. I was soaked to the skin and so was my poor
BlackBerry. The screen flashed anemically but there was no cell
signal and no way to alert anyone that the cavalry was on the
way. The car started right away, on the twelfth attempt, and I was
off, fishtailing out of the driveway, shivering and shedding clumps
of snow onto the front seat. Despite the heater in the Taurus, I
still couldn't feel my legs.

On the ten-minute drive out to the Cumberland Motor Inn,
where I knew Angus would already be standing at the podium
announcing his retirement from politics, I had an epiphany of
sorts. I realized that there really was never any hope of sitting
this one out. If I were really honest with myself, for all my big
talk, I didn't *want* to sit it out. I'd already tried to leave the
brutal and cynical world of politics to nurse my public service
calling back to health in the relative serenity of academe. I'd
tried and failed. I'd always assumed that restoring my faith in
our democracy would be possible only away from the crucible
of Parliament Hill. It really never occurred to me that my political rehab might unfold successfully within the game itself. That
the alcoholic could dry out while still in the tavern. But that's
what the honesty and integrity of Angus McLintock seemed to

have made possible. Lindsay's stiletto questions and Muriel's glare had also helped.

I executed a perfect four-wheel drift into a snowbank in the parking lot and came to rest as close as I could to the door to the meeting rooms. The door was locked. I sprinted back around to the front of the motel and into the lobby as fast as my frozen pant legs and straight-legged gait permitted. I didn't stop to seek directions, I knew exactly where I was going, and goose-stepped my way, panting, to the other end of the building where the Confederation Room beckoned. I got some strange looks from the guests and staff milling in the lobby but I was beyond worrying about such minor considerations. I burst into the room at the point of passing out from exhaustion. Muriel was at the podium and Angus looked stone-faced standing behind her. This meant only one thing. I was too late. Angus had already announced he would not seek the Liberal nomination and Muriel was about to close the proceedings. It was 10:34. I was too late. Shit. What a failure I was.

I still couldn't speak. I felt sick but willed myself not to throw up, although it might have improved the look of the carpet. I bent over, feeling as if I might never breathe again. Then I straightened up and puffed for a time, holding my hand in the air to interrupt Muriel and claim the floor. Apparently, I was still completely covered in snow, as an expanding pool of water soaked into the carpet beneath me. One reporter later described my entrance as the first ever sighting of the rare and elusive Cumberland yeti. All eyes turned to me, including the bulging peepers of Angus and Muriel.

"Wait . . . stop! Please wait!" I gasped for air. "There's been a horrible mistake and a terrible misunderstanding," I said, slowly gaining control over my lungs and voice.

"Ignore what Angus has just announced. It's all my fault. Angus McLintock will, I repeat will, be seeking re-election as the Member of Parliament for Cumberland-Prescott and I'll be running the campaign again, with Muriel Parkinson providing her expert leadership and guidance as well." I heard clicking behind me. "Sorry about barging in late but I had a little run-in with a snowbank."

"Looks like you lost," a reporter in the back said.

"Muriel, back to you to finish up," I managed and dropped into the nearest empty chair.

"Well, thank you, Daniel, for your rather unorthodox entrance and declaration," Muriel replied. Something wasn't sounding quite right. Neither Muriel nor Angus looked as happy as I thought they would. Peter scurried over and whispered in my ear loudly enough to do drum damage, and for most of the reporters to hear.

"We had a problem with the PA system so we couldn't start on time. We just got it fixed now. Muriel was just about to start the news conference when you landed," he hissed.

Excellent. Fantastic. I looked up at Muriel and Angus and brought my hands together in prayer, mouthing sorry, while trying to make myself as small as possible. Though moving was difficult with still-frozen pant legs, I lurched to the back behind the cameras. André Fontaine gave me a sarcastic thumbs-up, his Nikon hung around his neck. I then realized what the clicking sound earlier had been.

"Um, good morning, everyone. Why don't we just start all over again. As I was saying, I want to thank you for coming up to our little gem of a town on the shores of the Ottawa River. I am Muriel Parkinson, secretary of the Cumberland-Prescott Liberal Association. Some of you may know that I also carried the Liberal banner unsuccessfully in five elections against the seemingly insurmountable Tory tide. I figured I'd seen it all in Cumberland-Prescott. That is until Angus McLintock let his name stand in last October's election. At eighty-one, I had thought that I'd exhausted my capacity for shock. I was wrong. When this wonderful man, Angus McLintock, found himself the new MP for Cumberland-Prescott, I was very nearly overcome with as strong a sense of contentment and joy as I've ever experienced. And not because a Liberal had finally won this seat. But because Angus McLintock had won this seat. We've never seen an MP like him. Canada has never seen an MP like him. But it is my fervent hope that we will have many MPs like Angus McLintock in the coming years. His honesty, his integrity, his commitment to the national interest above all else is what we need to restore Canadians' faith in our democracy. Though he doesn't see it, I believe Angus McLintock is the vanguard of a new political movement for which so many of us have been longing. Yesterday, my happiness at his October election victory was matched when he told us he wanted to run again. The whole country is the better for his decision. Canadian democracy needs Angus to run and to serve again. I cannot tell you how proud I am to introduce the current and future Member of Parliament for Cumberland-Prescott, Angus McLintock."

It sounded to me like he was going to run, regardless of my position.

When Muriel finished and stepped back from the mike, she wobbled slightly at the knees. Angus moved fast and made it to her side before the swaying moved to its logical horizontal conclusion. He armed Muriel to a chair in the front row, and the room actually applauded, helped along by the enthusiastic clapping of Pete1 and Pete2. Having organized and endured more news conferences than I cared to remember, I knew it was rare, and bizarre for that matter, for journalists to applaud.

Muriel sat and fixed her eyes on Angus as he stood at the microphone applauding her. She gestured for him to stop clapping and start talking, but Angus wasn't quite ready to shift the focus to him. Muriel had hit it out of the park without even a note. Eventually, the room calmed and Angus stepped forward, no notes, no cue cards. He'd tamed his hair and beard so that they looked merely dishevelled rather than chaotic. He'd given up on ties and just wore a suit and a pale blue open-necked dress shirt. Television likes pale blue shirts. I'd been there when he'd bought the suit. But whenever he wore it, it always seemed as if it belonged to someone else. He rocked from one foot to the other until he was ready, and then looked at Muriel.

"Are you absolutely certain you haven't a sixth campaign left in you, Ms Parkinson?" Angus inquired to the chuckles of those assembled. Muriel looked cross and wagged an index finger at him.

Angus took a deep breath.

"It is tough to follow Muriel Parkinson as a speaker, and as a candidate. As I have said before to some of you, I will always carry with me regret that events should have conspired to place me in the House of Commons with the ink barely dry on my nomination form, when there had already been five previous opportunities for good fortune to smile similarly on Muriel. It should, by rights, and by history, be Muriel in the House and not I. Nevertheless, the milk is spilt and here I am. Muriel, I thank you for your introduction and I'll do whatever I'm able to honour the high standards your public service has set." Angus paused now before continuing.

"Most of you will by now know the story, but four months ago I had no desire to seek public office. On the contrary, nothing could have been further from my mind or my heart. It was only the promise of escaping a duty I loathed, that of teaching English to first-year engineering students, that advanced my name as the Liberal candidate in this riding. It seemed a paltry price to pay to shed an unwelcome burden. History guaranteed that I would lose, thus restoring in mid-October my quiet but satisfying life as an engineering professor. Well, history is not always trustworthy, as I discovered last October 14.

"To be truthful, which I strive always to be, I was angry with my fate and with myself for ever allowing such a scenario to come to pass. I was also quite upset with my co-conspirator, Daniel Addison, though I know he was dealt a shocking hand same as I. But in the intervening weeks, we've been on a journey together. I tell you today, that journey has opened my eyes and infused me with a renewed energy and spirit I thought was lost to me. I have always believed that public service is important and should figure in every citizen's life. I always thought I'd make my contribution as an engineer in the Third World. It seems fate has given me the rare chance to serve in a different way, in the House of Commons."

Angus spoke with a relaxed honesty that rang so true that not even the most hard-bitten reporter considered his words to be anything less than genuine.

"I had not expected to be fulfilled by my work on behalf of the citizens of Canada and the voters of Cumberland-Prescott. But I was. I've long been dismayed by the practice of politics in this country. It has always seemed that logic and reason are shunted to the sidelines to make way for polls and media coverage as the drivers of policy. I think there is another way. I believe that Canadians want their government to make the tough decisions we confront based on the best interests of the nation as a whole. Not on what is right for one party, for one region, for one riding, or for the short horizon of one election campaign. I think the voters have seen enough of the cynical opportunism that today passes for politics, on all sides of the House. And I'm betting my candidacy that Canadians and the voters of Cumberland-Prescott agree.

"No need to prolong this any further. I'm a candidate for the Liberal Party of Canada in Cumberland-Prescott and I pledge in all that I do to put the interests of our country and our citizenry first, even if the voters of Cumberland-Prescott may not always agree. I know the people of this community can lift their eyes beyond the Ottawa River to see the vast potential of this great nation."

Angus paused and lowered his eyes to the floor as if reviewing in his mind the list of items he wished to cover. He seemed to put a mental check mark in each box and lifted his head again.

"I told Muriel and tardy Executive Assistant Daniel Addison yesterday that I'd not run again were they not beside me, and I meant it. I was honoured when Muriel reported to me early this morning that both she and Daniel were with me. I offer them my deep gratitude. Here endeth the sermon," he said, triggering a few snickers among the reporters. "I'm told that I must now entertain your questions, whether I want to or not. So, fire when ready."

I slipped into the chair next to Muriel as Angus scanned the room for reporters' questions.

"You told Angus this morning that I'd be there for him?" I asked her, still perplexed. She didn't even have the courtesy to look sheepish.

"I know you, Daniel Addison, and I knew what you'd ultimately decide. What does it matter that I realized it before you did?" she replied, looking at Angus the entire time. "And I was right, wasn't I?"

I too turned my attention to the Liberal candidate at the mike. This was not the first time most of the gathered reporters had been exposed to Angus McLintock's uncommon approach to politics. When Angus had initially laid out his beliefs on election night back in October, the reporters just weren't ready and had no idea how to react. Angus had finished his eloquent, powerful, yet impromptu acceptance speech to stunned silence and then stepped out of the scrum and headed for the car for the ride home. I hustled to catch up, mentally and physically, as did the reporters. Now, some four months later, the scribes were ready. A reporter from the *Ottawa Sun* piped up first.

"Angus, do you really think the voters of C-P are ready to turn their backs on over one hundred years of traditional Tory rule in this area and send a Liberal back to Ottawa?"

"I frankly think it's a long shot, but we're going to find out," responded Angus. Short and sweet.

"Just between you and I, are you planning on using the hovercraft in your campaign?" asked another reporter.

"Hmmm. I hadn't really thought about that but I imagine *Baddeck 1* may well see some action in the campaign. And for the record, I'm sure you meant to say 'Just between you and me' in your question. But you need not feel too bad, the 'Just between you and I' construction is probably one of the most oft-made grammatical mistakes, so you're in very good company, laddie," Angus soothed, as I winced. Embarrassing the reporters at your own news conference was definitely on the "Don't" page in the candidate's handbook. I furrowed my brow in Angus's direction but he wasn't looking my way.

"There's a rumour that Emerson 'the Flamethrower' Fox will toss his hat into the ring for the Tories. As he is the father of negative campaigning, how do you feel about facing him?"

This was the first I'd heard of Fox running for the Tories. This was definitely not good news for our side.

"Well, I hadn't heard that, and I've never met him," Angus replied. "I'm not one to prejudge a man but I can tell you that if Mr. Fox does run, he need not fear that I will spend the campaign in the gutter engaged in 'negative campaigning.' The voters of Cumberland-Prescott, indeed all Canadians, deserve a campaign that discusses the issues and challenges we face as a nation."

"Knowing that Fox is going to delve deeply into your past, are you worried about anything you've done that might come back to haunt you in the campaign?"

"We all have our weaknesses – heaven knows, I surely do. But this is already a somewhat foreshortened campaign. There really isn't time to explore all of my faults, imperfections, and many indiscretions," Angus deadpanned. By the guffaws and head-shaking, the room liked his answer.

"I figure most of us have some regrets as we look back on lives lived but I sleep mercifully soundly most nights. I spent nearly forty years married to a paragon of virtue. My late wife set very high standards that I still strive to meet. I frequently fall short, yet I strive still. In the end, the voters of C-P will be the final arbiters and I'm at peace with that."

"How goes the fundraising?" inquired a smirking reporter from *Maclean's* magazine.

"I actually haven't a clue, but as far as I know, we'll be living on a shoestring again." Angus looked my way, and I pulled my thawing pants pockets inside out and nodded in confirmation.

A reporter for Canadian Press pointed my way when she asked her question.

"Has Daniel already started researching the Flamethrower's life in the hopes of finding a grenade to lob his way during the campaign?"

"Whomever we face, there'll be none of that on our campaign. We simply refuse to partake in that kind of effort. Call me old-fashioned but we have too much respect for democracy to go tearing it down in that way. When you hear me speak about any of my opponents, it will only be to question, oppose, or support positions they're advancing in the context of the platform I'll be promoting."

"Aren't you being horribly and fatally naïve about all this? You're talking about changing how politics has been conducted in this country for the last fifty years," exclaimed a press gallery skeptic.

"My goals are not nearly so ambitious. I'm merely passing on to you how we intend to conduct our campaign. Call it tilting at windmills if you wish, it makes no matter to me. I'm just going about things the way I think they should be gone about," Angus concluded with a faint shrug. Any nervousness had dissipated. Despite the tailored suit that looked too small and too large depending on the body part examined, Angus actually seemed completely at ease in his own skin. I can't imagine anyone else being at home in it, but Angus clearly was.

"I wonder if you'll still be singing that tune after Emerson Fox launches his first incendiary offensive," said a reporter, sitting at the back and out of my view.

"Believe me, laddie, you don't want me singing under any circumstances. Just be happy I've not brought my bagpipes with me."

After a few more questions, Muriel took the stage to thank them for coming and to invite them to call me at any time for campaign updates.

So it was official. Angus was back in the play. And so was I.

Angus embraced me in the parking lot when it was all over.

"I knew you'd be there. Aye, I knew it," he said, beaming.

"Well, I'm glad you and Muriel knew it. I just wish someone could have told me earlier so I didn't have to spend a sleepless night wrestling with a dilemma that was already resolved." I said it with a smile.

Angus drove Muriel home. I got into the front seat of the Taurus and dialled Bradley Stanton, a man who doesn't apply antiperspirant without first checking polling data. Take-no-prisoners partisan politics runs in his veins and oozes from his every pore. I owed the centre a call about Angus and this little change in plans, before they read it in the papers.

Bradley and I had locked horns quite a few times over Angus McLintock's rare take on politics and public service. I wasn't looking forward to continuing our tussles but you take the bad with the good, I guess. To be clear, Bradley is the bad. He walks around all day, every day, with a Bluetooth earpiece lodged in his ear canal so he doesn't waste any of his valuable time unholstering his cellphone and raising it to the side of his head. He answered on the first ring.

"Stanton!" he blasted in his clipped, drill-sergeant tone.

"Addison!" I mimicked, immediately regretting it.

"Very funny, jackass. Just calling to say goodbye to all this?"

"Actually, Bradley, I wish that were why I was calling. There's been a slight and unexpected turn of events. I wanted to let you know that Angus had such a good time on the Hill that we've just announced he's seeking the Liberal nomination in C-P and will run for re-election." Three, two, one . . .

"What the fuck, Addison! I thought you and your noble warrior would take the hint and get the hell off the field when the opportunity presented itself. You told me yourself you were done! Why would McLintock put himself, and all of us, through that sanctimonious, 'do the right thing' stuff all over again? It's getting old. It's time to walk away, Addison. Just walk away."

This was why I'd needed to leave politics in the first place. Perish the thought that our party might, just once, give the "do the right thing" approach a try.

"I'm as surprised as you are, Bradley. And I've kept a well-travelled piece of Swedish meatball to prove it."

"Meatball? You lost me."

"Forget it. Look, you know that this is still a deep blue riding, and winning it again would mean a second lightning strike," I reminded him.

"You know the party's constitution gives the Leader the authority to appoint candidates. We may just throw someone else in C-P," Bradley threatened.

Ah, the old cut-off-your-nose-to-spite-your-face gambit. I was ready for that one.

"You can put away the big guns, Bradley. We both know that Angus is the only candidate who stands even the slightest chance of keeping C-P red. We need this seat."

I let the angry silence simmer for a moment or two before changing course.

"What have you heard on the street about any Tory candidates?" I inquired. "We've just heard a rumour that I didn't like very much."

"You don't want to know. I've heard only one name and it keeps coming up over and over again from different sources." Stanton paused for dramatic effect. "The Flamethrower." Bradley heard my sharp intake of breath and waited to let the name sink in. "So you'd better trick out your guy McLintock in some asbestos underwear, Danny boy, it's going to be a wild ride."

"So it's really true, Emerson Fox is coming out of the backrooms to run?"

"That's the word. Have a nice day." Stanton hung up.

Emerson Fox. The Flamethrower. Shit. Fox had been a backroom commander of the Tory election machine for nearly forty years. He earned his nickname by pioneering and perfecting what he called "scorched earth negative campaigning." In Canadian politics, whenever any candidate "goes negative" and tosses mud, or worse, in the general direction of his or her opponent, they really should send Emerson Fox a royalty cheque. When Fox figured out the power of negative campaigning and first deployed it strategically in a federal election twenty-five years ago, his colleagues in the Tory war room gave him the name Flamethrower. It stuck, as all perfect nicknames do. Frankly, I thought Flamethrower didn't quite capture Fox's power and ferocity. But "thermonuclear bomb" doesn't exactly roll off the tongue. His specialty was invasive and intensive research on his opponents, stopping just short of B&E and wiretapping. Richard Nixon is one of Fox's heroes. The point is to uncover even the slightest indiscretion in his opponent's lifetime so it could be trotted out in mid-campaign. It didn't have to be anything too serious. Fox's theory was that you didn't have to release incriminating photos of a candidate snorting cocaine while robbing a convenience store in the company of his kids' scantily clad sixteen-year-old babysitter to have an impact on the campaign. Rather, you really only had to sow and nurture just one seed of doubt in a voter's mind as to the candidate's morality or integrity.

One of Fox's Tory candidates had famously come from twenty points back to win a riding after it came to light that the Liberal incumbent MP had passed his Royal Conservatory of Music Grade 8 Piano exam by letting his more talented twin brother play the test piece in his place when they were both fourteen years old. That's all the Flamethrower needed. How did he know about the incident? One of his attack dog researchers had interviewed two of the Liberal MP's high school hockey teammates who had heard the story and laughingly passed it on as a great joke. No joke. To add insult to injury, when the MP admitted the story was true and apologized, the Royal Conservatory actually stripped him of his Grade 8 certificate. It was over then and there.

If there were something to find, a hidden illness, a padded resumé, a shoplifting charge, an illicit affair, a quirky interest in hamsters, or a shoe fetish, Fox would sniff it out and blow the lid off it in public. He earned his nickname every campaign, leaving a string of singed and charred Liberal candidates in his wake.

Coincidentally, I'd just finished reading Fox's autobiography, creatively entitled *Flamethrower*, featuring the catchy subtitle *Going Negative and Winning in Canadian Politics*. In the book, he lays out his theory of negative campaigning and illustrates it with enough examples to turn the most ardent and idealistic optimist into a jaded quivering heap of cynicism. Bradley Stanton kept a copy of the book on his bedside table where he read a passage from the Fox gospels every morning.

I knew that Emerson Fox had retired several years earlier and lived just inside the C-P boundary in the northeast corner of the riding. It never occurred to me that he'd ever come out of retirement, and certainly not to stand as the candidate. And why would it? He'd always inhabited the dimly lit and smoke-choked backrooms. I didn't feel so good. I knew that sometimes Fox would embarrass his opponent by revealing something untoward about the campaign manager. I wondered if Fox knew about the naked woman I'd sketched on the back of my arithmetic notebook in Grade 3. I'd been sent to the principal's office for that. My mind automatically turned to what key messages I might employ to explain my sexist scrawlings. Not good for the manager of a candidate whose late wife is a bona fide feminist icon.

The Flamethrower. Great. Just great.

After changing my still damp clothes, I stopped by Words, Cumberland's only bookstore, and picked up several copies of *Flamethrower*. Pete1, Pete2, Angus, Muriel, and Lindsay would need to read it. Know thine enemy. After lunch at my desk in the Angus McLintock constituency office in Cumberland, I made a careful review of the campaign file I'd compiled from the October election. Then I ducked out again to make one more stop.

Muriel was back in her regular chair in the lounge looking out on the river, a book open in her lap. She saw me approaching and patted the chair next to her.

"You don't look happy to see me, Daniel. That can give a girl a complex, you know. I thought that went very well this morning, other than your little escapade at the start."

"Sorry about that. You wouldn't believe the night and morning I had. When I finally came to the conclusion that I'd give politics one more try, everything went wrong. Luckily, you seemed to know my decision already."

"It was hilarious, though. I can't wait for the *Crier* tomorrow."

"I'm thinking of buying André off. But we have bigger problems than another funny front-page photo."

In response, Muriel just lifted the copy of *Flamethrower* from her lap so I could see the cover.

"I've known for two weeks now," she replied, still holding the book up in the air and away from her as if it might set her dress alight. "I'm reading his tripe now for the third time in the last ten days. His approach is despicable, deceitful, nefarious, regrettably effective, and fully laid out for us to see. We know what he'll do and we'll be ready."

"When were you going to tell me about Fox?" I asked, a little hurt that she'd kept me in the dark.

"I was planning on telling you as soon as Angus announced that he'd be running again with you at the helm. I had no desire to give either of you any reason to back out."

I saw her point.

"But the Flamethrower is going to smoke us. Pun intended. Isn't he?" I whined.

"Emerson Fox is a little pissant Tory brownshirt who enjoys pulling the wings off flies and barbecuing Liberal candidates. We have his game plan right here. We know what he's going to do. And I think Angus is going to have him for breakfast. Angus won't play Fox's game because he knows it will nourish the voter's disrespect for Parliament and politics. But that doesn't mean Angus won't fight back. But he'll change the game on Fox. You don't always fight fire with fire. Sometimes water works pretty well."

"Poor Angus," I sighed.

"Poor Emerson!" countered Muriel.

What a marvel this eighty-one-year-old Liberal stalwart was. I was coming to realize that Muriel relished the fight as much as the victory. We laid out a strategy that protected and promoted Angus's high-road politics and rendered all elements of our campaign fireproof. At least that was the plan. To make it work, we needed honest answers from Angus to the very same questions about his life that Fox's team would be painstakingly researching.

The Fox issue aside, Muriel and I were worried, now that Angus actually wanted to be elected, that he would regress towards typical candidate behaviour and try to please the voters at all costs. Angus was way ahead of us and had talked about this very issue with Muriel the day before. He accepted fully that the root of whatever political success he'd had so far was found in his rejection of what André Fontaine had called "politics as usual." To win, he had to be the honour-bound Angus McLintock who put the national interest above all else, even his own constituents' interests. That was the only way Cumberland-Prescott might, just might, consider re-electing Angus. The voters seemed to like "Angus the maverick" even though he was also "Angus the Liberal" in what had historically been the safest Tory riding in the land. Victory was still a long shot, even if the last few months had improved the odds.

I felt better heading home after cooking up political strategy with Muriel. When I'd arrived at Muriel's, our humble campaign seemed destined to go up in flames at the hands of a skilled political pyromaniac. Now I thought we might well be singed during the campaign, but not fatally. If all went according to plan, Emerson Fox might well get burned. That happens sometimes when you play with matches.

Angus was in the workshop when I made it to the boathouse. He was upside down in the cockpit fiddling beneath the dashboard of *Baddeck 1* while his feet waved in the air. I was impressed, but figured holding such acrobatic positions was eased by his low centre of gravity. When he returned to his normal upright position, I handed him his own copy of *Flamethrower* and displayed my most serious countenance.

"I'm now wearing my campaign manager's hat. Your homework is to read and study this tome as if your future depends on it. Why, you may ask? Because your future depends on it. Meet Emerson Fox, founding father of the negative campaign and almost certainly your Tory opponent in the race."

Angus eyed the book and nodded as recognition dawned.

"Aye, I seem to recall throwin' something at my television when he was yammerin' away on some talk show recently. I figure he's done more to turn our citizenry off politics than anyone else in Canadian history."

I liked the combative tone Angus had adopted. Campaign managers seem to have an easier time when candidates carry a healthy dislike for their opponents.

Twenty minutes later, I headed upstairs, exhausted and hungry. Lindsay was still in Montreal. It was quiet and lonely in the boathouse. A can of minestrone soup and then I was down.

DIARY
Saturday, December 28
My Love,
'Tis done. Daniel gave us a scare but he was there when it counted. Aye, 'tis well and truly done. In hindsight, I'm even glad the negotiations with the NDP collapsed. The two leaders were left standing amidst a great heap of ideological rubble from which nothing of value could be salvaged. So the game is on again. It seems that I may be the only aspirant for the Liberal nomination. Muriel says it would be exceedingly bad form for an incumbent to be challenged in his own riding. Bad form or not, I'll be relieved when the papers are duly signed next Wednesday.

Word is that an infamous rogue from the underbelly of Tory politics will stand against me in the election. They call him Flamethrower for the indiscriminant scorching he lays upon his victims. Knowing that this Emerson Fox is to be my opponent has steeled my spine and stiffened my resolve. But I must stay in control of my emotions. The battle is joined.

AM

CHAPTER FOUR

Lindsay came home on Sunday afternoon from her Montreal sojourn. She came sailing through the door and into my arms as if we'd been apart a year, not a weekend. I cooked dinner for us. She was very impressed. I played it very cool, leaving the impression that I shop, plan meals, and cook all the time, even though I'd ruined two batches of spaghetti sauce before getting it right on the third. I also needed three trips to the grocery store. Third time's the charm. I doubt the Apollo moon landings had more elaborate work-back schedules and checklists than my spaghetti dinner. I knew, of course, that my chef charade wouldn't stand for long. Within a week or so, it would become clear to Lindsay that I was much more adept at making reservations than I was at making dinner. No matter. It was wonderful to have her home and she seemed to feel the same.

"So you made your call. You're back in the race with Angus," she warbled through a mouthful of garlic bread. I took it as a sign of our utter comfort with one another that she would pose a question with her mouth brimming with buttered baguette. "I knew you'd come through. I just knew."

I put down my fork.

"How is it that everyone knew before the guy actually making the call knew?" I asked, genuinely interested in the answer.

"That's easy. You're honourable, ethical, and you care about doing the right thing. With that kind of baggage, you really had no choice. Simple deduction. Plus, you can cook."

I'd also made crème caramel. Really I did. But in the excitement of having Lindsay home, I lost track of time and cooked it just a little too long. It tasted fine, but was packed full of so many air holes it had the texture and look of a melting Aero bar. We skipped dessert and just talked, and talked.

Monday morning, Angus and I headed into Ottawa for a meeting he'd already arranged for us.

The Vice President, Administration, of the University of Ottawa, met us in her office. The campus was virtually deserted, as it usually is in the dead zone between Christmas and New Year's.

"Gentlemen, gentlemen, Happy Holidays to you both," she greeted us warmly as she waved us into her office. We all sat down.

Brenda is a compact woman with tight symmetrical grey curls. Though French is her first language, you'd never know it. In our prior conversations, I'd never detected even the faintest trace of her hometown of Trois-Rivières. A French literature scholar, she is tough, fair, and, according to Angus, very skilled at navigating the sometimes simmering, sometimes seething politics of the modern university. I was glad she was on our side.

"Brenda, I thank you for interrupting your holiday to see us. If it could have waited until after the break, I'd have let it. But I fear it won't keep till then," Angus started.

"It's no trouble, Angus. You know I live just across the way so coming in was an easy call, particularly if you bring the news I'm hoping to hear," she replied.

"Well, I hope we're on the same side of the fence with this. I wanted you to know that I've decided to seek re-election in the upcom –"

"Yes! Now that's what I'm talking about!" The VP Administration jumped to her feet and punched the air, catching us a little off-guard. Angus paused, unsure of how to proceed. It didn't matter, for Brenda continued.

"Angus, that's wonderful news for the riding and for the university. I hoped for this possibility but didn't dare to assume it would unfold this way. In hopeful anticipation, I've already prepared the paperwork to extend your earlier leave of absence, yours too, Professor Addison, with no loss in seniority for however long you both choose to spend in public life. I could not be happier for you."

I kept my mouth shut. This was Angus's show.

"Brenda, you're very kind, and the university's been very good to us both. We're grateful." Angus looked at me. I took the cue and nodded in assent.

"Very grateful," I echoed.

"The one remaining fly in the ointment is probably just arriving in the outer office right now," she said, inclining her head towards the door.

"The Rumper?" Angus asked.

"None other," Brenda confirmed.

Angus was on his feet, rubbing his hands in anticipation.

Defying Darwin somehow, Roland Rumplun had ascended far above his rightful station to hold the lofty position of Dean of Engineering. He is very short and very wide. As near to spherical as any human I've ever encountered. I'm sure it was an optical illusion, but his sprawling belly made him look as if he'd be taller lying down. His black hair was really . . . black, chemically assisted, I assumed. Truculent, miserable, and conceited, he detested Angus with an alarming intensity. It was rumoured that a special task force of engineering graduate students had spent months in a futile secret search for even the slightest circumstantial evidence of Rumplun's sense of humour. Apparently, they'd found nothing yet. My theory is that he'd had it surgically removed in adolescence. Enough lily gilding. Roland Rumplun is, quite simply, a bloated and blustering asshole, period, full stop.

When Angus had shocked the nation and himself by winning the election the previous October, there was very little that could comfort and console him in the immediate aftermath. But discovering that Roland Rumplun would have to take over teaching his first-year English for Engineers course almost made winning worth it.

Angus and I signed the documents Brenda had prepared and rose to leave.

"And thanks for your voice mail the other day, Brenda," I said. "It helped me in my decision. I assume Angus reached out to you."

Angus looked puzzled.

"No problem, Daniel," she replied. "And it was Muriel who called me. She was covering her bases and taking nothing for granted."

"That is what Muriel does."

I think Angus was starting to see what had happened, but he kept his own counsel.

"We'll welcome you both back here whenever you choose to return. In the meantime, keep doing what you've been doing in the House since you landed there. That place needs a swift kick, and I like the boots you're wearing."

Angus and I smiled, shook Brenda's hand, and then headed out the door.

"Rumplun! What an unexpected nightmare it is to see you," cooed Angus as we exited the VP's office. "Have you missed us these last few months?"

Rumplun's crimson face took on a distinctly evil look as he hoisted himself out of the chair in the waiting area.

"Stow it, McLintock. Your English for Engineers students are breathlessly awaiting your return to the classroom, and so am I. Now that this parliamentary insanity is behind us, I trust you'll be back on campus next week to immediately take back your infernal class," Rumplun spat.

I just stayed silent in the background through all this, watching the duel unfold – though "duel" really isn't the right word. It suggests at least a reasonably balanced battle. Rumplun wasn't anywhere near Angus's league. I could tell that, from her office doorway, Brenda was enjoying the encounter, but she made an effort not to let it show.

"Well Rumper, I see without me around you've regressed to splitting infinitives again. I am so sorry."

You know in those old Warner Brothers cartoons when Yosemite Sam would get so mad that steam would stream from his ears? I swear I saw a few puffs issuing from Rumplun's fleshy flaps. Angus continued.

"I would hate to deny you the exquisite pleasure of force-feeding literature to beer-addled engineering freshmen, so I've decided to seek re-election."

Rumplun's eyes met mine. "Don't look at Addison. He can't help you," Angus chided. "He'll be on Parliament Hill at my side all the way. I admit I was all set to come back, but then the vision of you teaching Atwood and Richler to hungover engineers in hard hats was just too much to resist. Good day."

Rumplun wobbled for a minute as the news sunk in. He looked as if he'd just taken a baseball bat to the forehead. Brenda, only just concealing a smirk, shooed us out before escorting the shattered, swaying dean into her office. Angus was quite light on his feet as he glided from the waiting room, with me in tow.

"I derive pleasure from so few things in life these days, but periodically going a few rounds with Rumplun is one of them," Angus declared as we headed for the car and the drive back to Cumberland.

Muriel and I met with Pete1 and Pete2 at the new campaign head-quarters. On twenty-four hours' notice, Muriel had asked our constituency office landlord to rent us the vacant store next door for the McLintock election campaign HQ. By then, we had raised a grand total of $147.32, which, for the Cumberland-Prescott Liberal Association, set a new high-water mark. On the strength of such impressive fundraising, the landlord agreed. The store-front actually had an adjoining door to the constituency office, so moving into the campaign space consisted of the two Petes loading up wheeled office chairs with various bits of campaign-related debris and rolling it next door. By Monday afternoon, Cumberland Graphics had installed a simple red sign that shouted "Re-Elect Angus McLintock!" The exclamation mark had been Muriel's idea to ensure that voters read the sign with the appropriate enthusiasm. There was no reference to the Liberal Party on the sign. Angus's personal popularity easily surpassed that of the party, particularly in C-P, so we played to our strengths.

Muriel, Lindsay, and I had agreed that the two Petes were ready to assume more onerous responsibilities on this campaign than they shouldered the last time around. They managed the canvass back in October largely because I really had no other option then. If you have only two volunteers, they do the canvass. It had taken a while for the citizens of Cumberland-Prescott to accept two canvassers who looked like they'd auditioned for the Sex Pistols and been rejected as too extreme. Despite hypnosis, dream therapy, and hours of counselling, I'd still not been able to exorcise the vision of the two Petes door-to-dooring in the early part of that campaign. Okay, I'm exaggerating, but barely. They eventually evolved into quite good canvassers by the end of the campaign, uncovering at least a dozen Liberal voters despite Mohawks, facial piercings, and, occasionally, cosmetics.

This time, the plan was to have the two Petes coordinate all the campaign volunteers. We thought they were up to it and they agreed. By working on Angus's staff in the constit office for the last few months, they'd come to know many in the community, and more importantly, the community had come to know them (rather than fearing and fleeing them, as many had at the outset). Muriel's prodding had worked, and they'd toned down their punk wardrobe, particularly when they were working. In our meeting, Pete1 sported just an eyebrow piercing, a tongue stud, and *Angus!* stencilled in red on his hairless head. Pete2 wore nice khakis, an oxford cloth button-up, a Liberal red nose ring, fluorescent pink Doc Martens, and blue hair coiffed neatly. Clearly they were in transition.

The news that Angus was in the race spread quickly. In fact, when we'd finished our meeting elevating the two Petes to volunteer coordinators, there were ten volunteers waiting patiently in the reception area to report for duty. I was stunned, and initially I couldn't believe it. But after interrogating the assembled mob for ten minutes I was forced to admit that it all seemed on the up and up. Unsolicited Liberal volunteers showing up on day one of the campaign . . . in Cumberland-Prescott? Maybe the local political landscape was shifting beneath our feet – except, of course, that the local Conservatives could count on volunteers in the hundreds. Still, Pete1 and Pete2 leapt into their new duties and took control of enrolling the volunteers. Muriel, the den mother and hard-headed political strategist, just sat back and beamed.

But winning the riding was not the first priority. Angus hadn't yet even been nominated as the Liberal candidate. Incumbents are rarely challenged for their own nominations but it had happened in the past. And these were strange times politically. We could take nothing for granted. By moving ahead and opening the campaign office, we hoped to discourage any other closeted Liberals from jumping into the nomination race. It was perhaps a little aggressive to hold a news conference and then open a campaign office without the official nomination. I worried briefly that we might be violating Liberal Party rules. I raised this concern with Muriel. "Don't know, don't care" was all she said. Good enough for me.

As the only surviving executive member of the nearly moribund Cumberland-Prescott Liberal Association, Muriel had the authority to call the nomination meeting for Wednesday. We reserved the Cumberland Community Centre next door to the Riverfront Seniors' Residence.

I slid behind my desk after closing my office door and reached for the phone. Yes, I actually had an office with a door. If this had been broadly known, I'd have been the envy of most other campaign managers across the country regardless of political stripe. Most had only a trestle table in the middle of a cramped and crowded room.

"News desk, Fontaine here," crackled over the phone.

"André, it's Daniel Addison."

"Hey Daniel, I was just going to call you. What did you make of my piece in the *Globe* last week?"

"It was a great story, André. You nailed it. I particularly liked 'Quixotic dash up to Ottawa' and 'potent political partnership.' Loved it," I gushed. "You must have been thrilled to get it into the *Globe*."

"It's always good to go national. My editor here likes the profile it gives the *Crier*, and it brings in a bit more coin," he explained. "So what have you got for me? What's the word?"

"Well, you've always done right by us so I wanted to give you a heads-up about the Liberal nomination meeting."

"Wednesday at the community centre? I already heard about it. I'll probably be there, but if Angus is running unopposed, as I've heard, it's somewhat anticlimactic. Not much news there after we ran his news conference story this morning."

"I think it'll be worth your while to be there. And I'd have your camera with you if I were you. The meeting is in the community centre but I think you're going to want to be outside, on the shore beneath the meeting room window. And don't be late or you'll miss it."

"I hear you. Is any other journo getting this message?" André asked.

"Nope. It's all yours," I confirmed. "And André?"

"Yo."

"Thanks for not splashing my abominable snowman shots from the news conference all over the front page. I'm sure you got some great photos that I'll gladly take off your hands."

"Well, I don't make the photo calls, the editor does. But, you know, she can only choose from the shots I provide. You're welcome. It looked like you'd had quite a morning. But I think I'll hold onto the pics just the same, in case Angus wants them for his next newsletter."

On Wednesday afternoon we all gathered in the Panorama Room of the Cumberland Community Centre. Like most Cumberland buildings on the shore of the Ottawa River, the Panorama Room had a wall of windows overlooking the ice. The clear sky let the sun stream in, warming the room. In the previous two days, the membership of the Cumberland-Prescott Liberal Association had swelled from five to nearly sixty. Most of them showed up for the meeting. Forty-five of the new members lived next door with Muriel in the Riverfront Seniors' Residence. We'd chosen the community centre for the nomination meeting to make it easier for our elderly contingent of staunch McLintock supporters to be there. By the time of the meeting, no other candidates had filed nomination papers so the path was clear for a McLintock coronation.

I armed Muriel up to the microphone and retreated to the back of the room.

"Friends, we have a historic opportunity in this campaign to end, once and for all, the Conservative stranglehold on Cumberland-Prescott. Many have argued that it was a fluke, an aberration, a violation of the natural order that our Angus McLintock won this seat last time around. If we're honest with ourselves, perhaps it was a twist of fate. But this time, let's make it real. Let's stop the Tory juggernaut in its tracks and send honest Angus McLintock back to the House of Commons."

At this point, Muriel gave me a subtle nod before continuing to whip up the crowd. I slipped out the back door and dialled Angus's cellphone as the prearranged signal. Angus briefly answered and then ended the call. I stepped back into the room, and seconds later, through the window, I could hear an engine turning over.

"Back where he belongs. Angus McLintock brought down a deceitful and duplicitous government when against all odds, he made a courageous journey up the frozen river to cast his vote – the very vote that broke the deadlock and brought the

Tories to their knees. Friends, out on that same river, I give you Angus McLintock, the Member of Parliament for Cumberland-Prescott."

Muriel stepped aside and cast a trembling hand towards the window. All eyes turned towards the river. But all we saw was ice. All ears, even the many with hearing aids, could now hear an engine struggling to start. It would sputter to life, idle briefly, and then die out. After a pause, the engine sprang to life again and revved at what sounded to me like full throttle. Uh-oh. Even I knew that full throttle probably wasn't the way to go.

An instant later *Baddeck 1* shot along the ice from behind a point of land to the east. The crowd creaked to its feet and cheered. I couldn't see Angus in the cockpit where he normally resided when driving the hovercraft. Then I saw why. He was being dragged across the ice by the hovercraft as he clung for dear life to the stern rope. He managed to look our way and raise a hand in a feeble greeting as he hurtled out of sight beyond an outcropping of rock to the west. The audience just kept cheering wildly as if it were all planned. One look at Muriel would have told them it was not. She had one hand over her mouth while she gamely returned Angus's wave with the other.

I burst out the door, flew down the outside stairs to the ice, and took off after *Baddeck 1*. In the distance, I heard the engine abruptly change pitch and then stop. When I rounded the point, I found Angus, caked in snow, leaning into the engine compartment.

"Damn Canada Post to hell and back!" he cried when I arrived on the scene. Angus seemed none the worse for his harrowing trip along the ice.

"What's Canada Post got to do with it?" I asked, looking around for a malevolent letter carrier.

"I've been awaiting the arrival of a starter motor from Illinois, but in its infinite wisdom, Canada Post has seen fit to hold it at the border to make sure it's not infested with anthrax or any number of other life-threatening substances."

"Right . . ." I prodded. I still didn't get it. "Go on . . ."

Angus looked impatient as if further explanation was unnecessary.

"If the starter had arrived when it was supposed to, I'd not have been thrashed over the ice by my own creation. I could have started the engine from the comfort of the cockpit rather than standin' astern to yank on the blasted pull cord."

"But why did it take off on its own?"

"Well, I'm not guiltless in the affair, I suppose. I managed to flood the engine, so you of course know the remedy for that."

"Of course I do. Doesn't everybody?" I paused thoughtfully. "Okay, no, I really don't know."

"I figured not. You must fully open the throttle to dry out a flooded carburetor. So I opened her up and the damnable engine started right off the bat. The possessed craft took off and I had only time to snag the stern painter and hang on."

"What's painting got to do with it?"

"You don't spend much time around boats, do you? The stern painter is the nautical term for the rope at the back," Angus explained, ever the teacher.

"Okay, I get that part now, but how did you stop it?"

"I pulled myself up the rope, shoved my hand under her skirt, and managed to spill enough air from the plenum to make the beast settle on the ice and grind to a halt. Then I reached up and knocked one of the spark plug leads off the engine and the cursed thing died."

"We'd better get back. Muriel may have resorted to card tricks by now," I suggested. "And if you ever tell this story during the campaign, please don't repeat the phrase 'I shoved my hand under her skirt.'"

"Aye. Surely no good can come of that," Angus agreed.

On his signal, I pulled the starter cord while Angus stayed in the cockpit. Naturally, it started immediately. I climbed into the passenger seat without falling, and we hovered back to the community centre. The Panorama Room's window hung over the ice and I could see many wrinkled foreheads pressed against the glass and many leathery hands clapping. Angus was still covered in snow from his ordeal so I grabbed a corn broom I'd found leaning near the back door and had Angus stand with his arms outstretched. It looked like he was being scanned with a metal detector by super-vigorous airport security as I swept the snow off him.

I finally noticed André Fontaine standing on the outside steps with his camera in his hand and his index finger twitching. Uh-oh.

"Don't tell me, André. You were standing right there for whole show and now have half a dozen good shots of Angus and his unique approach to piloting a hovercraft," I said.

"Nope, you're wrong. I actually got about twenty-five good ones. The shutter speed on this thing is great."

I didn't feel I could call upon his generosity twice in one week. I just nodded in resignation.

Two minutes later Angus was standing before the Cumberland-Prescott Liberal faithful.

"Well, that was a wee bit of a drag," he started. Laughter all round. "Happy New Year to you all and I thank you for coming out on what is traditionally a holiday. This hastily called election just doesn't give us much flexibility on timing."

He went on to cover the major points of his principled approach to representing the riding by putting the interests of the nation ahead of all else. But he was preaching to the converted, and it didn't really matter what he said. They loved him and very nearly derailed his talk by interrupting every third sentence or so with a spontaneous outburst of applause.

Then Angus sprung the red ribbon idea on them. And on us. Muriel and I had been wondering how we were going to produce lawn signs when we really hadn't raised any money yet. Angus solved that problem for us towards the end of his remarks.

"I've been thinking a lot about how campaigns are usually run. At the end of the race, our local landfill is the recipient of thousands of cardboard or, worse, plastic lawn signs. I'm not happy about that and I venture to say that you probably aren't either. So here's how we're going to handle it. We will manufacture no lawn signs. None. If any of you, or any other voters, care to express public support for my candidacy, you have only to tie a red ribbon on your car, or to the tree in your front lawn, or to something in your front window. Just a simple display of red will suffice. Let's change the way things are done."

In the last campaign I had brazenly spun our lack of lawn signs as an environmental initiative. At the time, only the most naïve had bought what I was selling. But four months later it turns out it wasn't such a bad idea after all.

With only fifty or so members in attendance, the vote didn't take long and Angus was acclaimed as the Liberal candidate. It was official. Of course, a Liberal winning in this riding, even Angus McLintock, was still the longest of long shots. No political pundits in their right mind would ever predict a second Liberal victory. The fluke Liberal win last time was such a shock to the local political system that re-electing Angus carried hole-in-one odds. But here we were.

As Angus and I extricated ourselves from the meeting, a group of boisterous women from the Riverfront Seniors' Residence started to chant "Angus! Angus! Angus! Angus!" They needed only pompoms to consummate the surreal scene. I doubt many other candidates in the country had their own squad of octogenarian cheerleaders. I think Angus was touched by the show of support.

After dinner, I left Lindsay to work on her Master's thesis as I headed up the path, intent on taking at least one game from Angus.

I had my regular Coke while Angus sipped a third of a tumbler of Lagavulin. I could smell its strong iodine-tinged aroma from my side of the board. Angus had already dismantled me in two games but I was holding my own in game three. I was playing white and had managed to sacrifice a bishop to set up a knight fork that claimed his queen. His queen for my bishop and knight was a solid return on my investment.

"Well played, laddie!" he thundered. "I must realign my thinkin' if you're able to plan and execute a stratagem of that calibre."

I tried to remain calm but when you take a superior opponent's queen, it's cause for celebration. I kept it low key and broke into a disco classic, complete with dancing hands and very rhythmic shoulders.

I crooned "That's the Way I Like It," complete with all the jubilant "uh-huhs." It just wasn't the same without the mirror ball, but nevertheless it was quite satisfying.

"If you're going to do that each time you win one of my pieces, I cannae promise you safe passage back to the boathouse."

"Don't worry, I don't imagine I'll get the chance to do that very often," I conceded. "Besides, I've had many compliments on that number over the years."

Thirty-two minutes later I finally took him down, confining his king on the back rank with my two rooks. No big celebration this time. That would have been unseemly.

"How is the fair lass Lindsay now that she's ensconced in the boathouse?"

"She is, quite simply, amazing," I replied with more emotion than I'd planned on deploying.

"Aye, she is. Providence has shone on you. But she's not doin' too badly in your company, I daresay."

"It's difficult to explain. We seem to connect on a different plane. It just feels different. Better. Deeper. I don't know. I'm not sure I'm being clear."

"You're comin' in loud and clear to me." He paused, but then continued. "Forty years or so ago, I'd probably be describin' my bond with Marin using similarly vague and imprecise terms," Angus confided. "It was very odd. I felt utterly changed yet still myself at one and the same time. It was almost as if my life had been fuzzy, slightly out of focus. Marin seemed to adjust my lens so that everythin' was brighter, sharper, more vibrant and vital.

Where I'd only seen murky shadows, she let me see a riot of colour. Where my view had been cut short, she gave me a distant horizon. I really didnae know what being alive actually meant, until I met her."

He stopped talking suddenly. I kept my eyes on the river, not daring to look at him. A few minutes passed.

"You dinnae need to attempt to give form and order to that which defies explanation and confounds understandin'. Just let it be. And hold onto it for as long as you can. I'm very happy for you both."

DIARY
Wednesday, January 1
My Love,
The year has turned. "Happy New Year" they all say. I cannot fathom it. It is odd that it's no longer officially the same year in which you left me. I think I was waiting for this day so I could finally be free of such a miserable year and what it brought us. I thought I might feel different. And I guess I do in some ways. But my life is different not because the year has turned over. Simply changing the number when I write the date has done nothing. It was folly to think otherwise. You are still gone. That part of me, that part of my life, remains . . . numb. But don't fear for me. There are glimmers in the distance to keep me from wallowing.

But for a spot of drama, the deed was done today. I am the Liberal candidate, for better or worse. It felt much different signing the nomination papers this time around. A busy couple of fortnights beckons. We will not succumb to the temptation to campaign as most others do. That is the one wan and wispy hope we have. I'm determined, as the old song says, to "Take the High Road."
AM

CHAPTER FIVE

When clouds blocked the morning sun, it was chilly in the boat-house. Lindsay, *Cumberland Crier* in hand, ran into the room and vaulted back into the double bed like a gymnast off a mini-tramp, plowing her elbow into my stomach as she came down beside me.

"Oooooff!" was my articulate response as the air left my lungs in a hurry.

"Sorry, sorry, sorry. I thought I was clear of you," Lindsay said as she rolled and propped herself up on the guilty elbow. "I'm not as coordinated in the air when it's so frickin' cold. We really need at least a queen if I'm going to land those safely."

When you're unable to breathe, you're unable to speak. So I just nodded. Lindsay spread out the *Crier*.

"Uh-oh. André has done it again," she warned.

I turned to scan the front page. Oh good, two photos of Angus. The first covered nearly the whole front page, above the fold. André sure had a knack with a Nikon. There, in full colour, was *Baddeck 1* dragging Angus behind as he looked right at the camera and waved. The caption: the very predictable "What a drag!" Nice. The second picture, as I feared, was a shot of a snow-covered Angus, arms outstretched in apparent political crucifixion as I appeared to attack him with a corn broom. The cutline on it: "McLintock hopes to sweep to victory." So the headline writer's a comedian. I rolled back over and managed to groan with what little breath I'd regained.

An hour or so later, Lindsay headed out to the U of O library to work on a paper with a looming deadline. She claimed she was unable to work at home. She said it casually, but I liked the way "home" rolled off her tongue and hung in the air between us.

As soon as Lindsay had gone, I switched into campaign mode and checked in with the two Petes, who were staffing the campaign HQ. All was well. In fact, seven more volunteers had shown up. Muriel was also there helping to slot the new recruits into appropriate roles. She had a gift for identifying those who were cut out for the perils of door-to-door canvassing, and those who should be isolated behind closed doors, licking envelopes and assembling poll kits. I chatted with Muriel for a while after hearing from Peter. It was actually beginning to feel like a legitimate campaign complete with real volunteers, bad coffee, stale doughnuts, uncomfortable chairs, and riding maps on the wall. But if I didn't deal with the money situation soon, we'd shortly have another staple of many political campaigns, debt.

I was a few minutes early for my ten o'clock meeting with Angus, but I was keen to get going and I sensed he was too. I knocked on his front door and it swung open before I'd connected on the third rap.

"There you are, laddie, I thought you'd forgotten," Angus opened. "We're burnin' daylight."

"I'm five minutes early," I pleaded. "I didn't want to interrupt your morning primping now that you're going to be in the public eye at least for the campaign."

"This is as primped as I get."

Wonderful. Angus looked as if he'd coiffed his hair and beard by thrusting his head inside a screaming jet engine. He desperately needed his own hair traffic controller.

"Uhmm, I wonder whether we might consider a hair cut and a beard trim, or at the very least some industrial-strength gel?" I ventured, fearing for my safety.

"What are you sayin', man? My hair has always looked like this. I like it and it takes me no time at all when I get up in the mornin'."

"You don't say," I commented. I corralled my resolve. "Angus, let's at least try to open a fledgling relationship with a hairbrush of some kind. We want your image to say *principled maverick*. But to those who don't know you, sometimes your look can veer a little too close to *crazed psychopath*."

He said nothing but was quite eloquent with the glare he sent my way before turning to a mirror in the hall. I pushed just a bit more.

"Angus, if we scare the voters, or even their children, they're less likely to mark the little X next to your name on E-day."

Angus stared at his reflection and sighed.

"All right, all right, you've made your point. I'll think about it," he concluded. The subject was closed. "So what's on our agenda? Where do we start, now that I'm runnin' on purpose this time?"

"Why don't we cover off some local issues that we're likely to face in the campaign? Nothing undermines a candidate's credibility more than being asked a question by a voter and knowing nothing about the topic."

"Grand. Lead on."

"Well, the first local issue is plastered all over the front page of today's *Crier*," I said as I handed him my copy.

Angus eyed the front page, and dropped onto the fluffy chintz couch, losing his right hand in the morass of his hair.

"Damnation, and the race hasnae even yet started," Angus groaned. "I've tripped over my own feet on the way to the startin' blocks."

"Angus, calm yourself. It's not that bad," I soothed. "There are many veteran campaigners who think that the worst kind of media coverage is no coverage at all. Here we are on day one of the campaign and you've dominated the front page." I didn't subscribe to the "all ink is good ink" theory but I wasn't about to mention that to my candidate.

"Aye, I surely dominated the paper, but as a snow-covered laughin' stock. I thought I had a good rapport with that Fontaine fellow."

"Angus, don't blame this on André. He likes you and respects you. That much I know. But when we offer up shots like these" – I waved my hand over the *Crier* – "his photo editor has no option but to run with them. It's not André's call, he just pushes the button. But you have to admit, it's outstanding news photography."

I took back the *Crier*. Time to move to safer ground.

"Onwards!" I rallied. "Sanderson Technologies is a great local story and we own it. It showcases your creativity, ingenuity, and foresight."

"I like the sound of that but what does it all mean?" Angus asked.

"When Norman Sanderson came to see you last October, he was looking for you to deliver federal subsidies to keep his aging shoe factory limping along on fallen arches. The path of least resistance would have been for you to work with the government to get those subsidies, whether or not it was good policy. Knowing it was in fact bad policy, you refused. Instead you persuaded him to stopping making shoes and start manufacturing Professor Khanjimeer's Internet wave router. It was brilliant, and Sanderson Technologies is now a bona fide high-tech success story, signing new supply contracts every other day. You did that!"

"Well, it was the sensible thing to do. It was obvious!" Angus waved his hand in dismissal.

"Obvious to you, but to most everyone else, you came through with a creative and innovative solution to an intractable industrial-policy dilemma. You cracked it first time out. And the icing on the cake was getting Sanderson to hire the workers displaced when you shut down Ottawa River Aggregate Inc. Talk about a win-win."

"Fine, but that's water under the bridge. Cleaner water, I hope, but what's next?" Angus asked.

"Well, what's next is, we hit up Norman Sanderson while he's still flush with gratitude and cash and see whether he'll spearhead our fundraising efforts. Even without lawn signs to buy, we're going to need to raise some cash to finance the campaign."

"Aye," grunted Angus, sounding very Scottish. "I've precious little to donate."

"As well, we do need to find something to do with the abandoned aggregate operation. Everybody knows shutting it down was the right thing to do but we just can't let it sit there as a monument to environmental degradation," I noted.

"What about that young lad who came in to see us about turnin' it into an environmental education camp for school kids? I liked that idea." Angus leaned forward, resting his elbows on his knees.

"It's a great idea if we can help them find some funding to bring the building up to code and get them connected with the schools. I just don't know what department to hit up for dough."

"Well, I want to be supportive of this initiative. It feels like shuttin' down the mill was the easier half of the problem. There's more to do, and I like the thought of kids learnin' about the river and sustainable development in a facility that used to dump toxins in the water. It'll bring home the message."

Angus and I kicked around a few other local issues, including the deterioration of Cumberland's roads and the highways leading in and out of it. We worked out some positions and key messages to use.

"You can totally blame the Tory government and your predecessor for neglecting Cumberland's infrastructure," I said.

"I'm not hankerin' to blame anyone. There's enough blame to go around. The Liberals did nothin' about it when they, er . . . we, were in office. I just want to talk about solutions and help citizens feel like their vote actually means somethin'."

"That's all very nice, Angus, but Emerson Fox is going to toast you every chance he gets with whatever ammunition he and his dirt squad can dig up on us," I replied.

"Okay, you're gonnae have to explain to me what you mean by dirt squad. And I'm not certain I even want to know."

"Emerson Fox created the dirt squad concept some twenty-five years ago and all major parties now have them. The aptly named dirt squad is a team of committed partisans who dig deep into the backgrounds of their opponents in the hopes of turning up that one embarrassing, humiliating, illegal, unseemly, and horrific event, deed, or even photograph that can kill a campaign cold. It is the very foundation of negative campaigning. It is what allows Flamethrower Fox and his acolytes across the country and around the world to *go negative*," I explained. "And the worst part about this whole sorry and often tragic approach is that it usually works. Many voters buy it. Even those who don't are often so disgusted by the entire process, that they simply withdraw from democracy and fail to exercise their franchise on election day."

"Well, I'm not gonnae play his game. I won't," Angus intoned.

"And that's what will separate our campaign from anything Flamethrower Fox has ever encountered. He's used to opponents who counterpunch fast. And by the middle of the campaign, no one can remember who started it all."

"I cannae promise I won't punch out his lights at an all-candidates meetin', but we'll not be havin' a dirt squad in this campaign," Angus decreed.

"Just to be clear, I was using 'punch' as a metaphor. You will not, I repeat will not, ever physically strike Fox, even though he'll surely deserve it. Skipping in*sult*, and moving directly to in*jury* is not a winning strategy."

Angus seemed to be biting his tongue. He just nodded in resignation.

"While we're on this topic, Angus. Have you ever been arrested?"

Even though I considered it a formality, I had to ask. I'd run a dozen campaigns in my political past and had always asked this question. I am pleased and relieved to report that I'd never ever received an affirmative response to this important question. No campaign manager ever wants to discover after the writ has dropped that the candidate had actually done time for shoplifting, impaired driving, B&E, fraud, or tax evasion. It would make for either a very long or mercifully short campaign.

"Now, why would you be askin' me that?"

"Flamethrower Fox has probably already compiled an investigative dossier on you that would set J. Edgar Hoover all aquiver. I just want to know what's in it so we can be ready," I replied cheerfully.

Angus paused, considering the question. My heart rate soared. No, no. This is not happening.

"Do you mean have I ever been convicted of anythin'?" Angus asked in earnest.

Oh no, no. You have got to be kidding. I tried to remain calm, or at least give the impression that I was calm.

"No Angus, I mean have you ever been arrested? Emerson Fox doesn't need convictions to launch his offensive. Arrests easily suffice. So should I be worried? Do you have an arrest record?"

I confess my voice was operating in a higher register than normal, though I tried to control it. Angus eventually sighed.

"Aye, I have been arrested, but not for quite some time."

And there it was. The elephant that I didn't even know was in the room had just sat down on my chest.

"Did this happen in Canada or was it a youthful indiscretion from your cricketing days in Scotland?" Remain calm. We can get through this.

"Well, there were a few times in Scotland, but most of my arrests occurred on Canadian soil," Angus said casually.

Holy crap, there was more than one arrest. Okay, breathe. Relax. Don't let on that this is a problem. Stay calm. Think Zen, yoga, transcendental meditation. That's it. Just relax.

"Holy crap, there was more than one arrest!"

Angus recoiled at my outburst.

"Don't be leapin' off the deep end, man. I'm proud of all twenty-three of my Canadian arrests, and I'd not change a thing were I to live it over."

69

What a joker. I laughed and shook my head before returning my "you almost had me" gaze to Angus. He wasn't laughing. He wasn't even smiling. Then the room shimmered in front of my eyes and my knees turned weak and wobbly. Then I dropped onto the couch beside Angus. Breathe.

"Sorry, I must be hearing things in the trauma of the moment. It almost sounded like you said you'd been arrested twenty-three times and I know that can't be right. I'm calm now, and I'm seated, and I'm listening carefully. How many times have you been arrested?"

"Your hearin' is fine, laddie. I've had the cuffs on twenty-three times."

"Wonderful. That's just great news. And you're worried about a funny photo on the front page of the *Crier*. This isn't just tripping on the way to the starting blocks. It's more like a double leg amputation. Fox is going to crush us with this, and it'll happen soon."

We sat in silence for a few moments. I cradled my forehead in my left hand. Angus crossed his arms over his not inconsiderable chest and looked at the ceiling.

He spoke quietly.

"Daniel, I was part of a pro-choice alliance with some other young academics. All twenty-three of my run-ins were civil disobedience arrests in the sixties, protestin' Canada's archaic abortion laws. It wasn't drug dealin', racketeerin', or prostitution, it was civil disobedience. Twenty times we were forcibly removed from the lawn in front of Centre Block, and thrice from the House of Commons visitors' gallery."

He was still looking at the ceiling as if it were a portal to the past.

"Did you know that under the legislation of the day, offenders could be imprisoned for life? It was an outrage. It could not stand," he said. He paused for a moment and when he spoke again, his tone had softened. "It was a long time ago and we were never convicted. You know, the first time I met Marin, we were both in handcuffs. When Trudeau brought in the new laws in '69, we retired from the front lines. The new law wasn't perfect, but it was a great leap forward. I have nary a regret."

We sat in silence for the next five minutes or so, mulling. It was time to start sewing a silk purse. Time to start making lemonade.

"Okay, we have to be ready to hit this head-on when Fox presses the big red button," I started. "He'll think this will sink us. I think this can lift us up if we play it right."

"I don't see it as a strategy that we have to play right. I intend to answer all questions truthfully. I'll not apologize. I'll not recant. I'll not soft-pedal my own convictions. In fact, I'm proud of what we did."

I nodded.

"Say it just like that, but without using the word *convictions*, and we might just turn the tables on him," I commented. "Okay, I'm now back from the brink. Clearly, you've been involved in a series of perfectly respectable arrests."

"Aye, that's how we always viewed it."

"So Marin dragged you to your first rally?" I asked.

I could tell by the way he turned on me that I may have misinterpreted his story.

"Why does everyone always assume Marin turned me into a feminist? I was at that particular rally of my own volition. I didn't meet her until the end of the demo," he thundered. "I'll have you know Marin earned only nineteen arrests and never spent a night in jail."

"Okay, okay, I'm sorry. I just have never met a male feminist who got there on his own, particularly an engineer."

"Watch yourself there, laddie."

"So after all these years, why haven't you sought an official pardon so that your arrest record is expunged? I figure you'd be a perfect candidate for a full pardon," I suggested.

"You seek a pardon when you're ashamed of somethin' you've done. There'll be no pardon."

I left an hour later after working through several scenarios in which Flamethrower Fox and his team might spring Angus's twenty-three arrests on him. My money was on the first all-candidates meeting. "Strike early" was a credo sprinkled throughout Fox's book.

Though many businesses were still shut down for the holiday break, Sanderson Technologies was hopping. There were still two Dumpsters in the far end of the parking lot filled with sensible-looking shoes of varying sizes. A big truck from Goodwill was backed up to them and two men were literally shovelling shoes into the back of it.

Norman Sanderson's office was on the second floor with a wall of glass overlooking the manufacturing line below. I had a quick glance as I entered his office and saw that the shop floor was cleaner than my boathouse apartment. I half-expected the workers to start eating off the floor now that it was nearly time for the afternoon coffee break. Workers in pale blue smocks and funny hats staffed the conveyor belt, adding the final few parts to the wave router by hand. It seemed that even the state-of-the-art automated assembly line had its limits. Nevertheless, it was an impressive sight.

"They're so much happier and more productive making the router than they ever were making desert boots," observed Norman Sanderson as he watched the afternoon shift of workers below. He'd arrived behind me as I stared out the window.

"Hello, Norman. This is quite a place you have here. It looks totally different than it did when shoes were on the menu." We shook hands. Norman was all smiles.

"This is for you," he said as he pulled an envelope from his jacket pocket and slid it across his desk to me.

I opened it and glanced at the cheque inside. Jackpot. It was for the maximum amount allowed under the Elections Act.

"This is wonderful and very generous of you, Norman. Angus will be very grateful. Thank you."

"It's the least I can do after what Angus has done for me and for future generations of the Sanderson clan."

"Well, Norman, I'm delighted to hear you describe it as the least that you can do because I have a favour to ask," I said, getting ready for the pitch.

"Of course, what can I do?"

I liked the sound of that.

"If we're going to run a successful campaign in the safest Tory riding in the land, we're going to need a lot more dough than your much-appreciated donation," I opened. Norman nodded, so I barrelled ahead while I still held the floor.

"What we really need is someone to take on fundraising and to put the touch on the other local businesses and wealthier citizens. You are one of Cumberland's most successful business leaders, so I can think of no one better qualified to take on this responsibility than you."

I tried to make it sound like he was winning out over a dozen other viable candidates when, in fact, I could literally think of no else for this job.

"Hmmmm. Well, I did raise money for the Cumberland Fall Agricultural Fair and that wasn't too hard."

"It's almost the same raising funds for the Cumberland-Prescott Liberal Association, and there's not as much manure shovelling involved. There's certainly some, but definitely not as much," I assured him.

I walked Norman through the current regulations governing political contributions for businesses and individuals while he took meticulous notes.

"I'm hoping that we can raise about $25,000 to cover the cost of our campaign office and operations, and to pay the two Petes for the duration of the campaign. Muriel won't accept payment and I'm still on the House of Commons payroll so I'm fine. Do you think we, and when I say we, I kind of mean you, can raise that kind of beanery in the next four weeks or so?"

"That's it? We only need $25,000? I think I can raise that by

73

the weekend," Norman replied.

"Norman, this is Cumberland. It's not exactly the promised land for Liberals."

"Not to worry. I'm hosting a Cumberland Chamber of Commerce luncheon here on Friday to show off the new facility. And I'll be laying the credit for this company's turnaround squarely at the doorstep of Angus McLintock. When I'm done, I'll spring the fundraising on them. We're raising dough for Angus. I won't dwell on the Liberal connection. I think we'll do quite well."

It seemed a logical approach.

"Thank you, Norman. I think my job here is done." I rose and shook his hand.

I left Norman hunched over the phone to some of his Cumberland business cronies, eager to start the process. I asked him to pass any cheques along to Muriel, our official agent for the local campaign. In the decades of Tory rule in this riding, I doubt whether a single businessperson in all of Cumberland-Prescott had ever been asked for a donation to the Liberal Party. I hoped donors might at least be attracted to the novelty of it all.

I was back in my aging, beat-up rust bucket of a Ford Taurus wagon when my phone chirped.

"Starbucks?" the voice asked.

"I just left Norman's. I'll be there in five," I said and flipped the phone closed.

Lindsay was already seated with her standard double tall latte. I stood in line for a moment to land my tall no-whip hot chocolate and took the seat opposite her.

"Hello, stranger," Lindsay said as we kissed over the table. In my head, the kiss seemed to play out in slow motion to the mellifluous strains of a violin chorus that encircled only us. She had a strange and welcome effect on me.

"What a nice way to interrupt the campaign," I replied, lowering myself onto the wooden chair. By then, the fiddle section had eased out the door to make it to their next romantic encounter.

Even in U of O sweats and an Ottawa Senators ball cap, she looked amazing.

"How goes your paper?" I asked, unable to look anywhere else.

"Arrrrrgh. Despite constant pleading, it simply will not write itself," she answered.

"Do you want me to take a stab at it? I would, you know," I offered.

"I know you would, and I love that you've offered, but I'm just not certain that writing a student's paper is the right way to start off your career as a professor. I'm not sure, but the university may well take a dim view of it."

"Well, when it comes together, I'm happy to review and edit. You know, fix any esoteric grammatical crimes that may have been unwittingly committed," I said.

"That would be great if you could, in all that spare time I know you have right now. What's new on the campaign?"

"Oh, not too much, beyond learning that Angus has twenty-three arrests in his past and Flamethrower Fox is surely going to make us pay for it."

"Ouch! You're kidding! What has Angus been hiding in his history?"

"That's the thing. He hasn't been hiding anything. In fact, he's proud of them," I replied. "He was never convicted, but he was arrested twenty-three times at pro-choice rallies back in the day, when our laws weren't quite as enlightened as they are now."

Lindsay just smiled and shook her head in admiration.

"I love him. I think I'll vote for him," Lindsay said. "So what's the plan for when Fox drops that bomb on us?"

"Angus doesn't really care. He's happy to talk about it. But I think we need to take the initiative away from Fox. I haven't quite figured it out yet, but if we play it right, we'll turn what the Flamethrower thinks is dirt into gold."

"So how did your little chat go with Normy?" she asked.

"I was all ready to pitch early, hard, and often but he stepped up before I was even into my wind-up. It was the easiest sell job I've ever done," I reported. "He's agreed to raise funds for the campaign and he doesn't think it'll be a problem to bring in $25k."

"Wow. Well, he *does* owe Angus big time."

My phone again. I looked at the display and saw *Lib. of Parl.* on the small screen. I looked sheepishly at Lindsay and pointed at the phone. She waved me onto the call.

"Daniel Addison."

"Hi, Daniel, it's Lucille at the library," said a familiar voice.

"Hey, Lucille, and how's my favourite bookworm?" It pays to be nice to those who toil in obscurity.

"I'm just fine, but I thought I'd break every privacy protocol in the book and give you a heads-up now that the battle has started."

"Hmm. That sounds ominous. Has my library card been revoked?"

"Nope, you're fine, but I thought you might like to know that someone has just checked out about ten books by a particular author you might have heard of," she said, drawing it out.

"The suspense is killing me."

"Some hefty guy has just walked out of here with every book we have written by . . . Marin Lee." She let it sink in.

"It's started. Fox isn't even nominated yet and it's already started. Can you bend the rules a little more and tell me who signed them out?" I asked ever so politely.

"Bend the rules? I broke the rules when I picked up the phone to call you. I forget the name, but he works in Tory Research. Hang on a sec." I waited and held up my index finger to Lindsay to indicate I was almost done. "Ramsay Rumplun. That's it. That's all I've got. Just wanted you to know."

"Thank you, Lucille. I really am grateful. And don't worry, I wouldn't give you up if they tore off my fingernails."

That night before I fell into bed, I picked up *Flamethrower* and flipped to the index. Whenever a political figure writes a memoir, everyone on the Hill rushes to the bookstores and scours the index, searching first for their own names, and then for those of others in their circle. Eventually, a few people may even end up reading the book. The name Ramsay Rumplun rang a bell, and not just because he shared a rather uncommon surname with the miserable Dean of Engineering. I discovered why soon enough. Ramsay was mentioned on several occasions in the book and appeared in one group photo. He was a shortish, youngish, chubby man with jet-black hair slicked straight back with enough petroleum product to lubricate a V8. Not that one should draw conclusions on the basis of a single photograph, not to mention family lineage, but he did not look like a nice man. So I switched over to Google and uncovered about a dozen more images that made me much more comfortable declaring him a jackass. Over the years, I've become quite adept at spotting the jerk, based purely on appearance. Ramsay Rumplun sure looked the part. He was the spitting image of his father.

DIARY

Thursday, January 2

My Love,

What a blessed flash of luck that the police should have stuck us with one another in the dark. Smart of them to cuff our wrists together behind our backs. It made escape impossible, not that we'd ever have bolted anyway. There we were, two strangers, sitting back to back on the floor of that police van. The jostling of the journey literally brought us together with every bump, with every curve. The exhilaration of the moment loosened our reserve and our tongues. We talked. Before I ever laid eyes on you I fell for your voice, for your mind, for the feel of your hands, and the arc of your spine pressed against mine. In the twenty-minute drive to the station, something passed between us. Even when released from the handcuffs, still I was bound to you. Rubbing my raw wrists, I finally turned to see you for the first time, but the die was already cast. I knew. Aye, I just knew. Pure certainty is a rare and wonderful gift. A lightning strike.

But lightning has its own dangers too. I learned today that the civil disobedience that first drew us together is double-edged and perhaps still sharp after so many years. Unless I miss my mark, my Conservative opponent will exploit the very arrests in which you and I have always shared a quiet pride. It's dawning on me that I'm now a public figure, which, by default, makes my entire life public. Nothing is mine alone, or ours alone, any longer. It has taken me some time to resolve my feelings on this but I reckon I'm nearly there. I'm proud of you and all you've done. I'm happy with my station. So if a light is to be shone on my life, on our life, let it shine. We've nothing to conceal, have we?

AM

CHAPTER SIX

The look on the Hair and Makeup woman's face was priceless as she first laid eyes on her next subject or, more accurately, her next project, perhaps even her life's work. Angus and I had just arrived for a taping of CBC's flagship public affairs program, *Face to Face*. As Angus settled in the chair facing the light bulb–bordered mirror, Sally, as her name tag revealed, stood behind him and just shook her head.

"Time to break out the heavy artillery," she said before disappearing out the door.

Angus gave me a puzzled look in the mirror.

"Sally clearly hasn't worked on anyone lately with quite your sense of style," I ventured.

Angus looked at himself in the mirror and tried in vain to quiet the riot roiling on his head.

"I cannae help it. My hair has always been a wee bit . . . mutinous."

Sally returned, rolling a cart with an array of tubes, jars, and aerosol cans, some of them still wearing their Home Depot price tags. That wasn't a good sign. There were also a few plug-in devices, including what appeared to be a giant industrial curling iron and what I took to be a hair straightener, its large, flat paddles poised for battle. Jammed in the corner of the cart was a cardboard box filled with what looked like bathing caps of various sizes alongside a paper coffee cup of bobby pins.

Sally had slipped into a green smock and was pulling on rubber gloves when a younger woman, similarly smocked, arrived on the scene drying her hands on a towel. She, too, donned rubber gloves. They faced Angus and me with their hands held up in front of them like surgeons before operating.

"I'm Sally and this is Rebecca. We're in tough this morning, so she'll be assisting me every step of the way," Sally intoned.

"Are you fixin' to give me a heart transplant?" Angus inquired.

"I wish it were as simple as a heart transplant, but our first priority this morning is to tame your hair so that we can actually get it all into the shot without having to rent an IMAX camera. And we have exactly thirteen minutes. Battle stations!"

Sally turned to Rebecca and nodded her head in my direction. Rebecca immediately grabbed my elbow and ushered me out of the room.

"I'm sorry, Mr. Addison, but unless you're a family member, you won't be able to stay for this. I assure you Professor McLintock will be just fine, but it's best if you wait in the green room."

I sat down on the couch and watched the TV monitor on the wall as the clock ticked to the top of the hour. In the meantime, Sally and Rebecca sprang into action and did their thing. And they did it very, very well. Despite what I imagine were howls of protest from Angus, they worked a miracle on his unruly cranial shrubbery.

On the monitor, the show opened as usual with the host, Brett Palmer, sitting across a sort of counter from his guest. It took me a minute or so to recognize Angus. He still resembled Angus, but he somehow seemed . . . smaller. His hair was quite neatly sculpted with what actually looked like a part demarcating the eastern hemisphere of his head. Whatever had been applied to his hair shone under the lights. His usually scraggly beard appeared to have been combed out in a Robertson Davies kind of style.

"Welcome to *Face to Face*. I'm Brett Palmer, and I'm pleased to be joined today by maverick Liberal MP Angus McLintock. Thanks for coming in today, Professor McLintock."

"I'm happy to be here, but you can just call me Angus, everyone else does."

"What made you decide to jump into the race and run for re-election when you really had no intention of winning the first time around?"

"'Tis a fair question. You're right, sitting and serving in the House of Commons was the furthest thought from my mind last October even though my name was on the ballot. But my unexpected stint on Parliament Hill was a revelation to me. I enjoyed it. I felt as though I were making a contribution. I was surprised that I felt fulfilled. And strange as it sounds, I was unhappy at the prospect of surrendering my seat to another when I was feeling as if I were just getting started. When you reach my age, it's not often that a completely new and interesting strand in your life presents itself. It's a gift to be explored."

Angus's hair still looked pristine. Sally joined me in the green room to watch the interview and fidget.

"So you're confident you can win re-election despite the very strong Tory tradition in the riding," Brett probed.

"Balderdash. It would be the height of arrogance for me to be confident about a Liberal winning this seat again. To be clear, I wasn't elected on my own merits the last time around. A flash of fate put me in the House. This time, I'd like to win the seat in the more traditional fashion, by persuading the voters of Cumberland-Prescott that I am worthy of their support over all the others. I expect it to be a very tough fight, whomever the Conservatives put forward."

The first signs were imperceptible to me but Sally picked up on them right away.

"Left temple, at the midpoint of his ear. We've got a bulge. Shit, we've got a bulge," Sally snapped at the monitor. "In ten years, I've never had a stage 4 shellac failure, but there it is."

And she was right. If you looked closely, you could see asymmetry emerging in Angus's hair. We were only two minutes in. Beads of sweat appeared on Sally's upper lip.

"How would you feel if you were to face Emerson Fox in the campaign, as is rumoured?" asked Brett.

"I'm less concerned with the candidate I might be facing than I am with the many challenges Canada is already facing as this recession takes hold. But I have been encouraged to read Mr. Fox's memoir and it is quite enlightening," declared Angus.

"Right bulge now," hissed Sally. "It's only a matter of time at this point. They'd better cut to commercial soon."

Of course, she was right again. Angus's hair was starting to lose its sleek and sculpted look and now had more of a Bozo the clown vibe to it. But according to Sally, it was a very dynamic situation. And it would get worse before it got better.

"But Angus, a typical Fox campaign is comprised of . . ." Brett started before noticing that Angus had instinctively raised his hand. Brett stopped, as Angus quickly lowered his hand again. "Sorry, Angus, go ahead," oozed Brett.

"'Twas nothing, carry on," said Angus.

"No, no, what is it?"

"Well, since you've asked, the verb 'comprise' is very commonly used incorrectly as you have just done. No problem, though. Just restart the question with 'A typical Fox campaign comprises' and you'll be fine," Angus said a little sheepishly. "Carry on."

I watched Brett's knuckles whiten as he gripped his pen. Nice, Angus. Very nice.

"Uhm . . . okay. A typical Fox campaign *comprises* muckraking, innuendo, and backstabbing. Aren't you a little daunted by the prospect of being in the Flamethrower's crosshairs, given his reputation for politically dismembering his opponents?"

"I don't intend to play that game. The voters deserve to hear about the issues this country must confront. I really don't think they're interested in a campaign driven by personal attacks. We want them to vote, not turn away from democracy. I'll have no part in a negative campaign regardless of what my opponent might have in mind. And if he does try to appeal to our baser instincts, I'll be doing my level best to stay on the high road, however much I may want to punch out his lights."

Very subtle. Back in the green room, Sally was about to climb the walls. The two side bulges on Angus's head had burst into a full rebellion. It was as if every hair Sally and Rebecca had carefully flattened was now struggling, with considerable success, to stand straight out and break free from his head. It looked, well, bizarre and other-worldly. And there were no Hollywood special effects. This was one hundred per cent, all-natural Angus.

Sally and I both saw them at the same time.

"Uh-oh," Sally whispered.

"What are those things?" I asked, squinting to identify the blondish streaks that suddenly appeared on both sides of Angus's head.

"Toothpicks," Sally sighed.

"Most people just carry them in their pocket," I observed. "How did they get in his hair?"

"We needed a little . . . or rather a lot of structural reinforcement to get his hair to . . . to comply. Those toothpicks were holding the bulk of his mop flat. It's a new technique recently developed in a small coiff college in Romania. The procedure is still being perfected."

"So you mean the toothpicks aren't supposed to pop out and stand up like that?" I asked, pointing to the screen. Sally said nothing. By this time his beard seemed to be moving all on its own as the fine, comb-straight lines began to vibrate and curl. "What's that?" I pointed to the screen again.

"Damn, I thought we got them all," Sally breathed. "This is heading south in a hurry."

"It almost looks like a kernel of corn," I said, squinting at the pale yellow nub in the lower left quadrant of Angus's beard.

"Yep. That beard is thicker than a Brazilian rain forest. For all we know, the cob could still be in there somewhere." Sally sighed.

Clearly the producer in the control room was no longer transfixed by the slow-motion transformation of Angus's hedge. I saw

Brett's right index finger zip to his right temple as if to prevent his earphone from flying out. Brett looked down, listening.

"Uhm . . . Angus we're going to take a quick break now," Brett said, before turning to face the camera. "So stay with us and we'll be right back with Liberal MP Angus McLintock."

I opened my mouth to say something to Sally, but she had bolted for the studio like a cheetah on a gazelle. I imagined her attacking Angus's hair and beard as an anxious producer counted down the commercial break. The monitor in the green room was not an inside feed but the standard cable output so I waited for the annoying Pizza Pockets ad to end before Brett eventually materialized before me once again. The camera shot had changed. I could no longer see Angus when Brett was posing his questions. Sally was probably still working on Angus.

"Welcome back to *Face to Face*. I'm Brett Palmer and I'm pleased to have renegade MP Angus McLintock with me in the studio today. Angus, there's a new rumour circulating on the Hill this morning that an ultra-conservative Christian preacher, Alden Stonehouse, will also seek the Tory nomination in Cumberland-Prescott against Emerson Fox. How do you react to that?"

"Well, I suggest Emerson Fox's view on the matter is more important than mine. I've heard of this Stonehouse fellow, but I was not aware that he might run. I assume he won't be campaigning on Sundays," Angus deadpanned. "Who opposes me for the seat is really not my primary concern. I'm interested in reminding, and in some cases maybe convincing, the people of Cumberland-Prescott that we all share democracy's principal obligation: to do first what is right for the nation before we consider what's best for our own community, let alone for ourselves. That may sound obvious but in my experience, it's not the way politics seems to work in this country. I aim to help change that."

Sally's emergency intervention during the commercial break must not have saved the patient because the camera shot of Angus had also changed. Throughout his thoughtful response, the TV screen was filled entirely with the face of Angus

McLintock. We saw a bit of his hair but the frame of the shot prevented the viewer from witnessing the real action taking place an inch or two off Angus's head. This particular camera shot was perfect for a remote dermatological examination, but didn't make for great TV. Angus delivered what I thought was a powerful answer. Unfortunately, the extreme close-up was more likely to prompt viewers to count his nostril hairs than focus on his compelling words. It sure made for strange TV.

Ten minutes later we were headed back to Cumberland with Angus at the wheel of his Toyota Camry.

"Well, beyond the histrionics of that possessed makeup artist, I thought that went rather well," he opened.

As a participant, Angus had obviously heard the show, but clearly he had not seen it.

"Absolutely! It was a great interview, Angus. Strong answers. And you looked . . . uhm . . . good."

"I could have done without those women wrestlin' with my locks every five minutes."

Oh no, you couldn't, I wanted to say.

"They were just doing their job." I glanced over and noticed a stray toothpick resting on his right shoulder. I brushed it off casually and shoved it down the crack in the seat.

"So tell me what you know about Alden Stonehouse," I asked. "I thought Emerson Fox was running unopposed."

"Aye, I'm surprised to hear that Stonehouse might enter the fray. I've met him once or twice in Cumberland, and he came in to the constituency office once a while back about graffiti."

"Right, I remember him now. Very polite. Nice guy. Has a way with words, as I recall," I ventured.

"Aye. He's very high on what he calls family morals, which I took to mean he's about as right wing as they come, but cloaks it in the civility and charm of a country clergyman."

"Well then, this is good news for our side," I noted.

"How do you figure?"

"Emerson Fox can't turn his flamethrower in our direction

until he's taken care of the opponent in his own party. That buys us some time to observe, learn, and plan," I replied. "But not too much time. The Tory nomination meeting is in a few days."

Angus was rifling through his beard as if searching for his house key. He found what he was looking for, lowered his window, and tossed out a corn kernel.

Later that night, while Lindsay slept beside me, Google, my laptop, and I got together to learn a bit more about Alden Stonehouse. He was the spiritual leader of the Assembly of the Divine Life of the Enlightenment. Yes, that does in fact become ADLE, an unfortunate appellation. ADLE had grown considerably in the last few years and now boasted a congregation of about 2,500 from the surrounding rural communities. Many of the congregants would be voters in Cumberland-Prescott. Some news reports I read, including an article by André Fontaine in the *Crier*, attributed a recent surge in new church members to the impending recession. A brush with death or the prospect of hard economic times often turned ambivalent church-goers into more devout followers. ADLE professed predictable views on the major social issues. Homosexuality: bad. Marriage between a man and woman resulting in the classic nuclear family: good. Premarital sex: bad. Post-marital sex: good, but only for procreation. Mothers who work outside the home: bad. A national child-care program: nope. Teaching *Slaughterhouse-Five* in high schools: no, I don't think so. Etc., etc.

But despite Stonehouse's living next door to Genghis Khan on the ideological spectrum, I found it hard to dislike him based on my online trolling. YouTube served up plenty of clips, from TV interviews to Sunday sermons. He was certainly doctrinaire in his right-wingedness, yet he sounded reasonable when espousing views I deplored. He accepted the right of others to hold their own opinions and relied heavily on lines like "Well, I understand your position but we're going to have to agree to disagree on that." He wasn't a screamer. He wasn't rude. He wasn't a

caricature of a corrupt TV evangelist. He was calm, polite, cour-
teous, well groomed, even handsome. And he could talk up a
storm. He was articulate, bordering on eloquent, with the
needle occasionally slipping into the charismatic zone. In other
words, he was a danger to us and, more immediately, to Emerson
Fox. His extreme views aside, he was much closer as a package
to the Honourable Eric Cameron, whom he sought to replace,
than was Emerson Fox. Most importantly, I assumed he enjoyed
the monolithic support of his congregation. If he were as smart
as he appeared, he'd be distributing Conservative Party mem-
berships to his flock on the collection plate Sunday mornings. If
I were Fox, I'd be a little uneasy.

Before I left YouTube, and against my better judgment, I typed
Angus McLintock into the search bar. Just as I feared, there were
already four separate uploads of that morning's *Face to Face* interview. As well, some online political junkie with far too much
time on his hands had produced a hilarious accelerated version
of the interview under the title *Angus McLintock's Hair: The 8th
Wonder of the World.* The wannabe filmmaker had zoomed in so
that Angus's head and shoulders filled the frame. He then sped
up the interview so the fourteen minutes zipped by in two minutes. I had to admit, watching the eruption on Angus's head in
compressed time was quite amazing. The pièce de résistance?
The entire two-minute clip ran accompanied by Tchaikovsky's
1812 Overture. The soundtrack so often really makes the film.

The next day, we got our first Emerson Fox wake-up call, and
we weren't even the target. Cumberland's two radio stations
started running the following two ads in heavy rotation, featuring a baritone movie-trailer voice-over with an alarmist tone.

"In every corner of the world, religious fanaticism has led to
anarchy, violence, and bloodshed. There is no place in Canada, and
no place in Cumberland, for religious zealots of any denomina-
tion. Who knows where it will end? This has been a paid political
message from the Committee to Nominate Emerson Fox as the

Progressive Conservative Candidate in Cumberland-Prescott."

"What do conservative voters really know about Alden Stonehouse? That he's the leader of an extreme Christian splinter group. That he's only lived in Cumberland for the last two years. That he rules his church with an iron fist. We've seen extreme religious leaders before, from Jonestown, Guyana, to Waco, Texas. Let's not add Cumberland to the list. This has been a paid political message from the Committee to Nominate Emerson Fox as the Progressive Conservative Candidate in Cumberland-Prescott."

I'd been waiting for Emerson Fox to fire his first shot across Alden Stonehouse's bow. I just hadn't expected him to fire directly *into* Alden Stonehouse's bow. Beyond how ridiculous and specious the ads were, it was odd for Fox to use such a public vehicle for his initial attack on Stonehouse when he was really only targeting PC party members who could vote in the upcoming Tory nomination. It was clear to me that Emerson Fox was not just lobbing a grenade, or more accurately a six-megaton cluster bomb, in Alden Stonehouse's direction, he was sending us a message, too.

Over the next two days, Emerson Fox and Alden Stonehouse waged a bitter and public battle for the hearts, minds, and votes of the Cumberland-Prescott Progressive Conservative Association. Both placed ads in the *Cumberland Crier* outlining their positions. Well, that's not quite accurate. Stonehouse's half-page ad laid out a series of policy planks that would make a hardcore libertarian blush. Fox's space in the *Crier* merely warned of the dangers of nominating a religious extremist-outsider-newcomer-cult leader as the PC candidate.

I kept the radio on in the campaign office, in the car, and at the boathouse as Fox's scorched-earth offensive played out before my ears. There were more incendiary radio spots, interview sound bites that were explosive enough to warrant hourly replays with each newscast, and a screen crawler on the Emerson Fox website that endlessly scrolled through troubling "facts" about the fanatical Alden Stonehouse and his messianic hold over his followers.

As I drove to and from the McLintock HQ, I saw choirs of Stonehouse supporters on busy street corners singing hymns, badly, and waving what I can only describe as blue campaign crucifixes with "Stonehouse" emblazoned on the horizontal crosspiece. It was the most blatant merging of church and state I'd seen since Jerry Falwell's Moral Majority and the pulpit politics he brought to the United States in the early eighties. For a good part of Monday, a Stonehouse choir swayed on the sidewalk outside the McLintock campaign office serenading our staff. Muriel sent out coffee to them and a request to sing one of her favourites, "Oh God Our Help in Ages Past." They did a commendable job of it, although Muriel thought they'd botched the descant on the last verse. We smiled and applauded anyway. The choir looked perplexed and broke up shortly thereafter.

Monday night, Lindsay and I were just finishing up burgers I'd brought home before another night on the door-to-door canvass, when the phone rang.

"Hi André," Lindsay opened. "Loved your photo in the *Crier* last week. I know you had to do it. I would have done the same thing."

Pause.

"Angus will get over it soon enough."

Pause.

"He's right here." She handed the phone to me.

Three minutes later my evening plans had changed. Despite some misgivings on my part, André had talked me into attending the PC nomination meeting at the Cumberland Motor Inn. Lindsay agreed to coordinate the evening's canvass in my stead.

"Okay, tell me again how the campaign manager for the Liberal candidate is going to gain admittance to the Progressive Conservative nomination meeting," I asked as I slid into the front seat of André's Subaru.

"Here, put these on," André replied, handing me *Cumberland Crier* ball cap and parka. "You'll be shooting video for the *Crier* website at the meeting so I can concentrate on taking stills."

I glanced into the back seat and saw a tripod and sparkling new HD digital camera.

"It used to be that newspapers were just newspapers," I observed.

"The damned Internet means we have to be broadcasters as well as writers and shooters now, so I could use your help. Plus, I thought you might want to be there for this."

"But what if someone recognizes me at the meeting? It could be embarrassing to be thrown out. You'd probably report on my ejection and plaster a photo on the front page."

"I probably would, but that won't happen. Nobody is going to recognize you. When you work for someone who looks like Charles Darwin in a force nine gale, no one remembers the clean-cut Joe standing next to him. You're safe."

We parked two blocks away in the closest spot we could find. It was going to be a long night. I donned the parka, pulling the cap down low, and grabbed the tripod with the camera already mounted on it. I tried my best to look like an experienced camera operator sauntering casually with it slung over my shoulder. In the five-minute walk to the motel, I inadvertently struck a stop sign and then André with the tripod. Curly, Larry, and Moe were smiling down on me.

I stood behind André, looking at my feet, as he signed us in at the media check-in table, and we then took our place at the back of the ballroom. After about ten minutes of tinkering, I finally figured out how to spread the tripod's legs and fix them in place. The breakthrough came when a miniature woman, who must have been about eighty-five, shuffled over and pointed with her cane to the release button where the legs locked together. I thanked her and looked around to see if anyone else had been watching. It was a breeze after that. I spent the rest of the time with my eye in the viewfinder, hiding my face in the lee of the camera. André just stood beside me, enjoying my anxiety.

The room and the lobby outside were absolutely jammed. There were probably 1,800 or so in the ballroom with at least another 500 trying in vain to get in. I thought back to our modest little community centre meeting that had officially nominated Angus as our party's candidate. As I counted the many gaudy yellow vests hustling about the ballroom, it occurred to me that the motel staff working this Tory nomination probably outnumbered the full membership of the C-P Liberal Association. Mercifully, the lights finally dimmed and three figures mounted the risers at the front. Emerson Fox and Alden Stonehouse took their seats while the president of the Tory riding association headed to the podium against competing chants of "Flamethrower! Flamethrower!" and "Stonehouse! Stonehouse!" Reverend Stonehouse's congregation was out in force. Judging on volume and energy, the split in the room seemed about even. The association president looked nervous and held up his hands for quiet. Eventually, I could hear his voice above the roar as I centred him in the shot.

"Please, please, quiet down, quiet down, please. We have a long night ahead of us so the sooner we get to the voting, the sooner we'll be able to declare our PC candidate." He paused as the last of the chanting died away. "I'm Herbert Clarkson, president of the Cumberland-Prescott Progressive Conservative Association and I want to welcome you all, new members and old alike, to the official nomination meeting. We are here to accomplish one thing tonight. To elect our standard bearer in this federal election who will then send Angus McLintock back to the engineering faculty at U of O. This riding has always been Conservative and on January 27," he thundered, "it will be Conservative again!" I know it's a bit of a cliché, but the crowd went wild.

The president of the riding association then opened the floor for nominations. Both Emerson Fox and Alden Stonehouse were nominated. No one else entered the fray and nominations were officially closed.

In the interests of time, each candidate was given only five minutes to speak. This was a sensible decision. There were likely very few undecided voters in the room so the speeches were really for the media and would have little bearing on who would be the nominated candidate. It made more sense to get the voting started.

With the ballroom lights dimmed, I no longer had to keep my face hidden behind the camera. I straightened up and focused on the podium, keeping a periodic eye on the video camera to make sure I recorded the proceedings. Given that I was masquerading as the media, I felt justified in choosing a few sound bites from the candidates' addresses rather than inflicting their entire scripts. One can only take so much.

Emerson Fox rose first and approached the podium. His supporters snapped to attention, leapt to their feet, then exploded in a rousing standing ovation. Fox arrived at the mike and lifted both hands in the air trying to kill two birds with one stone: accept the accolades and calm the crowd. It took a while, but eventually he had the floor all to himself.

"Friends, these have been bleak months since the last election when a candidate who abused the democratic process, a candidate who had no intention to serve, a candidate who had no desire to serve, wound up representing one of the great conservative constituencies in Canada. It was an electoral travesty that we must set right on January 27."

Requisite standing ovation and unrestrained cheering.

"And what do we know about Professor Angus McLintock? Not much. We know he shut down a local plant that had provided jobs for dozens of Cumberland residents for a quarter century. We know he stood between the citizens of this community and their own hard-earned money when he fought the government's tax cuts. We know he almost single-handedly defeated the duly elected Progressive Conservative government in an act of political conceit and caprice that will cost the taxpayers of this country millions of dollars for a needless election."

More wild applause and predictable audience gyrations. For strategic reasons, Fox was clearly ignoring his real opponent that night and was targeting Angus for the benefit of the scribes and cameras lined up along the back wall. As rhetoric goes, Fox was making the grade and his supporters were lapping it up.

"What else do we know about Angus McLintock? Well, my friends, we know he was married for nearly forty years to one of the most extreme and fanatical feminists Canada has ever produced, who, if you read what she has written over the years, tried to violently rip apart the very social fabric of our society with her dangerous ideas. That's what we know about Angus McLintock."

By this time I was so offended I hadn't initially noticed Fox's "to violently rip" split infinitive. I was shouting at the top of my lungs and shaking my fist in outrage until I felt the viselike grip of André Fontaine on my forearm. Thankfully, the crowd was so powered up in their reaction that my lone dissenting voice died in the din.

I should have expected such a malevolent diatribe from Fox. I'd already warned Angus that he was going to have to keep his cool and not take the bait Emerson Fox would surely be offering. But still it caught me off-guard, and I had that bait halfway down my throat before André intervened. He said nothing as he released me. He didn't have to. Though still fuming, I dipped my head to look through the viewfinder like the other camera guys.

Fox rattled on and never once mentioned Alden Stonehouse. He simply refused to acknowledge his opponent's existence. It was a common enough strategy, to focus his supporters on the real battle ahead with Angus.

When Alden Stonehouse took the stage, he moved the podium to one side of the risers and took the mike in his hands like an old-time evangelist.

"Whether you're here to vote for my accomplished opponent or to support me, I can tell you that there is far more that unites us here tonight than divides us. Let's not squabble among ourselves when the real enemy is sequestered in his workshop tonight, plotting the continued moral decline of Canadian society. Angus McLintock, an admitted agnostic, in his short time on Parliament Hill has left the people of Cumberland-Prescott to twist in the winds of a recession. It is not what he has done *for* Cumberland-Prescott. No, no. Rather, it's what he has done *to* Cumberland-Prescott."

He was a tremendous orator who knew just how to lift his audience with his own inflection. He paced the front of the stage, stopping and turning to face the crowd at dramatic moments when his words really mattered. He spoke quietly at times to draw his listeners forward in their seats. I had to admit, he was good. The Stonehouse contingent was alternately on their feet shouting or sitting transfixed in rapt silence as the preacher-turned-candidate skilfully piloted his rhetorical roller coaster.

"Yes, friends, it's what Angus McLintock has done to the people of Cumberland-Prescott that brings us here tonight in such numbers. He supported the opening of the Corrections Canada halfway house in Cumberland. He championed it! He even wielded a silver spade at the sod-turning with the Minister. He has opened the gates of our community and invited hardened criminals to live here among us, with our children, with our families. We must stop this heinous act against our community and the social decay it will surely bring."

Blah, blah, blah. It was nauseating. Yes, he was a great speaker. Yes, the crowd loved him, and even the Fox supporters cheered enthusiastically. But couldn't anyone see through him? He was a cartoon character, a stereotype, an archetype, and not in a good way. But looking around the room, I was clearly in the minority. The jaded journalists at the back were not taken in. They stood stoic as the crowd celebrated two barnburner speeches.

Fifteen minutes later, at 7:40, the voting booths opened in a separate room down the hall. The lineup snaked all the way out to the motel lobby. The voting at the normal garden-variety nomination meeting took about an hour. This was no ordinary meeting. By the time the haggard president of the riding association took the stage again with a sheet of paper in his hands, nearly five hours had passed. Most of the crowd had gone home and were probably already asleep. But about 500 diehard supporters, evenly split between Fox and Stonehouse, remained to the bitter end.

"Thank you for your patience. I can report that more members voted in this nomination meeting than ever before in the storied history of this association. There were 1,956 ballots cast and 24 ballots spoiled. So, 967 votes are required to achieve the 50 per cent plus one threshold and win the nomination. With 1,083 votes, the official candidate for the Progressive Conservative Party in Cumberland-Prescott will be . . . Emerson Fox!"

Bedlam. It was a crushing disappointment for the Stonehouse supporters. Many were in tears as the Fox fans square-danced in the aisles. Emerson Fox and Alden Stonehouse made their way to the stage. While the margin of victory had been slim, it was not slim enough to warrant a recount. After Emerson Fox delivered a mercifully brief victory speech, during which André had to caution me only once against excessive eye-rolling, Alden Stonehouse sought the mike.

"I congratulate Emerson Fox on his victory tonight and I wish him well in the campaign. But not too well. You see, I made a promise to my supporters that I would fight the daily assaults on the moral fabric of this community with every ounce of strength and every breath I have left within me. I hereby declare that I will run as an independent conservative in this election. Even as we speak, and in regretful anticipation of my defeat tonight, my nomination papers are being delivered to the Chief Electoral Officer. I'll be on the campaign trail bright and early tomorrow morning."

The Stonehouse disciples still in the room erupted and shot from down and out to do-si-do in two seconds flat. As the implications of Stonehouse's announcement sunk in, the Fox folks seemed intent on switching from square-dancing to slam-dancing. In short order, several Stonehouse supporters found themselves laid out on the carpet. Fox himself looked as if he'd been punched in the stomach. André told me afterwards that I'd just stood there through it all, pumping my fists in the air and shouting "Yes, yes, yes, yes . . ." until he restrained me, lest I were to blow my own cover. Two conservatives in the race were much, much better than one.

Monday, January 6

My Love,

It's been a day or two since I've held the quill but the campaign is not a part-time endeavour. Daniel, Lindsay, Muriel, and the two Petes have got my shoulder to the wheel every waking hour. Going door to door is a right pain in the arse as it means that I have to meet and talk with people, a pastime you know I've always considered overrated.

I was on TV the other day with that guy from CBC you always liked. I forget his name. The woman in the makeup department seemed to have met her match when she tackled the silver fleece on my head and chin. She put all manner of concoctions in my hair to make it behave. I've no idea what it was, but I was worried about spontaneous combustion sitting under those hot TV lights. I've not seen the interview yet but I thought I worked my oars in the water reasonably well. Mind you, it took the entire weekend before my hair felt like my own again.

By the morning we'll know my Tory opponent for better or worse. I don't really care who I'm against. One will surely shout from the rooftops many imperfections and indiscretions I've long forgotten. The other will publicly lament my dubious moral rectitude and ambivalent faith, and may even try to mend my soul. I care not who I face. My plan is to pay them no heed whatever.

'Tis late now, love, and our well-worn bed beckons. I've learned in the last two days that during an election, weekends just mean that more voters are home to pursue and persuade. Have an eye for me and lend me strength. . . .

AM

CHAPTER SEVEN

I rolled over and rested my hand in that amazing little curve that linked Lindsay's waist and hip as she snoozed on her side next to me. She sighed, in a good way, in a contented way. The morning light squeezed into the room along the borders of the blinds.

"I promised Muriel I'd meet with her this morning without Angus," I whispered.

"Hmmm. That sounds suspicious. What's up?" croaked Lindsay in full Brenda Vaccaro morning voice.

"Not sure. She said something about the high road still having gutters," I said. "Not sure what that means."

"If I know Muriel, I think it means she's about to get her elbows up in the campaign without involving our candidate," Lindsay opined.

Muriel wasn't where I usually found her by the window overlooking the river. One of the front desk staff directed me to the card room down the hall from the main lobby. She stood at the front of the room before about eight fellow residents who were so focused on Muriel they didn't seem to notice my arrival at the back. Muriel had written in her shaky hand the word GOUT on the white board beside her. I didn't know that Muriel was an expert on gout but I sat down and tuned in.

"Our only chance to win this riding is if Angus continues to practise his unique brand of politics. He may well squeak out a victory if he avoids the traps Emerson Fox is laying," Muriel opened. "Fox is coming after Angus with both barrels blazing. Angus is going to be pilloried. If Angus takes the bait, responds in kind, and jumps into the gutter to duke it out with Fox on his own terms, we will lose, sure as guns. Angus has to change the game and try to force the debate to a higher level. But, but, I still think the wily Fox deserves his comeuppance," Muriel stated.

"Hear, hear," voices in the group replied.

I didn't like the sound of this but still wasn't sure where it was going, and what it had to do with gout. In fact, what the hell is gout anyway? Muriel's voice brought me back.

"Angus can know nothing of this. He must be protected." Muriel looked my way then. "I see that our stalwart campaign manager, Daniel, has arrived. He'll just be staying for a few moments but then I'm going to throw him out. I don't even want Daniel knowing about the shadowy workings of this elite political SWAT team." She kept her eyes on me. Those in the room who could turn their heads far enough around looked at me too. I started to put two and two together, but I still missed the gout connection. Muriel took over again.

"Friends, welcome to the inaugural meeting of Geriatrics Out to Undermine Tories. Welcome to the GOUT squad."

The theme music for *The A-Team* TV series started up in my head. Four women and two men clapped. The fifth woman, sitting on the aisle, pumped her fist in the air and shouted, "Yeeee-haaaaa!" I have to say that it was a little creepy.

"You are not members of the Liberal Party. You are not volunteers on the campaign, at least to the untrained observer. The campaign will not acknowledge your existence, particularly if your cover is blown. You are deep undercover. Your mission, should you choose to accept it, is to ask Emerson Fox the tough questions."

"We're not doing anything illegal, are we?" one frail but strong-voiced woman asked.

"Of course not, for pity's sake," replied Muriel. "We're just exercising our constitutional right to organize, aggravate, irritate, and agitate. Your job is to get under Emerson Fox's skin. To keep him guessing. To knock him off balance. To flummox him. To force him into revealing his ignorance. To make him pay for what he's done to politics in this country." More applause.

That was my cue to leave. I stood and Muriel simply waved to me and smiled sweetly as I eased myself out of the room. I see nothing. I hear nothing. I know nothing. Muriel just wanted me to know that Fox would not be sailing through the all-candidates meetings unchallenged, even if it wouldn't be Angus who was going for his jugular. As I left, I heard the group debating nasty questions to hurl Fox's way. The GOUT squad. Nice.

I was to meet the two Petes and Angus at campaign headquarters at 10:30 to map out the week's canvassing priorities. I was early and grabbed a *Globe and Mail* before sequestering myself in the back office to kill half an hour. The campaign office was humming along and even though I was the campaign manager, I certainly had less to do this time around. The growing volunteer staff, selected and trained by Muriel and the two Petes, had the operation running like a well-oiled machine. Clipboards and coloured markers were involved. The canvassing team met each evening, after the door-knocking was done for the night, to map out the priority polls for the following day. They compared notes on voter reaction and which issues were coming up at the door. They brainstormed compelling response lines and rehearsed delivery. While doing all this, they were also cutting lengths of red ribbon to hand out when they stumbled upon a Liberal household. A smaller team worked with Norman Sanderson on the fundraising front. It was almost like a real campaign. Much of the time, I was merely taking up space, which was fine with me.

The newspaper was chock full of economic doom and gloom. It was amazing the speed at which the recession came upon us. Canada's economic fundamentals remained relatively sound and we seemed to be weathering the storm better than most other industrialized nations. Nevertheless, Angus was very concerned. He had already left to drive in to Ottawa to meet with a faculty friend in U of O's economics department for a briefing. Angus read the papers and was extraordinarily well informed, but he really wanted to dig into the economic situation. Being on the faculty of a top university gave him free access to leading independent economists who weren't on the payroll of the Department of Finance or the Bank of Canada.

After my session with the two Petes, I stayed in the campaign office and worked on the Angus McLintock website. I'm no programmer, but we'd chosen to build our site using blogging software rather than HTML so that even non-geeks like me could add new material. I spent some time uploading a digital recording of Angus's nomination speech. Then I scanned and uploaded André's piece in the *Crier* about Angus and me. I did not upload the front-page photo of Angus being dragged by *Baddeck 1*. Several times I had to ask for Pete2's help with some of the more esoteric technical procedures, like lifting the lid of the laptop, turning on the computer, and logging in.

When I was done, I looked around the campaign office and was gratified to see that it looked not that much different from any other Liberal campaign headquarters across the country. There were several volunteers hard at it, colour-coded riding maps on the wall, phones ringing, newspaper articles pinned to bulletin boards, fifty-year-old desks and chairs, the stench of coffee burning to the bottom of the carafe, and a box of day-old doughnuts as hard as pucks. Well, they'd been day-olds a week ago. What made our campaign office unique were the two pierced punk rockers holding clipboards, overseeing it all.

When Angus returned home from campus late in the afternoon, Muriel and I were waiting for him in his living room.

"How was your economics tutorial?" I inquired.

"Fascinatin'!" he gushed. "Bob is a first-rate teacher. I already had a reasonably good understandin' of why the economy has collapsed, but I really needed some help on what the options are for pullin' ourselves out of it."

"Why don't we just throw on another shift at the Royal Canadian Mint and print more money?" I joked.

"Because the value of our dollar would plummet and inflation would go through the roof," Angus countered.

"I know. Thank you, Angus, but I was actually kidding. Even I have at least a passing understanding of our monetary system."

"So what's the solution?" asked Muriel.

"Well, since we're discussing economics, there is no clear consensus on what we should do. Bob believes that Canada's infrastructure is its economic backbone. We're so large a country that we rely more than most nations on our roads, rail lines, ports, etc. He made quite a compellin' case," Angus concluded.

Muriel was starting to fidget and I could see that it was more than her Parkinson's.

"Love to hear more about that, but we're running up against the clock here, Angus. Are you ready?" I asked. The first all-candidates meeting was that night and we had only an hour to get ready.

"Aye."

We stood Angus up in front of us as Muriel and I stayed on the couch. Muriel started.

"Do you respect Canadian laws?"

Angus furrowed his brow.

"I'm not clear on what you mean."

"It's a simple question with a simple yes or no answer. Do you respect Canadian laws?" She sounded cold and hostile.

Understanding dawned on him.

"I do respect Canadian laws, including the laws that protect our right of assembly and our right to protest legislation that citizens deem to be unjust. That's called democracy."

Muriel wasn't done yet.

"But as I understand it, you were arrested more than twenty times. Arrested! Is that the kind of example our Member of

Parliament should be setting for our young people?"

Angus was into it now.

"I'm proud of the civil disobedience in which I partook to protest laws that I felt enslaved women in Canada. Had my late wife and I ever been blessed with children, I hope they would have had the conviction and the courage to challenge legislation that in their eyes promulgates injustice and inequality. To me, that is the essence of leadership in a democracy."

Okay, not bad. My turn.

"Your wife, Marin Lee, was a femiterrorist whose extreme views threaten our family values and social fabric. Do you support everything found in her books?"

Angus's face clouded and he bounced from left foot to right. I felt like a jerk but knew it was better for him to hear this for the first time in his own living room and not an hour later in the all-candidates meeting. Angus gathered himself and turned to face me. Calm now, and confident.

"I was married to Marin Lee for nearly forty years. She was a great woman: the most intelligent person I've ever known. She was greatly concerned about the state of women in Canada. Most of her work was in the service of equality for women in all respects. We still have a distance to travel, but she left us with a clear sense of our destination and the maps to get us there too."

Not so fast.

"But in one of her early books, she demanded that women working in the home be compensated for house cleaning, laundry, and cooking. Wouldn't that introduce a harmful distortion in the free market economy that has helped Canada to prosper?"

"It depends on your definition of 'distortion.' To me, when a businessman takes his shirts to the cleaners or hires a cleaning woman, he pays for the service. When a businessman takes a meal in a restaurant, he pays for it. These transactions fuel our market economy and drive wealth generation. If the woman who performs these very same services does so in the family home and is his wife, the businessman benefits in the same way, yet pays nothing. That to me is the longstanding distortion in our vaunted market." Angus paused and then continued. "I'm not proposing or promoting a policy change to address this anomaly. But I certainly support the underlying analysis my wife advanced."

"Nicely done, Angus," I said, and meant it. But something wasn't quite right. Now that the performance was over, Angus suddenly looked downright mean. His index finger was in my face.

"You'd be wise to watch your words, sir, when you're invokin' the memory of my wife."

"Angus! Don't you talk that way," Muriel scolded. "You're missing the point. You should be thanking Daniel. He just gave you a taste of what Flamethrower Fox is going to unleash an hour from now. Daniel did that for your benefit, not his enjoyment."

Angus sighed and collapsed into the chintz cushion next to me, closed his eyes, and rested his head on the back of the couch. No one filled what seemed an uncomfortable silence. Finally, he opened his eyes, nodded, and patted my knee.

"Aye" was all he said.

The phone rang, breaking the moment.

"Hello." Angus pressed the receiver to his ear.

"Ah, André. The man with the camera." Pause. "Aye, that's what Daniel argued. But do you have to take so many?" Pause. "Anyway, what's on your mind?" Pause. "What? On what earthly grounds? Excluding Stonehouse from the all-candidates meeting is unfair. He's a duly registered candidate, isn't he? Why should he not participate?" Pause. "Well, Fox can believe what he pleases, but I'm certainly not in favour of cutting out Stonehouse. We've some tough challenges ahead and I think the more heads tackling them the better." Pause. "You're welcome. See you later on. Perhaps keep that lens cap in its place a little longer this evening." He hung up the phone.

"Let me guess," Muriel sighed. "Emerson Fox is trying to freeze Alden Stonehouse out of the all-candidates meeting just because he's running as an independent, right?"

"Aye, but the Returning Officer is havin' none of it."

Angus drove Lindsay, Muriel, and me over to the all-candidates meeting. Halfway there Angus turned on the radio. His timing wasn't good. The fading tail of a song was overtaken by an angry woman's voice.

"Does a man who's been arrested twenty-three times deserve to represent Cumberland-Prescott in the House of Commons? Angus McLintock has twenty-three arrests on his rap sheet. You didn't know that, did you? That's because Angus McLintock doesn't want you to know. This has been a message from the committee to elect Emerson Fox, PC candidate in Cumberland-Prescott."

I turned off the radio, a little late. Cars honked.

"Angus, you can't just stop here in the middle of the road, we're blocking the intersection," I said quietly.

With white knuckles on the wheel, he eased forward and was soon back up to speed.

"Well, we knew it was coming. There should be no shock in this at all," Muriel observed from the back seat as she leaned forward to rest her hand on Angus's shoulder.

He looked straight ahead.

"Welcome to the Cumberland Chamber of Commerce all-candidates meeting," intoned the moderator from the podium. "We'll begin with two-minute opening statements from each candidate, Liberal incumbent Angus McLintock, Progressive Conservative Emerson Fox, NDP Jane Nankovich, and Conservative Independent Reverend Alden Stonehouse."

We were in the auditorium of Cumberland Collegiate. About 150 voters filled the theatre-style seating, with the media occupying their traditional space along the risers at the back. André was there, of course, but this time he had to work the video camera on his own.

The candidates had drawn straws and providence was with us. Angus rose, removed the microphone from the lectern mount, and walked around the podium to stand at the very front of the stage. His suit was a little rumpled. He wore no tie. In the pitched battle with his hair, waged in the car on the way over, the brush and comb tag team had clearly lost. He had no notes as he stood alone, as close to the voters as he could get without falling off the stage. He spoke calmly and quietly, but was heard by all.

"Thank you all for coming. Democracy works best when citizens take their civic obligations seriously. You're doing that by being here tonight, and I'm sure I speak for my fellow candidates when I say we're grateful. I've met my opponents for the first time this evening and I look forward to more discussions and debates with them, I hope on topics that are relevant to the challenges we face as a nation in the throes of an economic tailspin. I, and I hope you, have no interest in discussing issues that do not bear on the current and future state of our government, our economy, our society, or our country."

A few people applauded while Emerson Fox, beyond Angus's field of view, smirked and slowly shook his head.

"You will all know that I landed in the House of Commons somewhat unexpectedly. Not only was I shocked to be elected, but I was surprised to discover over time that I was actually enjoying the adventure. I like to think we made a few good things happen while holding the government to account, supporting that which earned our favour, and opposing that which rightly deserved our opposition. That is our duty to you.

"I'll not blether on much longer so we have time to try to answer the questions you have on your mind. But before we get to the truly important issues we're confronting, let me seize the benefit of speaking first by launching a pre-emptive strike of sorts. I want to tell you a few things that I'd much rather you heard from me. If you've listened to the radio recently, you might know something about this already. As a young graduate student shortly after I arrived here in Canada, I participated in demonstrations protesting laws I could not and would not countenance. Partly due, I believe, to the public awareness and support engendered by these protests, these unjust laws were eventually changed by the Trudeau government. I'm referring to legislation that allows a woman to choose, in consultation with her doctor, whether or not to continue an unplanned or unwanted pregnancy – a right Canadian women have enjoyed since 1969.

"So I peacefully protested the old laws and fought for the new legislation we now have. In that process, I was arrested for trespassing or unlawful assembly on Parliament Hill along with hundreds of other protestors. This scene repeated itself some twenty-three times. Yes, I realize in hindsight that it seems an excessive number. I ascribe it to the passion of youth, yet it has not dimmed much in the intervening years. Incidentally, and for what it's worth, I was never ever convicted.

"You should also know that I accidentally broke a window in my school when I was eleven, dented a car with a mudball at thirteen, and I may have parked my hovercraft illegally beneath Parliament Hill a few weeks ago, and I do apologize for that. These have been my only brushes with the law. I expected all of this would emerge in the campaign, so I thought I'd nip it in the bud. But I don't wish you to misconstrue my confession. As I look back across my life, there are certainly moments of regret, embarrassment, even shame. But to be clear, I look upon those Parliament Hill demonstrations so many years ago with nothing but pride."

Angus paused and lowered his head. A young woman I didn't recognize started clapping. Soon, at least half the room was applauding. Angus nodded once, laid the mike on the podium, and sat down. Lindsay squeezed my right hand and Muriel my left.

Jane Nankovich, the NDP candidate, was up next. She spoke well but had the unenviable task of following Angus. The audience drifted as soon as she opened with "brothers and sisters." If she'd been at a Canadian Auto Workers rally she'd have done well. But there didn't appear to be a union brother or sister in the room.

Alden Stonehouse really is a great speaker. His time in the pulpit had been well spent. His supporters seemed to have congregated on the right-hand side of the room. He tended to stay focused on them, which may have been a mistake. He already had their votes. He really needed to appeal to the rest of the room.

Stonehouse went on a rant, an eloquent and articulate rant, but a rant nevertheless, about moral decay. He seemed incensed that Angus would recall with honour and dignity his role in the abortion wars of the sixties and called it a sacrilegious assault on Christian values. There were a few boos as he said this, the loudest from Muriel, who expertly cupped her trembling hands around her mouth to help project her already bone-rattling voice. But you could hardly hear Muriel for the ovation from the literal and ideological right wing of the room.

What Alden Stonehouse was not accustomed to was having a time limit placed on his sermons. After only two minutes his vocal chords were barely warm. But rules were rules. The chair of the meeting first stood to signal that the time had expired. When this didn't work, the PA was turned off. But Alden Stonehouse doesn't need a PA to make himself heard. Finally, in a moment of desperate inspiration, the lights were extinguished, throwing the entire room into darkness. He stopped talking then and returned to his seat as the lights came back on.

"Just a gentle reminder that candidates have just two minutes for their opening statements. Unlike the Oscars, we don't have an orchestra to cue when speeches stretch into overtime. Our final candidate to speak this evening is Emerson Fox from the Progressive Conservative Party, and then we'll move to audience questions."

Emerson Fox, beanpole thin with a grey crewcut, approached the podium in a grey suit that looked like a hand-me-down from Richard Nixon's 1960 presidential campaign wardrobe. The notoriously taciturn and reticent backroom legend lived up to his reputation.

"No need for me to speak for long right now. I want to make sure we have plenty of time for questions from all of you. Let me just say that Cumberland-Prescott for over a hundred years has been represented by Conservatives. We all know what happened just prior to the last election that left us with a Liberal MP, but the time has come to restore the universe to its natural order. We don't need another tax-and-spend socialist union-loving lefty in the House. We certainly don't want to elect a religious fanatic who would have us dissolve that critical historical separation of church and state. And above all, we simply cannot elect a common criminal and feminista who abused the electoral process last time around by letting his name stand under false pretences. He should have been prosecuted under the Election Act, not ushered into the House of Commons."

Wow. He wouldn't even use the names of his opponents. In a brief pause, I heard two loud cracks in quick succession that sounded like a wooden yardstick smacked twice on a desk. We all looked up to see Angus standing and holding the now broken arms of his chair in his hands, having ripped them from their moorings. Angus found us in the crowd with his eyes. Muriel, Lindsay, and I were all instinctively moving our hands in front of us, palms down, wordlessly imploring Angus to breathe deeply, calm down, and banish thoughts of medieval dismemberment techniques. He seemed to find his peaceful place and gently put the broken chair arms on the ground beside him and sat back down. Emerson Fox was grinning and shaking his head before lifting his eyes once more to the crowd.

"It's time to let this government complete the job it was elected to do last October. It's time to put more money back into the pockets of Canadians, into your pockets. It's time to return the Progressive Conservatives to government in Ottawa. That's how we'll get out of this minor recession. That's all I have to say now. Let's get to the questions."

A large and boisterous group of young Tories leapt to their feet, clapped, and waved Fox signs that they had smuggled into the auditorium under their shirts, even though they weren't permitted under the rules of the meeting.

By the time order was restored and the offending signs collected, Angus had regained control and looked calm. Handheld mikes were given to each candidate as the moderator headed to the podium.

"The floor is open for questions from you, the voters."

As is often the case, most of the questions were pedestrian and boring, and the candidates generally responded in kind. Angus did well, but I think he was still a little rattled from the fierce but short Fox attack. After about forty-five minutes, the line at the mikes dwindled.

One of the teenage Fox supporters moved to the mike.

"My question is for Angus McLintock. The night you were, like, elected, you, like, basically admitted that you, like, didn't care what your constituents thought, that you were, like, going to do what you thought was right for, like, the country, even if it, like, hurt this riding."

She stepped back. Angus stood and lifted his mike.

"Well, I'm afraid you're wrong and you're right."

"No, no, I'm right. That's, like, what you said."

"If I may, you're wrong in describing your words as a question. There was no question. Just a statement no doubt intended to be, *like*, provocative."

He smiled as he said it. It wasn't mean-spirited.

"But you're right in recalling that I promised the voters of Cumberland-Prescott on election night that I would be guided first by what I think is in the best interests of Canada, and second by what I think is in the best interests of the voters of C-P. That is what I said because that it is what I believed then, and believe now. In my mind, that is what democracy is. The whole is greater than the sum of its parts. The nation has primacy over the constituency. So we must think of Canada first as a whole. Sometimes that means sacrificing short-term local benefits for longer-term national gains."

A smattering of applause.

An old woman made her way to the mike. She seemed somehow familiar, though I couldn't place her. She unfolded a piece of paper and stepped up.

"Mr. Fox. Some years ago after you apparently retired, you spoke to the Ottawa Board of Trade. During an interview afterwards you said the following:

> 'I could not care less about policy. I have no interest in policy. I know nothing about policy. I win elections through any means necessary. Policy doesn't win elections, politics does. And it's a blood sport. You win by cutting down the other candidates and driving them into the ground. Who cares what you stand for? It doesn't matter if you can sow the seeds of doubt about your opponent's character. That's all you have to do to win.'

"Mr. Fox, do you stand by those specious words now that you've come out of retirement?"

I now remembered where I'd seen her. The GOUT operative returned to her seat. She was sitting by herself and did not even lift her eyes when she passed us. André approached her and she gave him the piece of paper she'd refolded.

Emerson Fox had stayed seated and now looked as if he were in the middle of a prostate examination.

"Um. Well. Ahhh. Don't ever believe a reporter when they say it's off the record." He chuckled unconvincingly as he raked his crewcut with his left hand. "Ahhh, those comments were taken out of context and were not supposed to have appeared in the story. It was yellow journalism and I was the victim. I know policy is important but I still believe that policy doesn't win elections."

Fox looked chastened and dropped his mike to his side and

lowered his head to signal that he was done.

"That's your answer?" someone shouted. The moderator took Fox off the hook.

"We have time for just one more question. Yes sir."

Another familiar face approached the mike. It was the roly-poly young man with slicked-back black hair from the pages of *Flamethrower*. I hadn't seen him in the crowd.

"Mr. McLintock, I'm Ramsay Rumplun and I'm a lifelong Progressive Conservative. Sir, you brought down the government because you opposed tax cuts. You denied the citizens of Cumberland-Prescott money they could sure use right now. And you've put the country to the enormous and wasteful expense of running another election so soon after the last one. Two questions. Aren't you worried you'll get less votes because of what you've done. And second, if you don't like the Conservatives' budget, what's your prescription for getting out of this recession?"

Angus could not contain his smile as he rose and took the mike.

"Another Rumplun, eh? Like father, like son. I'm glad to meet you, young Mr. Rumplun. Your father and I, um, know each other. Let me start by saying that I may well earn *fewer* votes this time out, but never *less* votes. As for my prescription for the economy, I don't claim to have any real expertise in what some call the 'dismal science,' but I'm doing my best to learn about it. I've become convinced that tax cuts in this climate are fiscally irresponsible. In such times, I fear Canadians will sock away their tax cut proceeds rather than boost consumer spending.

"We've also sadly neglected our national infrastructure to pay off the deficit. We Liberals were in on that, too, but I'm not sure replacing a financial deficit with an infrastructure deficit was wise. We're going to have to rebuild our roads at a higher cost, refurbish our ports and bridges at a higher cost, upgrade our railroad system and power generators, all at a higher cost than if we'd sustained a measured infrastructure investment program and taken a wee bit longer to slay the deficit. So after researching this and talking to economists I've come to trust and respect, I think that instead of tax cuts, we need to embark on a program of infrastructure investment. This will immediately create jobs and put our economy on a stronger footing when the recovery takes hold. Now I don't have any particular influence over Liberal policy but that's what I'd be recommending. I'm hoping we'll see something like that in the Liberal platform when it's unveiled in a few days. Please pass along my regards to your father."

I passed André as we made our way out of the auditorium after the meeting. He leaned over and whispered to me.

"It was all square for most of the meeting, but after that old lady skewered Fox with his own words, I'd have to give the nod to Angus."

After the meeting, we dropped Muriel off and then drove home. Angus was still seething and did little to hide it, now that he was among friends. In view of how steamed he seemed in the car, I gained new respect for his powers of restraint during the meeting. The entire drive home he didn't talk much, but when he did, it was through gritted teeth.

We heard Angus enter the workshop below us at about eleven. The glow from the lights hung outside the front of the boathouse spilled into our apartment. Angus seldom turned on the outdoor floods, so Lindsay took a peek out the window and then beckoned me.

I was surprised to see Angus skating on the frozen river in the dim illumination offered by the lights. Up and back he'd go, striding then gliding. He wasn't a stellar skater, given that his childhood was in Scotland, but he held his own.

"His eyes are streaming," observed Lindsay as we sat together and watched.

"So would yours in such an icy January wind," I replied, putting my arm around her shoulder.

But the Canadian flag hoisted on the pole down near the dock hung lank and limp.

Friday, January 10

My Love,

He dared to call you a "feminista." I could have dropped him on the spot. I very nearly did. I cannot imagine conducting myself as he did tonight. He is truly a cancer on democracy. Sorry to appropriate your wretched disease but the analogy is sound. No one will have the stomach to vote, let alone serve, if the policies we should be creating and debating are shunted aside to make way for a malevolent wave of personal attacks and character assassination. It cannot stand. It is vexing to listen to his tripe and not be able to respond in kind without serving his very cause. I must hold my tongue, not to mention my fists, and let victory be my rebuttal. But it's hard. It's a right bastard, so it is.

Beyond an unhealthy desire to see Fox drawn and quartered, I thought I held my own tonight. There really wasn't as much about you as Muriel and Daniel had led me to expect. But perhaps they're keeping their powder dry for a later battle.

I had to skate tonight to calm myself. The ice was hard and fast. Do you remember that you were the first to put the blades on my feet? Of course you do. It was odd and empty to skate alone without your hand to hold. It also meant I fell twice, with no damage done. The second time I just lay there and looked in frigid peace at the stars for a time.

AM

CHAPTER EIGHT

The all-candidates meeting was given extensive coverage in the *Cumberland Crier* the next day. André's piece was balanced, as usual, and there were no compromising photos of Angus. It did describe how Angus broke the arms of his chairs in thinly veiled rage over Fox's comments. But it also painted a vivid picture of Emerson Fox's obvious discomfort in handling the GOUT agent's stiletto question. The photo accompanying the story was benign enough and just showed all four candidates standing together at the front of the stage.

There was a second shorter article on page two, also under André Fontaine's byline. The headline was "McLintock's 40-year-old arrests earn respect." Nice, André. The story quoted heavily from Angus's remarks, particularly his closing comment that conveyed how proud he remained of his involvement in the pro-choice demonstrations. André found and quoted a couple of members of the audience who'd been moved by Angus's explanation and respected him more for it. One woman declared the Fox campaign radio ads that referred to Angus as "a criminal" to be despicable. These very supportive comments were offset by a quotation from Ramsay Rumplun, who said that he could not support a candidate "who does not respect the laws of the land." On balance, I gave the round to Angus. This was reinforced by the last line in the story that revealed that both Cumberland radio stations had pulled the offending ad off the air.

Perhaps most interesting of all was the short editorial that appeared. The headline was "The political gets personal." The editorial decried Fox's decision to "go negative." It commended Angus for his restraint and forbearance and called on Emerson Fox to end the personal attacks and focus on the issues. Nice.

Everyone at the McLintock campaign headquarters was in a buoyant mood. What had seemed last night to have been a draw or at most a marginal victory looked this morning in the *Crier* like a slam-dunk win. But we had no time for laurel-resting. There was canvassing to do. The Liberal Red Book had arrived at long last. I flipped quickly through the party's platform document for any surprises. With the last election just a few months behind us, I hadn't anticipated many changes, although the economy had dipped into freefall since the last campaign. I was right. Most of it was warmed over from the October battle, including promises of tax cuts, albeit more modest than those proposed by the Tories. I cringed, knowing that Angus would have difficulty supporting tax cuts, particularly during an economic tailspin. There was a vague commitment to infrastructure renewal, which pleased Angus, but it wasn't exactly a fully formed program. The only concession to the emerging global financial crisis was the following sentence at the end of the book:

> *In light of the current and projected economic trends, and until we have an accurate and timely accounting of government revenues and expenditures, it would be irresponsible for the Liberal Party to commit to an implementation schedule for the proposals contained in this policy document. Should we form a government, our Throne Speech and Budget will lay out the timing.*

I thought this was a sensible, reasonable, and responsible declaration. But I feared the Tories would bludgeon us with it in the campaign.

We pulled into the designated canvassing neighbourhood and parked. The two Petes looked almost like average citizens, except for Peter's fiery red nail polish and Pete2's matching fiery red ear, nose, and tongue studs.

"Did you guys call one another this morning to coordinate your accessories?" I asked, genuinely interested.

"Well, yeah," replied Peter as if the answer was self-evident. "You don't want us clashing when the candidate is with us. It could put some people off."

As usual, Pete2 nodded in agreement, content to let Peter do the talking.

"Very thoughtful lads," Angus said as we piled out of the car into a typical January arctic blast. My eyes watered and my face hurt, yet we hadn't even hit our first house. Angus didn't seem to notice the cold.

The two Petes donned red ribbons, took a couple of stacks of our somewhat lame pamphlet, and headed up the street like the veteran canvassers that they were. They would take one side of the street and Angus and I would tackle the other.

I stepped up to the first house and reached for the doorbell. Angus took my arm and eased me behind him.

"You might just as well let me try this myself," Angus suggested as he rang the bell. He seemed in good spirits.

I stood aside with a be-my-guest arm sweep as I consulted the voters list in my hand.

"George and Yvonne Leonard" was all I could get out before the door opened to an unshaven man in ripped sweat pants, one sock, and a lovely stained undershirt straining to contain a belly of near planetary proportions.

"Ah, Mr. Leonard I presume," opened Angus, smiling and rocking on his feet.

"Yeah, well who are you, the amazing Kreskin?"

"Ah no. We have a voters list so that's how I knew your name. Speaking of names, mine is Angus McLintock and I'm your Member of Parliament seeking your support in the imminent election."

"Don't care about politics, goodbye," he said before turning back into his home.

Angus set his foot on the step to prevent the door from closing.

"Can I ask why you don't care about politics? You surely pay enough in taxes. D'ye not want to make sure your money is well spent?"

Mr. Leonard spun to face Angus with a look that suggested violence, not conversation.

"What I think or do makes no goddamned difference. You're all crooks anyway, so I'm sure not going to help you by voting. Now step away from my house," he hissed, his stubby index finger tapping Angus's sternum in time with the rhythm of his last sentence. That wasn't a good idea.

Angus's eyes narrowed to slits. That's not good. When Angus does his slitty-eyes thing, you want to get out of the way. He leaned in.

"Well then, you deserve the government you get, you half-baked buffoon!" Angus roared. "D'ye not understand how a democracy works? You've a duty to vote!"

Against all my very well-developed self-preservation instincts, I leapt in between them. I silently gave thanks for Mr. Leonard's monstrous abdomen as it kept his flailing arms and volcanic face farther away from us.

"Well, thank you for your time, Mr. Leonard. We'll leave you now. Right now, Angus. Call us if you need any more information," I croaked, shuffling Angus off the front porch like a linesman separating brawling hockey players.

"He called me a crook," Angus raged as we walked back to the road. "I admit I'm many things, but a crook is not one of them."

"Angus, calm yourself. Remember, most of the voters in this riding are Conservatives. And calling them half-baked buffoons is not exactly a winning conversion strategy," I said. "We're at the voter's door to engage, not enrage."

The very beginnings of a smile snuck onto his face.

"You're very quick with the clever quip, aren't you, Professor Addison?" he replied as he cooled down. "All right, once more into the breach." Angus climbed the front stairs of the next home and rapped on the door.

"Jonathan and Meredith Waxman," I said, scanning the voters list again.

"Good morning, I'm Angus McLintock, your Member of Parliam–"

"Honest Angus of hovercraft fame. I'm pleased to meet you. I'm Jon Waxman."

"Happy to make your acquaintance. This is my colleague Daniel–"

"Addison. I know, I read the story in the *Crier*."

Handshakes all around.

Angus still seemed a little rattled from our first encounter. He looked slightly lost for a moment and eventually turned to me.

"Now what happens?"

Jon turned to me with a quizzical look.

"Um, Angus is still getting the hang of canvassing. You don't mind, do you?" I asked.

"Not at all. I've been a teacher for thirty-five years and I can see that this is a teaching moment. Carry on," said Jon.

I turned back to Angus.

"Okay, since we have a willing subject here, we want to get a sense of what's on Jon's mind and whether he might consider putting an X next to your name on the ballot."

"Aye, I can see why that would be helpful," Angus replied. "So how about something like this?" Angus paused and then turned to face Jon. "So Jon, are you pleased with how you've been served in the House of Commons these last few months?"

"Well, Angus, since you've asked, I have been impressed with what you've accomplished, particularly since you didn't really want to be in the House in the first place."

"Aye, you've got that right. But the adventure seemed to grow on me and I think we had a few small wins in our brief time. So, do I divine by your at least polite response that we might be able to count on your support on election day?"

"Well, from our conversation you might reasonably expect that I'd support you, but I'm afraid not," Jon said with a smile. "I like you and what you've done, but I'm an ideological Conservative. I don't agree with your party's policies and likely never will. But I do like you." Angus just stared at him and nodded. We turned and left.

The morning wasn't a complete loss. Eventually, the extreme cold brought our canvassing to an end. A red blotchy face, wind-assisted crazy hair, frostbitten nose, and snot-icicled beard weren't really helping Angus make that all-important initial connection with voters on the front porch. In fact, it was more likely to lead to slammed doors and 911 calls. Still, we'd managed to hit thirty-seven houses. Twenty-eight of them were Tories. Two, I was shocked to discover, were NDP. And yes, we uncovered seven Liberal voters we didn't know existed. All of them had voted for Eric Cameron in previous elections but were drawn to Angus through his recent well-chronicled exploits on Parliament Hill. Still, the odds were twenty-eight to seven against us. Just another typical C-P poll, in other words. It was tough.

Oh yes, and Angus was propositioned by one middle-aged woman who seemed to me to be a few ministers short of a full Cabinet. She had a fixation for penguins. Hundreds of them crowded every square inch of display space in her living room. There were ceramic penguin figurines, stuffed pen-guins, penguin paintings, a penguin coffee table book, fittingly resting on a coffee table made from three carved wooden pen-guins supporting a circular plate of glass, even penguin can-dles. Her bookshelves were overloaded with orange-spined paperbacks from the only appropriate publishing house. The pièce de résistance was a cartoonish penguin wallpaper border encircling the room up near the ceiling. Had we known, we'd have worn tuxedos.

Getting the hang of canvassing, Angus simply said, "I've always enjoyed penguins. I hope we can count on your support on January 27."

Then we bolted after politely declining tea in, yes it's true, penguin mugs. As we fled down her front walk, she opened the door and shouted a heated invitation to Angus to come back later to join her for a screening of her special-edition director's cut of, yep, *March of the Penguins*. I gave a little shiver but Angus waved without really committing.

The two Petes had fared quite well, stroking their red highlighter through eleven more names on the voter list. We were also able to add three more Liberals to the tally for houses where no one was even home. The red streamers tied to front railings, or trees, or garage door handles, were evidence enough for us. Angus's red ribbon campaign seemed to be catching on.

My cellphone rang early Sunday morning while Lindsay and I were still struggling to get going. In other words, we were both still comatose. I sat up on the edge of the bed to cut through the cerebral cobwebs.

"Daniel Addison," I rasped, sounding like I'd just had throat surgery.

"Daniel? Michael Zaleski. Did I wake you?"

"Not at all, Michael. Just a bit of a sore throat. I've been awake for, um, quite a while. What's up?"

Michael Zaleski was once again running the Liberal polling operation for the campaign. Even though the Leader's office seemed to have a love-hate relationship with Angus and me, tending more often towards hate, Michael seemed to be a closet McLintock fan and had done me a few favours last time around.

"I'm not sure you knew, but on top of our national polling, we've over-sampled in some key ridings, and C-P is one of them," he opened.

"I hadn't heard that, but it makes sense. I was actually going to call the centre and ask."

"Well, we polled last night and found enough people at home in your riding to get some reasonably accurate numbers, including a solid number of voters who actually attended the all-candidates meeting Friday night."

"Nice, Michael. That's great," I replied. "I'm sitting down. Is it good news?"

"Well, it's better than I ever thought it would be deep in the heart of Tory country. Going in, you were a 100–1 shot. Against. Now, it's still a steep uphill climb, but you're headed in the right direction. The margins of error are a little high, given the sample size, but let's meet early in the week and I'll give you the full treatment."

"I'm there, Michael. I can wait till then for the whole story but can you at least give me the headline now?"

"Sure. Here are the voter reaction bullets so far. Three out of four voters are Conservative. But Emerson Fox is an asshole. Alden Stonehouse is pulling much better than we thought he would. And everybody loves Angus."

"So it looks like there actually is potential for Stonehouse to split the right-wing votes?" I asked.

"There's a long way to go, but if Flamethrower is still an ass-hole in two weeks, and preacher-boy doesn't fall off the 'calm, thoughtful, and reasonable' wagon, there could be two viable options for C-P Conservatives to choose between."

I silently rearranged his sentence so that it didn't end with a preposition.

"That's just great news, Michael. Thanks for passing it on," I said. "I'll drop in tomorrow and you can take me through the cross-tabs. Thanks again."

I hit the hang-up button on my BlackBerry and stood up to head for the shower.

"What's the great news?" Lindsay sighed with her eyes still closed.

"Stonehouse may be siphoning right-wing support away from Fox," I responded. "If that continues, Angus may be able to slip up the middle."

"Hmmmmm" was all she said as she appeared to drift back to sleep. But she was smiling.

———

Shortly after one o'clock, I met Angus in the driveway and we climbed into the Camry for the short drive over to Muriel's.

"So what's this first appointment?" Angus inquired.

"Just a brief talk to the Riverfront Seniors' Residence that Muriel has arranged," I said. "I think we already have the votes there, but Muriel is a big believer in never taking anything for granted. I don't like to throw my weight around so I chose not to overrule her."

"Do you really think you could have shut her down on this?" Angus smirked.

"Not for an instant," I sighed. "That's why I decided not to throw my weight around."

"Smart lad. So I should just try to, what do you call it, 'connect with them' or 'engage' them?" he asked with the slightest sarcastic edge.

"Yep, you've hit the haggis on the head," I confirmed.

Angus turned to look at me for longer than any driver should shift their eyes from the road.

"What?" I asked, pointing my index finger out the front windshield to remind him where his focus should be.

"You'd best rethink your Scottish metaphors, or one day you might find yourself wearin' the haggis."

"You'll get your kilt bunched up. I was just making conversation," I countered, still working my finger towards the road. Still he eyed me. "Um, you're drifting a bit out of your lane." He ignored my observation.

"While we're on the topic, the 25th is Rabbie Burns Day, as I'm sure you already knew," said Angus. "That's just two days before the ballots are to be marked. So I'll be courtin' the Scottish vote that night. The Prescott Robert Burns Society has asked me to speak, givin' The Immortal Memory."

"I think you've already got the Scottish vote in the bag . . . pipe."

Angus winced.

"Sorry. That was bad, I know," I conceded. "But we might need you to do some other events that night with fence-sitting voters. We have to use you where we can get the biggest return. Is this haggis-eating event really necessary?"

"Daniel. Hear me. On Rabbie Burns Day, I'll be in my kilt being piped in to a dinner that happens but once yearly. It's important. I'll yammer with the fence-sitters at any other time."

We drove in silence until we neared Cumberland and started traversing the newer subdivisions encircling the centre of town.

"Well, look at that, will you now," Angus said, shaking his head.

I could say nothing, though my mouth was open. We were greeted by a sea of red. Well, for a Liberal in Cumberland-Prescott, bunches of red ribbons and the odd red bandana tied to trees and veranda railings on every fifth house or so easily constituted a sea. Clearly the canvass was going well. I made a mental note to buy beer and pizza for the two Petes and their crack canvassing crew.

"It looks so much better than the conventional lawn signs that just seem to fade into the background by mid-campaign," I observed, craning my neck from side to side to take it all in. "Great visual impact."

I reached for my cell and left a message for André, suggesting he take a quick drive through this neighbourhood.

Inside the Riverfront Seniors' Residence, the common area overlooking the river ice was filled to capacity. Lunch had just ended and some sixty-five or so sated residents populated the oddly coloured couches and chairs. Several pulled up in their wheelchairs, parking in the areas most likely to cause traffic jams and irritate others. I realized that having Angus speak right after lunch would require him to be scintillating beyond all measure to forestall naps among his audience.

Muriel stood.

"We've talked before about what this Conservative government has done to us as seniors and pensioners, and not done for us. It makes my blood boil. It seems we're to be cast aside and ignored. It is so disrespectful," Muriel railed. "At a time in our lives when many of us have more time, more knowledge, and more perspective, we are rendered invisible, purposefully or inadvertently, it matters not. The effect is the same. After sixty-five, we disappear."

Muriel paused and waved Angus up to the front.

"I know Angus McLintock. He's only sixty-one, so he's not yet one of us. But I can tell you, we are not invisible to him. Angus McLintock, the very first Liberal MP for Cumberland-Prescott." She clapped as she closed and the applause gathered strength as Angus stood before them, looking more comfortable than I'd seen him in a while.

"I cannot imagine anyone or anything making Muriel Parkinson invisible. She is always a force with which to be reckoned," Angus opened.

"But she's such a bossy-boots," complained a grizzled man slumped in the corner of a couch towards the back, his elbow sitting on the armrest, his chin reclining in his palm.

"Oh hush up, Ralph!" Muriel shot back.

"See!" he replied, his hands now lifted in supplication.

Ralph seemed to settle down when the woman next to him, who looked twice his age, backhanded his forearm, never once taking her eyes off Angus.

"I can see that this is a tough and impatient audience so I'll not tax your time unduly," Angus started.

"Let me start simply by saying that I cannot stand here and tell you that if you elect me, and if the Liberals form a government, your lives will immediately change for the better. In fact, despite Muriel's well-meaning, albeit somewhat partisan words of support, I can find nothing in the Liberal policy book, the so-called Red Book, about seniors and the issues and challenges you're confronting.

"What I can promise you all is that my eyes are working well. I do see all of you before me. Though I'm not far behind you, I do understand that you've lived through times that I've not seen. That you've already crossed thresholds that still lie ahead of me. That you have insights that I don't. I also know that it is never too late for us old dogs to learn some new tricks. And I'm the living proof of it."

Angus paused and looked down for a moment before lifting his eyes once more.

"Less than a year ago, I lost my wife. She was my better half through nearly forty years of marriage. I looked up to her. I learned so much from her. I didn't think I had any living or learning left to do when she died. But all of you know that I was wrong. Aye, and now I know it too.

"For an old dog like me, serving in the House of Commons, initially against my will and certainly in defiance of history and logic, is surely a new trick. But I feel I am learning it. I think I'm getting the hang of it. And it has me feeling alive again, which I can assure you is far preferable to the alternative.

"Now we won't always agree. This is not a monolithic community. There will always be differences of opinion. But I'll promise to tell you my view, and when we disagree, I'll always tell you why. Now, what say all of you?"

Angus stood there eyeing the group, looking for a hand or someone slowly getting to their feet. A woman sitting near me, whom I'd first seen at Muriel's inaugural GOUT meeting, piped up. Both Angus and I recognized her from the nasty question she'd asked Emerson Fox at the first all-candidates meeting.

"Angus. What you say is all well and good. And Lord knows politics in this country needs a good cleaning-up and a kick in the keister. But Emerson Fox is evil incarnate. He won't be stopped till you're lying by the side of the road to be spat upon by Tory followers."

"Well, I'm not certain that's an accura–" Angus interrupted.

"I'm not finished yet," she said holding her hand up.

Chastened, Angus nodded and waved to cede the floor back to her.

"I just think you're going to need some help against that scoundrel. And I want you to know that we've . . . um . . . we've . . ." She stopped to whisper to her co-conspirator seated next to her, who then whispered back. "Right," she said, turning back to Angus. "We've got your back, Angus. We've got your back."

"I thank you, I think," responded Angus. "I'm not interested in defeating Emerson Fox using the same nefarious weapons of political battle that he seems to wield. I've no interest in that. We need more Canadians to vote, not fewer. So we have to win in a way that actually enhances voters' respect for democracy and reminds us all of our obligations and duties in the democratic bargain."

"Yes, yes, that's all well and good, Angus, and we're with you on all of that. But still, when the flamethrower is ignited, we've got your back."

"Ahhh, I thank you," he said. This time, the "I think" part was only etched in his face.

By 3:30 we were back on the road to the editorial offices of the *Cumberland Crier*. Angus and I had been invited to a rare Sunday afternoon meeting with the editorial board. I wondered why Sunday? André said it was just a little quieter on Sundays and they could deliberate as an editorial board in relative peace. Fine by us. Angus was parking when an aging Cadillac lumbering by let loose a long and loud blow on its horn.

"Jehoshaphat, that's a racket!" erupted Angus.

We spun around to see an older man at the wheel with his window open despite the below-freezing temperature.

"Go get 'em, Angus!" he shouted, waving his fist and then leaning again on the horn. He had red ribbon tied to all four door handles, woven throughout the front grille, and wrapped the length of the radio antenna. Finally, he had several longer pieces of ribbon streaming from the windshield wipers that he inexplicably had operating at high speed in the sunshine, as the great boat floated by.

"Aye, I will," Angus said, looking a little sheepish when he turned to me as we parked. "What have we done?"

Alerted by the partisan Caddy, a few pedestrians stopped on the sidewalk when they recognized Angus walking by. One booed and gave us two thumbs down. But the others clapped. Angus was headed the other way when I grabbed his arm and nudged him over to the sidewalk supporters to glad-hand a bit.

We were about to climb the stairs to the *Crier* offices above the venerable Reg Paterson's Mens Wear when Angus pointed out that the thirty-year-old mannequins in the store window each sported red ribbons in their lapels. It took me a moment to notice the flashes of red as it was difficult to see past the dummies' garish pants, shirts, and jackets. The bold checks, stripes, and paisley combination would have been quite at home in a second-rate golf club pro shop.

"If only they could vote," chuckled Angus as he took in the mannequins.

"As your campaign manager, I decree that you are forbidden to shop here," I said. "We want Reg's vote, but not his clothes."

"Agreed. Although I understand the two Petes never miss his Boxing Day Blow-Out Sale."

That didn't surprise me.

The *Crier* isn't a big operation but it takes its role in the community seriously. Angus and I sat on one side of the boardroom table while André, the executive editor, the news editor, and the managing editor sat along the other. It felt a little like defending my PhD thesis.

The meeting went reasonably well, for the most part. Angus made a few opening remarks touching on the now familiar themes that formed the core of what you might now call his stump speech. Even when baited by the news editor, Angus refused several invitations to trash Emerson Fox. They asked some questions about the Liberal Red Book that we'd just seen for the first time the day before.

"I cannae say I support every plank in the platform but in general I am comfortable with the direction," Angus stated.

There was the opening. The executive editor filled it.

"Is it not incumbent on every Liberal candidate to stand behind every policy promise made in the Red Book?"

Uh-oh. I was about to jump in but Angus shot me a look so I held back.

"I'd say that's a rather extreme interpretation of a candidate's obligations," Angus started. "I support the party. I support the Leader. And I support all but a couple of the proposals in the platform released yesterday. The few with which I have some concerns, I would gladly support if our economy were booming as it was eight short months ago. So I will invoke the caveat that you'll also find in the Red Book that grants us flexibility in implementing the measures when the economy and the government can afford them."

Not bad, Angus, I thought. Not bad at all. I exhaled. They let it pass.

"One more question, Professor McLintock. You may have read our series on health care a week or two back. We're quite concerned with the state of our health care system, the mounting costs, the long wait times, and the frequency of collective bargaining breakdowns, be they with nurses, doctors, physios, or hospital orderlies. What's the answer?"

Great. Health care was one of the few areas Angus, Muriel, and I had not covered in our several policy briefings last week. The meeting had gone so well, only to close out on a policy area certain to reveal Angus's ignorance.

"I see you leave the easy lob until the end," Angus noted. The table chortled.

"I'm no expert on health care, as will almost certainly become clear, although your recent articles were instructive. I have no ready solutions for some of the challenges you've described, like wait times and hospital overcrowding. It seems to me we should probably look at the root causes of the current problems and not be distracted by the symptoms. If we can address the underlying causes, the symptoms should resolve themselves."

Not bad, Angus, I thought to myself. So far so good.

"I do think the way most doctors are compensated could be part of the problem. The fee-for-service model ensures that public costs and doctors' incomes rise with the number of tests done, diagnoses made, and treatments started, whether all are absolutely necessary or not. Doctors make more when their patients require more services. I'm inclined to look favourably on the roster system where doctors make more when they keep their own roster of patients healthier, and out of hospital longer. The incentives then shift to practising healthier lifestyles and illness prevention. Now, I don't think all doctors like this more integrated approach, and the longer-term evidence is certainly not yet in to show the superiority of one model over another. In the end, I suspect some kind of blended model will ensure that Canadians have access to the health care they need and that doctors are encouraged to keep their patients healthy. I've prattled on too long already. The brains of smarter thinkers than I are required," Angus concluded. "Besides, it's really more of a provincial responsibility."

We were in the car pulling away from the curb after the meeting when I finally asked him.

"So did you just pull that health care answer right out of your . . . um . . . head?"

"What are you drivin' at, man? I told you and Muriel already that I knew very little about health care and that we'd have to bone up on it before the next all-candidates meetin'. I thought I'd made that quite clear," Angus protested.

"Angus, whether you believe it or not, your last answer in there revealed quite a deep knowledge of health care policy, certainly deeper than they or I were expecting. You were very impressive. Just the right blend of knowledge and self-deprecation. But where did it come from? We've never really talked about health care."

Angus looked puzzled.

"Well, I can read, you know. Even quite large words. And I can ask questions. So I did some readin' online and spoke to a few colleagues. That meant I knew enough to get by. It's fascinatin' stuff, but I now know just enough to realize how little I really know. And I dinnae like that feeling."

André called when were halfway home to confirm my read on the meeting. Angus had impressed them mightily. He said he thought we'd be pleased with tomorrow's editorial.

I passed all of this on to Angus as we neared home. Then I turned on the car radio. The final ultra-harmonious refrain of Starland Vocal Band's "Afternoon Delight" was just dying out. Then the grating voice of that same angry woman resumed.

"Brainwashed by the writings of his ultra-feminist wife, Angus McLintock has a secret extremist feminist agenda ready to rip apart Canada's social fabric. He actually wants housewives to be paid for baking cookies and vacuuming. If you thought affirmative action programs were unfair, you ain't seen nothing yet. So don't give Angus McLintock the chance. Vote for Emerson Fox. This has been a paid political message on behalf of the Cumberland-Prescott Progressive Conservative Association."

Uh-oh. I looked at Angus. For about thirty seconds after the radio ad, he seemed to be calm and to take it in stride. Then I noticed his white knuckles on the wheel and he promptly drove us into a snowbank.

DIARY
Sunday, January 12
My Love,
I skated again tonight, for over an hour. I needed to, and you know why. (I fell only once, I might add.) How did you become such a part of all this? He is really testing my patience, my civility, and my long-standing belief in non-violence. But laying the beating on him he deserves would

be but a pyrrhic victory. So I breathe deeply, skate, and lift my eyes above the moment, the day, the week, to see the future. Aye, that's what you'd tell me . . .

AM

CHAPTER NINE

Michael Zaleski was waiting for me in the offices of National Opinion, the official polling firm of the Liberal Party. He had earned the loyalty of the leader and Bradley Stanton by always and only delivering the advice his principal clients needed to hear, not what they may have wanted to hear. He wore a staid grey suit, white shirt, and a tie that shattered even the most avant-garde conceptions of good taste. The design seemed to me to depict the botched autopsy of a small two-headed neon bird, spread and splayed. But it was hard to look directly at it for long enough to be sure. It was so bright, it hurt my eyes. It was so loud, it hurt my ears.

"Whoa, that's some cravat you've got going on there, Z-man," I said, looking away. Everybody called him Z-man. You know you've made it in politics when you get a nickname. "I didn't think those were allowed in Canada."

"I know. Isn't it great?" he replied, holding it out perpendicular to his chest. "It keeps everyone awake in our morning staff meetings."

"Awake or away?" I asked. "Can you pop out the batteries until we're done? You can turn it back on when I'm gone."

He ignored my last comment. I seem to have this unerring habit of making one remark too many.

He turned his laptop around so we could both see the PowerPoint presentation he had cued up, ready to go. A pollster without a PowerPoint is like an Albanian diplomat without an interpreter. They could both speak, but you just would have no idea what they were saying.

"So thanks for coming in. I thought you'd be interested in these numbers," he started.

"Well, thanks for the invite, Michael. Fire when ready," I said as I opened my Moleskine notebook. I could still see the reflection of his tie in the laptop screen.

"Look, you know you're really up against it in C-P. It's been Tory-blue for so long, the idea of voting red is completely foreign to most residents," he cautioned.

I nodded. The title slide gave way to the first of the colourful graphs and charts, standard fare for pollsters around the world.

"Okay, as I mentioned in our call, Alden Stonehouse is pulling much stronger numbers than we expected. He's just shy of 14 per cent of decided voters, which is big for an independent. Really big."

"That's just block-voting within his congregation, isn't it?" I asked.

"That's what we first suspected, but that's not all that's going on. Every respondent in our sample who admitted to being in his congregation is voting for him, but that only accounts for about nine points of his fourteen," the pollster explained. "It seems he's actually pulling Tory voters away from Fox."

"How can that be?" I inquired. "It makes no sense in C-P."

"That's what we were wondering, too. So we've probed a little deeper in the last two waves. For the most part, there are three interconnected reasons for at least some local Tories bailing on Fox. One, Stonehouse has easily exceeded voter expectations. They're surprised he's so articulate, thoughtful, and reasonable. He just doesn't sound like the religious nutbar voters thought he'd be. Two, his policy positions and political views are very closely aligned with the Progressive Conservative party's and the prevailing sentiments of the average C-P voter. Third, and most importantly, Fox's attack ads seem, at long last, to have crossed some kind of line in the voters' minds. He's finally gone too far with the personal stuff."

"Wow. Fascinating. Great work, Michael." I was impressed with the analysis. "Are the numbers in motion? Where's the trend?"

"They're still very loose, but the movement from Fox to Stonehouse has been sustained since the first all-candidates meeting."

"So what are the voter intention numbers?"

"Right. Here you go," he said as he clicked to the next slide. I took in the figures.

Fox	34%
McLintock	23%
Stonehouse	14%
Nankovich	8%
Undecided	21%

I was amazed we were as close as we were, even with the Stonehouse factor.

"What's going on with the Undecideds?" (Angus would never accept this pollster-invented word, but I was in a hurry, and besides, he wasn't there.)

"You'll like this. Of the regular Tory voters who are abandoning Fox, a third are going to Stonehouse, another third are going to Angus, and the final third are parking in Undecided."

"But what are the demos of the Undecideds?" I asked.

"I'm way ahead of you," he replied. "It cuts quite evenly across the sample. No one group seems to stand out except that Conservative voters are skewing higher than usual for the reasons we've already discussed."

"So the story is, without Stonehouse, Fox would be leading by twenty-five points and we'd never be able to make up that much ground," I reasoned.

"Yep. The numbers tell us that virtually every one of Stonehouse's votes is either a church member or a disaffected Conservative."

"So the right-wing split is actually real. It's really happening," I said, excitement creeping into my voice.

"In spades." Zaleski nodded, smiling.

"Awesome. But what about the national numbers?" I asked.

Zaleski skipped a couple of slides.

"Well, it's very tight. But since your man's hovercraft heroics, the Tories have dropped six points and we've picked up five of them. The remaining one per cent went to Undecided."

"And you think Angus helped that shift?"

"He didn't help it, he caused it," he declared. "We specifically asked, and the numbers are solid."

I sat in silence taking this in.

"But there's more you should know," he said before moving to the next slide. It was entitled "The Angus Effect."

"There's actually an Angus Effect?" I asked, genuinely perplexed.

"Not *an* Angus Effect, *The* Angus Effect," Zaleski responded. "Let me explain. We always ask what issues are most important in the minds of respondents as they consider their candidates, and then we prompt them with a rotated list. The national gen pop results look like this." He clicked the numbers onto the screen.

The economy and jobs:	27%
Health care:	22%
The environment:	17%
Education:	13%
The candidates' integrity, trust, character:	12%
The deficit:	9%

"Yeah, makes sense to me," I said, not quite understanding. "So what?"

"Well, here's the same list for Cumberland-Prescott," Michael fingered his mouse, then sat back and watched my face as the numbers took root.

The candidates' integrity, trust, character:	28%
The economy and jobs:	23%
Health care:	19%
The environment:	12%
Education:	10%
The deficit:	8%

Michael just smiled and nodded before adding some colour commentary.

"On the national list, candidate integrity has never risen above 7 per cent, and it's now riding at 12. And after Cumberland-Prescott, while there's not a single riding in Canada where candidate integrity is seen as the most important issue, let alone pulling 28 per cent, it is steadily moving up the list. And the ridings surrounding C-P have shown the highest growth in the candidate integrity numbers."

"Um . . . you've got to be kidding . . ." I mumbled, realization dawning on me.

Like P.T. Barnum in the centre ring, the official pollster of the Liberal Party lifted his hands and his voice.

"Ladies and gentlemen, I give you . . . The Angus Effect."

When I arrived in the boathouse workshop, Angus was already there tinkering in the cockpit.

"The blessed starter motor finally arrived this morning," Angus opened. "The damnable excise tax and duty cost me near as much as the motor itself!"

It looked like he was nearly finished installing it, but what did I know?

"Can I give you a hand with the installation?" I offered.

Angus visibly recoiled at the thought, then realized he'd visibly recoiled at the thought, and tried to soften the blow.

"Ahhhh, no thanks, lad, I'm nearly done," he stammered. "Why don't you have a seat way over there? I'll just be a jiff." He pointed with what I thought might be a screwdriver, or perhaps a wrench of some kind, to a stool over in the corner, as far away from the hovercraft as was possible while still being within the same building.

"Angus, I'm not a complete klutz," I replied, feeling a little wounded. Of course I'd have had more credibility had I not been looking so intently at him that I missed the stool, settling on the concrete floor next to it and knocking a steel pail from its hook on the wall. Angus pretended not to notice, though my ears were still ringing from the clatter.

While he worked, I talked to him about Michael's briefing on the numbers, concluding with a detailed description of The Angus Effect.

"Piffle and codswallop," he muttered under his breath and under his dashboard. "Sounds more to me like The Stupid Arse Fox Effect, combined with The Better Than Expected Stonehouse Effect. I guess we owe the good reverend our gratitude if it keeps up."

"We may well owe him our victory, so we should hope he continues to do well," I said from the safety of my stool in the corner.

"Undiluted hyperbole," Angus snorted after a moment or two. "*The Angus Effect*. Mercy. You know, laddie, the last time I heard that phrase, I was at boardin' school in the Highlands. My bunkmates regularly invoked that term, particularly after we'd been served cabbage for dinner. Or turnip," he added thoughtfully.

A half-hour later, we'd muscled *Baddeck 1* down the boathouse ramp onto the ice. Angus donned the supple leather flying head gear and goggles I'd given him some months earlier. They'd been worn by my great-grandfather when he flew in World War I. Not many could have pulled off such a retro look, and neither could

Angus. I pulled a bright Liberal red toque down over my ears. The plan was to cruise up the river and to do some dock-to-dock canvassing while the two Petes and their crew of volunteers went door to door in another part of the riding.

"Shall we give her a whirl?" Angus asked as he settled into the cockpit next to me. I placed the large spool of red ribbon I'd brought with me on the floor beneath my seat.

"Fingers crossed," I said.

Then, in cinematic slow motion, Angus aimed his index finger at the shiny black button that was freshly mounted on the dash, and pushed. The whine of the new starter motor kicked in, soon to be overtaken by the thump-thump of the main engine as it roared to life. Even his goggles couldn't obscure the satisfaction in his eyes, despite how ridiculous he looked.

Angus fingered the throttle and the engine wailed at his touch. I felt us rise off the ice. You really could feel yourself being lifted as the rubber skirt filled to capacity around the perimeter of the hovercraft. With Angus working the foot pedals and the steering wheel, we actually rotated on the spot, then headed out onto the ice. The noise was fearsome, and I wondered how we were going to engage voters in meaningful conversation, or even in canvassing's more typical mindless chatter, when we'd need at least twenty minutes after killing the hovercraft engine before the ringing in our ears died away.

I had the voters list for the poll we were in opened on my lap. It was of course laid out by address. But the house numbers were usually by the front door, not on the back of the house, let alone on the dock. So I wasn't exactly sure where we were when Angus slowed and stopped by the shore at the first house. What lovely homes these were, strung along the river. The nicest real estate in all of Cumberland. Very tony. Very Tory.

Baddeck 1 settled to the ice and we both clambered out. Our noisy approach had aroused some attention as a tall and very patrician older man in a dark blue ski jacket and a fur hat sauntered down the shovelled path and onto the dock to greet us.

"Well, if it isn't the famous Angus McLintock and his even more famous hydrofoil," the man said in greeting, his face fractured by a warm smile.

He looked familiar to me but I couldn't quite place him. I stood a few paces behind Angus, as loyal servants do.

"Greetings to you, sir," Angus said as he climbed onto the dock and offered his hand. "It seems I need not introduce myself, but this is my trusty companion, Professor Daniel Addison."

"Oh, I know who he is. The Robin to your Batman. I'm pleased to meet you too, Daniel," he said as we shook hands.

"And to be precise, 'tis a hovercraft not a hydrofoil," Angus noted with a patient smile and a wave towards *Baddeck 1*.

I was still trying to figure out which house we were at, so I needed either a name or an address to find out where we were on the voters list.

"Nice to meet you, too, Mr. uhm . . ." I prodded, looking to land his name.

"Call me Bert," he replied before turning and heading back off the dock and onto the path. "You must be frozen. Come on up and we'll take the edge off and chat for a while."

"We'll not outstay our welcome," said Angus as he followed.

A faint alarm bell was ringing but I couldn't quite figure out why. The man did look familiar. Bert. Bert. I racked my brain. We were on the heated stonework of the back patio just about to head into Bert's palatial home when my memory finally betrayed him. Herbert Clarkson. Herbert J. Clarkson. No time to lose. We were almost at the door.

"Angus, my watch seems to have stopped. What time is it, just before we go in?" I asked, stopping them both on the grey flagstones.

Angus looked annoyed but checked his watch.

"It's just quarter of two. We've plenty of time."

"Actually, we don't," I said, boring into him with my eyes.

"Oh, you must come in to warm up and talk. I've got a few issues I'd like to raise with you," Bert implored.

"Well, that's why we're –" Angus began before I cut him off.

"It's very kind of you to offer, Mr. Clarkson" – I emphasized his name while making plenty of eye contact with him – "but it's later than I thought, and we really have to dash."

I took Angus by his forearm, something I'd never done before, and gave a gentle tug. My firm grip on his muscular wrist seemed to register my message in his mind. He looked perplexed but held his tongue. By this time, Bert was smiling and shaking his head.

"You've got a keeper there, Angus," Bert said, nodding my way. "Good luck on E-day. You're going to need it."

Bert entered his house and closed the door behind him.

Angus was steamed as he pounded back down the path to the ice and *Baddeck 1*.

"You'd best explain why we walked all the way up there only to cut and run when we got to the door," Angus demanded, stopping with his arms crossed over his chest. "Bert, or whatever his name was, seemed a nice enough lad. I think we could have got his vote."

"Herbert Clarkson. That was Herbert Clarkson. I didn't figure it out until we were on the patio. But that was Herbert Clarkson," I explained.

"I actually heard his name the first time you said it. My hearing and my mental faculties are still with me, mostly."

"Herbert Clarkson? It doesn't ring a bell?" I asked. Angus said nothing, but his face creased. He looked about ready to blow. "Herbert Clarkson is the president of the Cumberland-Prescott Progressive Conservative Association. He just attempted the oldest ploy in Machiavelli's manual." I shook my head in disgust. We stood on the ice in what I thought was mutual distaste for Clarkson's gambit.

"Were you plannin' any time soon on sharin' the ploy with your candidate or am I to read your mind?"

"Oh, um, sorry Angus, I forget that you're still a political greenhorn. Bert was trying to get you into his living room so he could ply you with booze, probably stuff you with some home baking, and engage you in long and tedious political discourse, ideally until the sun sets. He was trying to take you out of play for the entire afternoon. In a close campaign, canvassing hours count. It's standard operating procedure."

Angus shrugged.

"A wee single malt to warm the core might have been nice" was all he said as we climbed back into the hovercraft.

The next home hove into view five minutes later as Angus throttled down and glided up close. The sun was shining in a near cloudless blue sky so it looked milder than it actually was. Angus climbed from the ice up onto the dock and I followed. We both noticed that the dock was not what you would call rock solid. It listed to the east and moved when we did. I trotted off it and was halfway up the path to the house while I scanned the voters list when I noticed that I was alone. I turned around to see Angus sliding under the dock on his back so that only his legs were visible. It looked as if the dock were swallowing Angus whole. I reversed course and was soon lying on my stomach on the dock looking down between the deck planks.

"Paging Angus McLintock. If there is an Angus McLintock under the dock, could he please identify himself?"

"Keep yer kilt on," Angus grunted from the middle of the dock's crib. "The deck teeters like a sailor on shore leave. I just wanted a quick peek."

"Well, we're in deep now. Here comes Mr. Garrettson, and he doesn't look like he was expecting company."

"What's the meaning of this intrusion? This is private property," Mr. Garrettson demanded as he tiptoed onto his dock.

"Mr. Garrettson, I'm Daniel Addison with the McLintock campaign," I started. "Um, er, and the candidate himself, Angus McLintock, is just taking a quick nap under your dock before coming up to meet you."

It didn't look as if Mr. Garrettson shared my sense of humour, but then he focused on the hovercraft and it all fell into place.

"Angus McLintock is here?" he asked. "*The* Angus McLintock?"

I pointed over the side of the dock.

"Those are his legs right there," I assured him.

Then a disembodied voice drifted up through the dock.

"I'll be topside directly."

Needless to say, Mr. Garrettson was somewhat taken aback when the famous Angus McLintock emerged from beneath and extended his hand.

"It's a pleasure to meet you, Mr. Garrettson, is it?" I confirmed the name with a nod so Angus could launch into his spiel. "Would you happen to have a two-by-four stringer about six feet long and a couple of four-inch lag bolts?"

We hovered away from the house forty-five minutes later, the red ribbons tied all over the dock dancing in the turbulent air from the thrust vents of *Baddeck 1*.

As it turned out, Gil Garrettson and his wife, Lucy, were big Angus fans. They were even bigger fans when Angus fixed their dock, adding a support strut to replace the one knocked out of place by the ice. There were already red ribbons on the front of their house. They'd never thought to put them on the dock for the snowmobilers and cross-country skiers to see. That was a value-added suggestion from yours truly. So we spent nearly an hour convincing a couple who were already going to vote for us that they should feel very good about their decision to vote for us. Excellent use of time, a non-renewable resource the campaign had in dwindling supply. The Garrettsons also got their dock repaired in the deal.

In an exercise that pushed back the frontiers of inefficiency, we managed to hit four, yes four, houses on the river in our long afternoon of hovercraft canvassing. On the other hand, the two Petes' door-to-dooring team probably made contact with over a hundred voters in the same period. Angus had a great time. Other than the Garrettsons, we met no other Liberals. But Angus did play two chess games with a German landed immigrant who was not yet eligible to vote. At the next house, he spent twenty minutes arguing an esoteric point of grammar with a retired high school English teacher who didn't sound like she was going to vote for us anyway. He also took four cross-country skiers for rides, one at a time, only to discover afterwards that they lived in Ottawa-West, not in C-P. By the time we'd hoisted *Baddeck 1* back up the ramp into the boathouse, the light was fading fast. Angus was upbeat. I was just beat. And a little angry with myself. Hovercraft canvassing had been my idea. I should have known it would just slow us down.

"Well now, that was a grand way to spend an afternoon," said a happy Angus as we swung the big doors closed.

"Unless you hope to be elected," I replied. "It would be more efficient for you to single-handedly bake, ice, and hand-deliver a cake to each of the 35,000 voters in C-P."

"Aye, you may be right. But did you split that infinitive just to spite me? There's really no call for that."

It wasn't infinitives I was thinking of splitting right then.

"There'll be no more hovercraft campaigning. We can't afford the time," I said as I headed up to the apartment. "I'll meet you in the driveway in an hour."

Angus and I picked up Muriel to head to the second and final all-candidates meeting at Cumberland Collegiate. She had the *Cumberland Crier* with her.

"You both must be thrilled with the editorial," Muriel said as soon as she settled into the front seat next to me. Angus was in the back seat.

"Right! In all of the day's excitement, I haven't even seen it yet. And I don't think Angus has either."

"Speak for yourself, laddie. I read it this morning," Angus volunteered.

"You did? Why didn't you tell me about it?"

"I figured my campaign manager would already have seen it, so it didnae occur to me to raise it," Angus replied. "I would have preferred an endorsement."

Muriel guided her less than stable hand to push the dome light switch and then slipped on her reading glasses. Worsening Parkinson's was giving her an almost uncontrollable tremor much of the time.

"Let me give you the highlights, Daniel. You keep your eyes on the road," Muriel said as she brought the paper close to her eyes and tried to hold it still.

"The headline is 'No endorsement for any candidate this time.'"

"Yes!" I cried and pumped my right fist into the very hard metallic edge of the dome light. It survived the blow unscathed, only flickering briefly before the steady glow returned. But I wasn't sure I'd ever have use of my right hand again. My eyes watered, and to the extent my seat belt allowed, I rocked in time to my throbbing fingers.

"Owww," I howled.

"Hush up, we're nearly there and you should hear this. André will be there," Muriel commented, scanning the vibrating paper. "Okay, here are my favourite lines." She switched into her news anchor voice, which really wasn't that much different from her everyday voice.

"'Angus McLintock is as honest as his beard is long and brings a refreshing candour to Canadian politics. He's thoughtful, dedicated, and trusts his hefty supply of common sense.' Wait, here's another one I just love. 'Carrying a congenital aversion to praise, the modest McLintock has become a hero to Canadians across the country, an honour he neither sought nor accepts.' The last line sums it up beautifully. 'The jury is still out on Angus McLintock. He's still too new to the game. But after decades of supporting Progressive Conservative candidates, this time around, we give the nod to none of them, and leave it to the voters of Cumberland-Prescott to decide.'"

"Wow! That's more than I'd dared hope for," I gushed. "Congratulations, Angus!"

"Poppycock" was all we heard from the back seat. "'The jury is still out . . .' my kilted keister it is."

Just before Angus climbed the stairs to join the other candidates on stage, Muriel took both his hands in hers and brought her face well within Angus's personal space.

"This could get ugly, Angus. Fox is getting more and more desperate with every red ribbon he sees. Whatever happens tonight, you want to stay on the high road," she fairly pleaded. "Taking the bait will be our undoing. Leave the gutter to Fox. It's our best hope."

Angus listened intently and gave just the slightest nod when she'd finished. He waited one extra second, then turned for the stage. As the candidates settled behind the trestle table and the moderator made her way to the podium, I took in the crowd from my place on a bench along the side of the auditorium. All the seats were filled. If it wasn't a sea of red ribbons, it was at least a large pond. The red was surpassed by the traditional blue buttons. Spinning further through the colour wheel, the Stonehouse supporters, about a quarter of the room by my estimate, sported bright yellow T-shirts. Unless you lived in the Philippines, yellow meant nothing politically. No Canadian party or movement had ever claimed it, making it the obvious choice for Team Stonehouse over mauve and aquamarine, the other passed-over pastels. The shirts themselves were interesting, too. They featured the classic outline of a church and steeple with the stacked words within: *God's house. Your house. Stonehouse.* Not bad, I thought.

I was a little nervous at what I saw in the front row. There sat four familiar and elderly women from the GOUT squad, each wearing a bright red plastic fire fighter's hat and staring down Flamethrower Fox. Upon closer scrutiny, I saw several other GOUT operatives sprinkled throughout the crowd wearing grim and determined looks.

The opening statements unfolded as Muriel and I had warned Angus they would. The luck of the draw had Angus speaking right after the Flamethrower. Emerson Fox took a few shots at Alden Stonehouse but saved the bulk of his time to eviscerate

Angus. He actually waved a copy of Marin Lee's book *Home Economics and Free Labour* to justify his claim that Angus had some sort of secret feminist agenda ready to unleash on an unsuspecting nation. When he'd finished his vitriolic tirade, his troops cheered, ours jeered, and Angus steamed and stewed.

The crowd was settled and silent by the time Angus walked slowly to the podium. I could see his brow furrowed, his wheels turning as he stood for a moment, head bowed, pondering. Then, as if he'd made a decision, he raised his eyes to the audience, abandoned the podium, and walked to the front of the stage.

"I had every intention this evening of sharing my views on the important issues we confront as a nation, including our current economic travails, our crumbling infrastructure, and several other policy challenges that have caught my attention. And I had planned simply to ignore my opponent's specious attacks on me and, unconscionably, on my wife's memory and her contributions to equality in this country. But it seems I have changed my mind. My trusted friends and advisers have assured me that I must not take the bait Mr. Fox has been dangling in front of me since this campaign began. I think they are right in their counsel and may well have saved me the embarrassment, and all of you the spectacle, of a bare-knuckle bout that I was brashly inclined to instigate with Mr. Fox. My hot head has since cooled. So I will not stoop to my opponent's level, but if you'll indulge me, I will take the time allotted me this evening to clarify and expand upon what little substance there is in Mr. Fox's fixation on my apparently radical views."

Uh-oh. This was not the plan for the meeting. Notwithstanding his words, it sounded very much to me like Angus was about to take the bait. I looked at Muriel but her eyes were fixed on Angus. She looked calm and serene.

"To my way of thinking, a feminist is anyone who believes that men and women should be equal. That men and women should have equal rights. That men and women should have equal access to opportunity. That men and women should be

147

paid equally for work of equal value and should be equally free from the threat of violence. Being a feminist simply means believing in equality. Mr. Fox has said, and repeated with some vehemence, that he is no feminist. I should think by this definition that he is part of a very small and declining minority. Equality is not a radical idea. And equality should not be a distant goal."

Angus paused and I distinctly heard the sound of a pin dropping.

"Let me address one other point continually raised and brought down like a bludgeon by my opponent Mr. Fox. My wife of nearly forty years, Marin Lee, was a respected feminist theorist and scholar. She was one of the first to write about the economic contribution of women working in the home. It was her view, and it is mine, that in strict economic terms, the almighty free market theoretically considers the work of women in the home to be without value, to be worthless. It is recognized nowhere in the free market economic model. She presented this idea in the thoughtful book Mr. Fox is waving around tonight as if it were *Mein Kampf*. To be crystal clear, neither she nor I have ever believed that there is a simple and workable public policy solution to address this distortion. This historical inequity cannot be resolved by changes in policy alone. I believe that all enlightened social change through our history and in our future starts with the evolving values and beliefs of each one of us. And that is something legislation can never dictate. So what is this extremist agenda I'm purportedly about to spring upon an unsuspecting nation that will irreparably tear our social fabric? Well, Mr. Fox grants me far too much credit. For my diabolical feminist master plan is simply this. I will continue to advocate and agitate for women's rights, as I have my entire adult life, so that our daughters and granddaughters might one day enjoy the equality our mothers and grandmothers deserved. I hope Mr. Fox and all of you will join me."

Angus turned and walked back and took his seat next to Emerson Fox, who looked distinctly uncomfortable. The room erupted. I looked carefully and through a red ribbon riot saw several yellow T-shirts and Tory blue buttons participating in the standing ovation. It took the moderator another five minutes to restore order.

When the floor was finally opened for questions, all four front-row GOUT firefighters' hands shot skyward. Despite the moderator's efforts to ignore them, one of them eventually had to be recognized.

"Madam Chair, I have a very simple question for Emerson Fox," she started in a surprisingly strong voice. "What makes you think that you can win by attacking your opponents in such personal and reprehensible terms? What makes you think that the people of Cumberland-Prescott will reward such behaviour with our votes?"

Emerson Fox stepped over to the podium on the other side of the stage and leaned into the mike looking smug. He'd recovered his swagger after Angus's soliloquy and still held the Marin Lee tome at his side.

"Thank you for the question. We've conducted this campaign with the goal of winning. With over forty years of experience running campaigns, I can tell you that whatever you may think of this approach, it works. You promote your own party's platform and you tear down your opponents'. It is a time-honoured and amazingly effective strategy. It may not always be pretty, but it works."

I thought he was done with the question but the audience was finding its own swagger. And the chorus of boos from the red ribbons and yellow T-shirts seemed to get under Fox's skin.

"Oh come on, you can't be that naïve," Fox sniped. "Look, it's a proven formula. When I tell you that Angus McLintock is a self-proclaimed feminist bent on pursuing his wife's extremist agenda, even paying housewives to bake and clean, it's because the evidence is clear and compelling, it's all written down in black and white in this book! It says right here in the dedication, before the book even starts, 'To Angus. My partner, my co-conspirator, my love.' I believe it, and the voters deserve to know. I've got nothing against Angus personally. I just don't want some feminazi representing this riding. Not on my watch."

What an outrage. I was about to take on Fox myself when something whizzed by me on the way to the stage. I didn't see who threw the first one, but it must have been a signal of sorts, because a moment later a shower of home-baked cookies rained onto the Tory candidate. Emerson Fox cowered, arms over his head, as the cookies fell. Mind you, the attack hadn't been flawlessly planned. Some of the GOUT agents were sitting too far back in the crowd. Their aging and arthritic arms couldn't power the chocolate chip projectiles all the way to the stage, so some cookies landed amid the audience, where they were immediately devoured. Then, the climax. A full vacuum bag scored a direct podium hit, a veritable detonation of dust. I lost sight of the Flamethrower for a moment in the cloud, but the dust eventually settled, all over Emerson Fox, as he coughed and waved his arms about as if he were signalling a circling chopper overhead.

André Fontaine and the rest of the reporters, photographers, and camera operators at the back recorded the whole show.

We made a quick stop at the campaign office before heading over to the Riverfront Seniors' Residence to drop Muriel off. As soon as Muriel turned the key and opened the office door, we knew something was amiss. Two desk lamps were turned on, casting an eerie glow about the room. The filing cabinets were upended, drawers pulled open, with files spilling onto the floor. I dashed into my office where my desk lamp also burned. Yep. My desk file drawer, where I kept the most precious resource of any local campaign headquarters, the marked voters lists, had been pulled out and now sat on the floor. I knelt beside it. We had carefully tracked and identified all Liberal voters so that we could make sure they all made it to the polling stations on E-day. Without our marked lists, the odds were even longer than they already were for a Liberal running in Cumberland-Prescott.

Our marked lists were gone. All of them. Every last one. All that remained strewn on the floor and on my desk were empty file folders, one for each poll, where the lists had resided. I had actually locked them in my desk drawer. But we'd bought the desks cheap, at a second-hand furniture store, and mine was about as secure as a wet Kleenex box.

I slumped into my chair. Muriel and Angus stood just inside my office door.

"They've all been stolen," I moaned. "This is an unmitigated disaster."

"There is a wee bit of a mess to clean up, but calling it a disaster is a bit much," said Angus.

"Oh no, it's not," Muriel piped up. "We're nothing without our marked lists. It was our only hope to get out the vote on election day. Those bastards."

"What, you actually think Fox is behind this?" asked Angus, incredulous.

"I wouldn't put it past him," I replied. "But it's a moot point now. We are well and truly sunk."

I would have said more but I was too busy wondering why the air-conditioning unit, usually mounted up in a wall vent near the ceiling, was sitting on its side, leaking on the floor next to my desk. In the dim light, I hadn't seen it at first. Angus had just noticed it, too, and was already looking up. I tilted my desk lamp to shine the light upwards.

"Shit," said Ramsay Rumplun. "Okay, you caught me. Now get me out of here," he whined. "I've been stuck in the vent here for over an hour and I can't feel my legs any more." He sounded more desperate than a claustrophobe in a coffin.

Angus finally hit the overhead fluorescents and the room lit up. Ramsay Rumplun was stuck halfway through the narrow passage that normally housed the air conditioner. We were stunned into silence. I knew now why I hadn't seen him at the all-candidates meeting. With our entire campaign team attending the meeting, it was a perfect time for a burglary attempt.

Muriel pulled out her cellphone to call the police (or maybe the fire department), while I pulled out mine to call André Fontaine.

"No phone calls yet till we know what we're dealing with here," Angus commanded.

Muriel and I stopped in mid-dial. But I went ahead and aimed my BlackBerry at Ramsay Rumplun and snapped a photo in case we needed it. Plugged fast in the wall vent, he was quite a sight, as he twisted and strained to escape. He looked like a big-game trophy, stuffed and mounted on our wall after a successful political safari.

"Ramsay Rumplun, I presume," said Angus with a smile. "Is this part of Emerson Fox's Breaking and Mentoring program?"

"I'm so sorry. I'm so ashamed. My father is going to kill me. I was only after your marked voters lists. That's all, I swear."

"That's like the bank robber who claims he was only after the money," I said. "Our lists are the principal asset of this entire operation. So turn them over or we'll just let you stay up there."

"I already pushed the bag with the lists through the vent into the driveway at the back. You'll find them there."

Angus went out the back door and returned in an instant with a canvas book bag brimming with our precious lists. I took the bag from him and just held it to my chest, rocking it gently, as if I were burping a baby. Pure, unadulterated relief. Muriel walked over and looked up at our intruder, avoiding the perspiration dropping periodically from his flushed face.

"Maybe we should just leave you up there. You clearly make a better seal in the vent than that old air conditioner. It's usually quite chilly back here but right now, it's really quite toasty," Muriel quipped.

"Just stay where you are," Angus mocked. "I'll try to get you down."

When we took a flashlight out back and climbed up a step ladder we had in our closet, we could see what the problem was. Actually, I could see *that* there was a problem, but only Angus could see *what* the problem really was. As he had tried to back out through the opening, Rumplun's belt had become lodged and locked on the steel edge of the air-conditioner mounts on the outside wall of the building.

I returned inside with Muriel. We were emerging from the shock of it all and had started to enjoy ourselves.

"If you'd only called, I would have been happy to tell you how successful our canvass has been. There was no need to re-create the Watergate break-in," I chided.

"Ouch! That's my belt!" Ramsay cried. "What are you doing?"

We could hear Angus through the open back door.

"Hold still and stop your wriggling or we'll have to call the fire department," Angus threatened. "Okay, there you go."

"What have you done? I need those!" Ramsay complained.

"You'll never squeeze through with them on," Angus replied. "Okay, I'm pushing on three. One, two, threeeeeee!"

Ramsay Rumplun shot through the opening like the human cannonball and landed on the floor below, winding himself. The sight of the portly Ramsay Rumplun, writhing on the floor in search of his breath and naked from the waist down, was not the lasting memory I would have chosen for the evening. But our uninvited guest really gave me no say in the matter. Muriel raised her cellphone and took a photo.

DIARY

Monday, January 13

My Love,

I'm in a circus sideshow. I hadn't realized before tonight that my past life within the ivy walls really was rather dull. In all my years, I've never witnessed a platoon of aged women bring down a defenceless man with a barrage of home baking. Nor have I ever pulled down another man's pants. But both I did tonight. What next, I ask you?

I made Daniel and Muriel email me the photos they'd taken of the sorry sod. They eventually saw it my way. No police. No reporters. Not even André. No one will know of this youthful indiscretion. No one will know, that is, but Emerson Fox. I've no interest in giving the voters of C-P any fresh reasons to withdraw from their democratic duty, so Ramsay Rumplun's idiocy will be forever buried. Tempting though it is, I'll not tell Roland, either.

I called Fox at his home tonight and then emailed him the photos. I then deleted the pictures from my hard drive, leaving him with the only existing copies. He may not have believed me, but I told him I assumed he knew nothing of this stunt and that the unfortunate lad was acting of his own misguided volition. I also told him he'd hear nothing about the incident from our campaign. He either thinks I'm extraordinarily honourable or irretrievably demented. Enough of this tripe.

I spoke of you to a room full of strangers tonight. It was odd, almost surreal. I found it calmed me. Are you proud of me tonight? 'Tis tomorrow I dread. Let me make it through and put one more threshold behind me.
AM

CHAPTER TEN

The next morning, the *Crier's* coverage of the all-candidates meeting could not have been better for our side. That is, unless André Fontaine had been with us later the previous night when we'd discovered the rotund Ramsay Rumplun plugged fast in our air-conditioning duct. Though several hours had passed, that final image of him quivering on the floor was still so fresh, vivid, and constant in my mind that I was considering hypnosis to exorcise it. I hoped my appetite might one day return. Had Muriel and I been in charge, the front-page *Crier* photo would have captured the naked truth of our bloated burglar and his botched break-in. (Ex-speechwriters are often plagued with chronic alliteration, and I was no exception.) But Angus dug in his heels and simply would not be moved. No matter. Muriel's grainy cellphone snap would surely have made Cumberland voters queasy as they sat around their breakfast tables. I wondered if Angus might be taking this high-road sentiment a little too seriously. I was convinced Emerson Fox, knowing how devastating the loss of our marked lists would be for us, had put his plump protégé up to the burglary attempt, but Angus would hear none of it. He shut us down hard and fast.

But I could hardly complain about the front-page photo that ran instead. It was a great shot taken from the side of the Cumberland Collegiate auditorium. About a dozen GOUT agents could be seen standing amid the audience, their spindly arms either winding up or following through, as a distressed Emerson Fox took cover behind the podium from the volley of cookies arcing his way. The photo was timed perfectly as the full vacuum bag had just hit its mark with the dust cloud germinating, obscuring Fox from the waist down. André really did have a gift for photography. After such a priceless photo, it didn't really matter what the story said. Best of all, the shot hit the wires and went national. The political bloggers had a field day invoking what they coined the "Cameron Curse."

Lindsay was out on the canvass with the two Petes, a rose between two thorns, and Muriel and I were in the constit office with Angus. I'd tried to convince him to forego constituency work until the campaign was over so we could concentrate all our efforts on getting re-elected. But I knew I'd lose that argument, too. As it turned out, the few hours we spent on constit business that morning were well worth it and might even give us a solid late-campaign announcement to make – what Bradley Stanton routinely called an "announcible." Our poor, poor language.

Angus and I spent an hour or so with a local group to talk about their dream of opening a seasonal ecotourism operation, offering kayaking trips up the Ottawa River. They were looking for a base of operations. In another patented McLintock win-win, Angus picked up the phone in the middle of the meeting and brokered an impromptu discussion with the other organization we'd already met that wanted to open an environmental education school in the abandoned aggregate operation on the river. For Angus, the idea had been immediately obvious. It took the rest of us a little longer to catch up, but we got there eventually. Even though the call to the camp people was unexpected and unplanned, the next forty-five minutes yielded a brilliant solution, at least in principle. Angus proposed that the two groups join forces to refurbish and then share the use of the shut-down aggregate facility.

The ecotourism group really only needed a home base from June to September, while the environmental education school would be in full swing during the academic year. Neither group had the resources to spruce up the place on their own. But together, they could. This, along with the complementary timing of their operations, made the partnership a perfect arrangement. Both groups could have a home, and the old aggregate mill would be redeemed. Three birds with one stone. Not bad for a morning's work. Angus had suggested that the two teams hammer out a plan together and we would try to facilitate the transfer of the moribund property from the municipality to the new partnership at a reasonable price. I wanted to move as quickly as possible in the hopes of nailing everything down in the next couple of weeks so we could announce it for a last-minute boost before the election.

I walked over to Muriel's desk to report on the successful meeting. She was putting in her regular weekday morning shift.

"Angus seems down today," Muriel remarked. "He's more cranky and taciturn than usual."

(I liked a woman who could correctly use "taciturn" in a sentence.) I hadn't really picked up anything, but my radar is not particularly sensitive, and I'd come to trust Muriel's instincts.

"He seemed okay in the meeting, but now that you mention it, as soon as the ecotourism group left, he did go all quiet on me," I remembered. "Then waved me out of his office and shut the door."

"Something is gnawing at him today, I can feel it," Muriel replied. "By the look of him around the gills, I have a hunch it might be Marin-related. Maybe it's her birthday today. Can you use your magical googly thing and find out?"

"Google, Muriel. It's Google."

I opened my laptop. It took me under a minute on Wikipedia to determine that it wasn't Marin's birthday. I spent a few more minutes searching, without really knowing what I was looking for, when my BlackBerry chirped. I looked at the screen. Shit.

"Hey Bradley," I opened.

"Addison?" he said.

"Yes Bradley, it's Daniel. That's how it works. You dial my BlackBerry, and then I answer," I replied.

"Thank you, dickwad, that's very helpful."

I let the ice thaw for just a second or two.

"So how goes the national battle?" I asked.

"Well, you better fasten your seat belt because in an hour, the national battle will be coming to your backyard. So clear the decks and pull all the volunteers you can to greet the big bus when we get there."

"Whoa! Come again?" I replied, understanding dawning. "The Leader is coming here? To Cumberland? Today? Now?"

"I don't care what everyone else says, I really think you are a quick study," he mocked. "We were supposed to be glad-handing in Gatineau-South with Kerry Doorpat, but she's got food poisoning from one of her own coffee parties and is in the Ottawa Civic on an IV. So it's going to be main-streeting with honest Angus instead. And you know how happy that makes me. Where do you want us to go when we pull in?"

Our campaign office was a bit of a disaster with the damaged air conditioner leaking in the corner and the general chaos that comes with running an election with more volunteers than we knew what to do with. Add a little smoke and you'd swear we'd been hit by mortar fire.

"Ahhhh, it's kind of crazy here at HQ. Let's meet at Angus's home on the river. We can brief the Leader there and then head downtown for a walkabout," I proposed.

"You want me to bring the Leader, the press, and the bus to McLintock's house?"

"The journos can wait for fifteen minutes on the bus while the Leader sits down with Angus. They like downtime. Give them their lunch, or throw *All the President's Men* back on the DVD," I replied. "Then Angus and I will ride the bus with you back in to Cumberland."

This was a classic good news/bad news scenario. The good news was that a Leader's stop in Cumberland meant that the centre now considered C-P to be a winnable riding; it was worth it to come, even though we'd made Stanton's life a living hell in the last three months. The bad news was we were going to have a Leader's stop in Cumberland. Putting Angus together with the Leader was a crap shoot at best, and the odds-makers were calling for at least a mishap (5–1) or perhaps even a disaster (2–1). Either way, the trouble potential was off the charts.

I gave Bradley the directions and got him off the phone as quickly as I could. Muriel had been by my side for the whole call.

"He's really not, is he? Not here?" she asked with a hunted look about her.

"He certainly is, in less than an hour."

I briefed Muriel as quickly as I could. Then I took her arm and guided her to Angus's door. We knocked and entered without waiting for a response. Angus was sitting behind his desk, his left palm supporting his forehead as he twiddled a pencil in his right hand. He was the very picture of melancholy, but we had no time to put him on the couch and diagnose his demons.

"Sorry to interrupt, Angus, but we have a bit of a situation," I started.

I didn't want to tell him what it was right away. We needed to get him into the car. Muriel was in a stronger position to make that happen, so she shuffled over to him on her own (all part of the plan), whereupon she offered her elbow to him.

"Would you mind getting me out to the car, Angus?" she asked sweetly but firmly. "Daniel, bring it around to the front door, would you?"

Muriel swayed a bit next to him, perhaps even legitimately, so Angus had no choice but to leap to his feet and take her arm. I grabbed his car keys from the desk and dashed for the Camry out back. By the time I'd pulled up to the front door, they were there on the sidewalk in their unbuttoned coats.

"I'll get in the back. Why, thank you, sir," Muriel cooed as he helped her in. "Now please get in the front seat, Angus. We'll explain on the way."

Bewildered, Angus got in and I pulled away from the curb.

I let Muriel explain the situation to Angus while I drove and briefed the two Petes via my cell. I had no choice but to leave them in charge of mobilizing the volunteers to greet the bus when it eventually arrived downtown. By the time I hung up, Angus seemed to be taking the news in stride.

"No, no. Not today, not today. I cannae do it today," he whined. "Why doesn't the buffoon go somewhere else? Anywhere else!"

Well, he was sort of taking the news in stride.

As usual, his house was pristine. For someone who cared so little about his own appearance, Angus seemed to take great pride in his home. It really was beautiful and very tastefully decorated. Marin may well have been the driving force behind the interior design, but I'd long since learned the hard way not to make assumptions about the breadth of Angus McLintock's knowledge and interests.

We sat in the living room looking out over the frozen river, awaiting the arrival of the Leader's bus.

"This is great news for us, it really is. It means it's possible we could actually win C-P. They wouldn't waste the Leader's time in a no-hope riding," I explained. "We must be closing the gap."

"But how does this help us?" Angus asked. "Everyone knows I don't see eye to eye with the man. How does it help us?"

I tagged with Muriel and she jumped into the ring. My BlackBerry vibrated with a text message. It was from Bradley Stanton and read "5 mins out."

"You'll get national media coverage tonight. The voters of Cumberland-Prescott will turn on their TVs tonight and see the next Prime Minister of Canada walking and talking with the famous and respected maverick MP Angus McLintock. Whatever you think of the man, his presence in this riding at this time is only good news for us," Muriel concluded.

Angus fell silent and we kept the peace until we all heard the hiss of the air brakes as the bus pulled up. Angus bowed his head and then turned it slowly, side to side.

"I see no trap door that would release me from what I'm certain will be a tedious and superficial afternoon. So let's get it over with."

Muriel stayed on the couch while Angus and I headed to the front door and put our coats back on.

"You need to lead on this, Angus. This is your riding, your home, and your show," I noted as I peeked through the small leaded-pane window in the front door. "Wait, wait. Almost ready. Okay, the Leader is off the bus and headed this way."

I opened the door so Angus could meet the Leader on the stone steps out front amid the belching diesel fumes from what looked like a Depression-era bus. Most of the reporters, photogs, and vidcam shooters had already piled off to record the historic meeting. Wearing a pale-blue long-sleeved dress shirt, grey suit pants, a red ski jacket (surprise, surprise), and dressy black boots, the Leader looked like the classic downtown city-dweller come to the country for the day. But he looked confident and relaxed, striding up the clear, dry, and salted walk. Just as he came within about four feet of Angus, the shiny polished toe of his right boot didn't quite clear the small flagstone step. I'd already experienced far too many scenes with Angus that played out in slow motion. I didn't really need another. But I got one anyway. The Leader actually seemed to lift off the ground as if the flagstone had been spring loaded. His eyes and his mouth opened wider than seemed anatomically possible and his arms became propellers as he tried to regain his balance for landing. I wasn't close enough to do anything useful, so I opted for the traditional hands-over-mouth look of shock. The shutters clicked away as Angus caught the Leader just before he went down hard. It was over in an instant, but not fast enough, I feared. That's all Bradley Stanton needed, a Gerald Ford moment. He would surely find a way to blame me for it. He glared at me when our backs were to the cameras.

"Would you rather Angus had let him face-plant on the stone-work?" I hissed.

Five minutes later, Stanton, the Leader, Muriel, Angus, and I were safely inside. Outside, the reporters stayed in the relative warmth of the idling bus and did what they did so much of the time on the campaign trail: they sat and waited. We were all comfortably seated in the living room. All, that is, except the Leader. He walked around the room looking as if he'd just fallen in love.

"Angus, this is just spectacular. What a beautiful home you have. And what a glorious view of the river," he gushed. "It must be amazing in the fall."

"Well, I thank you, sir. Yes, we're very happy in this home," said Angus. "Or rather, I am."

"It looks like you've been preparing for my arrival for weeks," the Leader droned on, rubber-necking and snooping around. "It's absolutely pristine."

"Actually, it always looks like this, sir," I interjected. "We didn't know you were coming until half an hour ago. This is just the normal state of Chateau McLintock."

"Well, I'm bowled over by it. It's wonderful."

It took another twenty minutes and a full guided tour of the house before Bradley and I could corral Angus and the Leader and herd them back onto the bus. We left Muriel there to hold the fort. A suspect bus that seemed as old as she was no place for an eighty-one-year-old in the throes of Parkinson's, although she would have kept the scribes in line. We didn't really get around to briefing the Leader, but there wasn't much to tell. On the way into town, the Leader remarked on all the red ribbons on cars, trees, and front doors, and commended the community's enlightened support of AIDS research. I then remembered to explain our no-lawn-sign policy and that Cumberland's red tide was actually in support of Angus, who was of course all in favour of more AIDS research.

As we turned onto our block, about seventy-five volunteers, dressed in, yes, more red, milled about in front of the campaign office with red streamers at the ready. I counted quite a few of Muriel's fellow residents among the supporters. In my mind, I congratulated the two Petes on mobilizing such an impressive crowd on such short notice despite the January temperatures. I took back the kudos an instant later when I caught a glimpse of Peter and

Pete2 standing at the front of the melee. They must have thought the Liberal Leader's visit to Cumberland constituted a special occasion, so they had dressed accordingly. How they gathered such a mob and then achieved their own special "look," all in fifty-four minutes, I will never know, because I will never ask.

Pete1 seemed to have dipped his entire body, I'm talking full immersion, into a bathtub of Liberal red paint. "Go Angus!" was stencilled onto his forehead in white. He wore a red and black leather jacket, not unlike Michael Jackson's in *Thriller*, except this one looked like it had been dragged behind a jeep for the duration of Rommel's North African offensive. Through random holes in both shoulders (I'm still on the jacket here), there protruded several sharp chrome spikes that posed a threat to anyone standing nearby. Much to our good fortune, and despite the cold, Pete1 left the jacket unzipped. This allowed us all to see the gunmetal chain looped through both of his nipple piercings and meeting just above his navel, from which was suspended a portrait of the Liberal Leader himself in a small barbed wire frame. As for his pants, well, he wasn't wearing any. His red-dipped legs ended in black Doc Martens laced to the hilt, no doubt so his feet wouldn't get cold. If you must know, the other ends of his legs disappeared into what looked like a red fur Speedo. I'm sure it was fake fur. Both Petes were animal lovers. The crowd gave him plenty of room.

Pete2 was much more sedately attired. He looked up to Pete1 and, out of respect, would never try to out-punk him. His red Mohawk was outstanding, literally. It stood on guard, straight and tall, again with "Go Angus!" in white lettering on either face of the foot-high centre strip bisecting his skull. He wore a simple yet elegant white cape gathered around him with long vertical tears in the fabric every four inches or so giving him plenty of choices when he needed to poke his hands through to the outside world. Bare legs seemed to be the order of the day as Pete2 opted for a fluorescent red and green kilt with a black, iron capital "L" swinging where the sporran normally would. No Doc

Martens for Pete2. He went with his bladeless Bauer Supreme hockey skates, which I'd seen him wear once or twice before.

I looked at Angus, who had also just taken in Pete2's garb.

"Aye, I can see him. All in all, a nice ensemble, well put together," he observed.

By this time, we were nearly at the campaign office and the ·Leader and Bradley Stanton had taken a good long look at the two Petes. Both recoiled in their seats.

"Let's just drive on and we'll get out on the next block," suggested the Leader.

"Rubbish!" protested Angus. "Stop the bus, we're getting off here. This has all been put on for you."

"But who are those two . . . those two . . . frightening beings at the front?" asked the Leader. "They look . . . dangerous and deranged."

"On the contrary, sir, those are the two Petes, our Volunteer Coordinators," Angus explained. "They're harmless and have worked very, very hard for the cause. Aye, they have."

I knew Bradley was staring me down but I refused to meet his eyes. The reporters at the back of the bus all seemed to notice the two Petes at the same time and then realized in unison that they'd just been handed that night's TV visual and the next day's front-page photo.

Ten minutes later, Angus and the Leader were walking up Cumberland's main shopping street with the two Petes and the Liberal ribbon-waving chorus in tow. Several of the volunteers carried bright red plastic fire extinguishers, making a powerful statement about their party allegiance and their willingness to take on Flamethrower Fox. They were Muriel's idea. Simple and effective political symbolism. The reporters walked beside the group to get their shots and footage.

Angus and the Leader were shaking hands and answering questions from dozens of shoppers along the route. People seemed quite willing to engage with them and several even allowed Angus to tie red ribbons onto their coat zippers. Each time this happened, Peter would sidle up to the unsuspecting shoppers and get their names so we could update our marked voters list. None of them fainted. By the looks on their faces, most of them would gladly have given up much more than their names to satisfy Peter, though he was unfailingly polite.

The sun was high and helped us all forget just how cold it really was. It was going quite well when in the distance, I heard the staticky strains of a loudspeaker. I looked behind us in time to see a Tory-blue Hummer turn onto our street with a large speaker mounted on top. I'd expected this. Word of the Liberal Leader's arrival would surely have travelled fast in such a small town. This was Fox's predictable response. His crew was trying to disrupt the visit. As the Hummer approached, I could just discern the ranting and chanting from the speaker.

"Vote Fox! Angus is a criminal! Vote Fox! Angus is a femiterrorist! Vote Fox! Angus killed your tax cuts! Vote Fox!"

Angus and the Leader were still far enough up the road that they hadn't really heard the insults yet. As I watched the Hummer come closer, several GOUT agents in the crowd suddenly stepped off the sidewalk and into the middle of the road, forcing the gas-guzzler to stop. The driver tried to steer around the geriatric brigade but they shimmied to the left, then to the right, to block the Hummer at every turn. It wasn't exactly the lone, courageous student staring down the tank in Tiananmen Square, but it did the trick. But they weren't finished. The group then surrounded the truck so it could not reverse either. I saw plastic bags emerge from parka pockets and in the next three minutes or so, the gnarled but nimble fingers of the GOUT squad must have tied about four hundred ribbons on the immobilized vehicle, wherever they found purchase. The antenna, door handles, gas cap, wipers, hood vents, bumpers, grille, and even the roof-top speaker. So every time the Tories inside hollered into their mike, the sound waves made the long red ribbons on the roof-top woofer dance about in the air. The occupants wisely stayed inside. Had they opened their doors to challenge the GOUT

165

operatives, it would not have been pretty. The Hummer now looked more red than blue.

Then, on some prearranged signal, all the seniors just walked away from the Hummer and shuffled up the street to rejoin the rest of us. This seemed to flummox Fox's team. They realized they couldn't drive around with hundreds of red ribbons marring their Tory campaign Hummer. I started to laugh. I guess we could have let the air out of the tires instead, but the ribbons were more fun, more effective, and made for better TV. Eventually, the Foxites hopped out, trying frantically to untie the ribbons. It's hard to untie a knotted ribbon, let alone four hundred of them. I jogged up to the front of our crowd, grabbed André's elbow, and pointed out the spectacle behind us. He did the rest all on his own, along with sixteen other photographers and vidcam shooters. The Tory team was so humiliated, they finally gave up, piled back into their Hummer, pulled a U-turn, and squealed away. I didn't see their retreat live, but I watched it on the news that night. Every campaign needs a fearless GOUT squad.

Half an hour later, Angus and the Leader stood together on the sidewalk in front of our campaign office for a quick scrum. The bus idled at the curb. Reporters and cameras jockeyed for position as a dozen microphones filled the space in front of the two Liberals. It was standard campaign scrum fare.

Towards the end of the scrum, André Fontaine piped up with a question for the Leader.

"You've had Angus in the caucus and in the House now for a couple of months. Do you always agree with him?"

I sensed Bradley's hackles rising without even looking his way. The Leader chuckled and looked at his feet as he struggled to formulate a response. He would have come back with a solid answer I'm sure, but Angus seemed to think the question may have been directed to him.

"Now André, what kind of mischievous question is that to be hurling around," he demanded. "You know very well that the Leader and I have not always agreed. In fact, we've been on opposite sides of several rather fundamental issues. But that's the kind of party he leads. One that encourages discussion, debate, even dissent, until we've finally hammered out the very best position we can. We won't always agree on how to get there but you can bet we share a common view of the destination, and that's more important in the end, isn't it?"

Bradley intervened.

"Okay, we're out of time, folks," he said. "We're due back in Ottawa in less than an hour. So, back on the bus, if you please."

Angus tried to open the bus door for the Leader but it seemed stuck at the two-thirds open mark.

"It's been doing that more and more lately," volunteered the driver standing nearby.

Angus looked into the crack where the door met the bus. He turned to me.

"Will you apply your weight against this, lad?"

I leaned against it while Angus reached carefully into the hinge mechanism – about as technical a term as I can muster – frigged around for a second or two, then pulled out a bent and twisted metal Liberal campaign button that had somehow found its way in. Instantly, the door swung smoothly again. The reporters applauded. And yes, all the cameras had been trained on Angus as he operated on the door, while the Leader stood helplessly off to the side, yet still in the shot.

Finally, Bradley and the Leader followed the reporters back on the bus while we stood on the sidewalk to wave them off. I looked up and saw Stanton's enraged face and icy eyes boring into me from the window. Angus had upstaged the Leader, again, so I was not surprised Bradley was livid. He looked as if he were passing a kidney stone. Given to melodramatic gestures, he held two fingers up to his eyes and then quickly pointed back at me. I smiled and nodded. Then, since he was into hand-talking, I gave him the traditional Vulcan "Live long and prosper" split-finger salute as the bus pulled away. By his darkening facial hue, I figured a second kidney stone was just coming into the chute.

Angus, Muriel, the two Petes, Lindsay, and I met after dinner in Angus's living room. It had been a very long day, but we were less than two weeks out and needed to pound out our E-day strategy. Now that he was among friends, Angus gave the impression that he was among enemies. He was as morose and cantankerous as I've ever seen him. He just sat in the big chair by the window, looked out into the darkness, and unconsciously raked his beard with splayed fingers. Nobody would willingly pass a hand so deeply into the great unknown of his chin spinach, where lurk treasures and dangers alike. He was utterly disconnected mentally from the discussion. When the others were mapping out a plan to drive shut-ins to the polls, I bent over Angus.

"Are you all right?" I asked. "You seem distracted, depressed."

"Aye, it's been an enervatin' day and I'm feelin' it," he said without eye contact.

"Is that all there is? Muriel is worried about you."

"Today is today and it cannae end soon enough for me," he nearly whispered. "But tomorrow is tomorrow, and I'll be back. So fret not, lad."

"It's late. We don't really need you for this discussion. Why don't you sleep now? Peter can drive Muriel home and I'll lock up here," I suggested.

"Aye, I will, if you'll permit me."

DIARY
Tuesday, January 14
My Love,
While much happened today, I've had but one solitary
thought in my heart and my head. Happy anniversary, my
love. Forty it would be. I pray I've better to give on the
morrow, for I'm down deep tonight.
AM

CHAPTER ELEVEN

The last two weeks of the campaign were a blur as we finally settled into a disciplined routine. The two Petes took the canvass into every nook and cranny of the riding with their ever-improving and growing team. They also spent some time on campus organizing a little group of engineering students in support of Angus. They called their little group "Engus." A few engineering faculty colleagues also came on board. Small clumps of them would parade around campus with signs extolling the virtues of engineers in Parliament. Even though most members of the loose organization were not C-P voters, the moral support was welcome, and Angus got a kick out of it.

As for our candidate, he would mainstreet early in the morning to catch the commuters, do voter calls in the mid-morning, give a luncheon address somewhere in the riding over the lunch hour (hence the term luncheon address), mainstreet late in the day to catch the working crowd on their way home, canvass for an hour or so in the early evening in strategically selected areas, and then close with a nightly wrap-up campaign staff meeting at about 9:30 to plan for the next day. Then Angus would fall into bed, only to have the alarm rouse him all too soon to do it all over again. The days all melded together, making time seem like more of an elastic concept. But Angus hit his stride and actually seemed to enjoy some aspects of it, particularly the staff meetings and the going-to-bed parts.

In his stump speech, while never saying exactly the same thing twice, he stuck to the major themes that had always underpinned his approach to public life. Honesty, forthrightness, the national interest over the local interest, fiscal responsibility, and social justice. When asked esoteric and irrelevant questions he could not answer, which happened occasionally, particularly if one of Emerson's emissaries were in the crowd, Angus would never try to skate around it as most politicians would. He'd simply say something like "I really haven't the foggiest notion" and then look for another raised hand. When he did this at a gathering of the Cumberland Rotary Club, the woman who'd posed an unfathomable and obscure question about particular endangered species was not quite ready to cede the floor.

"Don't you think you should know the answer?" she persisted.

"Aye, it's likely I should know something about that, and in time, I hope I do. But there are some limits on what sits upstairs in my brainpan, so I'm concentrating first on the major issues that I believe are most significant to Canadians right now. The economy, equality and justice, our environment, jobs, and the prudent expenditure of our hard-earned tax dollars. When I have additional cerebral capacity, I'll turn what's left of my mind to the plight of the pygmy short-horned lizard and the Loggerhead Shrike."

Many in the audience clapped.

In general, the campaign had unfolded much better than expected. Norman Sanderson had really stepped up on the fundraising front. In week one of the campaign, he delivered $24,000. By the midpoint, another $19,500 came in. On the eve of election day, Norman came through with a final cheque for $27,200. Whatever happened on E-day, all of the campaign's expenses would easily be covered, with a nest egg left over for the C-P Liberal Association. Few ridings in the country were as flush. Notwithstanding the cash, I reminded myself that winning was still a faint hope.

We were able to nail down the ecotourism–science school partnership to breathe new life into the padlocked and abandoned aggregate operation on the river. We got great local coverage, and both partners in the deal laid all the credit at the feet of Angus McLintock. To come full circle, the stories also reminded everyone that it was Angus who had shut down the rogue polluter in the first place.

Towards the end of the campaign, it became quite clear that the Angus McLintock red ribbon initiative had taken on a life of its own. Some drivers tied such elaborate red ribbon arrangements on their cars that their vision was somewhat impaired by the flowing red streamers. It became an isolated but legitimate question of public safety, and the Cumberland Police Chief called and asked for our help. I wanted to get on top of this issue fast before the Fox camp caught wind of it and started accusing Angus of imperiling voters' lives. So I quickly drafted a news release with some guidelines for creative but safe automotive ribbon displays. As usual, I quoted Angus in the release. Everyone else on the campaign team was busy right then so I printed out a copy on our campaign letterhead and passed it to Angus for comments and a final check. As a speechwriter, my credo has always been two sets of eyes on everything. Good thing too. Five minutes later, an agitated Angus was standing nearly on top of my desk clenching the offending news release in a white-knuckle death grip.

"This whatchamacallit better not have yet hit the streets," he glowered. "I'd thank you to spell my name correctly. You've got all the right letters on your bleedin' keyboard. I can see them from here."

He dropped the crumpled news release on my desk and stomped out. I smoothed it out and saw that he'd circled the headline in thick red marker. Oops. Careless of me.

Tips for safely displaying your red Anus ribbons

"G" added. Candidate calmed. Crisis averted. Funny campaign story created. Funny at some point in the future.

———

Every day, our canvassers tallied the number of Fox lawn signs and Angus ribbons as a kind of bellwether read on the riding. By their estimates, we had at least as many properties represented as did Fox. As well, the Alden Stonehouse campaign had kicked out an impressive number of signs. The more of them the better. Unfortunately, only votes could decide the outcome. All the rest – the ribbons and so on – were just tea leaves for the reading.

Even in the final week, Emerson Fox intensified his nasty and deeply personal attacks on Angus in his speeches, letters-to-the-editor, and more and more radio buys. I thought it smacked of desperation. The Fox team seemed to panic as the campaign wound down, making wilder and wilder accusations about Angus's background. I kept waiting for them to link Angus to the Gretzky trade to Los Angeles and perhaps even the CBC's loss of the *Hockey Night in Canada* theme song. Even Angus got used to it towards the end, holding his temper to a slow simmer rather than the roiling boil of the early campaign. Then with six days to go, Fox woke up and realized that Alden Stonehouse posed a greater threat than Angus ever did. It took him a while to reach that conclusion but when he did, the crosshairs shifted to the ultra-conservative independent candidate.

To his credit, Alden Stonehouse seemed to get better and stronger as the campaign rolled on. He never wilted, never wavered, never wobbled under Fox's withering attacks in the last week. He joined Angus on the high road and looked almost noble, despite a platform that might even have given Jerry Falwell pause. Whatever you thought of his policies and positions, the reverend stayed on message for the whole campaign. As for Jane Nankovich, well, she suffered the worst fate that can ever befall a candidate. In Cumberland-Prescott, she was simply irrelevant from the opening bell.

True to his word, Angus addressed the annual Rabbie Burns Supper on the 25th. He was among friends, so I let him go by himself so I could meet with our E-day team to make sure all was ready for the big day. Angus made it home quite late in a cab, having enjoyed perhaps a little too much the single malt tasting that closed the evening. I'd been watching for him from the boathouse window and met him as he struggled to find his key in his sporran then stab it in the front door lock. Wobbling a tad on his stone porch, Angus turned to me and slapped one hand on my shoulder while he steadied himself with the other on the door handle.

"I can support that our report among the voters of Scottish descent is monolithic. The ethnic vote is solid."

"Good to know," I replied. I made sure he got inside the house.

The day before the election, I thought it was time to check in again with Michael Zaleski to get one more glimpse at the numbers before twenty or thirty thousand voters in C-P started marking Xs on ballots. He answered on the first ring.

"Hey Daniel."

"Hi Z-man. How are you holding up with one day to go?" I asked.

"I'm counting the minutes till this thing is done. It's been short but gruelling, and a week in Martinique is looking pretty good."

"I hear you," I commiserated. "Look, I don't want to take up your time, but I was just wondering if you might be able to give me a last look at the C-P numbers before E-day?"

"You got a writing instrument of some kind?"

"My pen is poised."

"Hang on," he said. I could hear him clacking away on his keyboard, calling up the spreadsheets. "Okay, the most recent wave is from E-day minus two. So that's yesterday. You ready?"

"Hit me," I replied.

"Okay. Fox thirty-two, McLintock twenty-seven, Stonehouse nineteen, Nankovich seven, and Undecided comes in still high at fifteen," Zaleski reported. "So the gap between Angus and Fox is closing. You're within striking distance depending how the Undecideds fall."

"Wow, Stonehouse is kicking ass," I said.

"He is, but he's taking his strength out of Fox, while Angus's growth is coming from the Undecideds. And that's good news. Fox is headed in the wrong direction. It's going to be tight. Angus could probably use another week of campaigning."

Michael didn't have to share those numbers with me. In fact, he was probably breaking protocol. It paid to be nice to people. I reported the numbers to Muriel and Lindsay, but no one else.

E-day. Finally. The day dawned cold but clear, with no snow in the forecast. Weather would not be a factor. I told Angus he could have an extra hour's sleep. He deserved it. From his reaction, you'd have thought I'd just given him a winning lottery ticket. I dropped Lindsay off at the campaign office, then headed over to see Muriel. She'd mobilized a phone team of fellow residents to call all Liberal voters. In the last campaign, the two Petes made all the calls themselves inside of a half-hour. This time around it was different. But we still had to get out the vote, that immutable and timeless imperative of all elections.

Muriel gathered about fourteen seniors in the meeting room, including some of the GOUTers. They were each sitting at their own card table spaced around the room to give them maximum privacy when the calling started. It looked like a high school exam room, only more boisterous. Muriel gave them their marching orders, and then, with her holding onto my arm, we ambled around to each table and presented the occupant with a voters list marked with red highlighter, and one of a dozen cellphones I'd requisitioned for the day from our volunteers at HQ.

The calling began when Muriel dropped her arm sharp at 9:00, as if she was waving the green flag at the Indy 500. False start. By 9:20, I'd finished my tutorial on basic cellphone operations and the calling really began. Most of the callers did a fantastic job. They could offer detailed information on polling station locations, when the polls closed, and even how to mark the ballot to avoid any challenges from opposing scrutineers. They could also talk a good game about Angus if necessary, to close the deal. Finally, we had a system set up to drive voters to the polling stations if they had no other way of getting there.

Muriel and I watched the operation from the front of the room with considerable pride. Demographically, it didn't look like any other E-day phone bank I'd ever seen, but it seemed to be working perfectly well. I circulated, gathering names, addresses, and pick-up times for those voters who needed drives. I then called Lindsay at HQ where she coordinated the master car-pool list and scheduled drivers.

"What do you mean, you've changed your mind?" sputtered Jasper in the far corner. He was wearing the only outfit I'd ever seen him in since we'd met the previous September, a peach safari suit, circa 1971. "You can't just change your mind, I've got you down as a Liberal." Pause. "Why do you want to vote for that whacko anyway? He's a nutjob in a nice suit." Pause. "Well, there's no need to get belligerent about it – I'm just trying to save you from yourself, you crazy old bat!"

That's how long it took for Muriel to get to Jasper's table, snatch the cell from his arthritic hand, and bring it up to her ear.

"Hello, I'm sorry for the exchange you've just had with one of our volunteers. He's very opinionated, as you could no doubt tell." Pause. "Yes, I do think that's a good way to describe him. Well put, Mrs. Knickerson," said Muriel as she stole a look at Jasper's list. "Of course, you have every right to change your mind and vote for Reverend Stonehouse. That is your prerogative." Pause. "Yes, that is the address for your polling station. Yes, I always find it easier to vote after dinner when the polling station is not as crowded. Yes, of course the polls are open late. The best time to go is in the last hour, between nine and ten." Pause. "Oh you're welcome. I've enjoyed it too." Pause. "My name? It's Cynthia. Goodbye."

Muriel handed the phone back to Jasper and spent a minute or two schooling him on proper telephone etiquette.

"Cynthia? What was that all about?" I asked when I helped

her back to her chair at the front of the room. "And by the way, the polls actually close at eight tonight."

"Thank you, Daniel, I'm well aware of the polling station's hours of operation."

"You are evil, Muriel Parkinson. Pure evil."

Just before I left Muriel and her merry band of phone bankers, I confirmed that we'd booked the dining room of the Riverfront Seniors' Residence, overlooking the Ottawa River, for our campaign party that night. In view of how much support Muriel had cultivated for Angus in the residence, having the party there at least guaranteed attendance. I desperately wanted it to be a victory party but we wouldn't know that until about ten that night, or perhaps even later if the race were really tight. The booking was fine, and we could get into the room right after dinner ended at 6:30 to hang some, yes, you guessed it, red streamers. After all this, I wasn't sure I ever wanted to see another red ribbon. Pete2 promised to bring his iPod and speakers so we'd have some tunes. He also agreed to cleanse his music collection for the evening so that the GOUT team wouldn't have to foxtrot to his favourite Canadian bands like Bile, Putrid Autopsy, and my personal favourite, Shit from Hell. He gave me his word he'd download some Bert Kaempfert, Benny Goodman, and Lawrence Welk too.

I made trips to the liquor store and the supermarket to stock up for the party. Norman Sanderson had popped in to the campaign office the night before and pressed a roll of bills into my hand to underwrite the cost of the party. It was his money. Very kind of him.

Back at HQ, everything was running as expected. In other words, it was a hybrid of pandemonium and bedlam. One can easily discern the subtleties separating the two when you're as experienced in such matters as I am. I briefly huddled with Lindsay, not so much because I needed to. I just felt calmer when I was close to her. I was really looking forward to peace reigning after the election so that our nights together revolved around something other than updating voters lists, assembling canvassing kits, and licking envelopes.

"The chauffeur line is ringing off the hook," she said when I arrived. "I've got my team of six drivers fully booked until 4:30 already."

"Linds, that's fantastic! Do you need more drivers? I can do a few runs in the Taurus."

"Ahhh, no thanks. I really think we should stick to cars that have floors." She held my wrist and scrunched up her face in sympathy to soften the blow as she delivered it. A wave of emotion washed over me at the gesture and I promptly forgot what she said. I kissed her forehead and left her to work her magic. She was just so efficient. It struck me that she might have been a star taxi dispatcher in a previous life.

Even Angus had gotten into the spirit of E-day. After his sleep-in, he spent the morning in *Baddeck 1*, flying some very excited voters from their homes on the river to their polling station in the Cumberland United Church a kilometre along the shore, and back again. All the voters had their own cars, of course, but how often did you get to ride in a famous hovercraft. I warned Angus that he was just to drive, not campaign. There were strict rules about campaigning on election day, particularly within sight of a polling station. He understood I was serious by my tone, and agreed. I called him to check in.

"How many trips have you made so far?"

"I'm at the kirk now in the middle of my fourth trek up the river," Angus explained. "She's handlin' like a dream today with barely a breath of wind out here. 'Tis truly glorious."

It was just like Angus to be more focused on the hovercraft than on his precious cargo.

"Don't get too caught up in your runs up the river. Remember, I need you back here at two for your polling station photo op," I reminded him.

"I'll not forget," he assured me. "By the way, two of the voters I drove earlier this mornin' have actually called me back wantin' a second blast along the ice to the votin' place."

"Angus, as far as I know, the law allows them to cast just one ballot in this election. 'Vote early and vote often' is just a figure of speech."

"Dinnae worry yourself, lad. I turned them down flat," he soothed. "Oh, I must sign off now, for my passenger is just out the kirk door and headin' this way."

I'd issued a media advisory the day before to make sure we had at least a couple of photographers there to record the classic candidate voting shot. At 2:30, as we made our way to the church where Angus had already spent part of his morning, I noticed a CTV satellite truck driving right behind us. It was obviously heading for the polling station to catch the scintillating scene of Angus disappearing behind the Elections Canada cardboard screens to mark his ballot, and then the heart-stopping moment when he re-emerges to have his ballot initialled, before the climax when he slips it into the slot, in slow motion of course. I hadn't expected the networks to show.

"I'm just going to pull over for a minute, Angus," I said as I turned into a Mac's Milk convenience store parking lot and stopped.

"Whatever for?" said Angus, checking his watch. "You can pick up your milk on the way home. We're runnin' a wee bit behind schedule already."

"The CTV satellite truck that just drove past us tells me we're running just a wee bit ahead of schedule," I responded. "We want network coverage, so let's give them a few minutes to get set up before we make our grand entrance."

We pulled into the polling station's parking lot ten minutes later, manoeuvring around not just the CTV truck, but the satellite units of CBC and Global as well. Nice.

Angus licked his hands and tried to calm his hair and beard as I pulled to a stop. I suppose fibreglass resin and a mason's trowel might have worked, but we had no time for that.

"Okay. We get out, smile, without artifice, then walk through the side door of the church and up to the registration table.

Engage the poll clerks. Hand over your passport to confirm your identity, as if there's any doubt, then proceed to our poll table – we're poll seventeen. Talk to the clerks there, then take your ballot, walk slowly but purposefully behind the cardboard thingy, mark your ballot, and come back to the table. Let them initial it, then make sure the cameras have the view they need of the ballot box. Don't just drop it in. Hold it in the slot for a moment so the photogs can get the shot. Then let it go. It's quite common to pat the top of the box for good measure. And don't forget to smile, in an Angus kind of way."

"Are you done now, laddie?" he asked sarcastically. "Now, do you think I should lead with my right foot or my left? What if I have to belch? What will we do?" He held his hands up to his face in mock horror.

"I'm just trying to get the most out of this opportunity," I sniffed, miffed.

Angus smiled.

"I'm just yankin' yer leg, so calm yourself," he said. "I heard every word you said and I've got it."

Without looking, he swung open the door and promptly knocked over a metal municipal trash can that I'd somehow failed to notice when parking. It sounded like a high-speed car accident and spilled garbage onto the sidewalk.

"Hell and damnation!" was his considered response.

Welcome to the flip side of the photo op coin.

At 8:00 p.m., Angus turned on his Electrohome console colour TV to warm up. It was old but still seemed to work quite well, although the colour was not quite right. The election coverage had already started. On the screen, Liberal red looked more orangey. Tory blue was purply, and the NDP orange was kind of yellowy. But the picture was clear and sharp.

Muriel, Lindsay, Angus, the two Petes, Norman Sanderson, and I squeezed into the couch and chairs as the returns trickled in. Angus seemed at peace and Muriel was calm and but sombre.

Lindsay was her usual wonderful self and was talking to a relaxed Norman. The two Petes, along with their tattoos and piercings, lounged quietly on the floor. And I was a quivering mass of stomach-churning anxiety, as I always am after the polls close. I have never got used to the stress of the ballot count and probably never will. For the hundredth time in the last week I reminded myself that, despite running a solid campaign, the polls still had us trailing in a riding with deep Tory roots.

By 8:40 the Atlantic numbers were coming in fast. We did better than expected in the east, although it was usually pretty solid Liberal territory. We gained three new seats there. When the CBC anchor asked the Halifax reporter about the Liberal wins, one of the several factors the local guy cited was Angus and his "hovercraft heroics." We broke into cheers. Except for Angus.

The first returns from Cumberland-Prescott arrived at 9:10, and then came in a steady stream as polling stations across the riding reported. As expected, given the order in which the polls were reporting, Fox opened a solid lead with Angus in second and Stonehouse in third, but showing astonishing strength. By 9:45, with 65 per cent of the polls reporting, it had grown very, very close but Angus was moving in the right direction, while Fox appeared stalled.

Fox (PC):   37%
McLintock (Lib):   36%
Stonehouse (Ind):   22%
Nankovich (NDP):   5%

As the night wore on, the numbers went up and down and my stomach acid followed in lockstep. Angus took the lead at 10:07, to a tremendous roar from the campaign team. At 10:12, Fox was back in front. Stonehouse continued to do amazingly well. He peaked at 25 per cent, which was an astonishing accomplishment for an independent. The panel of analysts in the CBC studio spent some time discussing Stonehouse's success. The consensus was that he provided a reasonable and viable ideological alternative to Emerson Fox, and that his election-day machine was outstanding. They'd done a great job getting out their vote. Every ballot marked for Stonehouse, they noted, was almost as good as a vote for Angus. I smiled to myself.

In my one secret concession to Machiavelli and the "win at all costs" philosophy he'd espoused, I'd helped the Alden Stonehouse team get their E-day act together. Ten days before the vote, the Stonehouse campaign office had received a plain brown envelope with no return address. Inside, there was no note or explanation of any kind. There was just a cogent, well-written, simple, and clear E-day manual, driven by the single goal of getting out their vote. The manual wasn't rocket science. It just laid out the basics with easy step-by-step instructions. I wondered whether they would use it. On election night, the strength of the Stonehouse numbers told me they had. Anybody snooping around my laptop would find no trace of the manual. Nothing.

At 11:09, Angus took the lead, and kept it. In the end, he beat Emerson Flamethrower Fox by 468 votes, a margin that would withstand even the most discriminating recount. An accidental MP the first time around, now Angus had actually won the seat, on purpose.

Muriel hugged me. Angus hugged me. Norman looked like he was going to hug me, but eventually settled for a classic hand-shake and hair muss. The two Petes punched me in both shoulders. Then Lindsay took me in her arms and I forgot where I was.

The party was packed and in full swing by the time Angus and I arrived. Norman drove the two Petes, Muriel, and Lindsay over first to survey the scene before giving me the signal. There were satellite trucks from all the networks there, an election-night honour usually reserved only for party leaders. But Angus had played so big a part in the events that brought us there that night, it was clear that now he was accorded special status.

On the way over, Angus spoke only once.

"Daniel, I'm happier tonight than I thought I'd ever be again.

be here were it not for you and Muriel. I've tried so hard
wl out of the vast hole in which Marin's passin' left me.
couldnae do it. I just couldnae. Tonight, I feel as though
I've just popped my head above the lip of that dark, dark abyss.
And I can see again. It feels as though Marin is now finally at
peace too, for she's been here and fussin' over me for the whole
ride. Aye, she has. I know you had other plans. I'm in your debt.
You have my gratitude. And you have my blessin', not that you
need it, to let this cup pass you by, and return to your teachin' if
you so desire."

I, too, spoke once only.

"I'll stay with you on the Hill. The university isn't going
anywhere."

As odd as it may sound, we clasped hands in the dark of the
car in a laddish sort of way, as the Riverfront Seniors' Residence
loomed ahead. It didn't feel odd in the least.

The room was packed. As soon as Angus entered, the crowd
simply detonated in a frenzy of applause. There was a lot of joy
inside those four walls. Angus needed no instructions from me
as he worked the room, looking more confident and relaxed in
a crowd than I'd ever seen him. Victory suited him. Pete2 was
surrounded by seniors complaining that they'd just about had
enough of Lawrence Welk and were looking to hear some Tom
Jones or Johnny Mathis, or maybe even Neil Diamond. I shrugged
and told him to improvise. I was too chuffed to worry about it.
The crowd around him dispersed after a compromise was apparently reached. Soon, blasting from the speakers was a bizarre
version of the Tom Jones classic "What's New, Pussycat?" I'd
never heard it before and instantly regretted hearing it then.
Beneath the heavy metal thrashing and yelling I could just barely
identify the tune. Usually a man of few words, Pete2 shouted to
me that it was a cover done by Chainsaw Lobotomy, a punk band
from Kingston. I told him he didn't need to explain that it was a
punk band. Several GOUT agents were dancing up a storm. At
least, I assumed it was dancing.

At the appropriate time, I armed Muriel up and onto the carpeted risers in front of the wall of windows. Reporters and video cameras crowded in front as Muriel gripped the podium to quell her tremors. She looked nothing short of radiant. The smile seemed permanent. The room slowly quieted as more and more celebrants noticed her.

"Tonight is not for speeches, especially from me. On this one night, Angus, you have our blessing to forget about the past, forget about the future, and simply revel in the extraordinary present. Tonight we celebrate the legitimate dawn of a new political era in Cumberland-Prescott, and I dare say in Canada. Ladies and gentlemen, Angus McLintock MP."

He embraced her when he reached the risers and guided her to a chair just off the stage. He took the mike from its stand and stood at the front of the platform, closer to the adoring throng.

Angus spoke beautifully and briefly. He struck the perfect tone, balancing humility, vision, grace, and strength. He offered heartfelt thanks and paid special tributes to Muriel, Lindsay, Norman, the two Petes, and me. He also recognized the tireless efforts of a certain band of political activists from the Riverfront Seniors' Residence. He was note perfect. This is how he closed.

"In the last month, there have been many a night, when in my private thoughts, this victory seemed nigh on impossible. Aye, and there were certainly many doubters who told us all it was never to be. The mountain, simply too high to scale. But a life without challenge, a life without hardship, a life without purpose, seems pale and pointless. With challenge come perseverance and gumption. With hardship come resilience and resolve. With purpose come strength and understanding. And tonight, with victory come elation, gratitude, expectations, and a wee spot of trepidation. All this we have achieved together. This unexpected triumph is shared with all of you, for I am so grateful for what you have done, and what you have given. It is the best of democracy come to life before our very eyes.

"Much lies ahead. We know not yet whether we're to govern or oppose, but either way, my simple promise to you is the same. I'll put Canada first, even when that means local sacrifice. I'll strive always to be honest, to listen more than I talk, and to do what I truly believe is right and just. I also pledge to explain my positions and decisions at every turn. I'll not be afraid to change my mind when persuaded by powerful arguments I'd not considered.

"The campaign was gruelling for all of us. But tomorrow, the work of public service begins afresh. And there's no more noble a calling."

As Angus finished and the standing ovation rang in my ears, I noticed Emerson Fox, unaccompanied, enter the room and make his way to Angus. I didn't want to miss the exchange so I moved closer to Angus. With hand extended, Fox reached Angus about the same time as I did, along with five cameras, their sun guns trained on the two combatants.

"Angus, I congratulate you on your victory tonight," he started. "You're a man of remarkable principle and high standards. It's always difficult to duel with such a candidate."

"I thank you, Mr. Fox, though I found your sword quite sharp enough," Angus said through a faint smile. "It's good of you to come, and I wish you well."

"You know, you taught me something about campaigning that I'll be considering carefully before I unsheathe my sword again," Fox confessed. "I'll leave you to your celebration, as I have another stop to make yet."

I thought it was a rather magnanimous performance from someone for whom magnanimity did not come naturally. I wondered if he were heading over to shake hands with Alden Stonehouse or propose pistols at dawn.

At 12:36 a.m., the CBC election desk declared a Liberal minority government.

Lindsay and I left Angus on his doorstep and finally fell into bed at 2:30 a.m., happy, contented, and utterly spent. We said little. Lindsay fell asleep almost right away with her head on my chest and my arms around her. I wasn't far behind.

At 2:40, after the final British Columbia ballots had been tallied, a Liberal minority government was confirmed.

Liberal:	146 seats
Progressive Conservative:	121 seats
New Democratic Party:	41 seats

Then, at 2:41, while we slept, the old Alexandra Bridge linking Ottawa and Hull groaned, shook, then gave up, and fell into the river.

DIARY
Monday, January 27
My Love,
I have few words left. Yet I am happier this night than I thought I might ever be again. It dawned on me tonight, as I spoke in grateful victory, that my call to public service may well be suspect. I cannot yet decide, but you were such a fixture in my old life, that I perhaps needed a new life to overcome my loss. So what has motivated me? Is it a desire to serve or an attempt to distract me from the heavy burden of grief I still shoulder? It is a new and intriguing question for me. Yet it is quite possible that the reason matters little. What I know is that not everything I do in the new life the voters tonight have granted me reminds me of you. That often makes my days pass more easily. Still, I remain guided in my beliefs and actions by what I think you would do. So am I just turning in circles?

Tonight, a dreamless sleep I pray. For tomorrow we begin anew.
AM

Part Two

CHAPTER TWELVE

In my nightmare, a stocky, blunt instrument of a man stands over my bed in the dark. Calm and deliberate, he stretches his hand towards me, obviously headed for my throat. I knew it was a dream, so I wasn't really that worried. The boathouse strangler then stopped short of my neck and gave my shoulder a shake. Hmmm. Vivid dream. I actually felt that. I then realized I was, in fact, not asleep. In a blink, my heart rate went from resting to "better grease the defibrillator."

"Daniel," he hissed in a whisper about as soft as a space shuttle launch. "Are you among the livin'?"

"Angus?" I gasped in the darkness. "What the hell! I was halfway to a coronary!"

I slid out of bed, mercifully in pyjamas, and led him to the living room, easing the bedroom door closed behind me. Man, could Lindsay sleep. She never even stirred.

"Why didn't you just phone me, or at least knock?" I asked when I'd turned on the lamp.

"I didn't want to disturb you," he replied, apparently seriously.

Angus, dressed to traverse the polar ice cap, wore his snowmobile suit and heavy boots. His thermal beard rendered the scarf redundant.

"But how did you get in? I locked up," I asked, still in a bit of a lather.

"Laddie, I've told you several times. There's a spare key hangin' under the porch railin'," he explained. "Have you not found it yet?"

I was about to ask him why he needed to wake me up at 5:05 in the morning, less than three hours after we'd all finally hit the horizontal, when my BlackBerry rang. I was surprised to find it clutched in my left hand. Apparently in life and death situations I instinctively reach not only, for the newspaper, but for my BlackBerry too. I held up my index finger to Angus, despite my instinct to hold up a different digit, and sent him a hold-that-thought kind of vibe while I hit the green button on my BB.

"Bradley, it's five in the morning! What gives! Somebody better have been assassinated."

"Addison, pop a Quaalude and shut the fuck up, this is important," Bradley Stanton replied.

I'd never had a call from Stanton this early so something out of the ordinary was going on. I looked up at Angus, who was pacing and starting to sweat off the pounds in his arctic garb.

"Okay, okay. I'm listening. What's going on?" I said into my BB.

"You know that bridge that connects Ottawa and Hull that nearly everybody who works in government uses every god-damned day?" he asked.

"Yeah, of course I know it. I nearly T-boned a bus on it last year. Not my fault, by the way. The Alexandra Bridge."

"Yeah, well, it's gone," Bradley said with some drama and a pause. "It collapsed into the river a few hours ago. No deaths, no injuries. It started vibrating and made some funny noises an hour or so before it fell, so the lonely people up at that hour got the hell off it in time."

"Holy shit. It just fell?" I asked. Angus nodded like a four-cappuccino bobble-head doll and cut in.

"Aye. That's what I've been tryin' to tell you. We're goin' there right now for a wee peek, so hang up and let's be off!"

I wasn't quite ready to get off the phone and held up my stop-sign hand. I was still missing something.

"Wait a second, Bradley. Why call me?" I asked. "It's not in our riding."

"Bright boy. Here's the thing. Your guy won tonight. Congratulations, by the way."

I then remembered that we'd beaten Fox, taken C-P, and won in the big national show, too. Funny how the mind works when it's trying to wake up.

"You too, Bradley. You'll soon be Chief of Staff to the Prime Minister. It has a nice ring to it."

"Whatever. So here's the thing. Angus is still big news across the country, though I wish it weren't the case. We got to find something for him to do because there's no goddamned way he's going into Cabinet or even getting a Parliamentary Secretary spot. There's no telling what might happen if someone with his overcooked moral compass made it into the Cabinet room. I shudder to think. Besides, we've got too many favours to return to even consider it."

"Wow, thanks for making us feel so welcome," I said in my eye-rolling voice. "Look Bradley, we had no expectations of getting anything this time around, so don't sweat it," I said.

"I'm not sweating it, Addison, but Angus is not just another backbencher. We need to be seen to be doing something with him. And as the big bridge went down, the perfect role came up. Angus is an engineer, right?"

"Yeah, why?"

Then it hit me, just as Bradley started to talk again. I nodded as I listened.

"Okay, here it is. I'm seeing a one-man commission to investigate the collapse of the bridge and to –"

I interrupted him, knowing exactly where he was going.

"Yep, and determine how and why it fell, then recommend measures to ensure it never happens again. Blah, blah, blah. Angus gets something contained, with a limited lifespan, but high profile in the short term. Everybody's happy and nobody gets hurt," I observed, as my brain processed the idea.

"And more importantly, the new Prime Minister is seen to be in charge and taking decisive action within hours of the collapse," Bradley reminded me. "Great optics from every angle."

"The McLintock Commission. Might work," I replied. "Let me kick it around with Angus and I'll get back to you."

"Danny boy, I'm not asking you to do this," he said with an edge. "I'm telling you. Have Angus in the Leader's office at 8:00 sharp. This one-man commission train is leaving the station so your guy better be on it. Trust me, this is the perfect solution. It's sheer genius."

Only Bradley Stanton could find a political silver lining in the collapse of a major bridge. He hung up. So I did too.

"Come on. Get yourself clothed, man, we've got a hovercraft to catch and time's a burnin'," pleaded Angus as he headed out and down the stairs to the main doors of the boathouse.

I pulled on long underwear and got dressed as fast as I could. By the time I'd left Lindsay a note and put on my fourth shirt and third pair of socks, Angus had opened the big doors. Though it was still dark, the thinnest gauze of light taunted the eastern horizon. It wouldn't be long.

"So just how did you find out about the bridge?" I asked as we worked together to position the two dollies under the hovercraft.

"The *Ottawa Citizen* website," he answered. "I'm over sixty now so I cannae sleep much past half-four."

"And why don't we just drive into Ottawa?" I inquired. "You know, in a car that has a heater and windows that roll up?"

"When we get to the scene, I've a yen to be on the more interesting side of the yellow police tape."

It took us fifteen minutes to get *Baddeck 1* down onto the ice and the dollies back into the boathouse. It should only have taken ten minutes, but I was there to help. I explained Bradley's one-man commission idea to Angus, as I squeezed the rubber bulb on the gas tank to feed the engine. It was the only remotely mechanical task Angus ever let me handle. And I'm pleased to report that I nailed it every time. Well, that's not exactly accurate. The first time, I was so eager to please that I pushed my finger right through the bulb, showering us both with gasoline. But since then, I'd been batting a thousand.

"So what do you think?" I probed.

"'Tis a sound plan, it seems, as long as we write and release our own report without any political interference from the Snake Oil Man."

That's what Angus often called Bradley Stanton. We took our places in the hovercraft cockpit and I rubbed my gloved hands together to warm my fingers.

"Well, you are in the driver's seat, and not just literally, so I figure we can negotiate our own terms."

"But I'll hear no jokes from you about Ottawa needin' to build bridges to Quebec," Angus decreed. "There's nothin' funny about a piece of our history lyin' twisted in the river."

I hadn't thought of that yet, but Angus was right. It was good to see his political instincts developing.

He hit the button and the engine screamed to life, putting an end to any further conversation. I'm sure more than a few of our neighbours were blasted out of their beds as Angus throttled up. We lifted off the ice and flew down the river in the early morning darkness.

It actually wasn't too cold in the cockpit. As Angus described it, the wind angling off the windscreen fed the thrust fan behind us and missed the driver and passenger sitting in our aerodynamic cocoon. It was a clear day and I regretted not being able to watch the sunrise behind us as we pushed west. It was ice most of the way, with just a few patches of open water that *Baddeck 1* negotiated easily, with only a bit of spray escaping from beneath the hovercraft's skirt. Other than the engine noise right behind us, it was a very pleasant ride and oh so smooth. It took about an hour, but we got there in one piece.

It made for a very strange sight. You forget how ingrained an image becomes through repetition. In the previous five years, I'd driven and walked over the Alexandra Bridge hundreds of times, from both sides of the river. The bridge had just faded into the background for me. It had become such a part of my memory's vision of the landscape that the bridge no longer stood out in my mind's eye. It simply blended in. I think my brain would have registered minor alterations in the scene, even if I might not have been able to put my finger on what precisely had changed. A new streetlight. Fresh paint on the bridge railings. A flock of birds on the ironwork. But nothing prepared me for the jarring image that emerged from the gathering morning light as we reached the scene.

Angus slowed *Baddeck 1* as we approached. I stole a glance at him and watched his mouth drop open and his eyes widen behind his goggles. Fire engines, red lights pulsing, blocked access to the bridge from either side. Police cordons kept back reporters and their cameras. From the south bank, the Ottawa side, the bridge looked completely normal for the first 150 metres or so until it reached the first of four foundation pilings, spaced unevenly across the river. The centre span then slanted sharply down into the ice and water, looking like a drawbridge that had plunged past its mark into the moat below. From the Hull side of the river, the roadway simply ended in mid-span, sprouting gnarled iron fingers.

Below, the ice was shattered, leaving chunks and floes competing for space in the black water. *Baddeck 1* was not exactly a stealthy craft. You generally knew we were coming ten minutes before we arrived and five minutes before you could even see us. We weren't about to sneak up on anyone. So we'd already aroused considerable interest by the time Angus guided us up close to the crippled span.

"It's definitely not a good idea to drive right underneath it, Angus," I shouted above the engine.

"I cannae hear you, lad," he screamed back. "I'm just going to drive underneath it to have a look."

Oh great. Good idea. I looked over at the Hull side of the river and saw about a dozen police and emergency officials scrambling down onto the shore. They were aiming a large megaphone our way and waving their arms like a rock concert audience that couldn't keep the beat. Of course I couldn't hear them, so I tried to convey in hand gestures and my own special pidgin sign language that we were there on official business and that they shouldn't worry. Judging by their reaction, it probably translated as "We're in a hovercraft and we'll go wherever the hell we damn well please. So back off."

I was still trying to read their flapping arms when they all of a sudden started pointing behind me as we inched under the bridge. I lost sight of them. I was a little nervous, okay petrified, that the bridge was still unstable and might yet break free completely, crushing us in the process. I honestly didn't think that was an unreasonable fear. So I turned back to Angus to give voice to this deeply held belief. But he wasn't there. I'm serious. He was no longer piloting *Baddeck 1*. You do strange things in such situations. I immediately looked under the dashboard where there was just barely room for our legs and confirmed that he'd not somehow squished himself underneath. There remained only one other option. Yes, ladies and gentlemen, Angus had left the hovercraft.

I looked all around, expecting to find him bobbing in the frigid black water. Then my eyes caught movement above. Two legs dangled from the iron girders under which we'd just passed. Angus was actually climbing up into the bridge's superstructure and I was actually beginning my first solo flight in *Baddeck 1*. I gaped behind me as Angus rooted around among the steel and iron, standing on a girder now, looking closely at bends and joints, and pocketing a few stray objects he'd found. By this time, I had passed beneath the bridge and emerged on the other side, still standing up in the cockpit. Angus popped his head below the girders and signalled that I should return for him. I just waved back to him in a bon voyage kind of way. I figured I'd stop when I ran out of gas. Angus beckoned more frantically and I finally snapped out of my bewilderment.

Fortunately, I'd sat next to Angus and watched him fly the hovercraft several times in the recent past, including that very morning. Unfortunately, I'd retained absolutely nothing from my close observation. But I did understand the basic operating principles of the garden-variety steering wheel. By then, I was well clear of the bridge and still puttering along about as fast as an exhausted slug. So, tapping into unknown reserves of calm and courage that are often available in moments of crisis, at least according to *Reader's Digest*, I dropped into the driver's seat, gripped the wheel, and turned. Responding to my decisive action, *Baddeck 1* cut a slow arc in the ice and swirling water. Actually, I made two complete circuits, as I forgot to release the wheel the first time around. On the third pass, at what I judged to be just the right moment, I eased off on the helm with a heart surgeon's touch to straighten my course. I set my bearing for the dangling boots of Angus McLintock. His timing was perfect as he let go of the bridge beam and dropped back into *Baddeck 1*, feet first. His aim was somewhat shy of perfect, scoring a direct hit on my dreams of future fatherhood.

We made it to shore without incident, or rather without further incident, and Angus let the hovercraft settle on the ice at the foot of Parliament Hill. I said nothing, preferring to wait for my voice to return to its normal register. The Library of Parliament rose above us as we made our way up the embankment. We ditched our winter gear in our Centre Block office, and just made it to the Leader's door by 8:00. In the outer office, a team of young political assistants was already packing boxes in anticipation of the move into the Prime Minister's Office. The PMO. Yes, the PMO.

The Prime Minister Elect (PME) leapt to his feet as we appeared in the doorway.

"Angus my man, congratulations on another upset victory," he opened. "It's wonderful news."

Angus stepped forward to shake his hand.

"I thank you, sir. And my congratulations to you. It feels a wee bit different than it did winning my first election, but this time, I'm actually pleased with the outcome."

"Well, you should be. Winning C-P again was an important part of our national triumph."

The Prime Minister Elect was dressed casually and looked tired. Bradley Stanton was in jeans and looked strung out on caffeine or something even stronger. It was a typical post-election look. He slouched in his chair and said nothing.

"And Daniel, you ran a great campaign. I knew we could count on you," effused the PME. "Defeating Flamethrower Fox is no easy feat."

I nodded and shook his hand, too.

"Thanks," I replied. "How does it feel to be the Prime Minister-in-waiting?"

"I'm not allowing myself to go there yet, we've more important things to do right now. Have a seat."

I'm pretty good at following simple instructions so I sat down with Angus next to me on the couch across from the PME and Bradley, who both sat in badly upholstered easy chairs. Time to get down to business.

"You saw the bridge on your way in, no doubt."

We nodded.

"It's been less than twenty-four hours since we won the election. I haven't yet decided on a Cabinet. We don't even know when the PM will step down and I'll be sworn in. But I want to send a signal to Canadians that there's been a changing of the guard. I want them to know that we'll act quickly and decisively when the situation demands it. Well, the collapse of a major arterial bridge, one that's supposedly maintained by the federal government, demands quick action. I've already spoken to the Prime Minister, and he's quite happy to cede responsibility for the investigation over to the government-in-waiting, where it rightly belongs. So it's our show from the start." He stopped to take a breath.

"I've also already spoken to the Deputy Minister over at Infrastructure Canada, and she's offered her resignation. Tempting though it was to accept it, we don't even know what went on out there, so I sent her back to work for the time being.

Besides, I'm not yet sworn in as PM so I couldn't accept it anyway."

Angus and I nodded.

"So here's what I'd like to do, and what I'd like to announce later this morning to the gaggle of reporters camped out on the Ottawa side of the bridge." He paused and looked directly at Angus. "You're an experienced engineer with a national profile. I want you to dig into what exactly happened, what caused the collapse, and what should be done to prevent such a thing from ever happening again. It's a miracle no one was killed. I want you, Angus, to get to the bottom of this and report back to me within thirty days." He paused again, as if trying to figure out what Angus was thinking. "You've got the credentials. Your stock is high right now. Canadians trust you. I'm asking if you will take this on?"

Angus didn't respond immediately. He nodded slightly as he held the PME's gaze. Then he leaned forward, closing the gap between them, to rest his elbows on his thighs.

"Aye, I'll do it. My engineer's instincts have been twitchin' since I heard the news, so I'd have looked into it whether you asked me to or not," said Angus. "But I have one stipulation to place on the table if our report is to be the official word on the fallen bridge."

Bradley cocked his head at this and sat up, ready to pounce.

"I see. Well, let's hear it then," said the PME.

Angus looked once at me before speaking.

"Our report will be publicly released, in its entirety, at the same time as we submit it to you," Angus declared. "In other words, I'm to report to Canadians, not just to the Prime Minister. 'Tis how it should be and how it will be if we're to undertake this."

"Out of the question!" Bradley interjected. "We need to control this situation for the good of the party and the new government. Who knows what you're going to find. No way. If it ever goes public, we'll be releasing it from this office, on our own schedule."

Bradley was still talking as Angus rose. I followed his lead and stood up, too.

"Well then, I'm sure you'll find someone else to look into it, but I'll not do it," Angus said as he turned towards the door.

"I accept the condition," said the Prime Minister Elect from his chair where he sat with his fingers steepled beneath his chin.

"I strongly advise against this. We're a minority governme . . ." Bradley started.

"Oh, put Machiavelli back in his cage, Bradley. We need to do this," interrupted the PME before he turned back to face us. "Angus, I accept. But I at least want a general sense of your findings before it hits the streets. And I'll need you to provide a big-picture briefing for Cabinet before you go public with the report, maybe even to caucus, too. This will allow us some time to plan and respond more thoughtfully when it is released."

Angus looked at me and I nodded.

"Very well," replied Angus. "Would you have a pen and piece of paper I could use?"

Bradley just fumed and glared at me as the Prime Minister Elect handed over a yellow newsprint pad and a cheap House of Commons ballpoint. Angus scrunched closer to me so I'd be able to read what he wrote. He scrawled a few sentences, signed and dated it, then turned the paper around to face the PME.

> *The Prime Minister Elect hereby directs Angus McLintock, MP for Cumberland-Prescott, to investigate the cause of the collapse of the Alexandra Bridge, and recommend related measures to protect the public and serve the national interest. Mr. McLintock's report is to be simultaneously submitted to the Prime Minister, and publicly released, by Wednesday, February 26.*

"I'd thank you, sir, to sign next to my name," Angus prodded.

"And this mandate must be included in the news release that announces the McLintock Commission," I added for good measure. Angus nodded his assent.

The PME read the lines, then signed and dated it. Bradley

stood up and left. So I wrote the PME's remarks. It brought back memories, not all of them happy.

An hour and a half later, Angus stood next to the Prime Minister Elect on Sussex Drive, with what was left of the Alexandra Bridge as their backdrop. Angus still wore his heavy boots, but one of the PME's newly arrived security officers donated his black trench coat so that Angus didn't have to appear before the nation in his snowmobile suit. Tough to be credible wearing a one-piece snowsuit.

From my vantage point standing off to the left, I counted fourteen reporters and six cameras. Bradley Stanton was still sulking in his office, but a communications staffer was there to run the show. She stepped up to the single microphone I'd helped to arrange. This wasn't to be a scrum, but a more formal announcement, with the journalists plugging into a multifeed box for the audio.

"Good morning, everyone. As you probably know by now, the Prime Minister Elect will make a short statement about the Alexandra Bridge and then will take questions along with Angus McLintock, MP for Cumberland-Prescott."

She stood aside and the man of the hour took his place at the mike.

"Good morning. I'm sorry that we've had to forego the traditional post-election sleep-in but clearly fate and this bridge had other plans for us today. Very early this morning, with little warning, the Alexandra Bridge broke apart from its moorings and fell into the river below. We do not yet know how or why the bridge failed, but we count our blessings that no one was injured. This bridge is operated and maintained under federal authority through Infrastructure Canada. So this is *our* problem now. This morning I've spoken to the Prime Minister, and although I have not yet been sworn in, nor have I assembled a Cabinet, this incident demands a swift response. The Prime Minister has ceded authority to me to initiate action." He paused and motioned for Angus to step a little closer to the limelight.

"I have directed Angus McLintock, MP for Cumberland-Prescott and a professor of engineering at the University of Ottawa, to undertake an immediate and thorough investigation into the cause of this collapse and to recommend appropriate measures to prevent future infrastructure failures. I've asked Angus to release his findings at the same time as he submits his report to me to signal a new transparency in government to which I am committed. Pending unforeseen circumstances, his investigation will be completed by February 26."

The PME then motioned with his hand to open the floor for questions.

"Angus, just what exactly happened here at 2:41 this morning?" a reporter from CBC Television asked.

"Well, we know exactly what happened at 2:41 this morning. The blessed bridge gave up the ghost and pulled away from its pilings," Angus replied. "What we don't know, and what I aim to discover, is why. The *why* is always more important than the *what*."

For most of the fifteen minutes of back and forth that ensued before the communications staffer shut it down, not a single question went to the Prime Minister Elect. Finally, a *Montreal Gazette* reporter asked him, now that he was about to become Prime Minister, what his plans were for bringing Quebec back to the constitutional table.

The PME switched back into campaign mode and delivered his response by rote.

"While it's early days, we promised in the campaign to reach out to Quebecers, to forge new partnerships, and to redress past inequities. We pledged to build new bridges from Ottawa to Quebec, and that's just what we're going to do."

I could tell by the pacing of his last phrase that he'd realized too late what he'd just said. He closed his mouth, grimaced once, and walked back to his car.

I hoped Angus realized that I hadn't written that line.

———

I spent the afternoon in the Parliamentary Library learning about the history of the Alexandra Bridge while Angus clambered about the broken span, spending as much time examining the parts that remained intact as he did the twisted wreckage. I'd also spent some time with very cooperative officials from Infrastructure Canada and I'd spoken to the two police officers who were first on the scene when the bridge started to make funny noises. I thought I'd learned a lot in a few hours.

In the fading light of the afternoon, Angus and I made the return trip to Cumberland in *Baddeck 1*. A rare east wind made the journey much colder than the morning's. My face was numb by the time we finally got the boathouse doors closed. Lindsay was teaching an evening class and would not be back from the campus until after 10:30. So I made a batch of Kraft Dinner and watched the news.

The PME's dumb bridge remark was played over and over, up and down the dial. A couple of the camera operators had the presence of mind to shift the focus from the Prime Minister Elect to the broken bridge carcass behind his left shoulder, as his metaphor fell to the ground like a lead ingot. As I suspected, there was also plenty of footage of Angus and me in *Baddeck 1* under the bridge. I was able to see just how I'd ended up by myself in the hovercraft. Angus simply reached up and hoisted himself into the steel maze while I looked the other way. It was actually quite funny, twelve hours later. I turned off the TV and headed up to see Angus.

"So what do we know?" Angus asked after wiping the chess board with me in three consecutive games. He looked quite content, as most anyone would after playing chess with me.

"Okay. The bridge was built in 1900 and is sometimes called the Interprovincial Bridge. It's about 575 metres long and made mostly of steel. Ironically, it's been designated as a National Historic Civil Engineering Site by the Canadian Society of Civil Engineers. As we already know, it's owned by the federal government through Infrastructure Canada." I paused to check my notes.

"Don't stop yet, laddie, you're doin' fine."

"Each day, some 15,000 vehicles pass over it along with 1,300 cyclists and over 2,000 pedestrians. There was a major overhaul back in 1975 and the whole thing was repainted in 1995. The Tory government hit the pause button on another major refurbishment slated to start two years ago, but not much has happened since."

"Right then, that's the history. What were you able to learn about the collapse?" he asked.

"The bridge apparently started groaning shortly after midnight, and an alert pedestrian called police. An engineer from Infrastructure Canada arrived by 12:45 to assess the situation. At 1:04, the engineer was worried enough about what he'd found to give the order to close it down. The police dutifully complied and cleared the bridge. In the next hour or so, the groaning intensified and a mild shuddering could be felt and seen by police and the onlookers gathered. A loud metallic snap sent the police sprinting off their respective ends of the bridge. Three minutes later at 2:41, the centre span of the bridge broke free at the Quebec end and plummeted into the river. Witnesses reported that it made a fearsome noise. One guy standing on the Hull shore said it sounded exactly as you might expect a mass of iron and steel girders to sound as they broke away from their mountings, twisted around themselves, and fell onto the ice. That's it. That's all I've got so far." I paused again before continuing.

"Did you discover anything, crawling through the steel maze?" I asked.

"I can tell you it was not a bomb, and it looks to me as if there was no sudden trauma that caused it. No bus rammed a support member. So I may not have learned much but I think I safely eliminated one or two possible explanations."

I was tired. It had been a long day. But Angus seemed up, alert, and talkative.

"You know, Marin once told me that an insatiable curiosity was my blessin' and my burden. Until she said that, I'd never noticed. But she was bang on the mark, she was. I don't care a fig for any political advantage we might gain by this little inquiry of ours. I just have to know why in blazes, after more than a century of service, a bridge would simply let go and fall. I have an idea, but I'm pushin' it from my mind."

"Why? What's your theory?" I asked.

"I'll not weigh you down with it just yet. We're better if we make no assumptions. I want the facts and our findin's to lead us to the promised land, not my suspicions and speculations."

Just before crawling into bed, I took a quick look at my BlackBerry. I'd switched to silent mode earlier in the afternoon and had a raft of messages waiting for me. As I suspected, Bradley Stanton had called several times, even into the evening, no doubt to deliver his finely wrought invective, insults, and threats. I chose not to listen to the three voice-mail messages he'd left me. I turned down Lindsay's side of the bed and left her light on.

DIARY

Tuesday, January 28

My Love,

Curiosity – my blessing and my burden. Your prophetic words came back to me tonight. In the careful hindsight I inflict on myself from time to time, I see the dominant role curiosity has played in shaping what passes for my life. Aye, I can see now it cuts a broad swath, curiosity does. Hiding in my shadow, it has been my constant companion, pulling my strings, taking me this way and that. I have found its faint and frail traces as I sift through the entrails of my last forty years. Now, it is with me still, as I sift through the entrails of a fallen bridge.

Why did it fail and fall? I'm on to the reason. But I'll keep my own counsel until my theory rests on more than supposition and conjecture. We saw today what happens when structures that look solid are not well supported.

The Prime Minister-in-waiting seemed relieved to have found something to keep me out of mischief, at least for a time. Less relieved was his young political operative, cynical well beyond his years, and with the apt initials B.S. In fact, the sinister glare Mr. Stanton routinely directs at Daniel and me seems laced with contempt, at times even hatred.

Muriel called tonight concerned that Daniel (not I!) is working too hard and too long for one in the throes of a budding relationship. I agree, though living together seems to make it more than a "budding relationship." He knows what he has in young Lindsay, but I'll keep a weather eye. AM

CHAPTER THIRTEEN

The next week blurred by. The Leader was sworn in as Prime Minister and set about the delicate task of assembling his Cabinet. Meanwhile, Angus and I were consumed with the investigation, taking only about half an hour off so the Clerk of the House could swear in Angus as the Member of Parliament for Cumberland-Prescott. Then it was back to the bridge.

I recorded interviews with the eighteen people who were eyewitnesses to the collapse. Well, really seventeen. One community college student, who'd spent election night in a bar in Hull with friends, wasn't that helpful. The group of them staggered out near closing time and lurched towards the bridge's pedestrian walkway. Just before they reached it, the bridge broke away and fell. Notwithstanding their blood-alcohol levels, his drunken friends provided surprisingly coherent accounts of the bridge's descent. But at the moment of truth, he'd been on his knees, head down, throwing up on the sidewalk. His most vivid memory is of the rather symmetrical splatter pattern his dinner made on the boots of his friends. I erased that part of the recording.

Despite the bitter cold, Angus spent much of his time clambering over the twisted iron with an aging blueprint always in his hands. On a couple of occasions, he had one or two engineering faculty colleagues in tow. No one could accuse him of taking the easy way out. He immersed himself in his work. Often, he'd don a safety harness and, with the help of several firefighters still on the scene, actually lower himself right over the edge of the

northern breakpoint and crawl up into the fractured steel girders. Sometimes he'd be up in there for a couple of freezing hours
at a time. I felt nearly frostbitten after a quarter hour standing
on the shore watching him. I cannot fathom how he could endure
the sub-zero temperatures for such long stretches. Welcome to
Ottawa in February.

Two days into the investigation, Angus complained that it was
hard for him to handle the sheets of interview transcripts he
needed to consult while climbing within the gigantic jungle gym
of the bridge's innards. So to free up at least one of his hands, I
transferred my eyewitness interviews onto my iPod as one large
MP3 file so he could listen while up inside the bridge. In addition
to the interviews, I recorded my own step-by-step chronology of
events that was based on the common elements in the seventeen
eyewitness descriptions. This gave Angus one clear and definitive
account of just what had gone down, when the bridge had gone
down. Angus said he listened to my recording more than any of
the others so I was glad I'd taken care not to dangle any parti-
ciples, misplace any prepositions, or use any words like "impact-
ful." I'd considered overlaying dramatic orchestral music, as if I
were narrating a documentary for the Discovery Channel's
Falling Bridges Week, but decided that was going a bit too far.

I would sometimes watch from the Hull shore as Angus
scrambled about above me in the spars and beams, listening to
my voice streaming through his ear buds. By watching his eyes
and the order in which he focused on different sections of the
ironwork, I could almost mark his progress through my moment-
by-moment audio tour of the collapse. Every once in a while,
he'd nod as if another piece had fallen into place. And every once
in a while, the wind would lift his beard up into his face, so he
could see nothing but swirling grey. It made him look momentarily like a geriatric sasquatch. But Angus never seemed too put
out and would calmly shove the unruly cascade back down into
the front of his snowmobile suit, to be constrained for at least a
moment or two. Through it all, the media camped out on either

side of the downed bridge and dutifully recorded his exploits.

Watching him, I could see that Angus was clearly focused on three important sites. He marked and numbered each with bright yellow painter's tape.

"What's with the yellow tape?" I asked when he'd finally hauled himself back onto the topside deck and I'd made my way back up the path.

"Just a jiff to catch my breath."

He wheezed. I waited. He said nothing until we'd entered the heated construction trailer that had been arranged so Angus could warm up between girder-grappling sessions.

"Based on how the bridge actually deformed during the collapse, I think I've determined the failure points in the superstructure," Angus explained. "The points marked with yellow are the stress loci. After stress locus number three failed, the bridge was doomed."

I nodded wisely.

"We don't get a lot of locusts in Ottawa, and never in the winter," I replied.

He didn't even have the grace to smile.

"Aye, you're a right laugh, you are," Angus said. "The stress loci trace the line along which a succession of failures in rivets, bolts, welds, and a few steel flanges brought the poor beast down."

"Um, just a reminder that I'm actually an English professor," I observed. "Everything I've learned about bridge construction came from a classic Bugs Bunny cartoon that climaxed with the Rube Goldberg journey of a red-hot rivet."

"Aye, it's quite clear to me, and to just about everyone else, that you're a wordsmith and not a blacksmith."

When Lindsay and I arrived at the Riverfront Seniors' Residence, peach safari-suited Jasper intercepted us and led the assembled residents in a round of applause. An anemic "Angus, Angus" chant surfaced briefly. Lindsay smiled and curtsied deeply. I just waved.

"Splendid job, you two!" he opened. "You really sent that jackass Fox packing!"

"Well thanks, Jasper, but Muriel and Angus had far more to do with it all than we did. I assume you give her a standing ovation whenever she arrives in the lounge."

Jasper looked over at Muriel by the picture window, her usual perch, to find her glaring at him. He waved his hand in dismissal.

"Awww, we get to see that cranky old bat every day. We like to see young blood in here. Next to hiding whoopee cushions in wheelchairs, welcoming visitors is the high point in my day."

"Speaking of jackasses," the piercing vocal stylings of Muriel Parkinson boomed from across the room, "why don't you let them pass and go iron your sock garters? They've come to see me."

Jasper bowed and waved us through with a "see what I mean" uttered under his breath.

Muriel had the paper opened on her lap. Lindsay leaned down to kiss her on the cheek and I followed suit, before we both settled on the couch across from her. She was a bit agitated.

"Now Daniel, you're supposed to be protecting Angus, even if it's from himself," Muriel scolded. "Why in hell's name is he swinging from a rope like some circus acrobat without a net? He's a Member of Parliament, not Karl Wallenda."

She could curse like a coal miner. She waved the *Cumberland Crier* at me. Another front-page photo of Angus. This one showed him suspended below the bridge in his safety harness, his beard bent horizontal by the wind.

"I've tried, but stopping Angus from doing something he's set his mind to do is kind of like sticking out your leg to stop a charging rhinoceros. The beast flies right by anyway, and you're left with a broken leg, if you're lucky," I explained. "I only have two legs and I need them to keep up with him."

"I must say, that was a colourful metaphor," observed Muriel.

"Simile, actually, but it was the best I could do on short notice."

"Well, do try to keep him safe. He's not a young man any

more and he'll do us all no good if he falls to his death."

"Grandma, I can testify on Daniel's behalf that he has tried," Lindsay piped up. "I was there yesterday when Daniel once again warned Angus about plummeting to the river below. True to form, Angus simply said with a smile" – at this point, Lindsay switched into a very bad Scottish accent – "'Will you stop worrying yourself, laddie, it's not the fall that hurts, it's the sudden stop at the end.'"

Muriel shook her head and looked out the window. It was overcast and the clouds seemed to crowd the sky, pushing down towards the frozen river. Chickadees dipped and darted about the feeder that hung from a tree by the shore. Upset birdseed lay scattered in the snow below.

"It's been interesting to be close to Angus in the last week," I noted. "He's like a man possessed with the task he's been given. He seems to know exactly what to do. I'm just following his daily instructions. He is Holmes and I am Watson."

"'Twas ever thus," Muriel said.

"Well, kind of you to say, but we've had our Laurel and Hardy moments too," I admitted.

"Do stay close to him, Daniel. He needs your political insight. I sense this little investigation of yours is going to yield more than the Prime Minister ever bargained for."

"That is my concern exactly," I replied.

We visited for an hour, covering off a range of topics. Lindsay reached across and held Muriel's hand for most of our stay. Our conversation was interrupted several times by residents, including several GOUT members, who stopped by to do a post-mortem on the Fox campaign. By the time we left, Muriel seemed buoyant. I made a mental note to visit her more often. When we left, Jasper appeared to be moving in on an attractive woman in a wheelchair. He pointed out something on her chair's footrest. As she leaned forward, I saw the whoopee cushion flash by, headed for the seat.

The next day was Wednesday, more than a week after the election, and the first meeting of the government caucus. As usual, I tagged along, as an adviser of my seniority on the Hill could. The government caucus room was much nicer than the rundown opposition caucus space. Despite having worked on Parliament Hill for the past five years, I'd never set foot in the spacious wood-panelled room on the second floor, just off the main Hall of Honour. At one end, an enormous fireplace with intricate iron-work gave it an old-world warmth. Large paintings depicting Canadians hard at physical work were intended to remind the caucus of whom they served. More likely the artwork triggered relief among the MPs that their jobs were not so laborious. It was set up much like the room we used in opposition – the green chairs arrayed in classroom-style with a long and quite ornate table at the front. Usually, the Whip, House Leader, Caucus Chair, Prime Minister, Senate Whip, and Deputy PM all scrunched in at the long front table. But since the newly sworn-in PM had yet to appoint any of these positions, he and Bradley sat alone up there. The Prime Minister was due to announce his cabinet and the other related appointments at the end of the day. This timing was deliberate. It would make the evening news, but leave insufficient time for newly minted ministers to be interviewed and screw up in the first hours of their appointments.

A new government's first caucus meeting was usually covered by the Parliamentary Press Gallery. But in view of the bridge situation and Angus's already sky-high popularity, Bradley Stanton had pulled the plug on the traditional day-one photo op, for fear we might again upstage the Prime Minister. Good call. At Angus's first caucus meeting after the previous fall's election, the reporters and cameras had filed into the room behind the Leader according to plan, to the frenzied applause of the Liberal MPs (all except for Angus, of course, who'd sat on his hands). Ten seconds later, all six cameras had swung from the Leader to focus on Angus, who'd just upset the popular Finance Minister in C-P. He'd obviously upset Bradley Stanton too. He was not amused and stared me down at the back of the room. If looks could kill, Bradley would still be fighting a murder rap.

Now, some three months later, Angus and I stood together in the foyer and watched the scene for a few moments. MPs arrived in clumps to a ritual display of handshakes, shoulder squeezes, and of course backslapping.

"Clearly, one's back plays an important role in politics," Angus said in a voice that I wish hadn't been quite so loud. "I daresay, if you took backslappin', back-scratchin', and backstabbin' away from politics as it's practised in this land, there'd not be much left over."

Angus left me standing at my post at the back of the room with a few other advisers and plunked himself down in the middle of the gathering pack of MPs. Soon after, the Liberal Leader, our new Prime Minister, strode into the room. He affected confidence, power, and leadership, while Angus affected boredom, impatience, and disdain. The room erupted on cue. Angus at least clapped this time but still had trouble with the standing half of the ovation equation.

The Prime Minister stood at the front facing the caucus adulation. His hands said "Okay that's enough, let's get down to business," but his face said "I can't hear you . . ." Eventually, the room settled.

"Friends, welcome to the better side of the House. Welcome to a new Liberal government. Welcome to a new era for Canada," intoned the Prime Minister.

Again with the standing O. Angus rolled his eyes in such a way as to make it clear that he didn't care whether his colleagues had seen him roll his eyes. He really had no tolerance for the orgy of self-congratulations that always, always followed election victories, regardless of political stripe.

The Prime Minister spoke well, without notes, for fifteen minutes or so, offering his analysis of the campaign and the victory. He paid tribute to his campaign team in general, and Bradley Stanton in particular, and congratulated the new and returning

MPs on winning their seats. He then lamented the defeat of several sitting Liberals MPs but didn't dwell on the negative. At one point, the PM actually declared "We have made it across the Rubicon to the promised land."

Angus winced, then turned in his seat to find me so we could both take offence at the fractured metaphor. Why not "We have buttered our bread and must now lie in it," I thought to myself.

Towards the end of his pep rally speech, the PM reached the part we'd all been awaiting.

"Friends, the collapse of the Alexandra Bridge has shaken us all. It marks the collapse of a Tory regime, but it also leaves us to pick up the pieces. We are fortunate to have returning to caucus Angus McLintock. He took down the Honourable Eric Cameron last time around, and then a week ago humbled Flamethrower Fox. But Angus is also an accomplished engineering professor. I have unleashed Angus McLintock to get to the bottom of the Alexandra Bridge collapse. He will find out just what happened early in the morning last Tuesday irregardless of the costs and consequences. Angus, may I impose on you to share a few words and bring us up to date?"

Bradley had warned us about this and Angus was ready. I knew he'd be appalled to hear the word "irregardless" fall from the new PM's mouth, but Angus held his tongue, stood, and made his way to the front as the room once again detonated into wild cheering and applause. Angus faced the raucous crowd. His hands said "Okay that's enough, let's get down to business," but his face said "Shut your bleedin' cake-holes, time's a wastin'!" Thankfully, his mouth remained closed. The room settled abruptly.

"Thank you, Prime Minister, and congratulations on the new title," Angus opened. "The Prime Minister has asked us to look into the bridge failure and to report to him by the 26th of this month *irrespective* of the costs and consequences. Our mandate is not just to discover what exactly happened last Tuesday morning, but more importantly to determine why. We're also to provide recommendations to ensure that such a calamity does not befall us again. Our investigation proceeds apace. It would be premature to speak of our findings to date. We have ruled out many theories, but one working hypothesis remains intact. I'll not discuss it now, but if it still holds when our analysis is complete, history may well consider the fall of the Alexandra Bridge not to be an isolated aberration, but rather a canary in Canada's coal mine. I thank you."

With that, Angus returned to his seat.

"But you're just focused on the bridge, right?" asked Bradley Stanton from his seat next to the Prime Minister.

"Of course we're focused on the bridge. Determining the cause of the collapse and preventing future failures would hardly be possible otherwise," replied Angus with an impatient edge to his voice. "That's what we've been asked to do, but we'll not paper over deeper implications should we find them in play. We're to be thorough and transparent, and that we intend to be."

"We understand all that, Angus," cut in the PM. "But we're not looking for a Royal Commission here, just an explanation for why the bridge fell."

"Fear not, Prime Minister, you'll soon have your explanation."

The PM and Stanton didn't look as if they'd completely bought into the "fear not" part.

That afternoon, Angus and I attended our much-anticipated meeting with the Deputy Minister for Infrastructure Canada, the department responsible for maintaining the Alexandra Bridge. It had taken some time to arrange the meeting because the outgoing government seemed to be stalling. It was only after our new Prime Minister was officially sworn in that the log jam was broken. After the ceremony at Rideau Hall, one call from Bradley Stanton on the PM's behalf gave us the access to the senior departmental officials that we needed.

Infrastructure Canada was housed in the Place du Portage complex of office buildings, ironically just a short distance from the fallen bridge. Angus and I were ushered in to the Deputy

Minister's office at 1:00 p.m. Rosemary Holden was a respected career bureaucrat, known for her intellect and integrity, who'd been DM at IC for nearly eight years. We shook hands. Despite a lumberjack's grip, she wore no plaid, but went with the standard-issue dark blue suit complemented by quite funky glasses. She'd come around her desk to greet us and seat us at a round table by the window.

"Mr. McLintock, it's a pleasure to meet you, and you as well, Mr. Addison."

"I'm pleased to make your acquaintance, Ms Holden, or should I call you Deputy?" Angus wondered aloud. "For the life of me, I can't get used to the honorifics attached to everything, so I insist you just call me Angus."

"Rosemary will do nicely for me," she replied. "I regret that it's taken us a while to convene this important first meeting. The delay was beyond my control."

"Aye, the long arm of partisan politics again, I hear. I think an amputation is in order," Angus suggested. "But no matter, we've been busy in the interim."

"You surely have. I have watched your work on the bridge from my desk, when I've lifted my head from the preparations for this meeting," she noted, and pointed out the window to the bridge a few hundred metres away.

Angus seemed quite at ease so I just kept my yap shut.

"Rosemary, let me place a theory before you and get your reaction," Angus proposed. "We've not the proof yet, but logic and mounting circumstantial evidence have us very much leaning this way."

Angus spoke as if I was totally in the loop and I reinforced this by nodding sagely. In reality, I had no idea what his theory was.

"Lead on, Mr. McLintock."

"Please, Angus, if you will. Only magistrates have called me Mr. McLintock before setting bail, and that was many years ago."

She smiled and nodded.

"I'll try, Angus. I actually live in your riding and so have heard all about your past brushes with the law. Let's just say I wasn't nearly as concerned about them as your opponents seemed to be."

It was Angus's turn to smile and nod. Then back to business.

"Based on what we've learned from close examination of the wreckage, and a quick review of the public accounts, in particular Infrastructure Canada's expenditures over the last ten years or so, we posit that the Alexandra Bridge would be safe and secure today had its rigorous maintenance schedule been assiduously followed."

"You are absolutely correct, sir. Wherever the nail is, you've just hit it squarely on the head."

"And I suspect that over the past decade or so, regular maintenance of federal roads, bridges, ports, and whatever else we manage has been sacrificed on the altar of deficit reduction, making the Alexandra Bridge just the first significant failure of a sadly neglected national infrastructure," Angus continued.

I now understood the coal mine canary reference Angus had made at caucus.

"Not quite, sir," she answered. "The steady reduction in infrastructure spending actually began twenty years ago, but you've got the rest of the story right."

I did the math on instinct.

"So this legacy of underfunding can be traced back to the last Liberal government, not just to the Tories," I calculated. "How inconvenient."

"What does it matter? This is not a partisan exercise. Are we not looking for the truth of all of this?" asked Angus.

I exchanged knowing looks with Rosemary Holden.

"Angus, I regret to say that the centre will very much want to make this a partisan exercise, regardless of our lofty ideals," I warned. "And Bradley Stanton will not be pleased to learn that it actually started on our watch, twenty years ago."

"Aye, 'tis surely the case. But we'll be telling the complete story before the spinning can start. Therein lies our only hope."

"So tell me more about this theory of yours," the DM asked.

"Well, 'tis nothing too advanced," started Angus. "It seems to me that we haven't at all eliminated our annual budget deficit, despite the nation's black balance sheet. Rather, all we have succeeded in doing is to transform our deficit from a monetary shortfall into a crumbling infrastructure. We may not strictly have a financial deficit, but it's increasingly clear that we have a roads deficit, a bridges deficit, an all-encompassing infrastructure deficit, that will cost us dearly in the coming years. In fact, I reckon it will cost the national purse much more than it would have had we simply followed the maintenance schedules as they'd been laid out."

Rosemary nodded.

"Dinnae misunderstand me," he continued. "I do not abide spending money we don't have. But saving a few billion dollars in one year by delaying investment in infrastructure maintenance is illusory. It will surely cost us much more dearly years later to rebuild those roads and bridges that are near ruined through neglect."

"Yes sir, the economics are inescapable. Short-term gain for long-term pain," she agreed. "Eight years ago when I started here, I was arguing for higher infrastructure spending. In the last three years, I've been warning of the kind of disaster we had last week," she noted, pointing to the bridge. "I very nearly resigned last year over it but ultimately decided I'd stick it out for one more election and see what might transpire."

We talked for an hour and a half, learning more than we'd ever expected to know about the state of our nation's infrastructure. She'd prepared detailed packages chronicling the whole sorry story, including several plaintive confidential memos to a decade of different ministers warning of the costs of infrastructure decay. Rosemary's staff had already developed a detailed briefing note on the Alexandra Bridge, including the maintenance schedule. Before the spending cuts began under the Liberals two decades ago, minor inspections of the bridge took place on a monthly basis. Major inspections were undertaken every six months, and comprehensive maintenance work was done on a quarterly schedule whether it showed signs of needing it or not. When the deficit became a national obsession, corners were cut. Well, more like entire blocks were cut. Now, twenty years on, minor inspections were done quarterly, major inspections every two years, and comprehensive maintenance yearly and only when prompted by visible evidence. This decline in infrastructure spending precisely paralleled the government's very successful deficit-reduction program.

"So our hypothesis is essentially correct," Angus commented. "The deficit was eliminated on the back of a sadly neglected and decaying infrastructure."

"Absolutely and undeniably," she confirmed.

"I thank you for these documents. We'll examine them closely," Angus said. "May I ask you one final question before we take our leave?"

"Of course."

"Who was the Deputy Minister here when all of this started two decades ago?"

"A civil service legend, Harold Silverberg," Rosemary reported. "He's long since retired but still lives in Ottawa."

I spent the rest of the afternoon comparing the increasingly lax maintenance programs with the steady decline in Infrastructure Canada expenditures across one Liberal and four Tory governments. No fewer than nine different finance ministers had wielded the knife. They may have aimed to trim fat but had cut much deeper, eventually right through to the steel of the Alexandra Bridge. It made for a troubling tale that should have been written years earlier. It had been hiding in plain sight until the day the bridge came tumbling down.

Lindsay, Angus, and I watched the eleven o'clock news that night in his living room. A crescent moon hung high in the sky. As expected, the lead story was the unveiling of the new Cabinet. The PM looked good in the clip. There were no shocks in the lineup, but there were a couple of minor surprises. The Prime Minister had decided to keep Infrastructure Canada for himself, signalling that the Alexandra Bridge file was important to him. I thought that was good news for us. But the bad news wasn't far behind.

A Montreal area banker and sophomore MP, Emile Coulombe, was named Finance Minister. Now that was somewhat unexpected – and not in a good way. I'd watched him for the previous few years and still hadn't divined why he even considered himself a Liberal. Fiscally, he was about as progressive as Milton Friedman. Politically, he reminded me of General Franco after he'd passed through his kinder, gentler phase. The joke around Ottawa was that Coulombe was so right wing, he'd been known to drive the long way home around the block just to avoid ever having to turn left.

"Well, the PM must feel he owes Quebec big time to give Coulombe Finance," Lindsay observed.

"All this repaying of supposed favours is a damnable way to run a country," snapped Angus. "Is merit such an outdated concept?"

"Angus, merit is a very important driver in many fields of endeavour. Unfortunately, politics isn't one of them and never has been. Paying off political debts with plum appointments is as old as democracy itself. How do you think Brutus landed the gig that got him close enough to Caesar to run him through?" I replied.

"Well, from what I've read about Coulombe, he's a more ardent proponent of tax cuts than any of the previous four Tory finance ministers," Angus continued. "That's all we need when we're trying restore infrastructure spending. What's he like as a person?"

"He's tough, partisan, and as ambitious as they come. And he has the sense of humour of a cadaver, but without as much warmth."

"So what's next, now that the Cabinet is set?" Lindsay asked.

"The PM should announce dates for the Throne Speech and Budget in the next day or so," I explained.

"Which doesnae leave us much time to pull Mr. Coulombe's head from his hindquarters so he can earmark some money in the Budget for infrastructure renewal," added Angus.

"Yep. And I'm sure Emile Coulombe will be only too thrilled to meet with us. I figure I may have to call in air cover from the PMO to make it happen."

DIARY

Wednesday, February 5

My Love,

I made another grave error today when I could no longer stare at the bloody bridge's maintenance schedules. I typed your name into the almighty Google. I've done that before without dire consequence. But this time, on a foolhardy whim, I clicked "Images" and released a tsunami of heartache and longing. I was thunderstruck at the number of photographs of you that lurk in cyberspace waiting to strike me down. There was even a snap of you beside a rather handsome and strapping lad, taken years before I arrived in Canada and met you. I know not who he is or what he was to you. Since I've always judged that my life really began when I met you, I was struck by the notion that you may have had a life before me.

No more work for me tonight. Google has ruined it for a time, at least until tomorrow. Perish the thought that I might one day pump your name into YouTube, or whatever they call it.

AM

CHAPTER FOURTEEN

The next morning, the PM announced the Throne Speech for Monday, February 24 with the Budget to come three days later on Thursday the 27th. He had the foresight to note that given the very tight timelines, there would be no glossy printed versions of either document, just simple and clean word-processed printouts. This would allow us to make changes right up to the last minute, flexibility that the new government wanted and needed. I liked this approach. I was not a fan of the trend in recent years towards producing something so glossy and over-designed that it was more like a coffee-table book than a federal Budget. It seemed as much time and money were spent designing and laying out the document as were committed to creating the content. This routinely led to ridiculous exchanges in the corridors of power like "I have no idea what the Canadian Pension Plan claw-back provisions for the wealthy are all about, but did you see that amazing cover? It was stunning!"

Angus and I had been sequestered in our Centre Block office finalizing the outline for what had come to be known as the McLintock Report, when news of the Throne Speech and Budget dates broke.

"That's in just over a fortnight," Angus noted. "And the Throne Speech will be read even before we're to submit our findings on the 26th. We can't expect our report to influence the blasted Budget if the Finance Minister only sees our report the day before."

"Realistically, the Budget will be put to bed at least two or three days before it's read in the House on the 27th," I replied. "So we have even less time to influence the Throne Speech and Budget. We have to move now."

"We need a meetin' with Emile Whoozits right now, today," said Angus. "We've got to get our infrastructure oar churning in his waters before he types up his Budget. I say we wander over there right now and camp out in his office till he agrees to meet with us."

"You've never met Emile Coulombe, have you? He's prickly enough already, so ambushing him in his own office won't help our cause," I counselled. "Let's at least start by trying to set something up with his office for today in the more conventional way."

I reached for the phone.

"Jean-Guy Duguay, *s'il vous plaît*," I said in my best high school French accent, and waited.

"Jean-Guy Duguay," said a voice after a moment.

"*C'est* Daniel Addison," I opened. "Congratulations, J-G."

"Tank you, Daniel," he replied. "What is it that you need? We are in the soup over here."

I assumed that being "in the soup" meant that they were busy, but I chose not to seek confirmation.

"I figured your guy would be up to his eyeballs giving interviews and buying a new pair of shoes to wear when he reads his Budget."

No reaction beyond heavy breathing so I just continued.

"You know I'm with Angus McLintock and that we're doing this bridge investigation thing. Well, we desperately need half an hour of your minister's time, preferably today. It's related to his upcoming Budget."

"Daniel, Emile hasn't even met his Deputy Minister yet and he's with the PM right now to talk about the Trone Speech and Budget. We've got no time to meet with backbenchers. I'm sorry," Jean-Guy replied.

"No problem. Another time. Gotta go, Jean-Guy. Nice talking to you," I said as I hung up.

"Angus, let's go," I urged even before the phone was back in its cradle. "Coulombe is at the PMO right now. So we're back to your ambush strategy."

We headed out the door.

"If Coulombe gets his way, his first Budget won't take long to write," I said as we headed for the PM's Centre Block office at a pace just shy of a jog. "With his near-libertarian outlook, he'll want to cut taxes and cut spending."

"Aye, that's what I fear," Angus replied. "Emile Coulombe, eh. I wonder if he's related to Charles-Augustin de Coulomb?"

"Friend of yours?"

"Ah, no. I'd like to have spoken to him, but he died in 1806. He defined the electrostatic force of attraction and repulsion, in the 1770s."

"Gee Angus, I can't understand why I haven't heard of him."

"You know, sarcasm really doesnae become you," he observed. "Anyway, politics is all about attraction and repulsion."

We burst into the PM's office and nearly collided with Bradley Stanton.

"Whoa, Danny boy. Where's the fire?"

"Hey, Bradley. Well, the fire we're looking for is probably crackling away in the PM's office right now," I replied. "Have you got Coulombe in there?"

"Yep. I just came out. He's just wrapping up with the PM. Why?"

"Bradley, we need ten minutes with the PM and Coulombe. It's not just urgent, it's important," I implored.

"Aye, young Mr. Stanton," Angus added. "If they're yammerin' about the Throne Speech and the Budget, we need in on that chinwag. It's about the wee bridge trouble."

Bradley looked at us for a moment as if trying to decide whether to take the red pill or the blue one. Eventually, he slapped on a look of resignation.

"You'd better not make me regret this, 'cause if this comes back to bite my ass, I'm coming after yours," he intoned with his index finger on my sternum.

He turned to the ornate wooden door, knocked softly, and went in, closing it behind him. Angus and I looked at each other. I quickly brushed sawdust off his shoulder and pointed to what I thought might be just a piece of whitish fluff in the lower left quadrant of his beard. Angus wrestled with it for a moment before wrenching it free.

"I wondered where that had gone," Angus said as he wrapped it in a piece of scrap paper from his pocket and tossed it in a wastepaper basket. "'Twas just yesterday's gum."

"You know, as far as I can tell, most people toss their gum in the garbage after chewing it," I chided. "I hope your new beard-based storage technique doesn't catch on."

"You're just a perpetual laughter machine, you are," he replied as Bradley cracked the door open again and waved us in. "Remind me to give you a good thrashing on the board tonight," Angus whispered as we entered the PM's office.

I heard Angus inhale sharply as we both marvelled at the beautiful wood-panelled office. If Chief Engineer Scott in the Transporter Room beamed you there without your knowledge, you might well guess you'd arrived in the Prime Minister's office. It just looked like it was designed with a head of state in mind. Wood and windows dominated the room. There was a fireplace, but no fire. The desk was really more of a large wooden table with an ornately carved base. There were hardwood floors underfoot. I wondered whether the PM met with the lumber lobby in that office. It would make sense. Building the PM's office alone would have kept the nation's loggers in plaid flannel shirts for months.

"I know. It's stunning, isn't it?" said a smiling PM. "Gentlemen, welcome. Angus, let me introduce the Honourable Emile Coulombe. Daniel, you already know the Finance Minister, I trust."

I nodded as Angus stepped forward and extended his hand to the newly minted minister. Coulombe didn't even stand up and looked as if he were fighting the act of offering his hand in return. His short and shiny brown hair was plastered flat to his head, making it look painted on. Although he wore round gold-rimmed glasses from the John Denver collection, there was certainly no "Sunshine on My Shoulder" happening, let alone "Rocky Mountain High." Instead, he looked like he'd rather Angus and I were "Leaving on a Jet Plane." He looked peeved and well on the way to pissed.

"Prime Minister, we have only a short time together. Is this interruption necessary?" Coulombe asked with only a slight French-Canadian accent.

"Emile, we're all on the same team here," soothed the PM. "Angus is undertaking a very important task on behalf of the government, and there may well be implications for the Throne Speech and Budget."

"I doubt it, Prime Minister. The formulation of the Budget is already well underway, as we have previously discussed," Coulombe replied, shaking his head.

"I'm heartened you have such an open mind about our work," Angus said through a forced smile. "Will you be good enough to hear me out?"

Coulombe looked past Angus and waved his hand in surrender.

"Please proceed, Angus. What have you to report?" asked the PM.

"I'll be brief, Prime Minister," Angus started. "When we submit our report on or before the 26th, it will present in considerable detail four simple and inescapable conclusions. First, the Alexandra Bridge collapsed because Infrastructure Canada did not and could not honour the recommended inspection and maintenance schedule. Second, we have evidence that virtually all of our national infrastructure has been similarly neglected. Third, two decades of underfunding in the name of deficit reduction have left our roads, bridges, and ports cracked and crumbling from coast to coast to coast. And finally, only steady and systematic investment in our national infra-structure over the next decade will ensure that the collapse of the Alexandra Bridge was a solitary calamity and not the first in a series of dangerous failures. I cannae make it any clearer than that."

"You're not telling us that we started all of this twenty years ago when a Liberal last occupied this office?" Bradley Stanton was leaning forward intently.

"Aye, that's exactly what we're saying," replied Angus. "Sorry about that."

"Well, we'll just see when we decide to start the clock on all of this. I have a feeling all of this started about sixteen years ago."

"I don't think so, laddie, the evidence is incontrovertible."

"So what does it all mean, Angus?" the PM asked. "What do you need?"

"Well, I'm new to all of this, but in discussion with Daniel here, it seems to us that we need a commitment to rebuild Canada's infrastructure in the Throne Speech and then enough funding in the Budget to honour the promise credibly and legiti-mately," Angus proposed.

"And don't forget the significant economic stimulus that a major public infrastructure investment will yield," I added.

The PM and even Bradley seemed to be listening. The Finance Minister clearly was not.

"*Impossible!*" Coulombe said in French before switching. "It simply cannot happen. What little money we have is spoken for already. We will be spurring the economy through tax relief to businesses and individuals. We will not be spending precious tax dollars on bridges and ports that already exist. There is no short-term political benefit in tightening a few bolts and repainting bridges that are decades old. May I remind you that we are a minority government? We simply cannot afford to waste our resources on something as boring as concrete and steel. Now if you'll excuse me, Prime Minister, I have another Budget brief-ing to attend."

With that, Canada's Finance Minister rose without even acknowledging our presence and left the room.

"Warm and friendly lad, he is," said Angus after the door closed.

"He is somewhat set in his ways and rather driven by ideology," the PM observed.

"Aye, but I'd have thought it might at least be a more liberal ideology driving him," Angus concluded.

"I'll see about adding something to the speech," the PM said. "Perhaps Daniel might craft something and send it to Bradley. I don't know how precise we can be, but we must say something about the damn bridge."

"But a sentence or two in the Speech from the Throne will hardly restore our infrastructure," Angus pushed. "The Budget speech is the place we really need to be."

"Well, Angus, the Finance Minister isn't exactly favourably disposed to the idea at this point in time."

Uh-oh. I winced and tried to stop Angus by bugging out my eyes in his direction and elevating my eyebrows to the middle of my forehead. Angus didn't seem to notice.

"It's either 'at this point' or 'at this time' but seldom both," Angus replied, unable to stop himself. "But more to the crux of the matter, is not Mr. Coulombe beholden to you for his position? Does he not serve at your pleasure?"

The PM was still processing the grammar lesson but eventually caught up, and to his credit, didn't even seem offended.

"Uhm, thanks for the tip. As for Monsieur Coulombe, one doesn't appoint a minister and then hobble him with too tight a leash before seeing what he produces," countered the PM.

"Right, the tight-leash approach didn't work so well for the last Finance Minister," I offered, forgetting for a moment or two that I was speaking to the Prime Minister of Canada. Angus turned again to the PM.

"With or without a Throne Speech reference, our report will be as impotent as a castrato in tights if the Budget is silent on the infrastructure investment. Can you not step in and dictate terms to him?"

"Angus, the power to do just that comes with the office. But knowing how and when to wield it comes only with time," replied the PM, with uncharacteristic wisdom, I thought. "I will see drafts of the Budget and will certainly have my say, but we can't simply commit billions of dollars because you've informally joined us at a meeting and said we need more money for bridges and roads. Get me the report."

Angus nodded and stood. I rose too.

"You'll have your report, and before the deadline."

Angus was three strides in front of me most of the way back to our office. I drew even with him for the long walk down the main corridor.

"Our researching must end soon. We must get to the writing," Angus said, still in full flight. "Our report will be meaningless if we don't get it finished and in the Prime Minister's hands before the Budget is set in stone. Even then, in the variable light of his mercurial judgment, who bloody knows whether he'll act on it?"

"He's not a complete idiot, Angus." I tried to defend my former employer. "And he is the Prime Minister. I think he'll listen to our report, but I also believe we must give him some added incentive by complementing your voice with a few others from the outside world."

Angus stopped in the middle of the corridor and turned to me.

"Lad, we've got precious little time. Do you think we can really muster the groundswell we need and get the report written, as well?"

"Angus, we don't have a choice. You can't be the only public advocate on this. We need support from beyond the Hill, or we're sunk."

"Aye. Well, do it in haste. We'll soon need your pen to share in the writing, and the clock is not waiting on us," replied Angus, as he started down the hallway again.

"Give me a few hours for my spadework, and I'll be back at

the keyboard again. We'll get it done."

We dashed the rest of the way back to our office in silence. I was planning my campaign.

"I'm on it!" I shouted to Angus, as I shut my door and stuck the phone in my ear. First, a receptionist put me through to Norman Sanderson. We did the small-talk thing and I thanked him once more for his stellar fundraising job during the campaign. We were one of only a few debtless campaigns – a miracle for a Liberal candidate in C-P. The conversation soon exhausted our common ground, so I moved in for the pitch.

"Norman, let me ask you something, and I'm serious about it," I started. "Just how important to Sanderson Technologies is the state of Canada's infrastructure – you know, our highways, bridges, ports, etc.?"

Norman paused. I could hear him breathing, his gears grinding.

"Well, in this competitive market, product delivery time is almost as important as product quality and price," he began. "If computer manufacturers can buy a slightly inferior but perfectly workable alternative to our component, but can get it faster with uninterrupted and perfectly timed deliveries, they would probably choose it. So getting our product to market quickly and reliably is critical."

"Okay, I'm with you so far. Keep talking."

"We've nailed our manufacturing process in the last month. We think it's as efficient as it's going to get. So the issue now is not how fast can we produce our wireless wave router, but rather how fast can we deliver it to our buyers. So when you think about it, if our infrastructure is superior, it gives us a competitive advantage."

"Right. And if the wrong bridge collapses, or a port shuts down for major repairs, your product may be late arriving, abrogating contractual delivery obligations, leading over time to the loss of contracts, plummeting sales, laid-off workers, shut-down plants, personal poverty and penury, all-round societal chaos, and the decline of Western civilization as we know it," I concluded.

"Well, that might overstate the consequences somewhat. But you're on the right track," Norman conceded. "Our product is trucked all the way to Halifax for shipping even though we could ship through Montreal. But trucks travel faster than ships so it makes it worthwhile for us to drive the product all the way to the Atlantic coast. If any of the major highways shut down for some reason, or worse, the port of Halifax, we'd be scuppered."

That's what I needed to hear. I made the "ask" and he readily agreed. We spoke for a while longer, shaping the kinds of messages that would be most helpful while still being truthful, then ended the call.

With the phone still crimped between my shoulder and jaw, I navigated the U of O website, then dialled again.

"Bob Philpot."

"Professor Philpot, this is Daniel Addison, I'm Angus McLintock's executive assistant."

"I know the name well. Angus spoke very highly of you when he popped in for a visit a while back."

"That's great. I remember Angus found his meeting with you to be very enlightening. Your view on the importance of our national infrastructure really hit home with Angus."

"I'm glad I was persuasive. Angus is not easily convinced and doesn't hesitate to report when he's not, often loudly."

"No need to explain. I've been to that party many times. Let me tell you why I'm calling."

I laid out my case, knowing that he was already well inside our camp. He readily agreed. I offered to write something for him but he declined, saying that if it were to have his name on it, he would write it. I then broached the deadline discussion. Still he agreed, though he knew that the timing was tight.

"For Angus, I'll make this happen," he noted as our call wound down. "It certainly helps that I believe in the cause he's pushing."

The next calls I made were to the Association of Canadian

Port Authorities, the Canadian Road Builders Federation, and the Canadian Trucking Alliance. These conversations took a while. I really had no contacts there, so with all three organizations, I started with the research staff, then moved to the communications staff, and ended up pitching the executive directors and/or CEOs. Understandably, they were all headed down the same path. The bridge collapse had left them shaken and troubled. I just helped them see it as a public policy concern and an advocacy opportunity. After I told them confidentially where the McLintock Report was headed, they were keen to help, as I figured they would be. I put them on to one another to coordinate the timing, and then I moved to the last piece in the puzzle.

Having media contacts is not always, or even often, enough. I'd managed to cultivate a few friendships with journalists and producers in my years in the Leader's office and I was glad I had. Even when I had to say no to them, I made it my mission to preserve the relationship. I also helped them out on stories whenever I could and passed along information that we usually wanted to get out anyway. I tried not to play favourites, and I like to think that engendered respect for me among the scribes. Alternatively, they may simply have been pulling my own strings for their own ends. Come to think of it, I did recall a few instances when I tripped, or was tripped, in the syncopated mambo that played out daily between reporters and politicos. Nevertheless, I dusted off my dancing shoes.

I made two more calls. One to the Ottawa producer of CTV's *Canada AM*, and one to the op-ed editor of the *Ottawa Citizen*. By mid-afternoon, the stratagem was in play. I wasn't fully in control of the timing, but was reasonably comfortable that we'd hit the right window. I figured we had a week.

If Bradley Stanton knew that I'd been freelancing without the centre's approval, I'd be in for any number of horrible fates at his hand. Quietly taking my leave was not one of the options he was likely to offer. It could be anything from live human taxidermy to the old naked spread-eagle, fire ants, and honey routine. Both were effective. If I were really lucky, I might get my own tiny ice floe and a bag lunch. I weighed the odds and decided it was worth it. I didn't tell Angus much, though. It was better that way. Preserving deniability for your boss was a time-honoured political tradition.

That night, I was to meet Angus at a swanky Ottawa restaurant to map out the report. I'd thought it a strange location and not exactly consistent with the Angus I knew. I saw her long before the maître d' and I arrived at the table for two.

Lindsay looked up, surprised.

"What are you doing here?" she asked as I leaned down to kiss her.

"I'm meeting Angus here to work on the bridge report," I replied, delighted to see her. "You?"

"I'm supposed to meet Muriel here for dinner. She had to come into Ottawa today," said Lindsay.

The maître d' hovering nearby seemed to be enjoying our exchange. He was smiling and finally piped up.

"I'm afraid neither Monsieur McLintock nor Madame Parkinson will be able to make it this evening. They have suggested that the two of you enjoy dinner together instead." He swept away back to his post at the front.

The penny dropped as we looked at one another.

"Well, I already knew that Muriel was capable of political sub-terfuge, but it seems she's been teaching Angus the ropes as well," I said as I sat down across from her.

"I've got to hand it to them, I was completely drawn in," Lindsay said. "How sweet of them to cook this up."

I'd been so consumed on the bridge file that Lindsay and I had seen very little of one another of late. We still shared an apartment, but we were seldom both there and conscious at the same time. It was a gift to be sitting across from her, so unex-pectedly. Lindsay has that rare ability to empty my mind of everything but her. Despite our looming deadlines and the pressures of always running against the political grain, dinner with Lindsay was exactly what I, what we, needed. I barely remember the food, though I expect it was amazing. Time flew by as we talked and held hands. We closed the restaurant. When I pulled out my Visa card to signal we were ready for the bill, the maître d' hustled over with our coats. He just shook his head and smiled.

"Your dinner has been taken care of already."

We awoke the next morning feeling happy, renewed, and blessed.

Over the next week and a half, Angus and I wrote and rewrote the report so that every word rested on solid cornerstones of research and reason. There might also have been just a smidgen of what some would call fear-mongering in it, though we both felt it justified. We considered the consequences of inaction to be a relevant, even powerful, consideration. Raising the spectre of more falling bridges and the occasional collapsing highway overpass served to focus the mind. We did not predict whole cities disintegrating around us in one deafening whoosh, but painted what we believed to be a plausible picture of steady national decay.

We struck three major chords in the report. First, what caused the bridge to fall? Second, what were the broader national implications of the collapse? And third, what must we do to prevent such a thing from ever happening again? We thought it was a simple and straightforward way to organize our findings and recommendations.

Rosemary Holden and her staff at Infrastructure Canada were indispensable, tireless, and timely in providing data, information, evidence, advice, and a balanced perspective as our report took shape. They were professional and thorough, and respectfully pointed out when we'd fallen down the rabbit hole and helped to haul us back out. They also laid out the policy options open to us and the evidence, support, and likely fallout for each. The officials were energized. Rosemary let her Deputy Minister's guard down long enough to tell me late one night that her entire senior team had been heartsick and enraged when the bridge fell. It confirmed what they'd been warning the government about for years. They were hopeful, but not yet confident, the new government would listen.

To save time, Angus and I each took sections to write, and then I would edit to make it appear the report had one author, not two. The editing wasn't as onerous as it sounds. Angus and I had eerily similar writing styles, though his vocabulary was broader and his sentence construction more varied. He was simply more eloquent than I, and it showed in his writing. As Angus said more than once in our sprint, the goal was to write so that even the Prime Minister would not just understand it, but be persuaded, moved, compelled, and convinced by it. It was a "hearts and minds" affair, written for the average Canadian, the person to whom Angus felt we were responsible. So it was not the dry, academic, mind-numbing treatise so common to government reports. If I do say so myself, it was a call to action, a dramatic story well told, with accessible conclusions and recommendations steeped in substance and research. We were almost there.

The timing worked out well. All three of the industry associations I'd quietly approached issued news releases on Friday, February 14, the day I'd suggested. The confluence of three major sectors calling for a significant investment in Canada's infrastructure resulted in considerable media coverage over the weekend, and not just in the major dailies. The head of the Canadian Trucking Alliance also appeared on Newsworld's flagship parliamentary program and the CEO of the road builders group did CBC Radio's *Cross Country Checkup* Sunday afternoon. Nice.

On Monday morning, after I spent two hours Sunday afternoon prepping him, Norman Sanderson appeared on *Canada AM*, the biggest morning talk show in the country. He skillfully used his own company as a microcosm of the Canadian economy. He mentioned the word "infrastructure" twelve times in his seven-minute interview. Best of all, they ran a clip of the interview in the show's frequent newscasts and also referenced the three industry associations' call for more money in the Budget for roads, bridges, and ports.

The pièce de résistance? Bob Philpot's 1,200-word op-ed piece ran in the *Ottawa Citizen* on Tuesday, bringing academe's depth and objectivity to the debate. I loved the headline.

CANADA'S ECONOMIC PROSPECTS FELL WITH THE BRIDGE

I hadn't really expected all of my overtures to have yielded such results. I had cast my net wide, believing that only one or two of my external support ideas would work out. I didn't know why I'd batted a thousand on them but Angus was certainly pleased. When I saw how chuffed he was at all the coverage, I revealed my hand and explained that there had been some orchestration behind the timely stories.

"You are a wonder" was all he said.

This was unfolding far too well.

I met with Bradley Stanton that evening. Our report was not quite there yet but the major sections were done. With no prospect of convincing Emile Coulombe of our position, we needed the Prime Minister to flex his muscles on the Budget. I brought an incomplete draft of the report for Bradley and the PM in the hopes it would prompt a call to Coulombe. We met in a dim bar on Bank Street not far from the Hill. It was not a popular spot for political types and that's why we'd chosen it. Bradley was already there in a booth at the back, thumbing madly on his BlackBerry.

"Danny boy."

"Bradley. How's life at the top?" I asked, genuinely interested.

"I gotta say, it's even better than I expected. You can actually feel the power of the office. I knew it was there. I didn't know it was so palpable – that it would vibrate right inside you."

I'd never heard Bradley use a word like "palpable." But then he was back to the old Bradley.

"It is too fucking awesome for words," he blurted, shaking his head and dropping his BB to the table. I paused for a moment, then slid over the stapled draft.

"It's not yet done, but the important part of our report is complete. It is not for anyone else's eyes but yours and the PM's. You wouldn't believe the gymnastics I had to perform to convince Angus to let you have this draft. But if we're going to have any say in the Budget, the PM needs to engage now on this."

"Bottom-line it for me," Bradley directed, leaving the stapled paper on the table between us.

"Twenty billion in infrastructure investment over the next ten years, front-loaded. So eight billion in the next two years, then twelve billion in the following eight years. That's the bottom line," I reported. "If we wait two more years and do nothing, like Coulombe is proposing, it'll cost us upwards of thirty-five billion over the following eight years, and who knows how many catastrophic failures. The choice seems clear to us."

"Fortunately, you don't get to make the choice," Bradley replied through gritted teeth. He looked mad. "Are you and mountain man dipping into the magic shrooms? You're not serious about twenty billion over ten, and eight over the first two. You can't be. Even you're not that twisted."

"Bradley, the bridge fell all by itself. No one blew it up. No one crashed into a major support column. There was no earthquake. It just fell because we didn't inspect it and fix it. That scenario is going to play out across the country and cripple our economy. You . . . we don't want that, do we?"

"So we toss around a couple billion, plug a few holes, change a few bolts, slap on some paint, and we're good for a few more years and can spend our dough on stuff that's going to keep us in power. Twenty billion over ten is a non-starter, so why don't you head back to the drawing board and sharpen your pencil."

I was speechless. Unfortunately, Bradley wasn't.

"And by the way, did you cook up this little infrastructure media fest? If you made all or even some of that happen, you're headed for pain and misery. We have a national media strategy already and you better not be getting in the way with your little 'save our bridges' crusade."

"Bradley, you think I'm that good, that I could have orchestrated such a perfect storm? You give me too much credit. I had no idea those stories were in the works."

"Not even your friend Sanderson on *AM* yesterday morning?"

"He was on *Canada AM*? I haven't seen or spoken with him since E-day. You'd think he'd have let me know." I shook my head with brows furrowed.

"Look, Daniel, just because Angus is still pulling some great numbers for us doesn't mean you have carte blanche. We've got stuff to do in this Budget and splinting aging bridges ain't on the agenda. So get with the program. We're in government now."

Stanton slid out of the booth and stood next to me, leaning down to whisper in my ear. He'd had garlic for lunch.

"One more thing. You're going to get a call from the Secret Service, so be nice to them and answer their questions," he said.

"The Secret Service? As in the United States? What for?"

"Well, just to complicate our 'To Do' list, the Pres is making a one-day stopover in Canada on his way to London to meet with the British PM, and wants to bring greetings to our newly elected Prime Minister, welcome him into the fold as it were, ensure that we'll still do whatever he says on international affairs, and so on."

"That's interesting. But where do we come in?"

"Well, the former PM hasn't yet moved his stuff out of Harrington Lake so we can't entertain the leader of the free world there. So instead, it's all going down at McLintock's house, largely because the PM loves it. From a security perspective, the RCMP guys think Angus's house, being right on the river, is very easy to defend. Anyway, the Secret Service squareheads are going to call you. They want to come up to do the advance work and we gotta keep the Pres happy."

With that, he walked out, leaving me agape with the bill resting atop the draft report, still undisturbed on the table. True to his word, they called a half-hour later as I drove home.

DIARY
Tuesday, February 18
My Love,

We're not quite finished, but we're close enough to know we'll be in time to make our case to the PM. But we don't know whether we'll be heard. While Daniel continued to write and weave his magic with the blessed reporters (not a word on that to anyone), I had dinner this evening with Harold Silverberg. I'd liked to have seen him earlier, but he just returned from a month-long family trip to Vancouver. He was the DM for what they called Public Works twenty years ago, when concern with the deficit overtook common sense within the halls of power.

Though it was never publicly known, he resigned when the Liberal government of the day cut back our public investment in bridges, roads, ports, and canals. He is a rare man of honour. He thought the cuts short-sighted and most costly in the long run. Even though he'd been out west, he seemed to know all about our investigation and was delighted and vindicated as I described our findings thus far. He just kept saying, "Dead on, Mr. McLintock."

The PM called an hour ago. His day ends as late as mine. It seems we're to have company on the weekend. The President of the U.S. and that odd wife of his are coming to visit on Saturday. The PM loves our home so much he'd rather hold private talks with the American mucky-muck here. Apparently, my blasted notoriety from a few months ago seems to have reached the ears of the President, and he wants to meet me and see *Baddeck 1*. I couldn't raise Daniel as he was caught in a trap with young Lindsay, expertly set by Muriel and me. They deserve some time together. So I

called my co-conspirator with the news. No disrespect
intended, but when I mentioned to her that the First Lady
had expressed keen interest in sitting in the hovercraft,
Muriel claimed the woman is attracted to virtually any
machine that vibrates.
AM

CHAPTER FIFTEEN

I kissed Lindsay goodbye as she assembled a banana smoothie in the kitchen. With one hand on the blender lid, one finger on the *Frappé* button, and her neck turned and tilted to complete the smooch, I taxed her early morning coordination. She was due on campus in an hour and was moving fast. I slipped out the door with the feeling that we'd been living together for two decades, not two months. Such comfort.

I climbed the snowy path to meet Angus. We were huddling at home to eliminate distractions and planned to hammer out our last unwritten section, the Executive Summary. I was pleased with the state of the report. Angus and I had spent hours and hours on the writing. We'd been brutal and hard-headed when it came to editing. There were no wasted words. Though our earliest draft had been over fifty pages, the entire report was now only twenty-two pages long. With full footnoting, it ran to almost thirty pages but the story was told in the first twenty-two. Reducing it to that length had been a struggle but we'd done it. The task brought to life a quotation often attributed to Mark Twain: "I apologize for the length of this letter. If I'd had more time, I would have written less." It may be apocryphal, but the point is valid. We wanted this report to be read. So making it short, but powerful, made sense.

With that in mind, this last piece of writing was particularly important. Many of the people who will claim to have read a report, any report, will only have read the Exec. Summary. It is perhaps not surprising that this is the reality of government reports, and had been for decades. I would guess that there have been more readers of the Cliffs Notes edition of *King Lear* than of the great bard's original text. So in two short pages of bulleted points we had to make our case in a compelling and convincing way, while ably supporting our conclusions and recommendations.

Our formal, public deadline was still eight days away, but we wanted to submit the report early to better the odds that our findings would influence the Throne Speech and Budget. We were close, and both Angus and I were happy with the way it was shaping up.

At precisely 10:00, not 10:01 or 9:59, but at the stroke of 10:00, there came a knock at the door. I could almost picture them on the front step counting down the seconds until "knock activation." I opened the door, leaving Angus at the dining room table where we'd been gathered around my laptop. I'm not sure exactly what I was expecting, never having met a Secret Service agent, but I was a little surprised to find Barbie and Ken standing before me. I looked over their shoulders expecting to see Barbie's Sports Camper in the driveway complete with surfboards on the roof rack, but there was only a dark blue, nondescript Ford sedan. Or maybe it was a Chrysler. The cars driven by Secret Service agents never actually have model names like Impala or Grand Prix. They're always simply referred to as sedans.

"Good morning, sir, I'm Clayton Leyland and this is Jennifer Fitzhugh, U.S. Secret Service."

"Are those your real names?" I quipped.

They looked bewildered.

"Ahhh, just kidding. Please come in. We were expecting you at, um, exactly this time. You're very punctual."

Ken, or Clayton rather, wore a white dress shirt starched to a plywood stiffness, a nondescript grey suit with a darker grey tie, black socks, and shiny black brogues. In other words, he was wearing the wardrobe equivalent of the dark blue Ford or Chrysler sedan he'd driven to the house. His dark brown hair was cut close to his head with a side part seemingly made with a T-square. His finely chiselled face ended in a solid chin lifted directly from Mount Rushmore. It would be an insult to describe his eyes as blue. Even sapphire seemed inadequate. He was built like a brick shithouse that had just undergone major renovations to reinforce perimeter security. When he shook my hand, it felt as if he could have killed me just by squeezing.

Barbie, sorry, Agent Fitzhugh, wore the feminine version of exactly the same outfit, although the bottom of her jacket flared to accommodate her narrow waist and perfectly proportioned hips. She didn't really wear a tie, but a more feminine version thereof that I'm not really sure I can describe, but think Colonel Sanders. Her hair was so blond I had to look away every few seconds or so, as if protecting my vision from a solar eclipse. It was piled high on her head in a bun, or rather in what looked more like a six-braid challah loaf. She wore just a touch of makeup on her lovely symmetrical face, which crossed Brigitte Bardot with Betty Cooper, my longstanding comic book crush. Her eyes, well, they were the same colour as Ken's. It made me wonder whether they were both sporting standard Secret Service–issue bionic blues. She was taller than Agent Leyland, and in a sympathetic gesture that confirmed she was in fact human, she wore shiny black flats at the end of her Amazonian legs.

I introduced Angus and offered coffee, which they both declined, before we all settled in the living room. It was essentially a security briefing. They explained that normally, such security reconnaissance would have been undertaken weeks ago, but the President's brief stopover in Ottawa had only just been added to the schedule. So the security preparations would be telescoped into three short days. The two agents described their approach to securing the immediate area and gave us important tips on how to avoid arousing the hypersensitive observational powers of the two dozen Secret Service agents on the presidential detail for the formal visit four days hence.

The list of restrictions placed on us was long, but seemed reasonable enough. To avoid being considered a "clear and present danger" during the power couple's visit, we were instructed to avoid sudden movements; to keep our hands out in the open at all times; not to carry swords, machetes, ninja throwing stars, or any object with a pin you could pull; and never, ever to pass a knife to the President with the blade presented forward. Good to know.

Then Barbie and Ken asked permission to explore Angus's plot of land. They pulled out the official municipal survey for the area, showing the property lines, and headed outside. After opening the trunk of their sedan and donning parkas, boots, and backpacks, they walked back up the driveway to start what they called a perimeter security audit.

Angus and I returned to our writing at the dining room table, but kept an eye out the window to track the progress of the intrepid Secret Service agents. We watched as they spent the next hour tramping around the property, crawling under the house, exploring every inch of the boathouse, clambering onto the roof with scopes and tripod, and slipping and sliding their way out onto the ice, presumably to check for sniper sightlines.

Eventually they came back and toured the inside of the house with Angus trailing closely. They asked a raft more questions but seemed satisfied as they took notes and spoke into what I assumed was a hand-held digital recorder. But who really knows what it was: visions of James Bond and his Q branch gadgets danced in my head. Agent Leyland asked whether Angus objected to the removal of a tall silver maple that hampered surveillance. He pointed to a beautiful tree on the east side of the property, visible through the dining room window.

"You'll cut me down before that tree falls," answered Angus. "That's always been my wife's favourite."

"May we please speak with her then?" Agent Leyland asked while Agent Fitzhugh caught his eye and shook her head in the negative. Clearly, she'd not only read the bio briefing note on Angus McLintock, she'd retained it too.

240

"I wish you could, laddie, but you're about eight months too late," Angus replied. "The tree stays."

The agent didn't need his super-acute powers of observation to see that Angus was not to be moved.

"We'll consider other security contingencies to avoid eliminating the tree and get back to you."

They were almost out the door when Agent Fitzhugh returned to open the well-stocked liquor cabinet. Several single malts stood ready.

"Can this be locked?" she asked.

"Mercifully, it cannae be. I managed to lose the key years ago," Angus replied, laughing. "Why anyone would want to lock that door is well beyond my ken."

"We'll call in a locksmith so that the securing mechanism is rendered functional again," she declared in a monotone that just seemed to fit the sentence.

"May I ask why that exceedingly uncivilized measure is necessary?" Angus asked.

"I'm sorry, I cannot answer that on the grounds that it would compromise national security."

They left soon after.

For my entire life, I'd laboured under the impression that the courageous agents of the U.S. Secret Service were congenitally emotionless, humourless, cold, by-the-book automatons. Now that I'd spent an hour or so with two of them, I was forced to conclude that for all those years, I'd actually been right.

We had lunch and spent the rest of the afternoon deep in the writing. We were so close.

The next morning, Angus and I sat in front of Deputy Minister Rosemary Holden in her Infrastructure Canada corner office just across the river in Hull. We'd brought with us the only printed copy of the McLintock Report, for her to review it. We wanted to leave nothing to chance, so having her set of eyes on the document was important to us. While she read the twenty-two pages, Angus and I watched out her window as workers with acetylene torches laboured on the twisted remains of the Alexandra Bridge. The engineering experts in Rosemary's department had determined that the damage to the bridge had been too severe to allow it to be salvaged. The bridge would be dismantled and replaced. I privately hoped they'd add at least two more lanes in each direction to ease the rush-hour congestion.

When I wasn't looking out the window, I watched Rosemary for signs of her reaction. She was nodding throughout, sometimes quite vigorously, and once slapped her hand on the desk. I couldn't tell whether she was agreeing with something she'd read or rejecting it.

She and her department had been paragons of professionalism throughout our four-week investigation. They'd responded quickly to each of our requests and had even provided very helpful information for which we hadn't asked when it was clear we needed additional context to ensure a balanced perspective.

About two-thirds into the report, I watched her eyes widen. She looked up at us.

"This is much broader than the collapse of the Alexandra," she noted.

"Aye, it is, and that was our mandate," Angus replied.

"It illuminates the core issue at play, not just the most recent and dramatic outcome."

"And that's been our intention from the outset," I added.

"You do remember that the Liberals were in power for the first four years of this era of neglect?" she asked. "That's when it all started."

Angus and I nodded in unison. She returned to her reading and we waited. Five minutes later she turned the final page and shook her head, with a faint, perhaps wistful smile.

"Do you think the PMO will really let this see the light of day?"

"As far as we're concerned, the report will be publicly released, and likely not by the hand of the Prime Minister," I responded.

"What is your reaction to the paper?" Angus asked. "Have we overstated or understated? Have we struck the right tone? Have we supported our findings adequately? Have we left anything unsaid – any stone unturned?"

"It's extremely strong. Well researched. And the funding numbers only slightly exceed what we've been proposing for the last twenty-three months. Overall, the report conveys to the government what this department has longed to say for many years without having had the voice," said Rosemary. "I don't think the tone is too strong and I do think the claims you've made and the conclusions you've drawn are all backed up by data and facts. But I think you're missing one critical piece."

"That's why Angus and I wanted you to see the draft. This has to be bulletproof if we ever hope to pull this off."

"I don't think you made it clear enough that the collapse was in no way caused by any kind of inherent flaw in the design of the bridge itself," she explained. "It needs to be hammered home that there are dozens, even hundreds of bridges of this design all over North America and Europe, most of which are actually older than the Alexandra. My staff has looked at every one, and none of them, not a single one, has collapsed. I'd advise you to close down that avenue of speculation very early on."

"Aye, that's a grand idea," Angus agreed.

"Can we footnote your department's research to back up our claim?" I inquired.

"I assumed you'd want to," the DM replied as she pulled a document from a file drawer and handed it over. "Here's the final report cataloguing every similarly designed bridge that we could locate. You may footnote to your heart's content."

"So, any other thoughts?" I asked. We were on a schedule and had to leave shortly.

"Just my gratitude for the piece at the end about the department," she noted. "It was gratifying to read that, and it will be very much appreciated by those who have worked here over the last two decades when this has been coming to a head."

As we rose to leave, Angus said to her, "I thank you for all the support you and your team have provided as we've worked through this labyrinth. We'd not have made it this far without you."

"That's kind of you, Professor McLintock, but we will be in your debt if you can get this report out there and actually have the government buy in to your recommendations. I'll be watching closely. It would certainly be something to see after putting in twenty-five years as a civil servant."

Angus and I headed for the car and the drive back to Ottawa.

"I can add a section on the design of the bridge towards the front of the report," I offered. "I thought she raised a good point."

"Aye, she did. She's surely not lacking in cerebral gifts."

"I'll draft the new section and have a final report for your sign-off by this evening," I proposed. "I still want to get the PM and Bradley an advance copy tomorrow in the remote chance that they'll love it and let us hit the streets with it. They can't stop us now, so we might as well give them a look at it."

"Young Mr. Stanton won't be very happy that we've not changed the recommendations since you shared the earlier draft with him. But I can see the logic in trying again," Angus conceded. "I think it would be wise to let Muriel have a pass through it before it leaves our hands."

"Well, the weekend is pretty well a write-off as you pal around with the most powerful couple in the world. So let's wrap up the report tonight," I concluded.

"Where to now?" Angus asked when we were driving back downtown.

"How could you forget? It's not every day we get to visit the U.S. embassy."

"Hell and damnation. I had managed to put that out of my mind."

I drove us down Sussex Drive towards the Prime Minister's residence. Long before we got there, I turned into the well-defended grounds of the United States embassy. At the guard booth I pulled up behind a car driven by the Chief of Staff to our Foreign Affairs Minister. I felt a bit sorry for her, as it had been decided between the White House and the Prime Minister's office that the Foreign Affairs Minister would not be invited to the quick stopover visit by the President and his wife. To add insult to injury, however, his Chief of Staff would still be fully briefed on what they'd be missing.

When it was our turn, the uniformed sentry, a marine I think, approached my open window and looked closely at Angus, then at me. He scanned his clipboard for a moment before looking back at each of us.

"Messrs Addison and McLintock, I presume," he said. "Passports please."

We'd been warned about this and I handed both passports over to him. He swiped them through a machine and we waited. Then he stacked our passports with several others he'd accumulated and handed me two lanyards with official-looking name tags, each embossed with the stamp of the Secretary of State for Foreign Affairs.

"Put these around your necks now and do not take them off for the duration of your visit. You'll be relieved of them by my colleague on the other side when you drive off the grounds. Please drive up to the official visitors' parking area just in front of the main embassy doors. You can go right inside, where you'll be met."

As instructed, neither Angus nor I said a word but just nodded in submission to signal that we understood but didn't want any trouble. We slipped the lanyards around our necks, drove up the road, and parked.

The embassy was amazing but we had no time for sightseeing.

"Mr. McLintock, you must be wearing your official lanyard, and it must be visible at all times," said the severe woman at the reception desk.

"Aye, and I've been wearing it the whole time, madam," Angus replied, somewhat indignant.

I looked over and saw no sign of the lanyard. I looked more closely and figured it out.

"Angus, it's buried under your grey cascade. You'll have to let it sit on top of your beard or we might soon be in an interrogation room."

He moved it out from behind to rest on his beard, where it looked slightly ridiculous. But neither of us was about to complain.

"Sorry madam, it seemed my lanyard, as you call it, had slipped from view. I trust this configuration is acceptable."

"Fine. Thank you" was all she said.

Eventually we were escorted to an enormous boardroom where we joined about two dozen other people sitting around the table. I recognized staff from the PMO and several bureaucrats from the Department of Foreign Affairs who sat next to the minister's Chief of Staff. They all looked ticked at being frozen out of the President's visit. It was odd, if not unprecedented, for the Foreign Affairs Minister to be excluded from meetings with a visiting head of state. As the briefing unfolded, it seemed a compromise had been reached. The minister would greet the President and his wife at the Ottawa airport for approximately forty-six seconds. Then the helicopter, Marine One, with the President and First Lady safely inside, would lift off for the short flight up the river to Cumberland. For the minister, forty-six seconds of presidential face time was some consolation.

Senior embassy staff led the briefing. They walked us through a minute-by-minute rundown of the entire visit, including presidential bathroom breaks and makeup touch-up times for the First Lady. Angus and I learned for the first time that the entire visit to the house would last about ninety minutes, including forty-five minutes for the one-on-one between the PM and President. During the official get-together involving the two leaders, Angus and I were in charge of showing the First Lady around the property and giving her the chance to see the hovercraft. Both the Pres and his wife would walk past the hovercraft on their way to the house after *Marine One* landed on the ice. But the First Lady would get a second, longer look at it, as she'd requested.

I had a bad feeling about this. Leaving the First Lady with Angus for thirty minutes was a great deal of responsibility for someone who couldn't even meet the U.S. embassy's lanyard-wearing standards.

As the briefing ended and the room started to empty, a young well-dressed woman with her hair pulled back behind her head in some kind of tortoise-shell comb-clamp device approached Angus and me.

"Professors McLintock and Addison, would you come this way, please? The ambassador would like to see you."

I tried to remember if I'd said anything vaguely anti-American in the last few years but came up empty. The ambassador's office was enormous, and really made you feel that you actually were deep in the heart of the U.S. of A.

"Thank you, Susan, but I'll take this meeting alone with our guests," the ambassador said.

"Certainly, sir," replied the woman known as Susan, and she left us, closing the door behind her.

Introductions were made, drinks were offered, and banal banter exchanged. The ambassador was a retired Republican senator from New Hampshire who had a reputation as a ball-busting neo-con with very strong ties to the White House. He and the President had fought together in the Republican trenches and served together in the Senate. He was the New England equivalent of a good ole boy.

"I won't take up much of your time, gentlemen, but I did want to thank you, Professor McLintock, for opening up your home to the First Family on such short notice. You'll get along just fine with the President. He's a first-rate guy with a first-rate mind. I'm sure the Prime Minister will be impressed."

The ambassador was huge. The term barrel-chested seemed to have been coined in his honour. And the barrel was big. Grey pinstripe, complete with vest and pocket watch. Blue shirt, red striped tie, matching red handkerchief in his jacket pocket. The full deal.

"Well, thank you, Ambassador. I'm really just the innkeeper. We don't expect any issues. With the number of Secret Service agents crawling about the place, I expect we could repel an invasion from almost any industrialized nation," said Angus. "Nevertheless, we're looking forward to welcoming them to my home."

"Yep, they're still a mite sensitive about that little incident in Dallas a few decades back, but you want your presidential security team to be seriously vigilant," he noted.

I held my peace. The ambassador removed his silver glasses and ran his hands through his flowing silver mane.

"Okay, now that we've exchanged a few pleasantries, it's time to cut the crap and get down to it," the ambassador suggested. "And this part of the meeting is on such deep background that I will deny we've ever met, let alone jawed about the presidential missus. Am I coming in loud and clear, gentlemen?"

"You can count on our discretion, Ambassador," I offered. I looked at Angus and he at me, as dread and curiosity mingled in the space between us. What had we got ourselves into?

"All right, boys, cards down. Plain and simple, the First Lady is a goddamned whack job who would beat up a priest to get her paws on his sacramental wine. There must be no alcohol of any kind on the premises when the First Lady is on site. Is that absolutely clear?"

Angus nodded.

"You can rest easy, sir, we've made arrangements to remove any and all liquor products, including beer, spirits, wine, rubbing alcohol, Aqua Velva, cough syrup, and even the fermented maraschino cherry juice that's been sitting in the icebox for a while now. There'll be not the least temptation for anyone beholden to the insidious liquid."

"Well, that's a relief. We've had a few unfortunate incidents in the last six months that we're, um, not eager to repeat. We're very lucky they haven't yet hit the press or we'd be dominating the goddamned news cycle and ducking calls from Larry King."

"Understood, Ambassador. My home will be dry as the Kalahari, but not quite so sandy and hot," Angus assured him.

"Don't forget to ditch any mouthwash you have lying around. You could make a mean Molotov cocktail with a bottle of Listerine," he warned. "Folks always forget the mouthwash, but FLOTUS never does. She makes a beeline for the crapper every time. Her breath is sure fresh, but that doesn't much matter if she's pissed to the gills."

Angus was still puzzling but eventually gave up.

"FLOTUS?"

"First Lady of the United States," I explained.

"And don't let her charm you into anything that wasn't on the plasticized agenda. I swear she could persuade a cobra to bite itself and enjoy the whole experience."

The ambassador stood up. We took the cue and rose, too.

"Okay, gents, I think we're done here. Thanks for this little chat that never ever happened."

After dinner, Lindsay and I drove to the Riverfront Seniors' Residence to consult the political oracle. Lindsay was guiding Muriel through the lobby, heading for our favoured couch by the window, when they stopped. Muriel's legs were vibrating but her feet weren't moving. She couldn't get herself going.

"Damn these shakes!" she snapped.

"Shall we invoke the speedbump protocol?" Lindsay asked.

"We might as well or we'll be here all bloody night."

"Daniel, would you mind lying on the ground directly in front of Muriel?" Lindsay asked. Both Lindsay and Muriel smiled sweetly at me.

I chuckled, shaking my head. They were joking, right? Nope.

"Come again?"

"Just lie down in front of my feet," said Muriel. "And trust that I've lived with this damned Parkinson's long enough to know what I'm doing."

I'd grown quite attached to Muriel over the previous several months. We'd been through a lot together. But I was still a little scared of her. I lay down on the ground on my stomach as casually as I could. Muriel and Lindsay immediately vaulted over me, then high-stepped all the way to the couch.

"Thank you, Daniel," Muriel said when I joined them. "Even when I've got the shudders, I can always step over something, but it actually has to be there to work."

We chatted about this and that for a few minutes before I pulled out two copies of our final, final report.

"It's done. I've read it over about 235 times and so has Angus. But we're far too close to it to see it objectively." I handed them each a copy. "Can you read it through for us before we send it in to the PMO?"

I played double solitaire with Jasper while Lindsay and Muriel read the twenty-two pages.

"How many of those peach safari suits do you own?" I asked Jasper.

"Just the one. Why?"

"It's very, um, stylish."

"You're telling me. The birds love it. It's Italian, you know."

"No kidding. Nice."

In the heat of the action, he kindly pointed out that I'd put a red six on a red seven. He then proceeded to beat me in three straight games. I was saved from further humiliation, at least related to solitaire, when Muriel and Lindsay closed their reports within seconds of one another.

"Well?" was all I said when I rejoined them.

"It's a compelling read presenting a simple and powerful story. There wasn't anything I didn't understand, except how government after government simply ignored their officials' advice," said Lindsay. "The writing is wonderful."

"But does it all hang together? Are there any chinks in the armour?"

"Everything was well supported. The footnotes put you on very solid ground. And the Executive Summary really presents the whole story succinctly, strongly, and clearly," Lindsay observed. "I read the summary last and it worked well for me."

I nodded, feeling better about it all. I trusted Lindsay's judgment and her academic perspective on the paper. Muriel was quiet and wore a vaguely concerned look. Lindsay and I both turned to her.

"It's the best piece of investigative writing I've ever read, and I couldn't be prouder of you," Muriel said. "But I hope you and Angus are ready, because the PMO is going to have all four of your chestnuts on display in the caucus room as a warning to others."

"Grandma!"

DIARY

Thursday, February 20

My Love,

Such a frenetic pace, a frenetic life. I cannot imagine how much fun we'd be having were you still here with me. It would be like those early heady days of ours. All those rallies and marches and police stations we shared. Days I cherish more now. The mix of love and outrage made for a strangely intoxicating combination. I think we're doing important work now, as we were then. But you are missing from it all. I'll stumble around in the void you've left until Daniel or Muriel or pressing work pulls me back to safer ground.

We've drawn our little investigation to a close. Daniel has taken our collective scribblings and fashioned a finely wrought piece of writing. He has a fine hand with the nib. Above all else, it says what we meant it to say, in the way we wanted to say it. There's fun ahead as the report conveys a wee bit more than many will want. No matter. We've been true, so we'll strap in for the ride.

Now I must tidy up a bit. As you know, we have company coming on the weekend.

AM

CHAPTER SIXTEEN

Angus, Lindsay, and I were all up early the next morning. We had to vacate so the Secret Service, the RCMP, White House staff, and the PMO could swarm all over the property doing whatever they do to prepare for the arrival of the President and First Lady. I had visions of land mines, Uzis, and laser tripwires but I tried to push them from my mind. Angus had been assured that no tree would be harmed in the making of this presidential visit, but he kept a weather eye on Marin's favourite silver maple just the same. Lindsay headed into campus to work on her thesis and mark undergrad papers. She was not looking forward to it. It being Friday and all, Angus and I made our way to the constituency office.

The two Petes were already en route to Ottawa for class but had a mission to complete first. They were delivering, through no intermediaries, two copies of our final report into the hands of Bradley Stanton. I'd warned Bradley they were coming and he had, in turn, arranged with the Commissionaires at the front doors of Centre Block to escort them up to the Prime Minister's office on the second floor. I'm sure when the Petes arrived at the Commissionaires' desk a few more phone calls were required to complete the transaction. Pete1 and Pete2 were in full punk regalia.

Pete1 called at 9:20.

"The eagle has landed" was all he said.

In case there's any doubt, that was our confirmation code that the reports had been successfully delivered from pierced and tattooed palms into the sweaty but unaltered hands of Bradley Stanton. I felt I should say something like "10-4" but just went with "Thanks, Pete."

Now I was nervous. It felt like a few dozen Lilliputians were playing lacrosse in my stomach, and it was a high-scoring game. Angus seemed completely at ease behind his desk, chowing down on a blueberry-filled doughnut, most of which made it into his mouth.

"Will you not fret yourself!" Angus chided. "We've done our job and we've done it well. We've nothing about which to be troubled."

"Right. No problem. We're about to derail a Throne Speech, the federal Budget, and perhaps even the government. I guess you're right, there's really no call for anxiety. None at all," I mocked.

"'Tis what we do. I should think you'd be getting used to it by now," Angus replied.

"I have no doubts about what we're doing. I just don't much like being yelled at. By the way, there's a blueberry off the port bow of your moustache."

"I thank you."

The ring of my phone ended the waiting about twenty-four minutes later. I hit the speaker button, wondering if anyone else could hear the pneumatic drill pounding in my chest.

"Daniel Addison," I croaked.

"Is this your idea of a fucking joke, because if it is, I'm not laughing and neither is the PM."

"You're on the speaker phone, Bradley."

"Oh."

"Our report is no joke, Mr. Stanton. In fact, I think it's complete, comprehensive, and fulfills our mandate signed and agreed to at the outset," noted Angus, as he smirked my way.

"I'd actually say it covers off more than your mandate, Angus. Much more. We asked you to find out what happened to the Alexandra Bridge and you come back with an indictment of our entire national infrastructure, which wouldn't be too bad if you didn't also blame a previous Liberal government for starting it all. You've given us a powerful partisan hammer to swing on page four, and then you bash us in the head with it on page seven. What the . . . hell?"

"Mr. Stanton, our mandate was, and let me actually quote it to make sure I've got it right . . ." Angus winked at me. He was having fun. "Let's see here, 'to investigate the cause of the collapse of the Alexandra Bridge and recommend related measures to protect the public and serve the national interest.'" Angus read the last phrase with real emphasis.

"Just a minute, I'm switching to speaker phone," Bradley warned before we heard a click.

"Hello, Angus," a tight-sounding PM said. "You delivered quite the little grenade to Bradley and I, haven't you?"

"Actually, sir, you mean I delivered a grenade 'to Bradley and me.'" I winced, and Angus went on. "I'm sorry, I cannae help myself. But I shouldn't think the grenade metaphor is at all appropriate, Prime Minister. We have submitted what I believe to be a balanced and thoughtful analysis of the bridge collapse, what led to it, and what we ought to do now and in the coming years to avoid any future calamities. The report presents only that which we were asked to consider."

"Yes, yes, you've done all of that, but I'd like to make a few suggestions for the final draft."

"But Prime Minister, you're holding the final draft."

"Just hear me out, Angus. Your report is very comprehensive, but it reaches back so far into history. Into *our* history, if I'm being clear. I'd like to suggest that we examine only the last fifteen years. This allows us to strengthen our position politically so that we'll have the support we need to redress this situation."

"Prime Minister, with all due respect, the underfunding story started twenty years ago and I don't care much who was in office at the time. The history is only there for context, but it is important. I'd rather we focus more on the recommendations."

"I could not agree more that it's the recommendations that are important, which is why I'm suggesting we abbreviate what you call 'context' so that we don't impugn the memory of a foregoing Liberal government. Why must we shoot ourselves in the foot?"

Not wanting to hog all the fun, Angus tagged me so I could go a few rounds.

"Prime Minister," I started, "we think the entire report will be more credible and legitimate because we haven't shied away from telling the whole story, including where it all started. Besides, it will take Tory Research about five minutes online to uncover the truth about which government really started the infrastructure negligence campaign. So why not take that revelation away from them and try to control how it's positioned?"

We debated the political pros and cons for another ten minutes or so before Angus grew bored.

"Was there anything else, Prime Minister?" Angus asked. Not a line often used in Ottawa.

The PM's polite façade was slipping. I'd seen it before when I served on his staff so I could almost picture the back of his neck flushing red as he struggled to remain prime ministerial.

"Angus, my direction to you is to limit your final report's view of history to the last fifteen years. The recommendations and everything else can stay."

Angus was no longer smiling.

"Prime Minister, your direction is clear and has been for the last twenty minutes or so. It seems I've not been clear. The report you're holding is the final report. We'll not be altering it on anyone's direction."

Knowing that two stubborn men had painted one another into their respective corners, Bradley went for the save.

"No need to resolve this finally right now. Let's get the Throne Speech and the Budget out there first and then we can hammer out what to include in the final version of the McLintock Report. There's no rush," Bradley soothed.

"Oh, but how wrong you are, Mr. Stanton," Angus replied almost in a whisper. "We need not have offered you this early look at the report. You'll recall that we agreed that Canadians would see it at the same time as we submitted the final draft to you. But we need you to alter the Throne Speech, and we require that Monsieur Coulombe alter his budget, to reflect this urgent public need. That's why we've delivered an advance copy of the report. It'll be too late if we wait until the Budget is unveiled. But I think you already know that, Mr. Stanton."

"I'm sorry, Angus, but we're already on a tight schedule and we can't change course right now."

"Very well, then we must change the course ourselves," Angus replied. "Either you let us brief caucus and Cabinet early next week, or we'll simply release the report publicly ourselves and let the chips fall. We need the Budget and Throne Speech to take this report seriously. I think you know I'll do what I say I'll do."

There was silence, so we waited. And waited.

"We'll call you back in five minutes," said Bradley before the line died.

"We'll be here," Angus replied.

We just sat there without speaking. Angus went back to the paperwork he'd been toiling over prior to the call. I closed my eyes and tried to quell my abdominal lacrosse game. About ten minutes later my cellphone rang. I knew who it was.

"Hi Bradley."

"Okay, you've got your fuckin' caucus and Cabinet briefings. Monday morning, then Wednesday morning," he hissed. I could tell he wanted to use my head as a piñata, and I don't think he cared much about the loot inside. "But the timing of the report's public release is still up in the air."

"Not as far we're concerned it isn't," I responded, trying to sound confident. Trying to sound like Angus.

"Yeah, well, fuck you and Angus too!"

He hung up, which seemed appropriate after delivering such a definitive epithet.

Angus looked at me and raised his eyebrows.

"Well, we got the briefings, and Bradley sends his regards" was all I said.

Twenty minutes later, my 10:30 arrived. She was a rather studious-looking middle-aged mannish woman, dressed in a beige suit that I assumed looked much better on the mannequin in the thrift store window. She actually wore brown suede Wallabees on her feet. I could barely remember Wallabees. They'd been part of the standard uniform of the high school audio-visual club, along with flood pants belted just south of the rib cage and, in extreme cases, a plastic pen-packed pocket protector. The unfortunate students I occasionally found hanging helpless by their underwear waistbands on bathroom stall doors were also often sporting Wallabees. Notwithstanding this ignominious heritage, in this case, they were worn by one of the most respected contract translators ever to ply her trade on Parliament Hill. We simply could not release the McLintock Report until it was available in both official languages. Yes, women sometimes wore Wallabees too.

Jeanette Leforme crossed the floor to shake my extended hand.

"Daniel, how are you, my friend?" she asked in her distinct French accent.

"Jeanette, it's great to see you," I replied. "I'm just fine and trying to keep my head above water."

"I find that when that's not possible, a snorkel works quite well," she joked.

Jeanette had that very literal sense of humour not uncommon to the translator set. We'd worked together for many years. Virtually every speech I churned out for the Leader, Jeanette had translated. She knew my writing, understood my sense of humour, and was skilled enough to mirror in the French translation the oral rhythms I had written in English. My French was passable but nowhere near advanced enough to support translation of speeches. The odd letter, perhaps, but not speeches. I came to trust Jeanette to the point that I wouldn't even review the French translation before releasing it to the media. Although she was a hired gun, a freelancing translator, I knew she was Liberal to the core. I couldn't imagine her giving quite the same quality to her Tory clients.

We sat in front of my desk, and as she settled in her chair, I handed her the final draft of the McLintock Report.

"I suspected as much," she said as she started reading.

"I'll leave you to it. Do you want coffee?"

"Just cream, please."

When I returned fifteen minutes later, she'd already finished her scan and sat with the report resting in her lap.

"Cream only," I said as I handed her a bright red Liberal mug from four campaigns ago. I sipped a glass of water.

"So the PM is actually going to release this publicly?" she asked.

"Nope. We are. And it may not be sanctioned by the centre, but we'll see."

"It's well-written, but not exactly in your style," she observed.

"Yes, well, I had a co-writer. Angus McLintock himself penned several major sections. His natural style is spare and elegant while I still hail from the 'why use three words when six will do' school," I explained. "So when I did the final edit, I kind of turned it into a hybrid of our two styles."

"It works. It works very well. I think Canadians are going to be shocked," she said.

"Well, that's the intention. They'll need to be shocked if they're going to support such a hefty infrastructure investment."

"I lose track of the years, but do you not lay the blame for starting the whole mess at the feet of a Liberal government two decades ago?" she asked.

"And there lies the rub."

"I've not heard that expression. What does it mean?"

"It's a lift from Hamlet and simply means 'and there's the problem.'"

"But still it will be released?"

"Yes, but unless there's a radical shift in our relationship with the PMO, we'll be doing the releasing ourselves, and paying the political price," I noted.

"You must be filled with faith in Mr. McLintock?"

"Well, I think that what I'm filled with changes from day to day, but in general, I know we're on the right track with this," I replied. "But this job really has to be done on the down-low, Jeanette, or we're history."

"If you mean that you're depending on my absolute discretion, you have always been able to count on me for that."

"I know, but I needed to say it out loud," I said as I handed her a slip of paper. "Don't email it to me here at the office. Send it only to the email address on that slip. Then eat the paper please. I'll need the final translation, formatted just as the English one currently is, by Tuesday at the latest. Does that work?"

I handed her a flash drive with the English final report as Jeanette stood and pulled her parka back on.

"I'm aiming for Monday," she concluded, before heading out the door.

I picked up the phone and called the National Press Building.

"Natalie, it's Daniel Addison. How are you?"

"Hi Danny, you've been busy. I keep reading about your man. You're doing some good stuff."

"Feel free to pass that on to Bradley Stanton. He's about ready to disembowel me."

"Don't worry, this too shall pass," she replied.

"Well, if I'm disembowelled, I don't think I'll be passing anything, but that's really not why I'm calling," I said. "I need you to put the media studio on hold for me next Wednesday from noon to about two. We'll probably need it for about thirty minutes some time in that window."

"Right now it's free at that time, so I'll put you down."

"Can you do me a favour and not hold it in my name?" I asked. "I don't want the world knowing – well, I don't want the PMO knowing – that we might be holding a newser then."

"No problem. I'll hold it for the Azerbaijani ambassador."

"Do we have an Azerbaijani embassy in Ottawa?" I inquired.

"I don't really know."

I stroked a line through one more item on my lengthy To Do list. Next, I drafted the news release to accompany the release of the McLintock Report. Because I'd been immersed in writing the final draft of the report, the news release pretty well wrote itself. Although when quoting Angus in this news release, I did take special care to spell his name and not an orifice. Finally, I reached for the digital recorder in my top drawer. I spent the next half-hour or so with Angus, recording his responses to seven or eight questions he would surely get from journalists when the report went public. I thought we'd issue a radio news release and make audio files of Angus in full rhetorical flight available for radio stations across the country to download. I edited the MP3 files myself and consigned the following pearls of Angus to the virtual cutting-room floor:

"Only a brainless jackass would ask such a question."

"I expect the Prime Minister would like to ram a red hot poker up my hindquarters so I'll not be turning my back on him for the foreseeable future."

"That young Mr. Stanton is greasier than a skid of bacon, but lacks the intoxicating aroma when in the fire."

"Oops. I'm sorry about that one. I blame the cabbage soup I had last night."

"The Liberals and Tories hold equal shares in the collapse of the bridge and the sorry state of our national infrastructure. The Liberals for starting the ball down the hill, and then the Tories for getting out of the way and letting it roll."

I very nearly included that last sound bite. It summed up the story quite nicely. But I feared it might push Bradley either into a straitjacket, or worse, to Googling "contract killers for hire in the National Capital Region."

I stacked the digital audio clips in a single MP3 file and used two of Angus's quotations in the news release. I'd distribute the audio file to reporters when the news release hit the wire. After Angus signed off on the release, which he did with only a few esoteric grammatical refinements, I loaded it onto a second flash drive so Lindsay could email it to Jeanette from her computer. I know. I was veering close to paranoia, but covering my tracks and taking no risks with only a few days to go just seemed the sensible approach. At least I'd learned something from Bradley Stanton. We were almost ready.

I'd seen very little of Lindsay in the previous few days and it was taking its toll on me. With all the pieces in place for the caucus and Cabinet briefings the following week and the report already in translation, I figured I'd earned an afternoon off. I met Lindsay at Starbucks. We lucked out and landed the two dark brown easy chairs right by the window. I set my backpack and its awkward load down on the floor beside hers. The sun was so bright it made the ice and snow of the river seem like a light source. The chairs were positioned in just such a way that we could hold hands. So we did.

"Guard this with your life," I said as I pressed the flash drive into her palm.

With a furtive and over-the-top look in all directions, she shoved it into her zippered coat pocket.

"What am I guarding with my life?"

"You're now in possession of the final, final version of the McLintock Report," I explained. "The complete French translation will be arriving in your email box sometime on Monday, Tuesday at the latest, from someone name Jeanette."

"Is that her real name?" she teased. "Should I be wearing gloves or dark glasses or something?"

"I know it sounds ridiculous, but we are not on the same page with the PMO. I think we're going to end up freelancing this ourselves just so we can get it out there."

I spent the next twenty minutes or so outlining our plan for next week. We'd need Muriel's help, too. I doubted we could keep her out of it anyway. Lindsay got into the spirit, or more accurately, the conspiracy of it all as she sipped her latte, and I, my hot chocolate. Angus and I no longer had the support of the centre. We'd decided jointly to stick to our guns on the report, even at the risk of being kicked out of the caucus. I thought it a long shot that the PM and Bradley would ever excommunicate Angus. Without even trying, the MP for Cumberland-Prescott had endeared himself to enough locals to win the election, and to a growing number of Canadians who seemed fascinated by this political anomaly. He was a hero to many. For this reason alone, it would be folly for them to make Angus sit as an independent and cause them to lose the reflected glow of his popularity. Or so I thought. Muriel and Lindsay agreed with me. Angus didn't really care. In the Liberal tent or out of it, he'd still be the Member of Parliament for Cumberland-Prescott. A fine line separated maverick and mutineer, and Angus was brushing up against it.

Even against the distraction of the afternoon rush and the stunning sun-soaked river view, I had a very hard time keeping my eyes off Lindsay. Other than the romantic dinner Muriel and Angus had arranged, we'd had very little meaningful time with one another, even though we actually lived together. With both of us working so hard, living together really meant we were just sleeping together. And by sleeping together, I really mean sleeping together, in the strictest sense of the term. But that didn't seem to matter. We both still seemed giddy at having found one another.

An older couple arrived, made it through the lineup, doctored their coffees, and then stood in the middle of the room, slowly rotating in a futile search for two empty chairs. Lindsay and I looked at one another and agreed in a glance. We both stood up and waved the couple over. They were relieved and grateful. After all, these were the best seats in the house. They were about to place their coffees on the small table when I grabbed my backpack. Somehow one strap snared the table leg. So in one motion I swung both the backpack and the table up onto my shoulder. Nice.

When I realized what I'd done and looked back, the old man looked flushed as he still held his coffee in one hand but used his other to massage his upper shin. His wife looked concerned. I fell over myself in apology. I mean "fell over myself" in the figurative sense, though I accept the need to clarify. They were very good about it. The fact that we had surrendered our plush chairs in their moment of need helped to soften the blow – the one I'd delivered to his leg with a hardwood Starbucks table. I was actually quite pleased that I'd timed it so that they hadn't yet set down their boiling hot beverages before my deft manoeuvre. Third-degree burns on top of the swelling contusion would not have helped. Lindsay watched it all with some amusement. I watched in hapless embarrassment.

I made one final heartfelt apology and backed away slowly. He just waved and joked about advancing his knee replacement surgery. At least I think he was joking.

"Smooth" was all Lindsay said.

In two minutes we were on a bench next to the river ice. Lindsay opened her backpack and I mine. Out came our skates. She favoured hockey skates, which made me love her all the more. I pulled on my CCM Super Tacks, while Lindsay donned her Bauer Black Panthers. She insisted on carrying her own boots in her backpack and I loaded my hiking shoes into my own. Then we were on the ice. I grew up playing hockey, so skating for me, even if I made it onto the ice only every couple of years or so, was just like riding a bike – or falling off a bike, as the case may be. I was a bit wobbly until I'd rediscovered the long-dormant leg muscles that seem to be used only for skating. They cried out in agony but I was too content to listen. Eventually, I found my stride and was able to keep up with Lindsay. Holding hands helped.

It was a stunning day to be on the river. Wispy cirrus clouds lay in the sky, artfully arranged on a cobalt canvas. In time, my eyes grew accustomed to the sun's glare and my perpetual squint faded. But it was cold. Both Lindsay and I pulled our hats down low and wound our scarves around our necks and faces, making our parkas look more like down-filled burkas. We didn't skate in a straight line but meandered, following the serpentine strip of clear ice. We saw not another soul as we carved our way towards the boathouse – our boathouse! – around the next point.

When we were even with the craggy promontory, I let go of Lindsay's hand and took off. She understood immediately that the Olympic speed-skating gold medal turned on who beat the other to the dock. My first inkling that all was not right with the world came when we were still about 300 yards from our boathouse. Lindsay was only three strides behind me and closing fast as our arms and legs pumped. To the average Canadian observer on the shore, it was a classic winter scene – two carefree skaters racing for some arbitrary finish line. But to the hair-trigger Secret Service lookout, trained to read evil into the most bucolic scene, Lindsay and I were a terrorist sleeper cell, our backpacks filled with gel-ignite, on a suicide mission to take down the smug and arrogant leader of the free world. Even though we were a day early.

The three snowmobiles came out of nowhere, driven by agents in arctic camouflage. Ever sensible, Lindsay apparently just stopped. I was ahead and just kept skating, trying to escape the snowmobiles. In moments of crisis, I've learned the hard way that I don't always think clearly, despite plenty of opportunities. I actually thought I just might be able to outpace state-of-the-art souped-up snowmobiles that were capable of speeds in excess of 100 kilometres per hour. See what I mean about my clear thinking challenge?

I was still streaking along the ice when the snowmobile pulled alongside. The driver looked my way and shook his head. His fellow agent sitting behind him leapt into space to close the gap between us. There was a soft and fluffy snowbank just to my right that would have been a nice place to land. But I managed to miss it. The flying agent wrapped his arms around my neck and down we went onto the ice. Intellectually, I know that diamonds are the world's hardest material. But at the moment of impact, I thought the frozen Ottawa River had to be in the running.

Ten minutes later I could breathe again and was able to confirm that I was not in fact a quadriplegic, despite the searing pain in my back.

"You're lucky your girlfriend talked fast or it might have been a bullet that brought you down, not Agent Dickerson," Ken explained.

A bullet might have been less painful, I thought to myself.

"We were just skating back to our own apartment. How is that a threat to Western civilization?" I asked, exasperated. My body felt like one gigantic sprain.

"If we've already set up our security perimeter, an old lady in a motorized wheelchair is a threat," explained Agent Leyland. "We are not programmed to take chances with the President's life."

"But the President is still in Washington," I insisted.

"But we couldn't know whether you knew that, so in your mind, you could have still been a threat if you thought the President was in fact here already," spun Agent Leyland.

"Okay, hold it. My brain is just not pliable enough to handle that kind of heroic convolution," I confessed.

Having found no C-4 in our backpacks or Uzis strapped to our inner thighs, agents Leyland and Fitzhugh eventually escorted us to the boathouse and warned us against any further unauthorized river cavorting. It was easy advice to follow. My body would need at least a week of recovery before I could even contemplate a return to cavorting of any kind.

Lindsay seemed to have a much easier time finding the humour in our little adventure than I did. Then again, she hadn't been body-slammed to the ice by a former Navy SEAL diving from a speeding Ski-Doo. She nursed me back to health for the rest of the afternoon and I felt better by the evening. As we'd

266

promised the Secret Service, Lindsay packed a bag and headed to her mother's for the night. They'd done security checks only on Angus and me, so Lindsay would have to vacate the property until after POTUS and FLOTUS had safely departed the next afternoon. We kissed and she was out the door, escorted to her car by Barbie, er, Agent Fitzhugh. I went over the itinerary for the next day again and practised my presidential small talk before turning in early. I read several sentences of John Irving's new novel before dropping the heavy tome onto my face as I nodded off. Awake again and nursing my tender nose, I was then able to read several more pages before sleep finally came.

DIARY

Friday, February 21

My Love,

Young Daniel has done a fine job as wordsmith on the report. It balances eloquence and clarity in a way that eludes so many writers. There's an economy to it. Simplicity and concision, with no wasted words. And that must have been a challenge for him, as political speech writers naturally tend towards hubris and hyperbole.

I wish I could report that the Prime Minister is happy with it, but no matter. I'll sleep soundly tonight even as we're pushed from the fold. We've done what we agreed to do, but Daniel thinks we're now on our own until the public leaps on our bandwagon. I did not know we were driving one.

Tomorrow, the President and First Lady. Ye gods, how did this happen?

AM

CHAPTER SEVENTEEN

I awoke to see the perfectly coiffed head of Agent Leyland framed in my window, speaking into the cuff of his jacket. He nodded ever so slightly. I waved him away and he descended out of sight as if he were on a motorized scaffold on the side of the boathouse. When I eventually got up, I discovered there was a motorized scaffold on the side of the boathouse. Agent Leyland, I found, didn't call it a scaffold. Scaffolds were for painting and window washing. No, this was an ESS, an Elevational Sniper Station. Of course it was.

As outlined in our pre-visit briefings, the President and First Lady's stopover was not an official state visit, so I did not have to rent a tux to greet the most powerful couple in the world for breakfast with Angus. It was to be casual attire. After all, it was a Saturday morning, and the President was a good old boy from Kentucky who'd grown up on a farm. I figured jeans and boots were his preferred clothes anyway. I pulled on just-back-from-the-cleaners Levi's cords and a black turtleneck, before heading out to walk up the path to the McLintock house. I was searched on my own porch and then escorted by four Secret Service agents to ensure that I had no plans for setting fires, launching rockets, or deploying deadly nerve gas. I really only wanted a glass of orange juice. But I confess it boosted my self-esteem to know that the Secret Service at least considered the possibility that I might be capable of some rash and monumental act of political violence. They seemed to think I was actually worth keeping an eye on. Cool.

Angus and I were just standing around trying not to violate the security perimeter or make any sudden movements when the Prime Minister and Bradley Stanton arrived. It was about 8:50, with forty minutes to go before the twelve-vehicle motorcade was to arrive.

The PM's plainclothes RCMP detail blended in with the Secret Service so that we couldn't tell them apart. It was the one time those silly scarlet tunics might have been helpful. The Prime Minister and Bradley pulled Angus and me out onto the deck. Bradley wore his standard-issue scowl, and the PM did not look happy as he turned to face us.

"I'm not happy. The so-called McLintock Report reaches well beyond the mandate I outlined. You've gone deeper in the investigation than I had intended and it's put us in a very awkward position politically. You do see that, don't you?" the PM asked.

I jumped in to give Angus a chance to cool down. I knew he'd be angered by the PM's opening gambit.

"Prime Minister, the report is comprehensive, built on irrefutable facts, and illuminates a national priority, the urgency and scope of which we were largely unaware before Angus started clambering among the twisted girders of the Alexandra Bridge."

The PM looked pensive and not ready yet to respond, so I just kept talking.

"I truly believe it gives you a great opportunity to do the right thing when the right thing is so obviously staring us in the face. This, to me, is an easy call, even politically. You can still score some big political points on the Tories' last fifteen years of underfunding. Yes, we started the ball rolling twenty years ago, but there's not a single Liberal MP, let alone minister, still in the House from that time. Canadians are ready for this kind of straight talk, for this kind of transparency. I think you should run with it."

The PM didn't look convinced.

"I understand your position, Daniel, but it's not that simple. I've got Coulombe crawling up my ass." He paused to look at

Angus. "Pardon my language, Angus. And we've also got a set of numbers telling us that Canadians want their damn tax cuts – you know, the ones we promised a few weeks ago, remember?"

I sensed that Angus wanted in, so I clammed up.

"Prime Minister, our situation has changed. A bridge has collapsed into the river and along with it any pretence that either the Liberals or the Tories actually slew the deficit. We are not rid of the deficit, we just hid the deficit. You can now find part of it in the Ottawa River."

The PM actually smiled at Angus's imagery.

"You've clearly been spending too much time with my former speechwriter. It's black and white to you two, but I'm the Prime Minister now, and decisions are seldom binary. I've still got some thinking to do, but let's get through this charade of a presidential visit first."

"I'm still back on slew," said Bradley, looking at Angus. "Slew?"

"Yes, slew. Are you not familiar with the past tense of slay?"

"Well, I'd have stayed with slayed," Bradley suggested.

"That doesn't surprise me in the least" was all that Angus said.

"Okay, it's almost show time," remarked the PM, checking his watch. "Angus, notwithstanding my, er, irritation over how this bridge business is unfolding, your home is wonderful and I'm glad to be welcoming the President and First Lady here. Thank you for indulging my desire to hold this gathering in your remarkable home."

"I'm pleased to host it, Prime Minister," Angus said. "I regret my wife is missing this."

I heard *Marine One* before I saw it. Looking up, we all focused on three helicopters heading our way from Ottawa in the west. *Marine One* was flanked by two smaller choppers that looked harmless enough but likely packed enough firepower to conquer a small republic. I think they actually call them gunships. On the river, a large square of ice had been cleared and four flares in tinfoil pans now burned brightly, one in each corner. *Baddeck 1* was resting on the ice next to the dock, like a stone lion in front of the New York Public Library. After all, for the President, seeing the hovercraft was one of the reasons he'd wanted to come.

The Prime Minister, Angus, Bradley Stanton, and I stood in the prescribed formation on the dock, just as we had during the seven rehearsals. I felt we'd all nailed our parts in only three rehearsals, but the protocol officials weren't quite convinced. As the trio of whirlybirds approached, I scanned Angus's domain. We'd heard no more about chopping down trees, and Marin's silver maple still stood tall, presiding over the scene. I did feel sorry for the Secret Service agent halfway up the seventy-five-foot tree, one arm clinging to the thick trunk, the other holding binoculars, ever-alert to threats. I thought it unfair that the term "tree-hugger" had become so closely tied to environmentalists.

As I surveyed the area, I saw dozens of Secret Service and RCMP officers. They were stationed every fifty metres or so along the shore, on snowmobiles out on the ice, on the roof of the boathouse, up trees, under the McLintock deck, on the road leading to the house, and quite likely under the McLintock matrimonial bed. Security was, to say the least, tight. If I'd needed to make an unscheduled washroom stop (I had two planned bathroom breaks in the master schedule), by the time the strip search and interrogation had been completed, my need for the bathroom would have resolved itself, and not in a good way.

Everyone seemed to stiffen just a bit as the helicopters drew nearer. As the PM had said earlier, it was nearly showtime. A separate, cordoned-off zone on the ice housed about two dozen reporters from the White House press corps, the Parliamentary Press Gallery, and a couple of local reporters, including André Fontaine. White House communications staff engaged in reporter husbandry stood along the perimeter of the area, keeping the journalists in their pen.

Marine One settled in the centre of the square landing area and shut down, the rotor blades spinning slowly to a stop. A red carpet was rolled over the ice to the machine and two marines, polished to an impossible sheen, marched to the end and waited. Then the hatch swung down to rest on the ground, steps and a railing magically unfolding with it. White hats gleaming, the marines stood ramrod-straight on either side of the hatch and stared dead ahead, oblivious by training to whatever happened on the four steps that descended to the ground between them. After Gerald Ford's several wipeouts, I'd have thought that they'd be ready with crash mats, airbags, and maybe a gigantic catcher's mitt in case of another presidential stair stumble. But no. The first out the door were two other chiselled marines, who formed a line at the bottom of the stairs. Then two more standard-issue Secret Service agents appeared. They were either eating snacks directly out of their sleeves or more likely were talking into their standard-issue cuff radios as they came down the steps. They immediately used their X-ray vision to scour the area for threats, their lethal hands clasped in front of them, affecting an air of extreme, even dangerous, vigilance. In the sunlight, they wore dark glasses but I could tell their eyes never stayed on the same object for more than a second – attention deficit disorder writ large.

Then, there they were. The President and the First Lady. He had a firm grip on her right elbow, and it looked as if she needed it. There was a slight sway to her gait, as if she were test-driving someone else's feet. She wore large dark sunglasses, a bright red ski jacket, black denim pants, gloves, and boots. No hat. You don't mess with the First Lady's *do*. All that talk about keeping alcohol away from the First Lady seemed moot. I thought she already looked as if she'd drained a few of those little airline bottles. The President looked . . . presidential, casually dressed for the rustic surroundings in black cords, a leather mid-length jacket, black scarf, and suede hiking boots of some kind. No gloves, no hat. He seemed a little concerned, but armed his wife down the steps onto the red carpet. A wooden set of stairs, built by a White House carpenter, painted white, and shipped north with the advance team, was put in place to bring the honoured visitors up from the ice to the dock, where we all waited. I expected to hear the strains of *Hail to the Chief* blast out from speakers hidden in the fuselage of *Marine One*, or even the fuselage of one of the marines, but it was eerily silent, other than the sustained clicking of cameras.

As practised, the Prime Minister stepped forward and extended his hand to the power couple.

"Mr. President, Madam First Lady, I welcome you to Canada and to the shores of our beautiful Ottawa River."

"Well, it's great to be up here, Prime Minister, and we thank you for your hospitality," the President replied, still holding onto his wife.

There were introductions and handshakes and all manner of smiling, nodding, and the occasional slight bow. The President seemed more relaxed now, and actually looked better in person than on TV. I stifled the urge to tell him. His wife perked up and was perfectly pleasant throughout the three and a half minutes of programmed small talk and banalities that seemed a mainstay of modern diplomacy. The photographers needed time to get their shots so the PM and his special guests turned to face the cameras and plastered on the photo op smiles.

A minute or two later – actually, by the schedule, it was exactly ninety seconds – a White House staffer nodded to Angus to signal the start of the next choreographed segment of the visit. On cue, Angus stepped forward slowly and deliberately so the Secret Service agents' hands wouldn't fly to the advanced hidden weaponry accessorizing their JC Penney suits. I saw at least one of the agents looking very carefully at Angus's beard, probably realizing for the first time that the grey whisker curtain could conceal almost anything from a grenade launcher to a sidewinder missile.

"Mr. President, Madam First Lady, would you care for a wee gander at the hovercraft before we head up to the house? I gather its modest exploits have reached your ears in Washington."

The President was about to respond when a newly animated First Lady leapt in.

"Why, Mr. McLintock, it is an amazing story," she drawled. "I'd love to see it."

The President just smiled and nodded, adding his endorsement.

As planned, I stayed on the dock with Bradley, while Angus led the PM, President, and First Lady back onto the ice and around *Baddeck 1*. He had precisely nine and a half minutes to explain the unique single-engine hovercraft before beginning the procession up to the house. When discussing his prized creation, Angus could chatter on for nine and a half hours. Cutting it down to under ten minutes would be a challenge. That's why the clipboard-bearing timekeeper from the President's staff was there. She moved down onto the ice at the seven-minute mark as yet another prearranged signal. Angus didn't even notice her. No matter, the President, and particularly his wife, seemed enthralled. They both asked several questions and leaned into the cockpit as Angus explained the craft's operations. Conversely, the hovercraft lecture seemed to keep the PM on the edge of his sleep. He tried to look interested but I knew him too well. He was bored stiff and probably resented how much attention Angus was getting.

I was about twenty feet away, but could still hear the conversation quite easily.

"Could we not go for a ride in it, Mr. McLintock?" the First Lady implored. "The sensation of flying so close to the ground must be exhilarating."

"Aye, it is quite uplifting," Angus quipped. "I regret our governments have thrown the shackles on us, Madam, but I'm told there's to be no spin in the hovercraft, despite what we both might like."

That earned a glare from clipboard woman.

"I hope we might have a chance for a flight on a return visit sometime, Mr. McLintock," said the President. "Thank you for showing us her. She's a beauty."

"Aye, she is that, sir."

The First Lady was miffed and climbed back up the stairs to the dock, much to the relief of the timekeeper. Angus had gone overtime by nearly six minutes. Not quite an international incident, but on the way there.

Five minutes later, we were all inside. The house was immaculate, as it usually was, and everyone oohhhed and aahhhed accordingly. Angus stood next to a bookcase filled with his wife's works, rested his arm on the top shelf, and beamed. Coats were stowed, coffee served, and brunch laid out on the table by the catering staff of ten, auditioned and approved by the White House. With body temperatures returning to normal, formal introductions were again made, without gloves compromising the handshakes. The President was very gracious and congratulated the PM and Angus on their electoral success. The Prime Minister presented the President and First Lady with an Inuit soapstone carving and a gallon of pure Cumberland maple syrup. The President then bestowed on the Prime Minister a bottle of Korbel Natural, the American champagne that was the official tipple of the last several presidential inaugurations. I was a bit unnerved at hearing "American" and "champagne" in the same sentence. The United States is known for many fine foods. Chicken wings, corn dogs, beef jerky, grits, and the Twinkie. Champagne? Not so much.

I remembered the ambassador's demand that there be no alcohol on the premises, but figured if the President had brought it as a gift, we were in the clear. As the ranking political staffer, Bradley Stanton was given the task of opening the Californian champagne. He immediately delegated the task to the second-ranking political staffer. Me. No problem. As a non-drinker, I'd opened precisely no bottles of champagne in my life, but how hard could it be? I peeled back the foil and then wrestled briefly with the little wire doohickey that was clearly installed to prevent someone who is already inebriated from opening the bottle. I passed the sobriety test, but wasn't sure what to do next. So I started twisting the cork while holding the bottle between my knees. The President stood about ten feet away from me speaking with the Prime Minister. I noticed Agent Leyland watching me and saw his facial expression transform from calm and passive to "what the hell are you doing, you idiot." He apparently caught sight of the full nelson I had on the neck of the champagne bottle and saw what I did not, the nearly imperceptible twitch of the cork.

"Down, Mr. President!" he shouted, and then launched himself into a swan dive in front of the U.S. head of state. While he was in flight, the champagne cork shot out of the bottle with the blast of a 12-gauge shotgun. The whole scene then clicked into cinematic slow motion. I felt a column of champagne strike my chin as I watched the ballistic cork strike the flying Secret Service officer perfectly in the family jewels. I don't mean kind of by his groin, or just below his navel. I mean a perfect, dead-on crotch shot. In a blink, the wordsmith in me conjured up "ballseye."

Yes, Agent Leyland took the shot that was headed for the President. It was every Secret Service agent's dream. He looked almost blissful as he writhed in pain on the living room floor. When we all realized what had happened and DEFCON 1 was dialled back to the standard peacetime setting of DEFCON 5, Angus brought us all out of our shocked silence, standing over Agent Leyland.

"I take it, laddie, that you didnae wear your Kevlar cup this morning. More's the pity."

A short time later, I'd changed from my champagne-soaked clothes and Agent Leyland's voice had returned to its traditional baritone. The brunch buffet had been exhausted and the timekeeper signalled the start of the one-on-one private talks between the PM and the President. It was scheduled for forty-five minutes. Twelve minutes on trade, fifteen minutes on defence, fourteen minutes on border control issues, and four minutes on joint space program efforts. Bradley would sit in, along with one of the White House staffers.

I was nervous about our role during this portion of the visit. Angus and I were to escort the First Lady on a tour of the property. She was not supposed to have been given any champagne, but in the melee that followed my inadvertent presidential assassination attempt, as the crowd gathered around the President and the fallen agent, she'd snatched the bottle from between my knees, turned her back on the group, and guzzled. Only I saw it. She'd winked at me after lowering the bottle and pressed her index finger to my lips, making me a co-conspirator.

I could tell she'd chugged more than a mouthful when I helped her put on her coat. It took her several tries – okay, thirteen tries – to find the right sleeve opening as I held her ski jacket. Angus offered his arm to her when she'd bundled up for the walk, and we headed out the door. We were barely down the walk when she stopped.

"Mr. McLintock, Angus I mean, would you show me the hovercraft again? I barely got a look at it before that hag with the clipboard shoved us up the path."

Angus looked at me and I just shrugged. That's what I always did when I had no idea what to do.

"I don't see why we couldn't do that. We were to take you around the property and I have to think that includes the dock and what lies beside it," Angus rationalized.

We turned left and headed down the path towards the river. Barbie, Agent Fitzhugh, walked a few paces behind. She was at least a pace or two too close for the First Lady's liking.

"Back off, Tammy, or Skipper, or whatever your name is," she snapped.

"I believe it's Jennifer," I whispered, instinctively locked into my role as a trusty adviser.

"Right. Back off, Jennifer, and give me some space to breathe," she pleaded. "I'm fine. I'm safe. I'm just going to look at the hovercraft with these nice, safe, gentle, and polite Canadians. There's no call to smother me. So just back off."

Agent Fitzhugh seemed momentarily stunned by the outburst, but eventually backed off a few steps and promptly buried her mouth in her sleeve, no doubt reporting in to Central Command.

I noticed the other Secret Service agents in the area taking two steps back. The First Lady noticed, too.

"Thank you," she purred.

I stayed on the dock as Angus showed the First Lady *Baddeck 1* again. She held his arm with both hands and seemed very happy. Very happy. Then she detached herself from Angus and, with considerable grace, vaulted into the cockpit and sat demurely in the passenger seat, rubbing her hands together in what I could only conclude was anticipation.

"Come and show me what all these little knobs are for, won't you, Angus?" she asked, patting the seat next to hers.

Uh-oh. I had a faint idea where this was headed and it didn't feel so good. I could tell that Angus liked her spirit. He stepped into the driver's side and sank into the seat. A ripple seemed to pass through the Secret Service. They all took two steps closer and were no longer just alert. They'd moved into super-ultra-alert mode.

I saw the First Lady reach into the space where the seat meets the padded seatback and she withdrew what looked like a silver flask. Surely she hadn't secreted it there when they'd first arrived. Angus took it from her and examined it before handing it back to her. I have no idea why he handed it back to her. I'm sure that, back on shore, the hair on the back of the neck of the U.S. ambassador to Canada just stood on end.

"That must have been left by a reporter from our local paper when we went for an unexpected ride up the river back in December."

Then she turned to me. "What was your name again?"

"Daniel Addison, at your service."

"Would you mind taking two steps forward and putting your hands on your hips?"

I did what I was told and in an instant, shielded by me, she'd unscrewed the top of the flask and without even taking a whiff first, downed whatever had been in there in one fell swoop (or sip as it were). In a flash, the empty flask was back under the seat.

"Ahhhhhhh. I think that was Johnny Walker Gold. Your reporter friend has good taste," she replied. "Okay, Angus, my man, rev her up and let's see what this baby can do."

"Madam, I'm not permitted to give you a ride, though I'd dearly love to. It's not in the blessed itinerary. And I'm already in trouble with your Secret Service friends for putting on my light coat when I'd already committed to wearing my blue parka."

"Oh come on, Angus. I live each day in a prison. I can never be by myself. I hardly ever see my husband, so having kids isn't looking so good. I'm bored and tired and I just want a little excitement once in a while." She looked at Angus with such a plaintive and forlorn expression that I think Angus may well have robbed a bank with her if she'd asked.

Uh-oh. This was not good. Not good at all.

"Ah, Angus, please don't do it. Do not even think about it, Angus. Angus," I found myself blurting, "don't do you dare, Angus. Ang–"

Yep, you have it right. Angus punched the newly installed and working-like-a-charm starter button. *Baddeck 1* lifted off the ice and headed towards the middle of the river. The engine couldn't quite drown out the First Lady's squeal of delight. I saw her punch the air with one hand as she held on with the other.

I decided the intelligent and prudent thing to do was to run as fast as I could after the hovercraft, waving my arms wildly and shouting "Annnnnnnguuuuuuuus!" over and over again, like an asylum escapee. I fell on the ice, twice. I hadn't remembered falling, but it came back to me when I watched it on the news that night, and then on YouTube, over and over again.

Secret Service agents are generally not known for their tolerance when it comes to kidnapping the First Lady of the United States. *Baddeck 1* was barely fifty metres onto the ice when a squadron of snowmobiles, or is it a drift of snowmobiles, was scrambled and in hot pursuit. Fifteen seconds later, both escort choppers were nearly on top of *Baddeck 1*. In the distance, I could see twenty or thirty cameras attached to journalists trying to get some newsworthy shots of the private presidential visit from beyond the security cordon. How about a renegade MP abducting the First Lady in a hovercraft? Is that newsworthy enough for you?

They didn't get far. Angus shut her down as soon as he saw the choppers. They hovered directly overhead, kicking up so much snow that all you could see below them was a white cyclone. The pilots eventually understood that the First Lady probably wouldn't appreciate what the choppers' downdraft was doing to her hair, so they backed off and landed on the ice fifty metres or so away. The scene and the snow slowly settled.

At first, I wondered where they'd gone. When visibility was restored, *Baddeck 1* was coated, stem to stern, in snow. It blended in with its surroundings very well. I was feeling queasy by this time. What seemed like an eternity later, but was probably just a few seconds, I saw first a mitten and then a frosted head pop up above the windscreen. Angus was not very happy. He disappeared below again and surfaced with the First Lady. She was completely white with snow, and red with rage. By then, the Secret Service in their snowmobiles had surrounded the snowbound hovercraft and were scrambling to "secure" or, more accurately, extract the presidential spouse.

For a semi-intoxicated, snow-encrusted First Lady, she seemed to have reasonable control over the uppercut she threw at the first agent to reach her. She landed it, too.

Had the President not intervened, the Secret Service investigation might still be going on. He lived with the First Lady and had no difficulty understanding how Angus might have been persuaded to take her for a ride in *Baddeck 1*. After *Marine One* lifted off with the President and the chilled First Lady, and the Prime Minister and Bradley Stanton had stomped to their limousine, it had taken Angus, the two Petes, and me an hour to dig out *Baddeck 1* and get her safely back into the boathouse. Angus used a hair dryer on the engine to combat the deleterious effects of melting snow. I had no idea Angus, of all people, knew how to operate a hair dryer.

The Secret Service needed a few hours to tear down their security installations and vacate the property. They didn't lift a finger to help us dig out the hovercraft. Well, actually, one of them did lift a finger our way as he drove by on a snowmobile. Nice.

"Can I just ask one simple question?" I inquired.

"Do you mean in addition to that one?" said Angus.

"Yes. It's very straightforward. Not complicated at all," I said. "What were you thinking?"

Angus paused to look pensive.

"I was thinking just how sorry I felt for that poor woman," he explained in a serious tone. "She's a prisoner as surely as an Alcatraz inmate."

"Well, that's her lot in life. She's the First Lady. It comes with the turf."

"I just didn't see what harm there was in taking her for a spin about the river."

"'A spin about the river?' Angus, come on. You knew that's all it was. The First Lady knew that was your intention. I knew you had no nefarious motivations. But the Secret Service is programmed to think that Girl Guide cookies are laced with arsenic and razor blades. That's how their brains work. And that's what keeps the President and his family safe."

Angus stared out the window and said nothing.

"So their reaction when you took off in the hovercraft was as predictable as it was effective," I said quietly. We sat in silence for a while. Eventually, I stood and walked to the chess table.

"Enough of this, let's play."

DIARY
Saturday, February 22
My Love,
What a cock-up I made of today. And I blame you. When that poor woman appealed to me, and asked for so simple a gift, your presence hung heavy all about us. Even when we were exchanging pleasantries at the outset, she brought you

to mind. One hardly thinks of the First Lady of the United States when considering the inequality of the sexes, or what John Stuart Mill called the "subjection of women." I know I reach perhaps too far to connect her plight to the broader cause of equality. She is a bird in a gilded cage. Yet I sensed it even in her, poor soul. She is at the very centre of the world, yet she seems so very unhappy and has so few freedoms. Despite her vaunted heights, I say the same timeless forces are in play. Wouldn't you?

You would surely have been compelled to respond to her as you so often did with the thousands of women you met, taught, and inspired. So, dear one, I blame you for my rash act. You, and John Stuart Mill.

Daniel was beside himself with incredulity and even anger. He took a few shots at me for my stunt, and I deserved it, I suppose. I was good and took it all till he was himself again. But then I gave it all right back to him on the board, and that felt better. Three games in succession. Aye, that felt better.

AM

CHAPTER EIGHTEEN

My cellphone rang. I was in a coma at the time but Lindsay nudged me with enough force to bring me to the surface. It was nice to have her home again, now that the Secret Service had finally vacated the property. I took an additional second or two to focus my bleary eyes on the phone's screen for the caller ID.

"Muriel, don't tell me you're up and about at this hour, it's still dark outside."

"It's nearly 7:30. It's always dark at this hour in February," she replied. "And yes, I'm up. I'm over eighty. At this age I don't sleep in. I can't afford to miss anything this late in the game."

"Don't be talking that way," I scolded. "You're going to out-live us all."

"Not with the gut rot they serve here I won't. It's damn hard to screw up Cream of Wheat but somehow they manage to, every day."

I was fully awake now, at least my head was. My arms, legs, and the rest of my body were still asleep.

"So which side are you on? Are you in favour of Angus abducting the President's spouse, or opposed?" I asked. "Right now, it's running two to one in favour."

"That woman is trouble. I knew it the moment she slithered into the White House," Muriel declared.

"Well, Angus feels sorry for her."

"He won't when he sees the front pages of virtually every U.S. and Canadian Sunday paper. And for pity's sake, do not turn on CNN."

After I'd hung up, I revved up my laptop and started browsing newspaper websites, just to indulge my masochistic streak.

Our photographic nemesis, André Fontaine, had hit the jackpot, again. His photo had been syndicated through Canadian Press and had by now appeared in dozens, perhaps hundreds, of newspapers around the country and beyond. Some were in colour, some black and white. But all were big.

André told me later that he'd been stationed on our neighbour's dock, still within the security cordon. He'd been lying on his stomach with a small table-top tripod and a humongous telephoto lens. It was just his good fortune that when the maelstrom of snow kicked up by the choppers finally settled, a gift from the Nikon gods revealed itself – a head-on shot at just the perfect angle and elevation. He snapped one perfect photo before the scene was overrun by Secret Service agents, snowmobiles, and helicopters. Amazing photographs get picked up. When CP put it on their photo-wire, it went viral around the world in minutes. One perfect shot.

Whether on the front pages of the *Washington Post*, the *Miami Herald*, the *Globe and Mail*, or the *Ottawa Citizen*, or every fifteen minutes or so on CNN, MSNBC, and CBC Newsworld, Angus was clearly abusing the fifteen-minutes-of-fame rule. There was plenty of video footage of the unauthorized joyride, but it was hard to argue with the power of André's perfect still. Like most compelling photos, his was simple in its composition. Calling it a head-on shot was really a misnomer. Filling the frame were the heads of Angus McLintock and his co-conspirator, the First Lady, frosted and frantic, poking up above what I knew to be the snow-covered windscreen of *Baddeck 1*. It literally looked as if their decapitated heads had been placed on a snowbank, yet the rage and shock on the First Lady's face made it all too apparent that she was alive, unhurt, and, well, apoplectic. In comparison, Angus looked like a shocked sheepdog who had run amok in a flour mill. Even in a vacuum, with absolutely no wind or air currents to trouble his tresses, it would still be tough to tame his hair and beard. So forgive me, but I do not have words to describe what the rotors of two helicopters did to his unique look. Yes, I am a speechwriter by training, accustomed to putting the impossible into words. But I do have my limits so I'll not even try. Virtually all the media coverage made it clear that Angus had no subversive intentions, but had wilted under the thrill-seeking First Lady's legendary powers of persuasion. When she explained her version of the unauthorized joyride, she exonerated Angus, and the Secret Service agents holstered their howitzers. There was some talk of recalling the American ambassador to Canada in protest, but cooler heads prevailed. In fact, it was the frozen head of the First Lady that prevailed. Just another day in Angus McLintock's orbit.

I spent the better part of Sunday, the traditional day of rest, talking Bradley Stanton down from a very high ledge. After about an hour, I succeeded in persuading him that sending a special undercover elite black ops military team to dispatch Angus and me would probably prompt some questions. I'm not absolutely certain his threat wasn't serious. But a quick and painless death would hardly satisfy his blood lust for vengeance.

He was most upset that there was barely a shred of media coverage of the quite productive and constructive talks between the PM and the President.

"The PM made real progress with the Pres. in a very short time on some thorny issues that have languished for years," said Bradley. "But there's no ink on that because idiot Angus and the First Freak went AWOL!"

"Bradley, I know it looks bad right now, but it could have been a lot worse," I replied.

"Yeah? Please tell me how it could have been worse? Just tell me! I'm serious. I want you to tell me just how this fucking debacle could have been any worse!"

Why I set myself up like that all the time, I will never know.

"Well, uhm, well, the Secret Service could have fired a rocket-propelled grenade and blown up the hovercraft."

"And just exactly how would that have been worse?"

I had nothing. The conversation cycled through the topic a few more times as eventually the fire in Bradley's vitriol died down.

"And to make matters worse, the PM and that asshole Coulombe are still duking it out on the Budget," offered Bradley. "If we weren't so vulnerable in Quebec, we'd have never put him in Finance."

"What do you mean, they're duking it out on the Budget?" I asked.

"Don't you play fucking coy with me. You know what I'm talking about. You and your hairy beast started all of this, and it's making my life a living hell."

Interesting. That was just what I'd wanted to hear. It seemed we might still be alive, despite the First Lady fiasco. Bradley eventually grew tired of fighting and hung up. I unplugged our phone and didn't dare venture out for the rest of the day. Lindsay's return home from her Secret Service–imposed exile made cocooning in the boathouse an easy call.

It was odd that caucus would be briefed two days before Cabinet, but the logistics in getting all ministers together in one room outside of the regular etched-in-stone Wednesday morning time defeated the meeting-makers. Plus, to accommodate Angus and his report, that week's Cabinet meeting was to start an hour early, conflicting with the weekly caucus meeting. The upshot? A special caucus meeting on Monday. Always concerned about controlling the message, Bradley instructed us to hit only the broad strokes of the report at caucus and save the details for the Cabinet meeting on Wednesday. He'd also fired off a stern memo to remind the entire caucus that the McLintock Report was highly confidential and any leaky MPs would pay a heavy price if their lips were loose.

On Monday morning, the ribbing started up as soon as Angus and I arrived at the special caucus briefing.

"Want to make some snow angels, Angus?"

"Hope this briefing isn't going to be one of your snow-jobs, Angus."

"Hey Angus, you really know how to show a girl a good time."

"I hear you've been snowed under with this report."

Etc., etc. What sparkling wit. I worried that Angus might just blow if one more ham-handed and futile attempt at humour were lobbed his way. But Angus seemed almost serene. He understood just how important this briefing was and seemed more than willing to suffer the slings and arrows of really bad jokes from backbenchers, most of whom were backbenchers for good reason. He just smiled and nodded as the primitive barbs flew and then died on the ground around him. The ubiquitous front-page Fontaine photo stared back at us from no fewer than nine newspapers resting on chairs and tables throughout the room.

"Aye, it's been a dream of mine to be buried alive with the First Lady of the United States. I can now check that off my list," remarked Angus to a chorus of guffaws.

As expected, no Cabinet ministers attended, so the mood in the room was a little more relaxed than it might have otherwise been. Two lower ranking PMO staffers were there to monitor and report back to Bradley, but most of the caucus members didn't even know who they were. I nodded to them when we arrived and they nodded back. The friendly banter continued for about ten minutes to allow a few stragglers to arrive, then, to business.

As planned, I took the podium first as the MPs and a few senators settled and took their seats.

"Good morning. For those of you whom I've not yet met, I'm Daniel Addison and I work for the Cumberland-Prescott MP, Angus McLintock, from whom we'll hear in a moment. This is a special meeting of caucus with a single agenda item. Angus will give you a big-picture briefing on the collapse of the Alexandra Bridge and then outline the general direction of his recommendations for ensuring that such a failure never recurs. Bradley Stanton has asked me, well more accurately, he demanded that I remind you all that this is a highly confidential briefing. I don't think you need to hear it again, but I'm supposed to remind you all that what you hear this morning is not yet public. So we are all sworn to secrecy until it is made public, we expect, later this week. For this reason, no hard copies of Professor McLintock's report will be distributed this morning. Finally, because of the travel schedules of some ministers, you're actually hearing this before Cabinet is briefed on Wednesday morning. So we're counting on your discretion."

"We can keep a secret, you know," whined one MP with a tinge of exasperation in his voice. "We're not children."

"I hear you, but I promised Bradley that I'd reiterate the importance of confidentiality on this until it hits the streets officially."

"And what's the big deal anyway? An old bridge gave way. So what."

"Well, now might be a good time to invite Angus McLintock to top-line his report and why this is in fact a big deal. Angus?"

I sat at the table across the front of the room as Angus came forward. He ignored the podium and simply stood before the government caucus. As usual, he had no notes.

"Good morning. I thank you for convening this special gathering. Daniel is right. This is a big deal. It has the potential to affect each one of us, every other MP from the other parties, and ultimately every Canadian."

He then pointed to the MP who had spoken up earlier.

"You, sir, just asked 'What's the big deal?' Let me tell you. Yes, a single century-old bridge has collapsed. But our investigation reveals that this is not an isolated event. This is not a single aberration predicted by statisticians and actuaries based on how many bridges we have in this vast country. I implore you, do not think of it in that way. Do not delude yourselves as past governments have, including Liberal regimes. You must understand and accept that if we sit idly by and do nothing, I promise you, the collapse of the Alexandra Bridge will be just the first in a long and tragic series of catastrophic infrastructure failures across the country that will surely cripple our economy and cost Canadian lives. Lives we could have saved. I can put it no more plainly than that."

Angus had the room now.

"We have the power to transform the Alexandra Bridge collapse into an isolated incident, but only if we muster the political will to act quickly in defence of the national interest."

Silence in the room. All eyes now fixed on Angus. Had the fire alarm sounded, I doubt whether anyone in the room would have noticed.

"Now, with that preface, let me tell you the story of the Alexandra Bridge so that you, too, will see it as a national warning we must heed."

Angus then proceeded to pace the room as he talked. He spoke so powerfully and eloquently that it sounded scripted, yet I knew it wasn't. He just had that innate ability to command the room: to combine eye contact, gestures, movement, and voice in such a balanced way that his audience was left somewhere between transfixed and spellbound. In fifteen uninterrupted minutes, he summarized his report. He covered the actual physical cause of the collapse using language and metaphors that the average Canadian could understand. He spent time on the maintenance records, on the steady decline in funding, on the systematic neglect, and on the mounting evidence that this was just the first collapse of many. He noted that the sad state of the Alexandra Bridge captured, in microcosm, the sad state of Canada's infrastructure. He did his "We haven't beaten, but just transformed, the deficit" routine, and it seemed to take root. Many were either nodding in understanding or shaking their heads in concern.

Angus concluded by outlining the general direction of our recommendations. He didn't give figures on the required spending to restore Canada's infrastructure but he did make it clear that it would take time and much more money than the government had ever intended to spend on such unexciting long-term initiatives as roads, bridges, ports, and canals.

Even though Angus was thorough, convincing, articulate, and passionate, not everyone was convinced.

"This just seems too far out there to believe," started one skeptic. "Is what you've just told us really entirely true?"

Although Angus was tolerant of many things, stupid questions that cast doubt on his integrity were not among them.

"No, now that I'm off my meds, this is entirely a construct of my very fertile imagination," sneered Angus, shaking his head. There was a limit to Angus's equanimity, and the backbencher had just blown right through it. "Of course it's all true. We've just spent the last three weeks getting to the bottom of this sorry story. I've hung by a rope in the guts of the downed bridge. We've met with dozens of experts who have spent their professional lives in this world. We've followed the paper trail to irrefutable conclusions. We've crunched the blessed numbers. Everything I've just presented has been documented, verified, corroborated, double-checked, and examined under a microscope and through a telescope in search of even the tiniest tear in the truth. This, ladies and gentlemen, is as close to gospel as we'll ever get."

"But it sounds like it'll cost billions to get back to where we need to be," complained one MP. "We just can't afford to cough up that kind of dough right now, particularly when we've promised tax cuts. We're screwed."

"I'm neither the Prime Minister, nor the Finance Minister, for which I'm certain you're all grateful," conceded Angus. "The power to resolve the spending dilemma our report undeniably raises rests largely with them. It will not be easy. But governing responsibly is seldom easy. If presented effectively, I believe Canadians will accept that infrastructure decay is not just a priority, but very nearly a national crisis, requiring extraordinary remedial measures. It is my fervent hope that the PM and Monsieur Coulombe will accept the dire findings and embrace the recommendations of our report."

"And what about the tax cuts we all rode to victory on?" asked a backbencher incongruously sitting in the front row.

"Aye. I know, I know. I suppose one option is to delay them for a few years until we've got a start on redressing our infra-structure," replied Angus.

"Don't forget that investing in infrastructure will also create jobs, which will bring in more tax dollars. In this economic cli-mate, such an investment will pay dividends, even if we suffer politically in the early going," I chimed in.

The discussion continued until the attention span of the caucus had been exhausted. There were many questions, some of them even good ones. Through it all, except for that initial sarcastic rebuttal, Angus maintained a calm and authoritative demeanour. I tried to read the room but there were quite a few poker faces. Some were trying to hide how they felt, while others were trying to hide that they didn't know what to think. I'm sure many were simply waiting to hear from the Leader's office before deciding how to feel about this issue. That's the reality of politics. Still, I was encouraged after the meeting. It seemed to me that Angus had turned at least a healthy portion of the assembled to our side. As the meeting broke up, the two PMO plants scuttled out the door on their way back to report to Bradley.

"Well, what's your read?" I asked Angus as we walked back to our office.

"I cannae tell for sure, but I think we may have turned a few minds," he replied.

"It was a good warm-up," I noted. "The real test is on Wednesday. Cabinet is where the decisions are made. Cabinet and the PMO."

That afternoon at four, after the markets had closed for the day, the Senate chamber filled to capacity for the Throne Speech. In a 600-year-old tradition, the Usher of the Black Rod, the Senate's ceremonial security officer, led the members of the House of Commons down the main corridor of Centre Block and into the red Senate chamber. MPs do not have official standing in the

Senate and so must stand behind a bar in the entrance to hear the Speech from the Throne.

Angus was there, of course, but I decided to watch the proceedings on television from our office. The PM looked pleased and proud to be sitting in the ornate chair at the right hand of the Governor General. A former Saskatchewan Cabinet Minister, the GG was seated up a few steps from the PM in the beautiful and ornate wood and upholstered throne at the very epicentre of the Senate. She wore a multicoloured dress that sparkled so much it looked as if she were wearing a sack of exploding fireworks. I could almost hear the Parliamentary Channel's producer cursing as the gown wreaked havoc with the television picture. Add a few munchkins and she could have stood in for Glinda the Good Witch of the South. Despite her Christmas tree fashion sense, the GG was an intelligent woman who took her role as as the Queen's official representative very seriously indeed. On my TV screen, classical music played in the background as she leaned over to chat with the PM. Soon they were both chuckling. MPs were still filing into the restricted area of the chamber so we were still a few minutes away. Eventually, the scene settled and the music faded to be replaced by the sound of a quieting crowd. A few coughs and throat clearings could be heard before the camera focused on the GG. She remained seated, put on her reading glasses, and opened a folder in front of her. Then she started to read.

"Honourable Members of the Senate, Members of the House of Commons, ladies and gentlemen, it is my great pleasure to greet you on this first day of a new Parliament. Today, we celebrate the unique bond between Parliament and its people, just as we have in Canada since 1867."

While it was a standard Throne Speech opening, I still found myself moved by the tradition and pageantry of it all. She welcomed new and returning members of the House of Commons and congratulated the Prime Minister on forming a new government. About four minutes in, the preliminaries seemed to be over with and she moved into the Throne Speech proper. Had I stayed in the Leader's office, it is quite likely that I'd have written a good part of the speech. I was wistful for a minute or two but then realized that I was in a much better place.

It was a good speech. Clear and clean, with some solid writing. The Throne Speech is one of those few opportunities to wax eloquent without being accused of being over the top. The speech was nearing the end and I was worried we'd be shut out. Finally, I heard what we were awaiting.

"My government promised during the campaign that we would reduce taxes and put more money in the pockets of Canadians. We intend to do just that, but the rapidly declining economy and the collapse of the Alexandra Bridge nearly a month ago has forced the government to confront a new reality. We must begin to rebuild our crumbling infrastructure and stimulate an ailing and failing economy. The government will keep its promises, but we must also do what is right for the country."

Yes. That was it. I recognized some of the words as my own, submitted to Bradley a few days earlier. We could have asked for little more. We didn't expect the speech to go into any more detail than that, so I was happy. He was not visible on screen, but I could imagine Angus standing at the rail in the Senate, smiling and nodding. We'd made it into the Throne Speech. The government was now committed to do at least something to redress a fallen bridge. I also imagined a stone-faced Emile Coulombe, quivering with rage and pushing pins into an Angus voodoo doll. He'd lost one battle, but the war was far from over. There were plenty of precedents for governments merely paying passing tribute to Throne Speech commitments. I felt good, but the champagne was still on ice. Not that I'd ever be allowed to uncork another bottle.

Lindsay had a night class, so after dinner I headed up the slope to see Angus, quite pleased with myself. Feeling athletic, I bounded up to the back deck, taking the stairs two at a time in three long strides. I'd forgotten that there were actually seven steps. I was never really that good at math. It's a long trip from *feeling* athletic to *being* athletic. As I lay on my stomach on the deck, my knees resting on that unaccounted-for last stair, I had the familiar feeling I was being watched. I turned my head to discover that I was being watched. Angus was on the chintz couch, sipping single malt from a squat tumbler and watching me through the window. He raised his glass to honour my perfectly executed pratfall. He then hoisted himself to his feet and came around to open the deck door.

"Will you have a drink of somethin'?" he asked, sticking his head through the doorway and looking down at my horizontal form.

There I was, perhaps paralyzed, lying on my face on the snowy deck, and Angus was taking drink orders.

"I'm not hurt, Angus, so don't you worry. I'm okay. I'm fine," I mocked. "Really, I'm just fine."

"I saw the whole thing, and you went down very gently, you know," he replied. "Were you expecting me to bring the backboard and call for the air ambulance?"

"No. But it's just nice to be asked if I'm okay."

"Och, stow the bellyachin'. I've seen you go down far harder than that and up you popped just fine."

By this time, I had had in fact popped back up and was brushing the snow from my pants. Ten minutes later I had a Coke in my hand and was prodding my white king pawn ahead two squares to start the good fight.

"I'm still feeling good that we pushed our way into the speech," I said as Angus considered his move. "It's no mean feat to get that kind of verbiage into the Throne Speech. Everyone and their cousin are clamouring to get their pet projects in there, but very few make the cut. Today, we made the cut."

"Aye, we did, but a few platitudes in a Throne Speech are not worth a tinker's curse if the Budget doesn't hand over the sterling to get the job done," Angus replied as he shoved his king pawn up two squares to meet mine. "We're not home yet, lad."

"No, we're not, not by a long shot, but the Throne Speech isn't meaningless. It commits the government to action. It remains to be seen how much action we're going to get, and what dollars are set aside."

The game progressed in the usual fashion. I made four sensible and reasonable moves in a row before offering up a humiliating blunder that luckily cost me only a bishop.

"Can you not carry on a conversation without your chess game going to hell in a handcart?"

"Not usually, no. Why do you think you always pound me into the ground when I start talking?"

We played three games. I lost the first two, yakking away the whole time. Actually, Angus crushed me in a handful of moves. In the third game, we maintained radio silence. I fought him to a draw. Clearly I'm not wired for multi-tasking. After the first two, a draw in the third game was as good as a win for me.

It was a clear night. The stars hung in the sky like backlit diamonds. We both sat on the couch so we could see the light show. I kept waiting for a shooting star to streak across the black, but they all remained fixed. On the coffee table in front of us, I noticed one of Marin's books lying open, a bookmark off to the side. I'd never seen Angus reading one of his wife's works.

"Are you holding up?" I asked.

He'd seen me eyeing the book and knew what I was asking.

"Most days," he replied. "It's not yet been twelve months. For some reason, gettin' to one year seems important, though intellectually I know that's rubbish. Still . . ."

"It's a loss I cannot imagine. I didn't know you when she was alive, but I think you're bearing up admirably."

"Now that the hovercraft is finished, the collapse of the Alexandra was the best therapy ever prescribed for an agin', grievin' engineer newly elected to the House of Commons. I know it could have cost lives had it dropped without warning us first, yet I think it may have saved mine. I was headed down into the darkness again. The task given us by the Prime Minister brought me back to the surface."

"You're supposed to grieve. It's unnatural not to."

"Aye, it is. But I'm still doing my fair share of grievin', every day. So don't fret. It may be that I'm left walkin' with a limp, but I'll still get around. Some days are worse than others but I'll still get where I'm goin'. Most of the time, where we're both goin'."

On cue, Lindsay's headlights flashed through the living room window as she drove up the driveway and parked as close to the boathouse as she could.

"If you hurry, you can meet her on the landing," Angus suggested. "But be careful. You've been down once tonight already."

I stood and slipped on my coat. Lindsay was rooting around in the trunk of her car, so it looked like I might just beat her to the staircase.

"Are you ready for Wednesday?"

"Aye."

DIARY
Monday, February 24
My Love,
He's a lovely man and a kind soul, he is. But I take nothing from him when noting that he's about as coordinated as a newborn giraffe. And not yet a stellar chess player either, mind you. But I can forgive him that. I purposely pursued an inferior line in the endgame and granted him a draw in our third tilt. He needed it more than I.

However ill-earned it is, the cursed spotlight on me persists. The papers remain filled with André's damned photographs. He seems to have a knack for laying me bare before the people, any pretence of privacy having fallen away. Mark you, 'tis the lot of the elected parliamentarian.

We briefed the caucus this morning, for what it was worth. A less impressive assembly of dolts and dullards you'd be hard-pressed to gather. Forgive me, I'm surely too harsh, yet the truth is nearby. Daniel called it a dress rehearsal for Wednesday's showdown with Coulombe in the Cabinet crucible. Some were with us today, but others were more inscrutable. Not that caucus has much say about anything on the Hill. The PM really calls the shots. Wednesday it is, provided the Finance Minister hasn't had me assassinated first. Tie a red ribbon around your crossed fingers, would you, love? It's about to get a wee bit more interesting.

AM

CHAPTER NINETEEN

Wednesday dawned dark and dreary. February is surely a bleak time of the year. I can barely stand that there is never light in the morning. I sat at the kitchen table eating a bowl of Cheerios and reading the *Ottawa Citizen*. The stories we'd orchestrated on the need for infrastructure renewal had pretty well dried up. Perhaps we'd shot our bolt too early. I turned to the editorial page in the hopes that the *Citizen* might come out in our favour. Nothing. But wait, there was something. The lead letter to the editor was headlined "Rebuild bridge, rebuild Canada." Harold Silverberg, the Deputy Minister twenty years ago, had weighed in with a thoughtful, articulate, and impassioned plea. Unlike the other unrelated letters that day, Silverberg's was long and accompanied by a head shot of the author. It was very nearly an op-ed piece rather than a garden-variety letter to the editor, and held pride of place above the fold. You want to be above the fold. I ripped the page down the centre crease, badly, and shoved it in my pocket to show Angus.

Lindsay emerged from the bedroom and dropped into the chair beside me. She shook out her hands and breathed deeply.

"Okay, I guess I'm ready," she sighed. "My stomach feels tight."

"Relax. You're going to be fine. This is a walk in the park," I soothed, taking her hands in mine. "There's no call for anxiety."

"Yeah, right," she said. "Should we synchronize our watches or agree on a secret coded message or something?"

"Good idea. Okay. When Angus and I are on our way, I'll call your cell and use the secret phrase 'Angus and I are on our way.' Got it?"

That earned a punch to my shoulder.

"You won't be by yourself. You know what to do. We've gone over our routine. You'll do fine. We'll see you at the appointed hour. And thank you for doing this."

I kissed her and headed out the door.

Angus and I drove to Ottawa in virtual silence. I knew he was mulling over his pitch and I didn't want to disturb him. Still, I'm sure he was somewhat distracted when the deer darted out in front of us. Mercifully, the deer had much quicker reactions than I. It leapt safely back into the woods at the last instant while I clamped my eyes shut, gritted my teeth, and drove dead straight.

"Excellent reflexes and fine evasive action, laddie," chided Angus.

That was my signal to open my eyes again.

"Would you rather we were on our roof in the ditch?" I asked. "I was counting on the deer's athletic prowess and will to live. And now that I can see again, I find I was right. That was a deer, wasn't it?"

In my office, I made a final call to confirm the arrangements before knocking on Angus's door.

"It's time."

"Must you make it sound as if you're leadin' me to the electric chair, laddie?"

I'd noticed that in moments of stress or in private conversation, Angus tended to drop his g's more often and become more Caledonian in his speech.

We walked through Centre Block to the Cabinet room. It was very quiet, even peaceful. Time for a little Vince Lombardi.

"Okay. Coulombe will not support this. He cannot support this. He's so committed to his tax cuts that he's left himself no room for retreat. He can't back away an inch. So don't even acknowledge him. Ignore him. Focus completely on the Prime Minister. We'll never have Coulombe, so write him off and bear down on the PM. You know what to say and how to say it."

"Aye."

My seniority in the party had earned me access to the Cabinet room for the show. We waited in the anteroom. Eventually, several senior Department of Finance officials emerged with bulging briefcases and the biggest binder I'd ever seen. It was large enough to deserve its own special trolley but a particularly strapping bureaucrat carried it instead, stopping to rest every twenty metres or so. That was undoubtedly the federal Budget, due to be presented the next day.

"Why wouldn't Cabinet hear our case before sending the Budget boys back?" Angus asked, a little ticked. "Makes our briefing seem moot."

"There's plenty of time to amend the Budget. Besides, maybe our stuff is already in it."

Bradley Stanton appeared at the heavy doors and waved us in. Just as we were headed into the inner sanctum, I sent Lindsay a prearranged text message from my cell. Timing was critical. Bradley looked like a coiled cobra sizing up his prey. I've always hated snakes.

"You've got twenty minutes, no more."

Angus needed only fifteen. He was so focused, the glory of the room seemed barely to register on him. The large table, upholstered chairs, wood panelling, and Canadian art made it a dignified and serene place to make momentous decisions about the nation's future. The full Cabinet had turned up. Angus stood at the head of the table and spoke to the PM as if they were alone in the room together. He'd refined his pitch since the caucus meeting. He spoke with power, conviction, the occasional flash of humour, but most often with a gravitas that demanded attention. I was very proud as I watched him get into his performance. He wore it like a comfortable jacket. Years at the front of the lecture hall had served him well. I watched the PM as much as I did Angus, and he could not conceal the impact the presentation was having. He caught himself nodding in agreement early on and stifled it. By the end of Angus's performance, the PM's face was impassive, but his eyes seemed brighter than usual. I also watched Emile Coulombe. For every slight nod from the PM, there were several emphatic head shakes from Coulombe. At one point, I heard Coulombe mutter in exasperation, "Oh come on, that's ridiculous." The PM heard it too, shot a glare Coulombe's way, and raised his hand to calm the waters.

Angus closed with this:

"Do you see this iron ring I'm wearing? You may not know the story. Each and every Canadian engineer wears an iron ring on the pinky of his or her working hand. The ring symbolizes the iron from a beam in a bridge near Quebec City that collapsed in 1907, killing seventy-five workers. It fell because the engineers who designed and built the bridge were incompetent. Each engineer in Canada wears this ring as a constant reminder of our commitment, of our duty, to serve and protect the public. We've just witnessed the collapse of another bridge. This time due to the incompetence of politicians, not engineers. This ring means a great deal to me. So you picked the wrong man to investigate the collapse of a bridge if you planned on doing nothing with my report."

Rather than sitting down at the same level as the Cabinet members, Angus stayed on his feet, above the fray. When he was finished, Coulombe was on his feet. Perfectly bilingual, with only the slightest trace of a French accent, he smiled and walked slowly behind his colleagues on one side of the table to calm himself.

"That is a lovely little story, Mr. McLintock, but we're not here to discuss history."

"Aye, you're right there, sir," Angus interrupted. "I'm not here to discuss history. I'm trying to make sure we don't repeat it."

That prompted some righteous nodding from a few ministers around the table.

"We cannot make the infrastructure investment that you seek, Mr. McLintock, for two reasons. Number one, we promised we'd cut taxes. And number two, we need the tax cuts to stimulate the crashing economy, and that's what will be in tomorrow's Budget. Period, full stop, end of story."

Angus had been calm up to that point but the flickering flame behind his eyes seemed suddenly to burst into an inferno. He was on him in an instant, yet kept his gaze fixed on the PM.

"Speakin' of *number two*, minister, with great respect, your argument is full of" – Angus paused – "it."

Snickering from many ministers had Coulombe glaring. But now Angus was too angry to care.

"Is there no beginnin' to your common sense, sir? Have you not been readin' the advice that's been comin' in from economists across the country? Have you not spoken to your own officials? Economists don't agree on much, but there seems to me to be a clear consensus that investment in infrastructure renewal is a better way to stimulate the economy than your much ballyhooed tax cuts. It will put more people back to work, it will put more money in Canadians' pockets, it will do it all faster, and in the end, we'll have the infrastructure this country deserves and needs to support economic growth. History shows that in a recession when you give citizens tax cuts, many of them just sock it away and don't head to their nearest Canadian Tire to buy that new washin' machine. Beyond all of the economic benefits of infrastructure renewal, we simply cannae wait until another bridge collapses, perhaps next time with no warnin' at all. Perhaps next time, with taxpayers amidst the rubble. We have four years to cut taxes. But in tomorrow's Budget, you have the opportunity to do what's right. Not because we promised it in a fluffy campaign brochure, but because the situation we've discovered since arrivin' in office utterly demands it."

Angus paused for a moment to gather himself before continuing. No one filled the silence. He returned his gaze to the Prime Minister.

"Sir, it may not be glamorous. It may make some people mad. It may give the opposition a reason to attack us. It may even yield a non-confidence motion that we could lose. But no one will argue that we did not act in the nation's interest. So we're not suggestin' we renege on our promised tax cuts. We're only proposin' that they be delayed until we can afford them, and until bridges stop fallin' into rivers."

Coulombe just shook his head and looked to the PM.

"Prime Minister, the Budget is put to bed. We can't change it now, and if we did, we'd be exposing ourselves to defeat in the House. And that surely is not in the nation's interest."

The twenty-minute allocation stretched to ninety minutes as the discussion went back and forth. Except for a few angry exchanges with Coulombe, Angus presented cogent and reasonable arguments in a steady and patient tone. Conversely, the Finance Minister grew more agitated as the meeting dragged on. At one point, the PM asked him to keep his voice down.

Several ministers actually spoke up in support of Angus, including some whom I had tagged as opponents at the beginning of the meeting. Never underestimate the McLintock powers of persuasion. The PM kept his own counsel, but listened intently, taking a few notes now and then. The debate raged for another hour. I was watching the clock and getting nervous. I caught Angus's attention and pointed to my watch. He checked his and visibly started.

"Prime Minister, I think I've done all I can here, so I'll leave you to it."

With Angus and Coulombe agreeing to disagree, and to dislike one another for the foreseeable future, Bradley Stanton walked us out to the anteroom and then played his last card.

"Just to remind you two loose cannons, now that you've presented your report to Cabinet, it becomes subject to all the rules governing Cabinet security and confidentiality. You must not release this report or discuss its contents with anyone. Is that clear?"

By the look of the gathering storm on his face, I thought Angus was going to have an aneurysm. His beard seemed to twitch and vibrate. Bradley took two steps backwards as Angus appeared ready to detonate. But when the words finally came, they were calm and quiet, but delivered through a locked jaw.

"No, it is not clear. We promised to release the report to Canadians at the same time as we delivered it to the Prime Minister. That was the agreement the PM signed at the outset. Well, the PM now has our report. Caucus and Cabinet have been briefed, and we intend to keep our promise, Mr. Stanton."

Angus turned on his heel and headed for the door. I saluted Bradley and left him standing there in stunned silence. Well, the stunned silence didn't last for long. I caught up to Angus as we exited Centre Block to the dying strains of Bradley's crazed cries.

"Don't you do it, Angus! You'll be out if you do. Danny boy, you're through too. You'll never . . ."

I watched the birth of a smile on Angus's face as we headed directly across the street to 150 Wellington. Had Bradley known where we were going, I'm certain he'd have done more to stop us, not excluding physical assault.

"Now this is getting interestin'" was all Angus said.

I made a quick call as we walked, delivered the prearranged secret coded message, then turned off my cellphone.

Lindsay and Muriel were waiting for us in the lobby of the National Press Building. Lindsay held two Kinko's shopping bags. When we reach them, she lifted first one bag, then the other.

"French and English. We're all set."

I gave Lindsay a quick squeeze. Angus seemed a bit surprised to see Muriel.

"I didnae want to drag you into the city for this."

"Are you daft? Pity the man or beast who gets in my way today," Muriel replied, while smoothing the shoulders of Angus's rumpled suit. "Now go forth and be Angus."

Fifteen minutes later, we were all set. Back across the street, the Cabinet meeting was breaking up. Ministers expecting to run the gauntlet of reporters as they tried to get back to their offices were surprised that not a single member of the press gallery was waiting outside the Cabinet room. That's because they were all with us in the main media studio, with cameras primed, notebooks opened, and microphones poised. Angus and I sat at the front table. Muriel sat near the back grinning almost maniacally at all who looked her way. Lindsay, looking stunning, had just about finished handing out freshly printed copies of the McLintock Report to the thirty-five or forty reporters in the room. At noon, I cleared my throat and raised my hand to quiet the buzz.

"Good afternoon, ladies and gentlemen, I think we're ready to begin." I paused to allow the cameras to turn on and the room to settle into silence. "I'm Daniel Addison, EA to Angus McLintock, Member of Parliament for Cumberland-Prescott. You will know that the Prime Minister appointed Professor McLintock to investigate the collapse of the Alexandra Bridge just over three weeks ago. The final report is being released today and I believe is now in your hands. The Prime Minister has reviewed the report, and the caucus has been briefed. We've just come from Cabinet where Angus presented his findings. I'll let Professor McLintock take it from here."

"Thank you, Daniel. Good afternoon. I've not prepared formal remarks but let me give you the headline and then I'll walk you through our findings. The Alexandra Bridge did not collapse because it was poorly designed. It did not collapse because of a buildup of ice. It did not collapse because of high winds. No, the Alexandra Bridge fell into the Ottawa River as a result of twenty years of federal government negligence in the almighty quest to slay the deficit. Had we adhered to the prescribed maintenance schedule set out by the officials of the department, the Alexandra Bridge would be serving us well for the next century. If we do not address our crumbling infrastructure, the Alexandra Bridge will be only the first of many bridges to collapse. In short, the deficit was not eliminated, it was merely transformed. The deficit lives on in our crumbling roads, highways, ports, bridges, canals, and every other part of our rusting national infrastructure."

Just as Angus was hitting his stride, an old man I couldn't quite place hobbled into the room and shuffled over to sit with Muriel.

"Courtesy of the four-year electoral horizon, we've made poor choices in government spending. We know we'll have to rebuild our roads. But we let them decay to the point that we'll need to disburse much more public money to fix them than if we'd sustained an appropriate maintenance allocation all along. But inspecting bridges and repaving roads don't seem interesting or exciting enough when the writ drops and the election campaign starts."

Angus paused to open the report.

"Here are the key recommendations:

- Immediate inspection of all infrastructure including bridges, highways, water filtration systems, canals, ports, nuclear power plants, and generating stations, whether or not they are in federal jurisdiction. After all, a classic method of trimming the deficit has been to download programs to lower levels of government and cut back federal transfer payments to pay for it all.
- Immediate investment in tomorrow's federal Budget to address some of the most urgent infrastructure problems, those that threaten public safety. We've recommended $20 billion over ten years with $8 billion of it committed in the first two years.
- A longer-term program of infrastructure investment to return our roads, harbours, power plants, etc. to the level Canadians deserve.
- Fund this infrastructure renewal by delaying the promised tax cuts and debt payment, while keeping the deficit at zero.

"I dislike deficits as much as the next person. But I dislike subterfuge even more. Canadians were told with great fanfare that the deficit had been wrestled to the ground. Tripe. Pure unadulterated tripe. We still have a deficit. It's all around us in our crumbling infrastructure."

Angus again paused for a moment. He looked out at the crowd and found Muriel and the old man sitting next to her. He nodded, almost imperceptibly.

"I wish to highlight a brief section in our report entitled 'The Role of the Civil Service.' Since democracy's earliest days, politicians, to shield their own ineptitude, have blamed their officials for bad advice, incomplete information, and incompetence. With this in mind, let the record show that for the last twenty years, the dedicated civil servants in Infrastructure Canada and its predecessor, the Department of Public Works, have steadfastly provided Liberal and Conservative governments alike with clear and consistent advice as to the consequences of this systemic underfunding, and have continuously recommended against it. Neither the Liberal regime twenty years ago nor the Conservative governments of the last fifteen years heeded their wise counsel. As a result, our infrastructure is decayed and, in some cases, unsafe. As well, one of the consequences civil servants have often cited, and which has now come to pass, is that it will cost the taxpayer much more to rebuild our national infrastructure than it would have had we maintained appropriate maintenance programs.

"I want to thank these men and women for their professionalism and service over the years. In researching this report, and in my many sessions with them, I found them always to provide balanced and unbiased advice, never partisan. They acted in keeping with the finest traditions of civil servants, when clearly they had cause to feel discouraged, if not angry. Like our politicians, there are some outstanding officials and some who are just along for the ride, putting in their time for their indexed pension. I've not met too many from the latter category but I can say from what I've read in the files and learned from speaking to senior officials from decades past, each government, whether Liberal or Tory, was served by talented and dedicated civil servants who acted responsibly and prudently at every turn. It is unfortunate that the same cannot be said for the politicians they served.

"Let me introduce the Deputy Minister of Public Works from twenty years ago, when this sorry saga of neglect began. Harold Silverberg fought the tide until he was swamped by it. Unable to support a government bent on undermining our infrastructure, he quietly and honourably resigned. His memoranda to the minister of the time foretell precisely what has happened."

As the cameras swivelled to find Harold Silverberg at the back, Muriel patted his hand on the armrest they shared, while his eyes blinked and glistened.

Angus closed the report and nodded to me.

"Professor McLintock will take your questions now."

Hands shot up and I started a list while the first question came.

"So how did the PM and Finance Minister take it when you told them you needed $8 billion in the next two years?"

"Well, I wouldn't liken it to Christmas morning. But I think they both understand the urgency and importance of this newly discovered national priority. I'm not certain I'll be a dinner party guest of Monsieur Coulombe's for the foreseeable future, but I'm not even a wee bit bothered by that."

"Will you get the funding you've asked for in tomorrow's Budget?"

"I regret that the decision is not ours to make. We've made our case as logically and forcefully as we could, and now we'll have to wait just like everyone else."

I pointed at a woman in the front row I didn't recognize.

"Sharon Stallworth, *Edmonton Journal*. Do you really think that by delaying and reducing expenditures on highway maintenance and bridge inspections we're in as serious a situation as you have indicated?"

"Yes, I do. That's the nature of infrastructure. It tends to look solid right up until the moment it collapses. It may look and feel as if the need is not so great, and not so urgent. But I promise you, the evidence will pile up fast if we do nothing. And the evidence may be more serious than mangled metal and cracked concrete. We need to act now."

I nodded to the reporter next on my list.

"You seem to have dug a little deeper than just determining why the Alexandra Bridge fell. Have you overstepped your mandate?"

"If you examine the mandate we were given, which is included in the report your hold in your hands, we have operated entirely within its confines. There is little value in reporting that a certain rivet snapped, starting a chain of failures that ended with a broken bridge in a river. Asking *why* is usually of greater moment than asking *what*. Guided by the question *why*, we quickly discovered that there were clear and pressing policy implications to this particular collapse and they are explored in the report. That was our mandate."

"Jean-Luc Beaubien, *La Presse*. Asking a new government that campaigned on tax cuts to give them up so we can fill a few potholes and repaint a bridge or two seems to me like an exercise in futility. Am I missing something?"

"Aye, you are missing something, sir. You are. From my perch, you're confusing politics and policy. You're confusing the political interest and the national interest. I understand that we promised tax cuts in the campaign. I'm not an ardent proponent of the measure but I can understand the appeal of tax cuts for politicians and voters alike. But our promise was based on incomplete information and a flawed premise. We had thought the deficit was dead. We've now learned that it's still very much alive. Like fiscal alchemists, we have transformed it from borrowed money into fallen bridges and crumbling highways and countless other examples of infrastructure decay. To a responsible government, that simply cannot stand."

Another thirty minutes of similar questions flowed and Angus handled them honestly and directly. I signalled "last call" and pointed to André Fontaine at the back.

"Angus, you've been a part of the national scene for a very short time, yet you seem to have found yourself at the very centre of a number of political hot spots. How do you keep emerging smelling like a rose?"

"Well, André, those who know me well may not share your view of how I smell," Angus replied, sending chuckles through the room. "But in serious consideration of what I assume is more than a rhetorical query, I would say that I have an overdeveloped sense of why I'm here and an underdeveloped interest in what others think of me. I assure you, the latter is quite a liberating gift."

Even though Muriel started the applause, as experienced political operatives commonly do, the reporters joined in too, which is not so common. Not common at all.

Just as Angus and I rose and the reporters came forward to scrum Angus, a breathless and red-faced Bradley Stanton burst in to the room. All heads turned his way. He saw the reporters and more importantly their cameras focused on him so he made a quick recovery. In an instant he looked calm as he sauntered up to me.

"What the fuck just happened here, Addison?" he hissed, through a large, white-toothed smile.

I smiled back.

"We just released the McLintock Report in French and English, and Angus answered reporters' questions after giving a compelling and eloquent overview of our findings," I whispered.

"You're fucked now, Danny boy. You have no idea . . ."

"Really. Well, don't look now, but I see cameras and sun guns heading your way."

In an instant Bradley Stanton, the Prime Minister's top adviser, was engulfed in a sea of microphones and jockeying cameras.

"What does the PM think of Angus's report?"

"Are you going to cough up the dough?"

"What about the tax cuts? Are they history?"

Bradley put up his hands in surrender.

"Hold on. I'm not here to respond to questions about the report. That would be premature. I'll say only this. The Prime Minister has received the final report on the Alexandra Bridge collapse from the Member for Cumberland-Prescott and is carefully reviewing it. We'll respond to the recommendations at the earliest possible opportunity and the Prime Minister thanks Professor McLintock for his thoughtful and comprehensive examination of the incident."

With that, Bradley delivered a smilingly deadly glare my way, then turned and headed out the door with several reporters in hot pursuit.

Angus helped Harold Silverberg move to the front of the room to sit at the table. Microphones were placed in front of him and the reporters scrummed him for fifteen minutes. They were gentle and he was forceful, articulate, and detailed in his responses. Angus stood with him for support and answered many more questions himself. By force of habit, I monitored his responses from a few feet away. He put not a foot wrong.

"You are a wonder," gushed Muriel as she embraced Angus when the reporters had moved on and we were left by ourselves.

Lindsay was holding on to my hand and beaming. It had all gone according to plan. I pressed my lips to her ear.

"We couldn't have pulled this off without your clandestine work. It was an honour sneaking around with you."

Angus brought us back to earth.

"Let's not get too carried away. We're not yet home," cautioned Angus. "Tomorrow will tell whether this was all twaddle and puffery."

DIARY
Wednesday, February 26
My Love,
Bless Harold Silverberg. He came. It was a struggle. It pains him to walk. Still, he came. Bless Muriel, too, for taking him

under her sparse wing when he arrived. Seems she knew him back then. My plan in having him there was to shift the spotlight that seems unceasingly to have me in its glare. It worked for a time at the news conference, or what Daniel calls a "newser," but the scribes eventually tired of the erstwhile Deputy Minister and returned with yet more questions for me. I ate my fair share of microphones, that's for certain. The questions came thick and fast. It was like trying to drink from a gushing fire hose. Oh, but it was fun, I admit. It was actually fun. Beyond flying *Baddeck 1*, I've not had *fun* in the true sense of the word since you and I hiked together in the Highlands a week or so before that damned doctor called you back. So rude and nonchalant, as you described it. I could have run him through had he been in the same room with us. But I did enjoy myself today.

The Cabinet room is glorious. The wood, the paintings, even the table, were wonders in themselves, though I had precious little time to admire them before the duel began. I'm certain Coulombe hates me but you know I'm not much torn up by that. I do think I was moving the PM our way, but he's an inscrutable fellow, he is. We've not long to wait to grade our harvest. Tomorrow. It all unfolds tomorrow.

What think you of my windmill tilting? My convictions always fed off yours, and still seem to . . .
AM

CHAPTER TWENTY

Every front page of every major daily in the country had it, most in full colour. Angus at the news conference in full rhetorical flight, with eyes ablaze, mouth agape, and finger cocked and pointing. It was a wonderful photo that I thought seemed to capture the real Angus McLintock – proud, honest, opinionated, and completely oblivious to the ancient art of hair styling. He must have been moving his head at the instant the shot was snapped as his beard was not resting on his chest as usual, but seemed to be floating in the air of its own accord. This made Angus seem quite dynamic, in the original sense of the word, as in not static. Thankfully, there was no visible projectile spittle and his beard seemed free of any foreign objects. Perhaps they'd already been shaken loose in the vigour of his informal address.

I was sitting at our kitchen table in my pyjamas with the papers spread out before me. My laptop was open so I could scan media outlets across the country by moving my mouse across the table. Lindsay had headed in to campus for an early class she was teaching.

The news coverage of the McLintock Report struck me as balanced and accurate. There were even quotations from Emile Coulombe, who dismissed the recommendations for infrastructure investment with a blithe "We'll get to infrastructure after we've fulfilled our campaign promises." The PM was a little more circumspect. He was quoted saying, "Angus has done just what I asked him to do and even a little more. His report is important and challenges us as a government to make some very difficult decisions, at a very difficult time." Nice.

More importantly to me, and perhaps to the Prime Minister as well, the editorials ran about 75 per cent for Angus and 25 per cent for Coulombe. I expected the Prime Minister and the Finance Minister both had long nights in anticipation of a very long day. The Budget was to be presented in the House of Commons at four o'clock. I had no idea what to expect and honoured my promise to Angus not to speak to anyone. Given the hoopla of yesterday, we decided to stay in Cumberland until it was time to head in for the Budget speech. I was just about to turn off my BlackBerry when it buzzed. I was expecting to see B. Stanton appear in the window. After all, it had been several minutes since he'd last torn a strip off me. I had very few strips left. But it wasn't Bradley. Curiosity trampled my pledge to Angus.

"Daniel Addison."

"Hi Daniel, it's Michael Zaleski."

"Z-man! Nice to hear from you. How are you?"

"I'm fine. More to the point, how are you?"

"Well, it's been an eventful day or so, but we're surviving," I replied. "It really does help when you actually believe you're doing the right thing."

"I hear you. Listen, I'm calling unofficially, so this is just between us."

"No problem, Michael, I'm in your hands."

"After your little media play yesterday, the PMO asked me to do a quick and dirty overnighter on how Canadians felt about trading off tax cuts to invest in infrastructure," the party's pollster said.

"I figured the centre might do that. Makes sense."

"Unfortunately, most Canadians really wouldn't have heard about it until today when the newspapers could dig into the issue. So we couldn't go the quantitative route and do a telephone survey. There just wasn't time. So instead, we pulled together a few fast focus groups last night. To simulate how Canadians might feel after reading this morning's papers, we played video from your news conference and then the 6:00 p.m. TV news pieces from CBC, CTV, and Global for all focus group participants."

"Right, I'm with you. Then you started the discussion," I said. "What did you find?"

"Well, I thought you'd like to know that there was consistency across all three focus groups. They were all evenly split. It's tough to pull back the tax cuts when people have been counting on them. But Angus convinced half the group that infrastructure investments were more important right now than tax cuts."

"That's encouraging. Did you ask why they felt that way?"

"We did. This is a bit of an oversimplification, but they actually believe Angus when he speaks. They seem to trust him. And as you well know, that's not the typical voter reaction to politicians. Canadians usually consider used car salesmen to be paragons of virtue in comparison."

"Wow. *The Angus Effect* strikes again."

"Right. Even most of those who favoured the tax cuts admitted that they were just looking out for themselves and that Angus had made a compelling and convincing case," Michael noted. "One more thing. We set up an Internet survey for our regular online panel to complete just to see if we could get a large enough sample for the numbers to be real. I just checked the rolling results and we still only have about 350 respondents, skewing heavily urban. This doesn't really give us a solid national read but for what it's worth, the numbers are splitting fifty-fifty there, too."

"Interesting, Michael. Thanks for letting me know. Have you briefed Bradley yet?"

"He was there for the focus groups. We didn't wrap up last night until close to eleven. He was heading right back to brief the PM. I gather it was a long night."

"Thanks again, Michael. I'm grateful."

He hung up, and I turned off my BlackBerry.

Angus was already at the board when I saw him through the deck window waving me in the back door. Chess seemed to calm Angus down a bit, even as it elevated my blood pressure. Angus's relentless pummelling, interspersed with timely, self-inflicted blunders seemed to have that physiological effect. But I suppose if dismembering me game after game left Angus more serene and relaxed, then there was at least one benefit to my shoddy and inferior play. Yes, that's it. That's why I only rarely won. I was subconsciously trying to manage Angus and his moods. Right.

Other than the games we played on Monday night, we'd had little time in the previous month to face off on the sixty-four squares. It was quite diverting to be angry and upset about my chess performance rather than be angry and upset over Bradley Stanton's politics. A change is as good as a rest, they say.

Angus looked good. He'd obviously dragged a rake through his hair and beard, so you could almost see where one ended and the other began. He'd put on his grey pinstripe suit that he'd bought off the rack. It was the wrong rack, but he looked quite reasonable with a white shirt and understated tartan tie, of course. He'd polished his shoes, several years ago, but they still looked quite presentable. I figured most observers could not take their eyes off his chaotic coiffure, so I seldom worried about the state of his shoes.

I had white again. I actually played quite well in the first two games, and even succeeded in claiming his queen in our second game, in exchange for my rook when I pinned her to his king. Angus was not happy and proceeded to make me pay. Despite playing queenless, he systematically destroyed me, resurrecting his queen when I was forced to promote one of his pawns in the end-game. It was all over then. I kept one eye on the clock but we had plenty of time.

We were several moves into our third game, deep enough that Angus was already up a knight and a pawn, when the doorbell sounded.

"Right on time" was all Angus said as he pushed himself back from the board.

"Who's on time?" I asked, but Angus said nothing and headed to the front door.

I heard him welcome the guest, who sounded very familiar when he spoke. I was still trying to connect the voice to a face when Emerson Fox strode into the living room, with Angus close behind. I knocked over my rook in surprise as I got up. He looked much more relaxed than when I'd last seen him on election night.

"Don't let me interrupt the battle," Fox said when he saw the chess board.

"No worries. I was about to surrender anyway, as usual," I replied offering my hand. "I'm Daniel Addison."

"Oh, I know who you are," replied Fox. "It's good to meet you in peacetime."

"Rest yourself, Mr. Fox," instructed Angus as he pointed to the chintz couch. "Can I get you a shot of courage as we welcome high noon?"

"No thanks, Angus. I know you've got a lot on your platter today so I won't be long," Fox responded.

I returned to my chair at the chess table while Angus dropped into the chintz chair across from the couch.

"I confess I was surprised to receive your call this morning," Angus opened. "Not displeased, just surprised."

"I can understand that after what I put you through in the campaign," said Fox. "I wanted to let some water flow under the bridge before I visited so that we were both at peace with the outcome. It took me a little longer than I'd expected, but peace is coming to me."

"Well, the water is still flowin' but the bridge I've been examin-in' is no longer where it's supposed to be," Angus observed.

"Indeed. Well, you delivered on your assignment, but I suspect the Prime Minister was hoping you'd not have dug quite as deep as you did."

"Aye, that may be, but I'm not bothered."

"Well, I wouldn't want to be the one advising the PM to renege on the tax cuts. But for the first time in my political experience

I see politics coexisting with common sense. I think he might just pull it off, thanks to you. You have risen above it all. Canadians trust you in a way they could never trust me."

Angus just nodded and let the silence hang there, I think to try to force Fox to his point. I said nothing at all.

"This is the kind of call I don't often make. I'm not accustomed to giving an inch when I'm in battle, or even when it's over and I've been defeated. I haven't lost very often, you know," Emerson Fox said as he looked at the floor. "But I don't feel I can close this chapter of my political career without having spoken at least once more to you. Professor McLintock, I've invested much of my life in developing and perfecting a style of campaigning that, while not for those with faint hearts and weak stomachs, has consistently delivered victories to my candidates. Until I crossed you."

"I cannae say I'm troubled by upsettin' your theory. You'll know that I'm not a supporter of slingin' mud and exchangin' insults. Somebody does win in the end, I concede, but in my mind, the country loses in the main."

"Regardless, I learned that there may be another way. Don't get me wrong. The negative campaign, I think, is still the way to go, but I wanted you to know that you'd opened the eyes of an aging warrior at least to the possibility of other approaches. And I never thought that would happen in my lifetime."

"I find that admission, sir, to be perhaps as rewarding as the election result," Angus replied with a smile.

"And professor, I will never forget what you did for me when Ramsay Rumplun broke into your headquarters. I hope you know his actions were not sanctioned, and I don't condone them for an instant."

"As I told you then, we kept it quiet not as a favour to you, but to protect the voters' tenuous and fragile respect for democracy."

"One final word of warning, if I may," Fox said. "Beware of Bradley Stanton. He's got a hate on for you that is seriously intense."

"Aye, I know he's none too pleased with us right now."

My curiosity prevailed, again.

"I wasn't aware that the animosity between us was public knowledge."

"It probably isn't, Mr. Addison. But my contacts on the Hill are still solid, and I'd be worried if I were you," Fox explained. "You've made a powerful enemy."

"All in a good cause, mind you," Angus concluded, smiling.

After another ten minutes of small talk, Emerson Fox took his leave.

"Well, that was illuminating" was all Angus said, before promptly forking my queen with one of his knights. I was done, again.

We waited until the last minute, and finally, Angus and I piled into his Camry and headed out. We found her where she spent most every afternoon, by the picture windows overlooking the river. As usual, she was staring intently out the window at the shoreline below. We caught the dying scent of lunch clashing with the emerging aroma of dinner. It was 2:30 p.m. We hadn't called but Muriel was touched that we'd stopped by on such an important day.

"You shouldn't be here right now, you should be getting ready for the big speech," Muriel scolded. "I'm crossing every appendage I have but I think you've done all you can."

"Aye, 'tis out of our hands now. I pray the Prime Minister astounds us with his courage and judgment, but I'll not be holdin' my breath."

Muriel returned her gaze to the river bank.

"Now, have a look out here, you two," directed Muriel as she pointed with a shaky finger. "I've been watching that marten by the shore gather bread the kitchen folk have been tossing out the back door. He snatches the pieces and then disappears underground. Now I'm no expert, but I think he's still supposed to be hibernating for a while longer. His routine has been upset by the smells wafting out the kitchen door."

We watched the marten's work for a time as it scurried back and forth. We could see two kitchen staff watching from the back door.

"But he looks healthy enough," I commented.

"Well of course, he's being fed with scraps from our meals. But it's not the accepted order of the earth. It's not how it's supposed to be," complained Muriel. "We're upsetting the balance, aren't we?"

Angus stood behind her chair and placed his hands on her shoulders.

"Aye, it may upset a time-honoured balance, but if you do it right, a new equilibrium can be found."

Then we were back in the car and on the road for Ottawa. We left the radio off and my cellphone too, and drove in relative silence. We pulled in at 3:45 with a quarter of an hour to spare. Perfect.

The Commissionaires nodded almost reverentially as we walked the main corridor in Centre Block and headed for the House. In the chamber, Angus stopped on the green carpet just inside the arch, bowed to the Throne, then climbed the tiers to his seat. I darted up the stone stairs, to the Members Gallery. A depression was worn into each step by nearly a century of political feet. I snagged the final seat along the front row of the balcony overlooking the House of Commons. My fellow political staffers all fell quiet when I sat down. I didn't care. I nodded to those I knew. I waited and fidgeted. I looked down to find Angus in his seat. He too waited and fidgeted. Thoughtlessly, I was stretching an elastic band I'd found on the floor under my feet. When it shot off my extended index finger into space, I was surprised at the graceful arc it cut in the air above the floor of the House of Commons. I leaned over the rail to follow its trajectory. Its gentle descent was very neatly arrested as it looped around the elephantine ear of a Tory backbencher from Manitoba. He lifted the rubber band off his ear, turning his eyes upwards to the gallery railing. He saw me carefully scrutinizing every inch of the ornate ceiling of the chamber. When an appropriate cooling-off period had elapsed, I looked over at the other Liberal assistants next to me. Yes, they had obviously seen the whole thing and were still staring at me.

At 3:55 p.m. Emile Coulombe was still not in his seat although the small lectern that Finance Ministers usually use when reading their Budgets sat on his desk at the ready. At 4:00 p.m. the recently elected Speaker entered the House with a sombre Prime Minister. They both took their places and the Speaker called for two pages. He pointed to the vacant seat of the Finance Minister and the pages walked there. I looked down at Angus, who'd been sitting up as high as he could to see this unfolding scene. Then he was smiling and looking up at me. It took me a moment longer to grasp but the penny then dropped and all was made clear.

The two pages picked up the special lectern and carried it to the Prime Minister's seat, placing it gently on the small parliamentary desk. The Prime Minister, who looked tired, nodded to the pages. There was an unmistakable tittering among the MPs and the press gallery. I heard a collective intake of breath from my colleagues beside me. Angus was beaming now.

The Speaker rose. "The Right Honourable Prime Minister."

We had won. Angus had won. Again. The Prime Minister rose.

"Mr. Speaker, before I read the formal Budget speech, let me begin by announcing the resignation this morning of the Minister of Finance. In the face of an increasingly complex and declining economic situation, and in light of the findings and recommendations of the Honourable Member for Cumberland-Prescott respecting the recent collapse of the Alexandra Bridge, the Finance Minister felt he simply could not continue in his role. I agreed. In his stead, I am presenting the Budget. And let there be no misunderstanding. I present this Budget myself, as Prime Minister, as a symbol of this government's solemn commitment to enact these measures, in the national interest.

"Notwithstanding our campaign pledges, since election day, our situation has changed. A bridge has collapsed into the river and, along with it, any pretence that either the Liberals or the Conservatives actually conquered the deficit. As the Honourable Member for Cumberland-Prescott said to me, 'We are not rid of the deficit, we just hid the deficit.' Mr. Speaker, and through you to my honourable colleagues, you can now find part of our deficit lying at the bottom of the Ottawa River in the twisted wreckage of the Alexandra Bridge. That will not be the legacy of this government.

"The recommendations in the McLintock Report released yesterday are included in the Budget. We are not proceeding at this time with the tax cuts to corporations and individuals. We simply cannot afford it right now. We expect to be able to introduce these promised tax cuts within the mandate of this government, but that will depend on the state of our infrastructure and the state of our economy. Had the Alexandra Bridge not fallen, the Finance Minister I appointed nearly two weeks ago would be presenting a different Budget today. But the government of the day must deal with the issues of the day. And that's just what we're doing."

He then proceeded to read the federal Budget to as quiet a House of Commons as I've ever heard. It took forty-eight minutes to get through it. There were some heckles but the decorum in the House lasted until the speech was nearly finished.

I've never been prouder of my Prime Minister. The allocations in the Budget for infrastructure renewal were slightly lower than we'd recommended. But then again, we'd recommended slightly higher numbers than we needed. Angus wasn't happy about our slight subterfuge, but in the end I convinced him, and we were both glad. The infrastructure investment announced in the Budget would suffice.

It was out of character for the PM to be so bold, so direct. He was a charter adherent to the try-to-please-everybody school of politics. I had no doubt his dealings with Angus had inspired this new approach. I looked down behind the MPs and saw Bradley Stanton through the curtains in the Members' lobby. He was looking directly at me. He pointed to me, then cocked his finger to the side of his head and fired with his thumb, before disappearing from view. I think he may finally have lost it.

After the PM sat down for the mandatory standing ovation from his caucus, I watched Angus haul himself to his feet to join in the applause. Then the PM did something I'd never seen in the House of Commons. While the ovation rolled on, he stood up, walked down to the other end of the House, turned, and climbed to the upper-most tier of seats, where Angus still stood clapping amid a sea of cheering Liberal backbenchers. Angus looked puzzled when the PM stopped in front of him and shook his hand while clasping his shoulder. He held his grip long enough to satisfy the cameras and make Angus distinctly uncomfortable. He then whispered in Angus's ear before returning to his seat on the front benches. Several giddy MPs around Angus stepped forward to shake his hand and cheer. Angus still looked as if he'd rather be somewhere else, anywhere else.

The rest of the proceedings passed in a blur. Of course, all the networks had set up mini-studios in the lobby of the House of Commons for post-Budget reaction. The Prime Minister gave brief interviews to all the networks and then slipped up to his office. Angus tried to avoid the cameras but was unsuccessful. We were seized upon by roving producers, and several live television interviews were given. He was calm, articulate, and very gracious in what was a clear victory for him and a devastating defeat for Emile Coulombe. He praised the Prime Minister for his courage and vision and appealed to Canadians to reflect on the difficult decisions the PM had made. At one point, one reporter asked Angus what he thought of the Finance Minister's resignation.

"Emile Coulombe is obviously a principled politician and he has made a principled decision. We need more women and men like him in public service."

Nice.

While Angus was doing interviews, curiosity drove me to the outskirts of the scrums surrounding the Tory and NDP leaders. Predictably, the Tories were having none of it. They would vote against this Budget because of the removal of the tax cuts. Politically, they really had no choice. That left the future of the minority Liberal government in the hands of the NDP. Never a great position to be in. I huddled closer to hear what the NDP Leader was saying.

"As you all know, we've never liked tax cuts and quite frankly, we're glad they're gone, at least for the time being. We can support the infrastructure investment as it will create jobs, mostly union jobs at that. I'm glad the Prime Minister has taken our advice on the need for spending on our roads, bridges, and ports. For these reasons, we'll hold our nose and support the government on the Budget," declared the NDP Leader.

Crisis number one averted.

We finished the round of interviews, and I steered Angus towards the corridor back to our Centre Block office. He took my arm, reversed course, and led me up the stairs towards the Prime Minister's office.

"He asked me to see him on our way out."

"Really. Hmmmm, that's interesting."

Angus gave me a look but said nothing. I figured I knew what was coming but decided to keep my yap shut in case I was wrong. And if I were right, and if Angus hadn't yet clued in, let it be a surprise.

Bradley Stanton was nowhere in sight as we passed the RCMP guard at the door and entered the PMO.

"You can both go right in. The Prime Minister is expecting you."

"Thanks, Gloria," I said as we opened the door and entered.

The PM was sitting near the fireplace. The flames crackled and looped around the logs. He stood up immediately and offered us the two chairs across from him.

"Gentlemen, welcome," he boomed, with arms outstretched.

He did not look like a national leader with the weight of the world on his shoulders. He looked as if he'd been somehow liberated, released from some unseen shackles. We all sat down. I positioned myself a little off to the side. This was really not my meeting.

"Angus, ever since you arrived on the Hill, you have been a veritable force of nature. It's been an impressive display."

"I know I've not always made your job easy, Prime Minister, but I'm too old to change, even if I had a mind to," Angus replied.

"Not always made my job easy? You've been a painful thorn in my side for the entire time. But upon reflection, I've come to realize that the gods of politics did not send you to test and try me as I first thought. Rather, I now believe that you were sent, in a way, to guide me. After this realization, the thorn has become decidedly less painful.

"Enough analysis. Let me get directly to the point. Despite our differences, I've been very impressed with what you've achieved and how you've gone about it in the relatively short time that you've been here. Your conviction and strong will have been a personal inspiration to me while occasionally making my leadership complicated and difficult. For instance, I spent most of last night reviewing focus group results that told me that half of Canadians would favour your recommendations at the expense of our damn tax cuts, and half would oppose them. Politicians don't much like fifty-fifty splits."

"Yet still you sacrificed your Finance Minister and delayed the tax cuts. Why?" asked Angus.

"In the silence and dark of night, while the city slept, I simply asked myself the one question that seems to have guided your foray into public life. 'What is right for the country?' It won't always be so easy to answer that question, but in this case, it was quite straightforward, as you know," explained the Prime Minister.

"Aye, the course was clear, sir. I commend your decision," replied Angus.

I stole a glance at Angus. He looked as serene as I'd ever seen him. He seemed . . . content.

"So Angus, to get to the real pressing matter at hand, Coulombe is gone. I'm sorry not to have his counsel, but not that sorry. So I'll be asking Aline Rioux to take over in Finance. But when you make one move, the dominos start to fall and you end up having to reshuffle the whole deck to preserve balance around the Cabinet table," the PM observed. "Angus, it seems I'm still left with one empty chair when the music stops."

Sitting there in the Prime Minister's office, looking at Angus, I could feel the political noose tightening around my neck. Somehow, I didn't care. This was going to be fun.

DIARY

Thursday, February 27

My Love,

I arrived home tonight to a handwritten note of congratulations from none other than Emerson Fox. He says he'll be watching me and learning. Strange fellow, but with softer edges now than he sported in the campaign.

My capacity for surprise remains intact. I daresay, the PM's performance today has caused me to reassess my earlier view of him. It is possible that he is growing into his role. That augurs well.

I spent a few glorious hours in the workshop tonight. At last, *Baddeck 1* is fully dried out after its ill-fated encounter with two military helicopters. It took longer than I expected but 'tis cold in the shop. I kept the heaters working overtime and the damp smell has now all but gone. I was planning on making some modifications to stabilize cushion pressure while accelerating, but I fear I'll be a little pressed for time in the foreseeable future, as will young Daniel.

I felt you with me tonight. You arrived suddenly, as if late for the meeting, though I suppose you were always with me. But all of a sudden, I was struck by your tranquil presence. I doubt the PM or Daniel noticed, but peace is what I felt. Even now, you, too, can still surprise me.

I don't mind being described as honourable now and then, but must they officially attach "the Honourable" to my blessed name for the rest of my living years? I'll not have it. What have I done, my love?

AM

ACKNOWLEDGEMENTS

I never expected to see my first novel published, so writing a second seems an undue privilege. I owe many for their support, encouragement, and guidance. I thank Douglas Gibson, whom I'm honoured to have as my editor, publisher, and, most importantly, friend. Beverley Slopen took a chance on me when no one else would, and I'm grateful to be among her flock. Publicist extraordinaire Frances Bedford kept me on the road and in front of readers for my first novel, an experience I thoroughly enjoyed. I look forward to doing it all again with this one. This is a better book for the eagle-eyes and copy-editing prowess of Wendy Thomas.

My thanks to a great ball hockey player, and an even greater artist, Jim Cuddy, and to a brilliant and funny writer, Ian Ferguson, for their kind words about this book.

I've never been clear on how far to take the Acknowledgements section, but for what it's worth, I've been inspired in my writing by many wonderful authors. In particular, Robertson Davies, Paul Quarrington, Mordecai Richler, Donald Jack, John Irving, and Stephen Fry, all set standards that I will only ever see shimmering in the distance. I doubt any book of mine could have been written without them.

Enumerating my blessings would be incomplete without acknowledging the pivotal role of the Stephen Leacock Association in changing my life as a writer, in the spring of 2008. I couldn't be more grateful.

And then there's my family. My father and mother created a home where the love of humour and language joined us every evening for dinner. From the very beginning, my twin brother, Tim, has been a stronger supporter, not to mention a halfway-decent author photographer, than I ever had a right to expect.

To my wife, Nancy, and our two boys, Calder and Ben, who inspired, nourished, and encouraged me with everything a writer needs, and more, even my most heartfelt words of gratitude simply fall short. So I'll just have to try to show you what it's meant to me.

T.F.
Toronto, 2009.

OTHER TITLES FROM
DOUGLAS GIBSON BOOKS
PUBLISHED BY McCLELLAND AND STEWART LTD.

THE BEST LAID PLANS *by* Terry Fallis
Winner of the Stephen Leacock Medal for Humour, Terry Fallis
brings us a terrific Canadian political satire. Thanks to a great scan-
dal, a crusty, old engineering professor is elected to Parliament.
He decides to see what good an honest politician with no aspira-
tions to re-election can do. The results are hilarious.

Fiction, 6 x 9, 336 pages, trade paperback

TOO MUCH HAPPINESS: Stories *by* Alice Munro
Ten astonishing new stories by the Canadian winner of the Man
Booker International Prize for Fiction. The reaction of her admir-
ers around the world may be summarized by the title.

Fiction, 5½ x 8½, 320 pages, hardcover

PAGE FRIGHT: Foibles and Fetishes of Famous Writers *by*
Harry Bruce
An impressively complete and witty history of the tools and tricks
employed by writers down through the ages to keep writer's block
at bay. "Delightful browsing!" – Edward O. Wilson

Non-fiction, 6 x 9, 352 pages, hardcover

GOING ASHORE: Stories *by* Mavis Gallant
As Alberto Manguel notes in his introduction, these thirty-one
hidden stories by the Paris-based Canadian legend "bear the most
merciless of readings." A superb collection.

Fiction, 6 x 9, 370 pages, trade paperback

HELL OR HIGH WATER *by* Paul Martin
Great events and world figures stud this memoir from Canada's

21st prime minister, which is firm but polite as it sets the record straight, and is full of wry humour and self-deprecating stories. Paul Martin emerges as a fascinating flesh and blood man, still working hard to make a better world.

Autobiography, 6 x 9, 504 pages, photographs, trade paperback

ROBERTSON DAVIES: A Portrait in Mosaic *by* Val Ross
Robertson Davies was a larger than life character whose books continue to fascinate readers around the world. Val Ross collected hundreds of stories from those who knew him. "Full of nuggets and small surprises, Ross's glance-back at the iconic Robertson Davies is greatly entertaining, a feast for the book lover." – *London Free Press*

Biography, 5 ³⁄₁₆ x 8, 400 pages, trade paperback

THE TRUTH ABOUT CANADA: Some Important, Some Astonishing, and Some Truly Appalling Things All Canadians Should Know About Our Country *by* Mel Hurtig
Mel Hurtig has combed through world statistics to see how Canada really measures up in this bestselling book. "Hurtig piles up oddly overlooked evidence to show exactly how we have become a much less enlightened country than we used to be." – *Winnipeg Free Press*

Non-fiction, 6 x 9, 408 pages, trade paperback

THE WAY IT WORKS: Inside Ottawa *by* Eddie Goldenberg
Chrétien's senior policy adviser from 1993 to 2003, Eddie Goldenberg gives us this "fascinating and sometimes brutally honest look at the way the federal government really operates." – Montreal *Gazette*

Non-fiction, 6 x 9, 408 pages, illustrations, trade paperback

STEPHEN HARPER AND THE FUTURE OF CANADA *by* William Johnson
A serious, objective biography taking us right through Stephen Harper's early days in power. "The most important Canadian

political book of the year." – Calgary Herald

Biography, 6 x 9, 512 pages, trade paperback

CHARLES THE BOLD by Yves Beauchemin, translated by
Wayne Grady
An unforgettable coming-of-age story set in 1960s and 1970s east-
end Montreal, from French Canada's most popular novelist.
"Truly astonishing . . . one of the great works of Canadian lit-
erature." – Madeleine Thien

Fiction, 6 x 9, 384 pages, trade paperback

THE YEARS OF FIRE by Yves Beauchemin, translated by
Wayne Grady
"Charles the Bold" continues his career in east-end Montreal,
through the high-school years when he encounters girls and
fights the threat of arson. "One of those 'great books.' No wonder
Beauchemin is considered Quebec's Balzac." – Montreal *Gazette*

Fiction, 6 x 9, 240 pages, trade paperback

A VERY BOLD LEAP by Yves Beauchemin, translated by
Wayne Grady.
In this third volume of the Quebec classic series, the teenage
Charles Thibodeau sets out to write The Great Montreal Novel,
only to discover that a writer's life leads in many strange direc-
tions. A triumphant successor to its two forerunners.

Fiction, 6 x 9, 352 pages, trade paperback

A PASSION FOR NARRATIVE: A Guide for Writing Fiction by
Jack Hodgins
The Canadian classic guide to writing novels and short stories,
with over 20,000 copies sold. "One excellent path from original
to marketable manuscript. . . . It would take a beginning writer
years to work her way through all the goodies Hodgins offers."
– *Globe and Mail*

Non-fiction/Writing guide, 5 ¼ x 8 ½, 216 pages, updated, trade paperback